THE MEASURE
OF A MAN

Look for these exciting Western series from bestselling
authors William W. Johnstone and J.A. Johnstone

The Mountain Man
Luke Jensen: Bounty Hunter
Brannigan's Land
The Jensen Brand
Preacher and MacCallister
The Red Ryan Westerns
Perley Gates
Have Brides, Will Travel
Guns of the Vigilantes
Shotgun Johnny
The Chuckwagon Trail
The Jackals
The Slash and Pecos Westerns
The Texas Moonshiners
Stoneface Finnegan Westerns
Ben Savage: Saloon Ranger
The Buck Trammel Westerns
The Death and Texas Westerns
The Hunter Buchanon Westerns
Tinhorn
Will Tanner, Deputy U.S. Marshal

THE MEASURE OF A MAN

Law of the Mountain Man
War of the Mountain Man

William W. Johnstone

PINNACLE BOOKS
Kensington Publishing Corp.
www.kensingtonbooks.com

PINNACLE BOOKS are published by

Kensington Publishing Corp.
119 West 40th Street
New York, NY 10018

Special book excerpts or customized printings can also be created to fit specific needs. For details, write or phone the office of the Kensington Sales Manager: Kensington Publishing Corp., 119 West 40th Street, New York, NY 10018. Attn. Sales Department. Phone: 1-800-221-2647.

PINNACLE BOOKS, the Pinnacle logo, and the WWJ steer head logo are Reg. U.S. Pat. & TM Off.

First printing: August 2022
ISBN-13: 978-0-7860-4858-8
ISBN-13: 978-1-7860-4859-5 (ebook)

10 9 8 7 6 5 4 3 2 1

Printed in the United States of America

CONTENTS

LAW OF THE
MOUNTAIN MAN

I feel an army in my fist.

Friedrich von Schiller

Chapter 1

He hoped this would be the last winter storm of the season. Probably wouldn't be, but there is that line about hope springing eternal.

He just wished it was spring. Period.

Smoke Jensen sat in a cave over a fire and boiled the last of his coffee. He knew he was in Idaho. He guessed somewhere south of Montpelier. All he knew for certain was that he was cold, and he was being hunted by a large group of men. He knew why he was cold; he didn't really have a clear idea why he was being hunted.

He poured a cup of scalding strong coffee and fed a few more sticks to the fire, then leaned back against the stone wall of the cavern and once more went over events in his mind.

Sally's parents had come out from the East for a visit. Why they had chosen to come to northern Colorado in the middle of winter was still a mystery to Smoke. It was so cold during the winter, that when someone died the body was placed in a cave until spring when the ground thawed and a hole could be dug.

It was colder here in Idaho, Smoke mentally griped, his big hands soaking up the warmth from the tin cup.

Dagger, Smoke's big mountain-bred horse, chomped on some grass Smoke had dug up for him.

Then the baby had taken sick—some sort of lung ailment—and Sally's father had suggested they go to Arizona for the winter. Smoke had no desire to go to Arizona and there were a few things he needed to tend to around the spread.

With the house empty and matters tended to, Smoke became restless. The pull of the High Lonesome tugged at him. He saddled up and rode out one cold but sunshiny morning.

He didn't have any particular place in mind. He just wanted to be one with the mountains again. Damn near got himself killed doing it. And wasn't out of the fire yet.

He had headed northwest out of Colorado, staying on the west side of the Continental Divide, angling northwest. He did all right until he came to a little town on the Bear River, just about on the border, he reckoned. He had stopped at the general store to resupply and then to have a drink of whiskey. Not normally a drinking man, Smoke visited the saloons more for news than for booze, although in this sort of weather, a shot of whiskey did feel good going down.

Smoke was tall, broad-shouldered, lean-hipped, and ruggedly handsome, with cold brown eyes. Smoke Jensen, called the last mountain man by some, was the hero of countless penny dreadfuls sold all over the country. He was also known as the fastest gun in the West. He wore two guns: on the left a .44 worn high and butt-forward for a cross-draw, on the right a .44 worn low and tied down.

When Smoke had been just a young boy, he was taken under the wing of a cantankerous old mountain man named

Preacher. Preacher had taught the boy well, watching him practice with those deadly guns as they traveled all over the Northwest.

Outlaws had raped and killed Smoke's first wife and cold-bloodedly murdered their newborn son. Smoke had tracked them all down and killed them, then rode into the outlaw town that had been their headquarters and shot it out with the killers' friends. His reputation was then carved in granite.

He poured another cup of cowboy coffee and let his mind drift back a few days.

"Whiskey," Smoke told the barkeep. "Out of the good bottle."

The saloon had quieted as Smoke walked in, something that did not escape his attention. He paid little mind, though. A stranger appearing out of the dead of winter always drew attention.

Especially one who wore his guns like Smoke wore his.

"We don't serve no Box T riders in here, mister," the barkeep warned.

Smoke's eyes turned colder than the weather outside. "I don't ride for the Box T. I don't even know where it is or what it is. Now pour the drink." He laid money on the bar.

A man walked up behind Smoke, spurs jingling. "I say you're a liar. I say you're one of that old man and woman's hands. And I say you ain't gonna buy no drink in here. I say—"

Whatever the loudmouth was going to say, he didn't get the chance to finish it. Smoke spun and hit the man smack in the teeth with one big, work-hardened fist. The cowboy's eyes were rolling back in his head and he was out cold before he hit the floor.

Smoke shifted positions, moving to the end of the bar closest to the door so he could keep an eye on the rest of the riders in the room.

"Pour the damn drink!" Smoke told the barkeep. "And make it out of a new bottle. Let me see you pry the cork and pour!"

"Yes, sir!" the barkeep barked. "Right now. Then will you please get the hell out of here?"

"I'll think about it." Smoke held the glass in his left hand. His right hand was hidden by the bar. His right hand was close to the butt of his .44. Out of habit, he always slipped the hammer-thong from his .44 as soon as his boots left the stirrups and touched the ground.

Preacher's lessons stayed with him.

"Mister," the voice came from a table near the back of the room. "That there is Jud Vale on the floor. He's gonna kill you when he gets up."

"If he doesn't handle his guns any better than he flaps his mouth he's going to be in for another surprise."

"You won't say that to his face!"

Smoke laughed at the man.

"You can't take all of us," another voice added.

"Bastard looks like Perkins, don't he?" yet another said.

Perkins? Smoke thought. Who is Perkins? "Maybe not. But I can kill the first six or eight. Anybody want to start?"

Apparently, no one did. No more voices were heard.

Smoke sipped his drink as Jud Vale moaned and stirred on the floor. "Isn't anyone going to help this stumblebum up?"

Several men stood up and warily approached the groaning Jud Vale. All of them keeping an eye on Smoke, who was standing by the bar smiling at their antics. Whoever this Perkins person was, he was respected, for sure.

"You a dead man, Perkins, or whoever you are," one of

the men said, helping Jud to his feet. "You got one boot in the grave now."

Jud Vale, his bloody mouth puffy, glared at Smoke. "I'm gonna let you ride, you punk!" he snarled. "Take this message back to Burden: I'm gonna kill him and then run that old broad off the land. You tell him I said that."

Smoke started to tell the man that his name wasn't Perkins and he didn't know anybody named Burden. Then he thought better of it. He'd play along for a time. The idea of somebody like this loudmouth Jud Vale bothering some old couple rankled him.

Smoke nodded, finished his whiskey and then backed away from the bar, finding the doorknob with his left hand. He stepped out into the cold blowing winds and closed the door behind him.

He stopped at a farmhouse a few miles from town, spotting a man carrying a slop bucket out to his hogs.

"Mister, where can I find the Box T spread?"

"South of here. It's right around Bear Lake. You got any sense you'll stay away from there."

"Why?"

"'Cause Jud Vale wants it, that's why. And whatever Jud Vale wants, he gits. Now you git!"

Smoke got.

Jud Vale's men came after him hard. So far, not a killing shot had been fired from either side, but Jud's men kept Smoke in a box, warning him back with well-placed rifle shots and causing Smoke to wonder what in the hell was going on.

He was south of Montpelier, a town settled by the Mormons back in '63, first known as Clover Creek and later as Belmont; Brigham Young gave it its present name. He was not too far from the Oregon Trail. Smoke was close to Bear Lake and the Box T spread, but could not figure out a way to get to the place without killing some of Jud Vale's men, and that was something he did not want to do. Not just yet, anyway.

How do I get myself in these messes? he wondered, drinking the last of his coffee. All I wanted to do was see some country, not fight a war.

He walked to the front of the cave and looked out. It was getting light, and soon the hunt would continue. Smoke sighed and did his best to keep his patience. He didn't want to get riled up. When Smoke Jensen got angry, somebody was sure to get hurt.

Dagger snorted and scraped a steel-shod hoof on the floor of the cave. The big horse was getting restless, and was letting Smoke know it.

"All right, Dag," Smoke said, turning to walk back into the wider area of the cave. "I'm getting tired of it myself."

Smoke packed and saddled up, then checked his guns. He led the big horse outside and swung into the saddle, riding with his Winchester across the saddle horn.

"We're headin' for the Box T, Dag. And come Hell or high water or Jud Vale, we're going to make it."

The big horse shook his head as if in agreement.

He had not gone a mile before he saw smoke from a fire. Dagger's ears perked up as he caught the scent of other horses. Smoke smiled grimly. "You wanna go visit that camp, boy? All right. Let's just do that."

When he got close, Smoke dismounted and slipped nearer—on foot. A half-dozen of Vale's men were huddled around a fire, drinking coffee and eating bacon. Smoke recognized several of them from the saloon.

He lifted his rifle and plugged the coffeepot, then dented the frying pan with another round. He put several more rounds directly into the fire, scattering hot coals all around the clearing and sending gunhands scrambling for what cover they could find.

He emptied his rifle into a tree where the horses were picketed and several of them panicked, reared up, and broke loose, taking off into the timber.

Chuckling, Smoke ran back to Dagger, swung into the saddle, and skirted the camp, heading for the Box T range on the Bear.

He had sure ruined breakfast for those ol' boys.

As he rode, he saw smoke from several more fires, but decided not to press his luck.

Twice he heard the sounds of horses and men and both times he slipped back into the timber and waited it out as the men rode past him. And they came close enough for him to see that Jud Vale really meant business. He recognized Don Draper, the Utah gunslick, and Davy Street, the outlaw from down New Mexico way. As the second bunch rode by him, Smoke picked out Cisco Webster, the Texas gunny; Barstow, a no-good from Colorado; Glen Regan, a punk kid who fancied himself a gunfighter; and Highpockets, a long lean drink of water who was as dangerous as a grizzly and as quick as a striking rattler.

What the hell was going on in this part of southeastern Idaho?

Smoke rode on as the day started to warm some.

He began to see cattle wearing the Box T brand, really no sure sign that he was on Box T land, for cattle wandered miles to grass, but Smoke figured he was getting close.

Then he found out why the cattle were so scattered—miles of cut fences. Somebody, probably Jud Vale and his men, had really caused some damage.

He topped a ridge and could see, far in the distance, a house and barn, and off to the south, a winding road leading to the house. He cut toward the road, riding slowly and cautiously, for if those in the house were under siege, he would probably be considered hostile.

He stopped several times as he drew nearer, taking off his hat and waving it in the air.

Nothing from the house.

He came to a closed gate and stopped, dismounting. He wasn't about to open that gate unless invited to do so.

But no invite came.

The snow was just about gone from the ground, but the wind was still whistling around him.

"Hello, the house!" Smoke yelled.

He was just about to call again when the response came. "What do you want?"

A female voice. And not an old voice.

"Some food and coffee would be nice," Smoke called.

"Have this instead," the voice said, sending him a bullet that had Smoke diving for the ground.

Chapter 2

Several more slugs cut the air above his head. Smoke noticed that none of the slugs came close to Dagger. The big horse trotted away a few yards and looked back at Smoke, his expression saying, "What have you got us into now?"

"I'm friendly!" Smoke called, crawling to his knees. "I mean you no harm!"

"You ride for the Bar V?" This time it was a man's voice.

"Hell, no! They've been chasing me all over the country for the last week."

"Why?"

"Because they think I'm somebody named Perkins!"

A full minute ticked by. "All right, mister." This time it was the female voice. "Get into the saddle and come on in. But you put a hand on a gun and you're dead. And close the gate behind you."

It suddenly came to Smoke. Perkins! Clint Perkins. The

outlaw that some called the Robin Hood of the West. He was always helping farmers, nesters, and the down-and-outers. He would rustle cattle from big land barons, butcher the carcass and distribute the meat to the needy. He'd been known to give the money to the poor, after holding up rich folks.

But what connection did Clint Perkins have with the Box T?

Well, he might find out . . . providing he didn't get shot first.

He swung into the saddle, leaned down and opened the gate, and rode on in, carefully closing the gate behind him. He walked Dagger toward the house. Smoke stopped at the hitchrail and sat his saddle. Damned if he was going to get down until invited.

"What's your name?" the voice came from inside the house, speaking from behind the open but curtained window.

"Mamma," a child's voice said excitedly. "I seen him on the cover of a book. That's Smoke Jensen!"

After a lot of apologies and much embarrassment on the part of those in the house, Smoke was invited to sit down and eat. A small boy took Dagger to the barn. Children could handle the big mean-eyed stallion, but Dagger would kill a grown man who tried to mess with him.

Smoke tried to put some family resemblance between the young woman and the old couple. He could not see any. And he didn't ask; none of his business.

Smoke put away a respectable bit of food and started working on his third cup of coffee.

"I like to see a man eat well," Alice Burden said. "Our boy used to eat like that."

Walt gave his wife a warning look that closed her mouth. Smoke picked up on the glance but said nothing.

"Just passin' through?" Walt asked, lighting his pipe.

"Something like that," Smoke sugared his coffee. "'Til I had a run-in with a loudmouth name of Jud Vale. I busted him in the mouth and put him on a barroom floor."

"I'd sure like to have seen that," Walt said with a sigh. "That man has sure caused us some problems."

"Why?"

The old man shrugged his shoulders. "He wants our land. Jud Vale wants everything he sees. Including her." He cut his eyes to Doreen, a slim but very shapely woman who looked to be in her mid-twenties.

Got to be more to it than that, Smoke thought. "What has Clint Perkins got to do with all this?"

Walt looked at his coffee cup. His wife busied herself at the sink, washing dishes. Doreen met Smoke's eyes. "He's my husband. Sort of."

Odd reply, Smoke thought. "Father of the boy?"

"Yes."

"Clint is from this area, right?"

"Not too far from here," she replied. "It's a long story, but I'll make it short. When Clint was just a boy he saw his father and mother killed by greedy cattlemen who wanted their land and didn't like farmers. The boy took to the high country and raised himself. He hates rich people to the point of being a fanatic about it. But he has a few good points. More than a few. I married him, but it just didn't work. He refuses to stop his outlawing. I just couldn't live like that."

"So you took the boy and left?"

"Yes."

Smoke didn't believe her. She was lying through her teeth, but damned if he knew why.

"This is a big spread, Mr. Burden. Where are your hands?"

"Don't have none no more. Jud's men run them off; killed a couple. They're buried on that crest to the east."

Smoke had seen the graveyard. More than two crosses there. "And Jud's men cut your fence?"

"Yep."

"Tell me about this Clint Perkins?"

"What is there to say?" Walt said. "Nobody 'ceptin' Doreen has seen his face in fifteen years."

"You two look alike," Doreen said. "I can see where someone might think you were him."

What to do? Smoke thought. All three of these people were lying to him. But why? What were they hiding? Walt and Alice Burden were too old for Clint Perkins to be their son. So that was out. So where was the connection? There had to be one.

"How'd you get here?" he asked Doreen.

"Runnin' from Jud Vale," she answered simply. "Walt and Alice took me and Micky in and let us stay."

Why? Had they known Doreen that well? Had they been neighbors? What? Too many unanswered questions. It made Smoke uneasy. Very uneasy.

"You have any idea how many head of cattle you have?" Smoke asked the old man.

"Not no more. Jud and his gunhands been runnin' 'em off for a year or more. The one herd they can't get to without a lot of fuss is west of here, next to the Bear River."

"How are you getting your food?"

The question seemed to make all three of them nervous. Walt finally said, "Friends slip food to us."

Smoke nodded, not satisfied with the reply but sensing he wasn't going to get much more out of the trio. Micky was outside, playing. Smoke figured the boy to be about eight years old.

"There is no point in my trying to restring the wire," Smoke said. "Without hands to ride fence, Jud's people would just cut it again come night."

"True."

"Do you have the money to pay hands, providing I could find some who'd work for you?"

"Oh, sure. I got money up in Montpelier. That's a Mormon town. Jud ain't gonna mess with them folks."

Smoke knew that for an iron-clad fact. Mormons tended to stick together, and folks who thought they wouldn't fight because they were so religious soon learned how wrong they were—providing they lived through it.

Walt was saying, ". . . You ain't gonna find no one to work for me, anyways, Mr. Smoke. Jud's got the folks around here buffaloed."

"You let me think on that for a few hours. You just might be wrong." He smiled. "However, the hands I get might not be the type you're used to seeing."

Smoke stowed his gear in the bunkhouse and fired up the old potbelly stove in the center of the room. Dagger was warm and content and chomping away on corn in a hay-filled stall in the big barn.

Smoke had noticed that at one time—not too long ago— the Box I had been a money-making spread. So why the sudden downfall? Was it just because Jud Vale wanted the land? Smoke didn't believe that for a minute. There was more to it than that; a lot more.

Smoke hated bullies. If it were just a simple matter of Jud Vale's greed, the problem could be easily solved—with a gun. Smoke wanted the whole story, though, before it came to that, if it came to that. And he sincerely hoped it would not. He, however, had a hunch that it would. Usually all loud-mouthed, pushy, bullying types could be handled without being killed, for bullies are cowards at heart. Give them a good beating and you've got their attention. But Smoke felt that Jud wouldn't go down that easily. If Jensen stayed around, he would have to drag iron against Jud Vale.

He felt pretty sure he was going to stick around. Nothing like a good mystery to pique one's interest.

Over supper, Smoke asked, "Lots of small farmers in this area, huh?"

"Oh, yeah," the old rancher said. "Most of them just barely hanging on. That's another thing that got me in trouble. I never minded farmers like a lot of ranchers seem to. Never had any trouble with them. I used to help a lot of them time to time. A little money, food, clothing, what have you. Used to hire some of the kids during the summer to work on the spread."

"Does Montpelier have a newspaper?"

"Sure."

Smoke nodded. "I'm going to be gone for several days." He noted the alarm that quickly sprang into the eyes of those around the table. "But I'll be back," he assured them. "And that's a promise."

"Jud Vale is a no-good," the farmer said bluntly. "And I'll say it to his face."

"Chester . . ." his wife warned.

"No, Mother," the man in the patched overalls shook his head. "Time for backing down is over. Mr. Burden is a good man who's hit on some hard times. We can't just turn our backsides to him and forget all the times he's helped us. 'Sides, we need hard cash desperate."

"Ralph is only twelve years old," she reminded him.

"And been doin' a man's work since he was nine. You seen how excited he is about Mr. Smoke's offer. And you heard Mr. Smoke say he ain't gonna put the plan into action unless the newspaper agrees to print the story and send it out to other papers."

"Well . . ." She shook her head. "I just don't know, Chester."

"Aw, Mom!" the boy finally spoke. "I can handle a gun good as the next feller!"

"No guns!" Smoke said it quickly and firmly. "If it comes to gunplay, I'll handle that. Any boy who shows up with a gun doesn't work."

"Yes, sir!" Ralph said. "You're the boss, Mr. Smoke, for sure."

"You pass the word around to your friends and neighbors. And keep it inside the circle. We want this to be a total surprise to Jud Vale when we spring it."

The farmer grinned and stuck out his hand. Smoke shook it. "You got it, Mr. Smoke."

The editor of the newspaper chuckled and rocked back in his swivel chair. "I like it, Mr. Jensen. I really like it. Jud Vale doesn't throw that big a loop around this town, but he's made life pretty miserable for those in his area. I've been curious about just why he hates Walt Burden so. Of course I'll print the story, and I'll send it out to newspapers all over the state. We want to be sure those young boys are safe. And there is nothing like the power of the press to insure that. Hire your . . . cowboys, Mr. Jensen, and put them to work. I'll ride down and do a follow-up on the story in a few weeks, to keep interest alive."

"Damnedest bunch of cowboys I ever seen in all my born days," Walt said, looking at the new hands.

"Looks like we better get to cooking, Doreen," Alice said. "Some of those boys look like they haven't had a decent meal in weeks."

The youngest was ten and the oldest was fourteen. Of the boys, that is. In Montpelier, Smoke had rounded up three slightly older punchers. Dolittle, Harrison, and Cheyenne were in their sixties . . . they claimed. Smoke suspected they might be a tad older than that. He didn't know much about Dolittle and Harrison, except that they could sit a saddle and knew cows, but Cheyenne was quite another story. Smoke remembered Preacher spinning yarns about a mountain man he knew by the name of Cheyenne O'Malley from back in the '40s. Cheyenne was one of those born with the bark on, he didn't have to grow into it; mean from the git-go.

Cheyenne was about seventy, Smoke reckoned, and looked so skinny he might have to drink a glass of beer to keep his britches up. But he still wore his Colt low and tied down and Smoke knew the old mountain man could and would use it.

"All right, Cheyenne," Smoke told him. "You're the range boss on this job." Cheyenne nodded. "You boys know what that means. Cheyenne tells you to make like a frog, you just jump as high as you can. You don't have to ask if it was high enough. If it wasn't, he'll let you know. Dolittle and Harrison will be carrying orders from Cheyenne to you boys, and you boys will be spotted all around this spread.

"Now then, the first thing we're gonna do is round up some horses and top them off; settle them down for you." Smoke glanced at the animals the boys had used to get over to the Box T. Mules and plow horses. "Then you boys can turn your own animals out to pasture and let them rest." He looked at Walt. "All right, Boss, what's the first order of the day?"

The old rancher smiled. "The wife says the first thing we do is feed these boys."

All the boys cheered at that.

Jud Vale balled the newspaper up and hurled it into the fireplace. "That no good—" He proceeded to cut loose with a stream of cuss words that almost turned the air blue.

When he had calmed down enough to try to catch his breath, his foreman said, "Boss, this is bad. If one of them kids gets hurt by a bullet, the governor will send the law in on us, that is, if some vigilantes from around here don't hang us to the nearest tree first."

"I know, Jason. I know. That damn Smoke Jensen! Jesus God, why didn't I recognize him right off and let him alone?"

"Didn't none of us recognize him, Boss. But we should have, I reckon." He wore a sheepish look. "Damn bunk-house is full of them penny dreadfuls writ about him."

"I better not see any of them around!"

"I'll pass the word."

"Do that. Damn!" Jud yelled. "Pass the word, Jason: stay off of Box T range and don't bother the boys. Don't even go near them. Jensen can't stay up here forever and them damn kids got to go back to school come fall. We can wait."

"Them high-priced gunhands is about next to worthless when it comes to workin' cattle, Boss. Most of 'em is just salivating to get a chance to brace Smoke Jensen."

"I'll give a thousand dollars to the man who kills Jensen. You pass that word along, Jason."

"That ought to get something stirred up, for sure!"

*   *   *

While in Montpelier, Smoke had arranged for a wire to be sent to Sally, advising her where he was, and for a courier to bring any reply to the ranch.

One was forthcoming quickly.

Darling Smoke stop Doctors say baby must remain in a warm dry climate for at least two years stop Mother and Father arranged to stay with me stop Father bought a bank here in Prescott stop We are fine stop Miss you terribly stop Come when you are finished stop Love Sally stop.

"Bad news?" Doreen broke into his thoughts. He had not heard her come up.

The girl moved like a ghost.

"Yes and no. Our baby has to stay down in Arizona for quite a long time. Lung problems."

"Then you'll be leaving . . . ?" She let that trail off with a catch in her voice.

"No. Sally knows I don't go off and leave a job half-finished. I'll see this through. If it hasn't ended by mid-summer, then I'll finish it."

She didn't have to ask how he would do that. She knew. "That is very kind of you, Smoke."

She moved closer. Doreen was a mighty comely lass. Smoke could smell the lilac water on her. Mayhaps, he thought, her middle name was Eve.

He moved back just a tad. "That is, I'll make up my mind about staying when and if you people ever get around to telling me the truth."

Her eyes turned frosty as an early morning chill. She spun around and stalked away, her rear end swaying like women's rear ends have a tendency to do.

Mighty shapely lassie. And Smoke didn't trust her any further than he could pick up his horse and toss him.

Chapter 3

On the first full day of work, Smoke didn't know whether to laugh or cry.

The boys were sure willing enough, but the trouble was that none of them knew diddly-squat about ranch work. They were farm boys, used to gathering eggs and slopping hogs and plowing and such as that.

Little Chuckie fell off his mount, and landed in a fresh horse pile. The only other britches he had were hanging on the line to dry. He had to work the rest of that morning dressed, from the waist down, in his longhandles. With a safety pin holding up one side of the flap.

Of the boys, Jamie was the oldest and the strongest. He was built like the trunk of a large tree. And he could ride and was a fair hand with a rope.

Matthew was a frail young man who wore glasses and was in dire need of boots.

Smoke was making a list of what the boys needed; and he was going to see to it that they got it. One way or the other.

Ed meant well and tried hard, but it was plain that he would never be a cowboy. Smoke put him to running errands and taking messages back and forth.

Leroy would do. He never complained, even after being tossed a half-dozen times. He just got back up, dusted himself off, and climbed right back in the saddle and stayed there until he showed the bronc who was running this show.

Eli was the son of a carpenter and, like Ed, was no horseman. Smoke put him to work fixing up the place, and there was a lot of fixing up to do. A ranch starts to run down mighty quick, and this spread had been neglected for a long time.

Jimmy and Clark and Buster would do fine, Smoke concluded.

Cecil was fourteen, like Jamie, and solid and mature for his age. A fair horseman.

Alan was a grown-up thirteen, from a hardscrabble farm family. A good solid kid.

Rolly, Pat and Oscar were all twelve and showed promise.

All in all, Smoke thought, a pretty good bunch of kids. But, he had to keep this in mind: they were kids. He could not chew on them like he would adults. He didn't want them screwing up their faces and bawling like lost calves.

"All right, Cheyenne!" Smoke called, with Dagger under him. "Take the men to work!"

Smoke rode over to a three-building town located on Mud Lake, leading a pack animal. He would buy the boys as much clothing as possible here. Maybe all of it if he were lucky. And he could pick up any talk about how Jud Vale was taking this new twist.

As soon as he walked in, he could tell by the barkeep's reaction that the name Smoke Jensen was known. Somebody had been talking about him, and fairly recently.

The barroom was separated from the general store by a partition, so the men could talk and cuss without bothering any ladies who might be shopping in the store. The only door connecting the store and saloon was closed.

Smoke ordered a beer and leaned against the bar, observing the very nervous barkeep draw the suds. Three men were sitting at a table in the back of the room. It was gloomy in the small saloon, and the men were shrouded in shadows, but Smoke could see well enough to recognize the men as part of one of the groups who had chased him all over half of the southeastern part of Idaho days back.

And one of them was Sam Teller, a gunfighter from over Oregon way. Sam wasn't known for his easy disposition and loving nature.

A local man, a farmer by the look of him, opened the door and stepped inside, closing the door behind him. He stopped cold when he saw the tall man at the bar. His eyes cut to the three gunslicks sitting at the table. He swallowed hard, then walked on to the bar and ordered a beer.

"All of a sudden it smells like a hog pen in here," one of the gunhawks commented.

The farmer's face hardened but he was smart enough to keep his mouth shut.

"What'll it be, neighbor?" the barkeep asked.

"Beer." The farmer took a position at the end of the bar, near the curve of the planks, so if matters deteriorated into gunplay, he could hit the floor and be out of the line of fire.

Smoke was a cattleman, so he could understand, at least

to some degree, why ranchers disliked farmers. But Smoke
Jensen was living proof that rancher and farmer could live
side by side and be friends. And he knew that not all of the
blame for the hard feelings could be laid at the doorstep of
the ranchers. Some farmers flatly refused to work with the
ranchers, fencing off the best water; homesteading in line-
shacks that the ranchers had built and maintained; and
sometimes rustling cattle, not always for food to feed hungry families. Sometimes just to aggravate the rancher.

The bartender had moved to the end of the bar, just as far
away from Smoke Jensen as he could get.

Smoke sipped his beer and waited for the gunplay that he
knew was just around the corner, lurking in those invisible
shadows that drifted around and clung to those who lived by
the gun.

"There ain't much to that pig slop, Burt," Sam Teller
said. "Hell, he ain't even packin' no gun."

Burt. Smoke searched his memory. Could be Burt Rolly.
Smoke had heard of him. A gunfighter of very limited ability, so he'd been told. Usually a back-shooter.

"You're a long ways from home, Jensen," Sam said. "I
figured you was still in Colorado, hidin' under your wife's
dresstail."

"You figured wrong on a lot of counts, Sam," Smoke told
him. "But then, the way I hear it, you never were very
bright."

"Huh?"

"I said you were stupid, Sam. Dumb. Ignorant. Slow.
Mentally deficient. Am I making myself clear now?"

The farmer moved further away from Smoke and if the
barkeep pressed any harder against the rear wall he was
going to collapse the entire end of the store.

"I don't think I like you very much, Jensen," Sam said, finally realizing he was being insulted.

"I don't like you at all, Sam. And I'm not real thrilled with those half-wits with you."

Burt pushed back his chair and stood up, his hands at his sides. "You take that back, Jensen! I ain't no half-wit."

Smoke smiled at him. "You're right, Burt. You're not a half-wit."

Burt relaxed.

"You're all the way a fool," Smoke finished. "The best thing you boys could do is pay for your drinks and ride out of this area of Idaho. Forget about Jud Vale and Walt Burden. And for damn sure, forget about trying to brace me."

The third man at the table slowly stood up and walked to another table. He sat down and placed both hands on the table.

Smoke recognized him. "Smart move, Jackson."

"The timin' ain't right, Smoke," the gunhand said. "Man, you're walkin' around with your tail up in the air, huntin' trouble. That ain't like you. What's got you on the prod?"

"I don't like Jud Vale." Smoke spoke to the man without taking his eyes off of Sam and Burt.

"Hell, I don't like him either! But he's payin' top wages for fightin' men."

Smoke laughed. "To fight an old man and an old woman? To fight a young woman and her eight-year-old kid? For that, Jud Vale hires two dozen gunnies? He must be a mighty skittish man."

"They's a lot more to this than that, Smoke."

"I figure so myself. One of these days somebody's going to tell me the whole story."

"I'm tired of all this jibber-jabber!" Burt shouted, just about scaring the pee out of the barkeep. "I'm a-gonna kill you, Jensen!"

Smoke stood tall and straight, facing the two men standing by the table. "No, you're not, Burt. All you're going to do is get buried. Think about it, man. I've faced more than a hundred gunhands, most of them better than you. They're all dead, Burt. Every last one of them. Pike and Shorty. Haywood and Ackerman and Kid Austin. Canning and Poker and Grisson. Clark and Evans. Felter and Lefty and Nevada Sam. Big Jack and Phillips and Carson. Russell and Joiner and Jeff Siddons. Jerry and Skinny Davis and Cross. You want more names, Burt? All right. Simpson and Martin and Reese. Turkel and Brown and Williams and Rogers. Fenerty and Stratton and Potter and Richards. And a half hundred more whose names I can't recall or never even knew. They're all dead and rotting in the ground. But I'm still here."

"Listen to him, boys," Jackson spoke the words softly. "I'm tellin' you, the timin' ain't right just yet. Back off."

"You could buy in!" Sam said hoarsely.

"Not just yet."

"Then you jist yellow!"

"No. But I'll be alive," Jackson told him.

The farmer was on the floor, belly down. The barkeep had slipped down to his knees and was peering around a keg of beer.

"Make your play, damn you, Jensen!" Sam yelled.

"Your deal," Smoke replied. "Bet or fold."

Sam and Burt grabbed for iron. Smoke's guns roared and belched fire and death. Sam stumbled back against the wall, his gun still in leather. Burt was plugged twice in the belly. He fell down on the floor and began squalling as the intense pain reached him. Sam cursed Smoke and managed to clear leather and level the pistol. Smoke shot him in the head. Burt tried to lift his pistol. He managed to cock it and fire, shooting himself in the foot, the slug tearing off his big toe. He dropped his gun to the floor and started yelling in pain.

Smoke glanced at Jackson. The man's hands were still on the tabletop, palms down.

"Holy Hell!" the barkeep hollered.

The farmer was praying to the Almighty.

"Can't say I didn't warn 'em," Jackson broke the silence.

"For a fact," Smoke replied, punching out empty brass and reloading. "Is there a bounty on my head, Jackson?"

"Thousand dollars."

"I don't have to ask who put it there."

"I 'spect you know."

"I imagine the bounty is gong to go up on me after this."

"It wouldn't surprise me none."

"What about them?" Smoke jerked his head at the dead and dying gunslicks.

"Don't ask me, Smoke. Hell, I didn't take 'em to raise!"

"I'll bury 'em iffen I can have what's in they pockets!" the barkeep said.

"Suits me," Smoke told him. He picked up his beer mug and drained it, wiping his mouth with the back of his hand. He set the mug back on the plank. "Fill it up, barkeep."

"Git it yourself! It's on the house. I ain't movin' 'til I know all the lead's through flyin'!"

Smoke walked around the bar just as the farmer was getting up off the floor. He looked at him. "You want another beer?"

"Hell, no!" The farmer hit the air and didn't look back.

"I'm gonna stand up now, Smoke," Jackson said.

"Go right ahead."

"Then I'm gonna walk out the door and get my horse and go."

"See you around, Jackson."

"Maybe. I ain't made up my mind about this job. You showin' up sorta tipped the balance some."

"Whatever pops your corn, Jackson."

The gunfighter nodded, turned, and left the smoky barroom. Within ten seconds, the sounds of his horse's hooves echoed down the short silent street.

Burt started hollering something awful.

"Ain't he gonna die?" the barkeep asked. "I'd lak to have them boots of his."

"Sooner or later. Is there any hard candy for sale in the store?"

"Hard candy!"

"Yeah. I got some kids working for me. They all probably have a sweet tooth."

"Hell, I don't know!"

Smoke shrugged and walked into the store area of the building. He was thinking that he'd better buy a couple boxes of .44's. Way things were going he'd probably need them.

The news of the gunfight had reached the ranch before Smoke returned. Walt and Cheyenne met him in the barn.

"Did you run into some trouble, boy?" the old rancher asked.

"Couple of two-bit gunhands who thought they were better than they really were." Smoke stripped the saddle off Dagger, hung up the reins, rubbed him down, and began forking hay into his stall.

Cheyenne and Walt were silent for a time. Walt broke it. "Swenson came by here, all flusterated. Said you cut them boys down faster than the blink of an eye."

"Like I said, they weren't as good as they thought they were."

Cheyenne grunted and spat a brown stream onto the barn floor. "I knowed Burt Rolly's dad. He wasn't no good neither. Utes kilt him years ago. Died bad. They never sung no songs about him. What was that other hombre's name?"

"Sam Teller."

The old mountain man and gunfighter shook his head. "Must not have been much to him. I never heared of him."

Cheyenne limped off. He still carried a Sioux arrowhead in his hip. Slowed him down when the weather changed.

"Doreen finally got around to telling me that you two had a little run-in, Smoke."

"Not much of one. I would just like to know why everyone is lying to me."

The rancher was silent for a time. "You want to explain that remark, Smoke? 'Cause if you don't, old man or not, I'm goin' in the house for my six gun and call you out!"

Smoke chuckled. "Yeah . . . you probably would, too, Walt. But I'm going to let my statement stand. None of you have leveled with me. I've seen the quick looks passed between you whenever I touch on certain subjects. What's going on, Walt?"

"Doreen is a good girl, Smoke."

"I never said she wasn't."

"She isn't married to Clint Perkins."

"I didn't think she was. The boy is a wood's colt, huh?"

"How'd you guess?"

"Just that, a guess. Is the boy's father Clint Perkins?"

"Yes. They went together for a time—on the sly. Then he got her all puffed up and ran out on her. He kept tellin' Doreen how they was gonna move to California and he was gonna change and . . . lies and lies, that's all they was. He'd climb a telegraph pole for a lie and leave the truth layin' on the ground."

"So Doreen figured that a make-believe outlaw husband was better than no husband at all?"

"That's about it. Clint is a no-good, Smoke. He started out doin' good, I'll give him that much; he really did do good. Then he turned bad. The young man is not right in the head."

"All that about him seeing his parents killed and running off into the timber . . . ?"

"Lies. You got to understand something, Smoke. I was the first white man to settle in this part of Idaho. Back in '38. The first one. I built me a cabin and got settled in and then went back for Alice. When we got here, the Injuns had burned the cabin down. We built again and fought off Injuns until they got to where they'd leave us alone. I prospered. Found some color and panned it. Found some more color and mined that out. I got money, Smoke. Plenty of it. I got money in a half-dozen banks. Hell, I don't need this ranch or the cattle. I kept on to it for my boy."

The old man paused to light his pipe and Smoke waited.

"But he married into trash. Pure trash. That woman—damn her black heart wherever she is—wasn't nothin' but a whore. That's all she was. Anyways, they had a son. Clint. His name ain't Perkins, it's Burden. But she run off with him and changed it."

"Wait a minute, wait a minute! This is getting confusing. Back up. Where is your son?"

"Dead. Ten years back. He turned into a drunk after that woman run off and left him. Staggered around here drunk and crazy in the head and heart for years. He never hurt nobody. He was just a fool there at the end. Jud Vale killed him. Shot him for sport one night over at the tradin' post where you was this day. Made it last a long time. Shot his legs out from under him, then busted his hands and arms with .44's. It was a awful thing for one human to do to another. Jud and that no-good foreman of his, Jason, just left my boy there in the mud to bleed to death. He ain't never hired nothing but trash over there at the Bar V. Most of them runnin' from the law somewheres."

"Where does Clint fit into all this?"

The old man laughed bitterly. "That's funny, son. Really funny. You see, I hired some fancy detectives to hunt that witch-woman down and bring my grandson back to me. They found her and brung him back. Bad seed, Smoke. He's just bad. But the more I got to lookin' at him, the more I began to suspect he wasn't none of my blood. The day he run off for the last time, he told me. My boy Clint didn't father him. Jud Vale did."

Chapter 4

Smoke walked outside the barn with Walt and paused to roll a cigarette. "Does Jud Vale know about Clint being his son?"

"Oh, yeah. That's why he wants Clint dead and Doreen his so bad. He suspects, and rightly so, that I changed my will leaving everything to Doreen. He don't want no wood's colt hanging around, messin' everything up. And with Doreen his woman, willing or not, he could produce a false weddin' license and claim it all. At worse, he could tie it up in court for years."

"Jud sounds like a real nice fellow."

"A regular Prince Charming," the old man said sourly.

"I'm glad you told me this, Walt."

"Me and the old woman talked about it last night. We agreed that it wasn't right for you to come in here and lay your life on the line for us, and us not to level with you. I'd have gotten around to tellin' you, son."

"You say you found gold around here?"

"A small pocket of it. I panned it plumb out. There was enough for me to invest in one thing or the other and become a well set up man. That's another thing, Smoke. Jud Vale knows about me panning the gold. But I never could convince the hard-headed no-good that there ain't no more gold. The gold I panned washed in here from God knows where, and the small pocket I mined is gone. Nature is a funny critter, Smoke. She'll sometimes put precious minerals in a place where they just ain't supposed to be. And when it's gone, it's gone forever. There just ain't no more."

"But Jud Vale doesn't believe that." It was not a question.

Walt sighed. "No. The man's a fool when it comes to money. Greediest man I ever saw in all my life. Got hisself a regular palace on his spread. And Doreen believes the man is in love with her; obsessed, is the way she put it. He's finally found something that he can't have; he can't buy it or steal it, and he's furious about it."

"He might try to take her by force."

"That thought has come to me from time to time."

"You going to tell her that you leveled with me?"

"Yes. Oughta ease the tensions around here."

"For a fact. Let's go all the way with it and then we'll speak no more of it. How were you getting your food in here?"

"Shoshone friends of mine. But rations was gettin' kinda sparse since Jud found the trail they was usin' and posted guards on it."

"Toward the end of this week, once the boys have settled in, we'll take a ride to the trading post and stock up. I imagine Alice and Doreen would like a little outing."

"I reckon so. Ain't none of us been off this spread in months. And them boys you brung eat like starvin' animals!"

* * *

The boys settled right in and soon needed very little supervison. They began stringing wire and doing a good job of it. Smoke took Cheyenne and several of the older boys and went looking for Box T cattle. He felt he knew where most of the cattle would be, and his hunch paid off.

"We been on Bar V range for a time," Cheyenne pointed out.

"And seeing more and more of Walt's cattle. Jamie, you boys start hazing them out and bunching them."

"Yes, sir, Mr. Smoke."

They hadn't gone another half-mile before Jud Vale and half a dozen of his hardcases came galloping up, punishing their horses needlessly. That was another way you could judge a man's character—by the way he treated his horse. Smoke's dislike for Jud Vale deepened as he looked at the lathered-up gelding he was riding.

"What the hell are you doing on my range, Jensen?" Jud demanded.

"Looking for Box T cattle, Vale. And finding them. You got any objections?"

Cheyenne had shifted positions so the muzzle of his Winchester was aimed right at a Bar V rider's belly, and the Bar V man didn't look a bit happy about it.

Smoke had pulled his Winchester out of the boot and had his thumb on the hammer. Jud didn't seem to be too terribly thrilled about that either, since the muzzle was pointed in his general direction.

"Yeah," Vale finally replied. "I got objections. I can't help it if that old coot's cattle wandered onto my range, eatin' up all my grass."

"Well, then, you should be glad to see us, Vale. We're going to take them back to home range and then you won't have to spend your nights worrying about them. Now we can either do that, or I can wire the territorial governor and ask for range detectives to be sent in here. How do you want it, Vale?"

The man puffed up like a 'possum and gave Smoke some dark looks. "Well . . . git your damn cattle and git the hell off my land then. I'm tired of lookin' at your damn ugly face, Jensen."

"Unless you want us over here every day for a couple of weeks, Vale, why don't you have your boys assist us? It would move a lot faster."

Cheyenne's leathery old face struggled to hide his grin. Smoke was pushing the big blowhard into a corner and the man couldn't find a way out.

Vale blustered and hissed like a spreadin' adder and shifted around in the saddle. "I ain't helpin' you do nothin', Jensen. I don't give a damn how often you come over here. You just make sure all the beeves you push across the crick are wearin' Box T brands, or by God, you'll answer to me."

"We can do that now, Vale," Smoke told him. He booted the Winchester and dropped his right hand to his thigh, close to the butt of that deadly .44.

Jud didn't like that idea at all. It was seven against two, for a fact. But it was also a fact that this was a no-win situation. Cheyenne was an old he-coon from 'way back. Jud's men might take him, but the old man was sure to empty two, maybe three saddles before he went down; and even down the old goat was as dangerous as a cornered grizzly. Even dying, if you got too close to the old bastard, he'd sure likely come up with a knife and cut you from brisket to backbone.

Smoke Jensen was quite another matter. Everybody knew he'd been raised by Preacher, and Preacher was a legend. Jensen had killed more than a hundred men—and that wasn't counting Injuns. Jud Vale knew the first thing to happen should he grab for iron, was that Smoke was going to blow him right out of the saddle.

And there just wasn't no percentage in dying.

"Round up your damn cattle and get off my range," Jud finally backed down. He savagely jerked his horse around and galloped off, his men following him.

"I hate a man treats a horse like that," Cheyenne said. "A horse or a dog. You show me a man who's unkind to animals and I'll show you a man that just ain't no damn good."

"I'm going to have to kill that man someday, Cheyenne. I can see it coming."

"I 'spect, Smoke, they's a long line of folks ahead of you thinkin' the same thing."

Saturday, they went to the trading post on Mud Lake.

Walt drove the wagon, with Alice by his side, and Doreen, all prettied up, and Micky sitting on boxes in the back of the wagon.

Doreen was a looker, no doubt about that, and a flirty thing, too. Smoke did his best to avoid her sliding glances. The heat coming out of her eyes could fry an egg. Although Smoke didn't think kitchen cooking was what she had on her mind.

Cheyenne, Winchester across his saddle horn, rode on one side of the wagon, Smoke on the other.

As they rode and rattled up to the big store, Cheyenne pointed out the two fresh graves out back of the building.

Doreen and Alice and Micky went into the store part of the building to shop, and Smoke, Walt, and Cheyenne went into the bar to have a beer.

"Not you agin!" the barkeep moaned, as Smoke stepped inside.

"I'm peaceful," Smoke grinned at him.

"Haw! You won't be when some of them no-count hard-cases from the Bar V show up. Just don't wreck my damn place," he warned.

"Why don't you just shut up and get us a bottle," Cheyenne told him. "You prattle on like a scared old woman."

The bartender looked at the skinny old mountain man with the wicked look in his eyes and shut his mouth. He placed a bottle on the bar and several shot glasses. Smoke pushed the shot glass away and ordered a beer.

Cheyenne downed one quick belt and poured another, taking the shot glass and moving to the far end of the bar where he could watch the door. He had left his Winchester in the saddle boot. If anything happened in the barroom, he would rely on the old Colt with the worn handles hanging low on his right side. Or on the Bowie knife sheathed on his left side. Or on the .44 derringer in his boot. Or anything else he could get his hands on. If it just had to be, the old mountain man would pick up a porcupine to use as a weapon and damn the needles.

Micky had a bottle of sarsaparilla and was sitting on a bench in front of the store. Coming to town was quite an outing for the boy.

Alice and Doreen were oohhing and aahhing over some new dress material in the store.

Two farmers were sitting at a table, nursing mugs of beer, talking quietly. They finished their drinks and left. A fat man, a drummer from the looks of him, was sitting alone at a table next to a window. He kept shifting his eyes to Smoke, stealing fast sly glances.

"Say!" he finally spoke. "Aren't you Smoke Jensen, the gunfighter?"

Smoke cut his eyes. "I'm Smoke Jensen."

"Well, I'll just be hornswoggled! I just read a big article on you in the *Gazette*. The writer said you've killed more'un five hundred men."

"Not quite that many," Smoke corrected.

"Kilt two right in here a few days back," the barkeep said with a grin. "This is my place. I'm Bendel." He pointed. "Kilt 'em right over yonder. They's buried out back."

"You don't say!" the drummer bobbed his head up and down. "I'm from St. Louis myself. I got the finest line of women's underthings and unmentionables on the market today, I do."

"How kin you sell 'um if you cain't mention 'um?" Cheyenne asked him.

The drummer looked startled for a moment, then burst out laughing. "Oh, that's a good one. I'll have to remember that." He stared at the old mountain man. "Are you somebody famous?"

"I have been a time or two," Cheyenne grumbled.

"That's Cheyenne O'Malley," Smoke informed the drummer.

"No kidding! You once fought off a hundred hostile savages."

"More like fifteen," Cheyenne told him. "And they wasn't savages or hostile. They was just mad at me 'cause I bedded down with the chief's oldest daughter. She was due to marry the war chief who led the band who come after me. Never could make no sense out of that. I enjoyed it and so did she. I went back about ten years later and looked her up. Sorry I did that. She was about the size of a tipi. Hit me up side the head with a rock and called me all sorts of vile names.

Damned if I didn't have to fight the same bunch all over again. But this time that war chief was mad 'cause I hadn't toted her off ten years back. I don't think they got along too well."

"That's incredible!" the drummer said.

Cheyenne belched. "Damn squaw follered me from the Sun River all the way over to the Bitterroot. Hollerin' and cussin' and raisin' hell. I finally lost her around Lolo Pass. Things like that tend to take some of the joy out of messin' with wimmin."

"What stories I'll have to tell when I get back to St. Louis!" He looked out the window. "Bunch of riders coming."

Smoke walked to the batwings and looked out. "Gunhands," he said.

"Is there going to be a Wild West shoot-out?" the drummer questioned.

"I hope not."

"Oh, that would be so exhilarating!"

"Not for them that gits shot," Cheyenne said, slipping the hammer thong from his pistol. "All they git is plugged."

Half a dozen Bar V hands began crowding into the barroom. They pulled up short and fell silent when they saw Smoke.

Smoke knew two of them. Blackjack Morgan and Gus Fall. The others might well be hell on wheels with a short gun, but they just hadn't made a name for themselves as yet. And if they decided to brace Smoke Jensen and Cheyenne O'Malley, the only name they were going to get would be carved on their gravestones.

"Jensen," Blackjack said, walking past him, his spurs jingling.

Smoke nodded his head.

Gus stopped by the bar and stared at Smoke. He shifted his chew around in his mouth and spat toward a spittoon near Smoke's boot. He missed the cuspidor, the tobacco juice striking Smoke's boot.

Gus grinned at him. "You can get the boy out front to come lick it off."

His grin was wiped off his face in a bloody smear as Smoke swung the beer mug, hitting Gus's jaw and knocking a couple of teeth slap out of his mouth. Gus was propelled backward, his boots slipping on the fresh-mopped floor. He slammed through the batwings, tearing one off, and fell into the dusty street, on his back, out cold.

Micky sat on the bench and stared, mouth open, eyes wide.

Smoke tossed the handle of the mug onto the plank. "Another beer, please."

"There wasn't no call to do that," one of the young so-called gunslicks told Smoke. "'Sides, Gus is my friend. I feel obliged to take up for him."

Cheyenne laid the barrel of his Colt against the young man's head and he dropped to the floor like a rock.

One of the young man's buddies thought it was a dandy time to grab for iron. He changed his mind as Cheyenne eared back the hammer on his Colt and put those cold old eyes on the kid.

"Boy," Cheyenne warned him, "I'll blow a hole in your gawddamn belly a horse could ride through."

"That's Cheyenne O'Malley!" the drummer blurted out as warning.

The young man's face turned gray and shiny with sweat. He let his eyes slide away from the eyes of death staring at him from the face of the mountain man. Slowly, very slowly, he let his hands drop to his sides, as far away from the butts of his guns as humanly possible. He would have grabbed the boards on the floor if his reach had been long enough.

Cheyenne eased the hammer down and holstered the Colt. He turned his attentions back to his shot glass.

"See about Gus," Blackjack told one of the men. He cut his eyes to Smoke. "You're right touchy today, Smoke. Who twisted your tail?"

"Two-bit gunhands have a tendency to annoy me." Smoke lifted his fresh mug of beer with his left hand and took a sip.

"When Gus gets up from the dirt, he's gonna kill you, Smoke."

"He'll try." Smoke turned his back to the gunfighter and sipped his beer.

Blackjack moved to a table and sat down, ordering a bottle.

The drummer was scribbling frantically in a notebook; he wanted to be sure to get all this down. He might write a book about this.

Gus was helped back into the barroom, his mouth bloody and his eyes wild with hate and fury. Smoke turned to watch him, his right hand by his side.

Gus shook himself away from the men on each side of him and faced Smoke. He was so mad he was trembling.

"Gus," Blackjack warned. "Back off, son. This is not the time."

"Go to hell!" Gus said, without taking his eyes off of Smoke.

"You better do what he says, boy," Cheyenne told him. "You're just about to step off into where the waters is deep and dark."

"You go to hell, too, old man!"

Cheyenne shrugged his shoulders. "Nobody can ever say I didn't try to warn you about the currents."

"You ready, Jensen?" Gus asked.

"I'm not finished with my beer, Gus. I would suggest you get you a cool one and calm down some."

"You, by God, don't tell me what to do, Smoke."

"I'm just trying to save your life, Gus."

Gus cussed him. "Here or in the street, Jensen?"

"It doesn't make a damn bit of difference to me, Gus." Smoke sat his beer mug down on the plank.

Gus reached for his guns.

Chapter 5

Smoke's left-hand Colt roared and bucked as his cross-draw flashed.

The slugs hit Gus in the chest and belly, doubling him over. He stumbled back and grabbed onto a table's edge for support. He finally managed to drag iron just as Smoke fired again, the .44 slug slamming into his chest. The light began to fade around him as the men in the barroom took on a ghostly appearance, drifting into double images as the sounds of the pale rider grew louder in his ears.

Gus looked down at his hands. What had happened to his guns? His hands were empty. But he had drawn them. He was sure of that.

Gus sat down heavily in a chair and the legs broke under the sudden weight, spilling him to the floor. The last thing he would hear was the sounds of the pale rider's horse galloping closer. And finally, the feel of that cold and bony hand reaching down to touch his shoulder.

"Did anybody even see Jensen draw?" the drummer asked, his voice filled with awe. "Jesus God, I didn't."

The young man whom Cheyenne had bopped on the noggin with the barrel of his Colt finally sat up and moaned, both hands to his head. "What happened?" he asked.

"Gus finally saw the critter," Blackjack told him.

The young man looked up into the cold eyes of Smoke Jensen. Right then, and unfortunately for him, only for a very brief moment, did the old homeplace farm back in Minnesota pull at him slightly.

The young man who had just recently taken to calling himself the Pecos Kid pushed those thoughts out of his head and began to think about how he could kill Smoke Jensen. Yeah . . . the man who killed Smoke Jensen would be famous all over the world. He'd have fame and money and all the women anybody could ever want. So he very wrongly thought.

Smoke stared down at him from the bar. His words momentarily chilled the Pecos Kid. "Put it out of your head, kid. Don't even think about it."

Smoke turned and Walt and Cheyenne followed him out of the bar and into the general store.

When Smoke was well out of earshot, Pecos said, "I bet I could take him."

Blackjack just shook his head in disgust.

It appeared that the bitterly cold and long winter had finally given way to spring as the warming winds began to blow. The syringa began to bloom, as did the balsam and lupine, and the marsh marigold and blue columbine lent their hues and fragrances to the cacophony of color. Harrison had ridden to the store by the lake and came back with bad news.

"That Clint Perkins done struck agin, Mr. Walt. This time he killed a man over on the Little Malad. Some big landowner over thataway."

Walt kicked at a rock and cussed.

"And that ain't all. Jud Vale—had to be him—done upped the ante on Smoke's head. Five thousand dollars to the man who kills him."

Smoke had walked up, listening. The news came as no surprise to him.

Walt looked at him. "Jud knows that with you out of the picture this whole operation would fold. Me and Cheyenne and Dolittle and Harrison could hold on for a time, but not for long. Maybe it's time for me to sell out and move on; take Doreen and Micky with me and the old woman and just get gone."

"Is that what you want to do, Walt?"

"Hell, no!" There was considerable heat in the man's voice.

"Then don't. But here's what we can do: round up the rest of your herds and sell off the older stuff. That would take some strain off the range. We could use the boys to drive them to the railhead at Preston. Me and Cheyenne would stay here on the place with you to make sure Jud's men don't burn the house down."

Walt thought for a moment, then nodded his head. "All right, let's do 'er."

Leaving Cheyenne in charge of the roundup, Smoke saddled up and headed for the nearest telegraph office to find a buyer for the cattle. He did not take the normally traveled roads or trails, but instead cut across country, blazing his own trail.

Smoke wasn't worried about the men Jud Vale had hired.

Most of them were stand-up, look-you-in-the-eye gun-fighters. They had a reputation to defend or to build, and back-shooters they were not. It was the bounty hunters that Smoke knew would be coming in who worried him.

That scum had no scruples or morals or anything that even remotely resembled those attributes.

And they would be coming in once that five thousand dollar ante on his head was spread about the country; that would not take long to accomplish.

He made the ride to the wire office with no trouble, and sent wires out until he found a buyer who knew him and was interested in the cattle. He made arrangements over the wires to meet the shipment at the railhead with a bankdraft.

He walked over to the hotel and checked in, then got himself a bath and a shave and changed clothes while his range clothing was being washed, dried, and ironed. Then he headed for a cafe for a meal.

Smoke was a handsome, striking-looking man, tall and muscular, and he turned many a female head as he strode up the boardwalk, spurs jingling. And he caused many a man to step back as he passed, for even though Smoke did not know it, and would have scoffed at it if someone had told him so, there was clear and present danger in those cold brown eyes. And by the way he wore his guns, there was no denying that he was very comfortable with those Colts, and knew how to use them. And more importantly, would use them.

He had changed into dark pin-stripe trousers over his polished boots, a white shirt with black string tie, and a leather vest.

He decided to have a beer before he ate his lunch and pushed open the batwings of the saloon, stepping inside.

The bounty hunters and the gunfighter locked eyes.

John Wills, Dave Bennett, Shorty Watson, and Lefty Cassell were sharing a bottle and playing poker.

Smoke told the barkeep he wanted a beer and walked over to their table, pulling out a chair and sitting down. "Deal me in, boys."

"You got a lot of brass on your butt, Jensen," Lefty told him. "Who the hell invited you?"

"You're hurting my feelings, Lefty. Makes me think I smell bad. And to think I just spent good money to have a bath and a shave."

"Very funny, Smoke," Wills said. "Notice how we're all laughing."

"I can see that. You boys gonna deal me in or not?"

"Closed game, Jensen," Shorty told him. "Just like you're gonna be soon. Closed. Like in a box."

They thought that was funny. Hysterically so. Smoke smiled with their laughter. They stopped laughing when they heard the almost inaudible click of a hammer being eared back.

"Is the joke over so soon?" Smoke asked, an innocent expression on his face. "Keep your hands where I can see them, boys."

"You can't shoot us like this, Jensen," Wills said, a very hopeful note in his voice. "That'd be murder!"

"And you law-abiding boys certainly don't hold with murder, now, do you?" Smoke's voice was low-pitched and deadly.

Lefty softly cursed Smoke.

"Boys," Smoke told them, as he tapped the barrel of his Colt on Shorty's knee, that action bringing a sheen of sweat on the man's face. "I'm going to have myself a nice quiet drink and then I'm going to the cafe for something to eat. While I'm having my drink, you boys finish yours. While I'm in the cafe, I'd better see you scum ride out of town and don't come back while I'm here."

"And if we don't?" Dave Bennett challenged.

"I'll come out of the cafe with both hands full of Colts and one thing on my mind: killing all four of you."

Wills swallowed hard and said, "This ain't like you, Smoke. You've usually had to be pushed into a gunfight."

"I came out here for a vacation. Soon as I crossed over into Idaho Territory, folks started pushing me. Now I'm pushing back. Keep another thought in mind, boys: if you ride out of here heading east, I'll know what side you're on."

"And . . . ?" Shorty asked.

"I will officially declare open season on bounty hunters."

Smoke holstered his Colt, much to the relief of all the men around the table. He stood up, turned his back to the men, and walked to the bar, ordering a drink.

Lefty exhaled slowly. "We got some talkin' to do, boys. We cross the Bear headin' east. This here job ain't gonna be no cakewalk."

"I say we take him as a group," Wills said. "Winner take it all."

"Here and now?" Shorty asked, doubt in his voice. "Standin' up and lookin' at him?"

"Hell, no! We'll ambush him. But we're gonna wait. The ante is sure to go up as Jensen puts more and more punk gunslingers into the ground. We'll just lay back and let them reputation-huntin' gunhands get kilt. Then we'll make our move."

Smoke sat at a table by a window, eating his meal, and watched the bounty hunters ride out of town, heading west. The move was not unexpected and didn't fool him one bit. He'd bet a sack of gold nuggets that Wills and his bunch would get a couple of miles out of town and then swing around and double back, try to get ahead of him and maybe set up an ambush. For sure they were going to head east where the trouble was, and the blood money was waiting for the man or men who killed Smoke Jensen.

Right then and there, over his apple pie and third cup of coffee—for Smoke was a coffee-drinking man—he made up his mind that he was in this fracus to stay, come Hell, Jud Vale, or that hot-eyed Doreen.

Smoke Jensen just did not like to be pushed.

Smoke left before dawn the following morning. He rode straight south out of town and did not turn east until he came to a canyon very close to the Utah line. He built a hat-sized fire and cooked his supper, then mounted up and rode until dusk before finding a place to bed down for the night. The bounty hunters might find him, but Smoke was going to make it as difficult as possible for them.

He was back in the saddle again before dawn, and did not stop to boil coffee until the sun had bubbled its way up into the sky and he'd found a place that was easily defended.

He crossed the Wasatch Range and pointed Dagger's nose north, keeping on the west side of Bear Lake. He was on home range by late afternoon.

"Any trouble?" Cheyenne asked in the barn.

"None. But I did run into four bounty hunters."

"More than that drifted in the last couple of days. And Jud Vale is hirin' more guns. I think the no-count is gonna hit the herd and to hell with whether the boys gits hurt."

Smoke smiled. At the wire office he had sent and received more than one telegraph. He handed a copy to Cheyenne. The man read it and his leathery face crinkled in a smile.

Received your wire stop Would be delighted to accompany the boys on a cattle drive stop Expect me at the ranch in three days stop.

It was signed by the editor of the Montpelier paper.

"Tomorrow morning, I'll ride over to the trading post and

tack this to the wall," Smoke said. "Jud will have it in his hands within hours. Then we'll see how he reacts to this news."

"Son of a bitch!" Jud shouted. Then he tore the wire to small bits, flinging the paper to the floor and kicking at the shreds. "Damn that Smoke Jensen to Hell!"

"This shore changes the plans," Jason said.

With a long sigh, Jud nodded his head. "Tell the boys to relax. We can't hit the herd with a damn newspaper man along. Public opinion would crucify me. The territorial governor would have this place swarming with U.S. Marshals if just one of those damn kids got hurt and it was reported."

"But they might not have a ranch to come back to," Jason said with a wicked smile.

"Yeah," Jud said softly. "You damn right!"

"You boys take 'er easy," Walt told the gathering in dawn's first light. "Ten miles a day is fine with me."

The editor of the newspaper had brought three men with him, a cub reporter from back East and two tough-looking men from his church. The men were heavily armed and ready for trouble.

Smoke knew there would be no trouble against the herd on this run. Jud was arrogant and perhaps crazy in the head, but he wasn't stupid. Smoke expected the drive to make it through with only the normal mishaps that took place on any cattle drive.

But he was equally certain the ranch would be attacked.

They stood and watched as the men and boys began moving the cattle out, the cattle setting their own pace.

After the dust had settled, Smoke began his preparations for the attack he was sure was forthcoming.

Cheyenne would stay in and defend the bunkhouse. The old mountain man and gunfighter had loaded up several rifles and half a dozen pistols. He had plenty of food prepared by the ladies and a couple of barrels of water to use against fire should it come to that.

Before the drive began, Smoke had fortified the horses' stalls with extra boards. The stalls were as safe from bullets as they could make them.

Both Alice and Doreen could handle a rifle or pistol as well, or better, than the average man. They would stay in the house with Walt and Micky.

Smoke would station himself in the loft of the barn. He had placed loaded rifles and shotguns at both ends of the building, and he had plenty of food and water to last out any siege.

Now all they had to do was wait, and sometimes that was harder than the actual battle.

The next move was up to Jud Vale and his men.

Probably forty or more men to wage war against an old rancher, his wife, a young woman, her eight-year-old son, three old men, a group of boys whose average age was twelve, and one gunfighter.

Smoke had to laugh and question the bravery of those who rode with Jud Vale.

Just before dark, Smoke did a once-around of the buildings, looking in first on those in the house.

"We're set, Smoke," the rancher told him. "We've got Micky in the basement, guardin' the potatoes and the canned goods."

Smoke grinned and nodded. "No bullet can reach him down there, for sure." He noticed that both Alice and

Doreen had changed into men's britches, so they could get around faster. Doreen did things to those jeans that the manufacturer never dreamed of.

She noticed the direction his eyes were taking and smiled at him.

"I got to go," Smoke muttered, and left the house.

In the bunkhouse, Cheyenne waved him toward the coffeepot. "I went over to the house about an hour ago," the old mountain man said. "Both them wimmin was prancin' around in men's britches. I never seen the like. This goes on, wimmin'll be votin' 'fore long and that'll be the ruination of the country." He was reflective for a moment. "Not that I ever voted that much myself. Quit altogether about a year after I cast my vote for Millard Fillmore. But, hell, anybody can make a mistake. I was gonna vote for that Abe Lincoln. But by the time I made up my mind and got to where I could vote, somebody had done up and shot him. Plumb disheartenin'. Damn shore ruined Abe's night out, too. You much on votin', Smoke?"

"I wasn't until I married Sally. Kind of hard to find a ballot box at Brown's Hole."

"For a fact. Fort Misery, we used to call it. But I 'spect Preacher told you that."

"Yes, he did."

"Ol' Warhoss is still kickin'. He's got to be eighty-five if he's a day. But them Injuns is takin' right good care of him. And I understand they's some old gunslingers and mountain men got together and in the process of building a retirement home for us old coots."

"That's my understanding."

"Won't that be grand! I'll have to go check that out—if I ever live to be old, that is."

Smoke laughed at him and walked back to the barn.

It was full dark when he crawled into the loft and made himself comfortable at the east end of the barn. He figured that was the direction from which the attack would most likely come.

Before taking his position, he watched the lamps go out in both the house and the bunkhouse as the defenders made ready for war.

Smoke settled down and waited.

Chapter 6

Arrogant! Smoke thought, as he heard the sounds of hooves drumming on the road. Jud is so sure of himself that he just rides right up the road to the gate.

He heard the gates being torn down and then the wild screams of the hired guns as they galloped up the road toward the house.

Smoke quickly shifted positions and sighted a man under the hunter's moon that illuminated the night sky. He took up slack on the trigger and the butt-plate slammed his shoulder. A saddle emptied just as gunfire from the house and bunkhouse roared, shattering the night and emptying half a dozen more saddles.

He heard Jud's voice, hollering for his men to fall back to the ridges.

Smoke fired again, and saw a man jerk in the saddle. He managed to stay on his horse, but one arm was hanging useless and flopping by his side.

The attackers had been able to fire no more than half a dozen shots before they were beaten back.

One man struggled to his boots in the road and began staggering and lurching toward the gates. The defenders held their fire and let him go. Just before he reached the gates, he collapsed facedown in the hard-packed dirt and did not move.

That sight must have done it for the riders. Someone shouted, "Hell with this! The luck ain't with us this night."

The attackers rode off, heading back for the friendlier range of the Bar V. They left their dead and wounded behind them.

Smoke and the others waited a reasonable length of time, to see if it was a trick, and then slowly and cautiously gathered in the yard.

Smoke and Cheyenne roamed about, checking on the men sprawled on the ground.

They found several alive. "What do we do with those still alive?" Cheyenne questioned.

"Patch them up and get word to Jud to come and get them," Smoke told him. "Maybe pile them in a wagon and send them back to Jud. We'll see." He was kneeling down beside a man who was alive, but not for long. He had been shot in the center of the chest.

"He'll never quit, Jensen," the dying man gasped. "Vale's a crazy man."

"Why is he doing it?"

The man ignored that. "As long as he's got a dime in his jeans he'll hire fighting men."

"Why?" Smoke persisted.

"King. To be king. Wants to control everything from the state line to Preston. Everything and everybody."

"Shut up, Slim!" another wounded man growled, mercenary and loyal to the gun right to the end.

"You go to hell, Lassiter!" Slim told him. He cut his eyes to Smoke. The light was slowly fading from them. "Vale's got gunhands comin' in on the train. This is shapin' up to be the biggest range war in . . . the state. He'll overpower you just by . . . numbers, Jensen. And he's just about reached . . . the point where he don't give a damn if the kids git hurt."

Slim groaned and closed his eyes. He did not open them again.

Smoke rose to his boots and took the blanket that Doreen handed him, spreading it over the dead gunfighter. Cheyenne had taken all the guns and ammo from the dead and wounded men. They would be added to the arsenal of the Box T. Smoke felt sure they would be needed before all this was over.

He knelt down beside Lassiter. The man had a bullet-burn on the side of his head and a slight shoulder wound. Painful but not serious. "I ought to call the U.S. Marshals in here and file charges against all of you, Lassiter . . ."

The gunfighter sneered at him.

". . . But that would take weeks and we'd have to keep you prisoner and look at your ugly face every day. It just isn't worth it."

"You better kill me, Jensen," Lassiter warned. "Davidson was a friend of mine."

"You should choose your friends more carefully, Lassiter. No, I'm not going to kill you. Not like this, anyway. Not at this time."

"Then you're a damn fool, Jensen!"

"Maybe. But I can sleep at night, and I don't make war against kids and women and old people."

"Who gives a damn what happens to a bunch of snot-nose brats!"

Smoke was a hard man in a harsh time and environment,

and he had killed many, many men. But he had to shake his head at the cold-blooded callousness of Lassiter.

"Back away and let me finish him," Cheyenne said, walking up. "We got it to do sooner or later."

Doreen stood looking at it all through wide and scared eyes.

Smoke had no doubts about the old mountain man's ability to do just what he suggested. And he knew the old man was right: they would have it to do sooner or later. But he just couldn't kill the wounded man that way.

He shook his head. "Get him patched up, Doreen. We'll put him in a wagon."

He walked over to where a young man lay, gut shot. The young gunfighter, no more than a couple of years out of boyhood, lay with both hands clutching his belly. The blood seeped darkly through his fingers, glistening wetly under the light of the hunter's moon.

"You got a mamma you want me to write, boy?"

He shook his head, wincing with the painful movement. "They throwed me out of the house a long time ago. I wasn't about to spend the rest of my life . . . sloppin' hogs and milkin' cows."

"Beats what you got now," Smoke coldy and bluntly informed him.

The young man cussed him. Smoke watched as his right hand slipped toward his large belt buckle. Smoke reached down and pulled a derringer from behind the buckle before the gunhand could reach it. The young gunfighter cursed him even more.

"How much was Jud Vale paying you, boy?"

"A hundred a month and found!" He moaned the words as the pain reached higher levels in his bullet-shattered belly.

"Maybe you can buy something in Hell."

"They'll kill you, Jensen! This is one fight you ain't gonna win. Your reputation . . . ain't gonna hep you none this time around. Jud Vale's better than you. His real name is . . . is . . ."

"Shet your mouth, you bastard!" Lassiter shouted at the young man.

But the admonition fell on dead ears. The young gunny's eyes rolled back in his head as his soul went winging to a fiery, smoky eternity. His boot heels and spurs drummed and jangled against the ground and then he was still.

Smoke walked over to Walt. "How long has Jud been in this area, Walt?"

"'Bout twenty-five years. He just appeared one day with that damn Jason fellow."

"He doesn't look that old to me."

"He's older than he looks. But he's one hell of a man still. Don't sell him short none. I'd peg him in his late forties. He might be fifty even. Hard to tell with a man like that."

"No idea where he came from?" Smoke got the strong impression that Walt was lying. But why?

"Not a clue."

Cheyenne walked up, hearing the last of the conversation. "He come up here by way of Texas," the old mountain man told them. "But I doubt he was Texas born. I 'member when he got here. Like all them hands of his, I think he's runnin' from the law somewheres."

"And you would guess . . . ?"

Cheyenne shrugged. "Back East. But that's just a guess. It'd be hard to read his back trail after all these years."

"What's the count on those still alive, Cheyenne?"

"Four dead and three wounded. None of them hurt too bad."

"Can one of them drive a wagon?"

"Oh, yeah."

"Let's hitch up a team and get them on their way. We'll pile the dead in with them."

"Beats the hell outta diggin' a hole," Cheyenne said with a wicked grin.

Walt, Smoke, and Cheyenne took turns standing guard that night, but as it turned out, they could have all slept soundly, for Jud Vale and his so-called fighting men had had quite enough of the Box T for this go-around.

"Four dead," Walt said, holding a cup of coffee in his hands, warming them against the early morning chill.

"They'll be more," Smoke told him. "This battle is just getting started. Now I'm afraid that some of the kids are going to be hurt."

"I don't think that even Jud Vale would do that. Not deliberately. One of those kids gets hurt, the whole area would turn agin him, and he knows it. But they might catch a bullet that was meant for one of us."

"The kids desperately need the money for their families," Smoke concluded. "I think what I'll do is ride around the area and speak to the mothers and fathers about it. Lay it on the line. Whatever they say, that's it."

Walt spoke around the stem of his pipe, "With most of the herd gone, we could do without the younger ones. Whatever the parents say, Smoke."

Smoke began seeking out and questioning the parents early the next morning, riding first to Little Chuckie's house; if that's what the shack could be called. It wasn't that his parents were rawhiders, they were just having a tough time getting the farm operation going—with Jud Vale and his men no small part of that struggle.

"It would really be a blow to Chuckie's pride iffen you was to send him home, Mr. Smoke," the father said. His wife nodded her head in agreement. "The boy is right proud of being able to bring in some money this summer. We'll leave it up to him."

Smoke rode over to the parents of Matthew, the frail little boy with the thick glasses. He got the same message as before. The parents were not unconcerned about their children; it was simply that this was still the raw frontier, and one grew up and pulled his or her weight from the git-go. It was called survival.

Smoke spent that day and most of another day talking with the parents of the boys. The message he got, albeit worded differently, came out to mean the same thing: it was up to the boys whether to stay or leave.

Smoke drifted on over to the railhead, arriving there about the same time as the herd. He watched through hard, chilly eyes, as the passenger car spewed forth a dozen or more booted, spurred, and two-gunned men. Smoke did not need a telegraph wire to tell him that these were the men the kid had told him about before he died in the front yard of the Box T spread.

Jud Vale was going for the brass ring this time, for Smoke recognized many of the newly arrived hired guns.

He watched as Gimpy Bonner limped off the train and made his way back to the horse cars. Gimpy was deadly quick and had no backup on him. He had a horse shot out from under him years back and the horse rolled on his leg, breaking it in several places, leaving him with a permanent limp.

Shorty DePaul, all five feet five inches of him, followed

Gimpy. Short he may be, but those guns of his, and his ability to use them, made him as tall as the next man.

The editor of the Montpelier newspaper had walked over to stand by Smoke's side and watch the gunfighters leave the train. "Who is that one?" he asked.

"Scott Johnson. From down Arizona way. That stocky fellow with him is called Yates. Right behind them is De Grazia and Jake Hube. They work as a team; they'll shoot you front or back. Doesn't make any difference to them."

"Looks like Jud Vale is pulling out all the stops, doesn't it?"

"For a fact," Smoke said, as he watched two gunfighters named Becket and Pike step out of the car.

Jaeger, the German immigrant turned gunfighter, stepped down right behind them. Molino was right behind him.

Smoke ticked the names off to the editor.

Chato Di Peso, the much feared and very dangerous New Mexico bounty hunter, stepped down, hitching at his gunbelt as he walked.

There were several young punks, with fancy guns and silver adorned gunbelts tagging with the better known gunnies. Smoke counted them out as two-bit never-would-be's with no sand in them.

"I think," the editor said, "that I shall inform the governor of this gathering of trash."

"Go ahead. But it won't do any good."

"Why?" the man asked indignantly.

"There isn't a man over there who is wanted for anything that I know of. And there is no law against hiring tough men to work for you."

"There is going to be a bloodbath around the Bear, Mr. Jensen."

"Yes. And the only way I know to avoid it is for Walt and Alice Burden to turn tail and run; just give up their holdings to a madman and leave the country. Would you want to see them do that, Mr. Argood?"

"No," the editor replied quickly. "I would not. Is there a joker in this deck, Smoke?"

Smoke smiled. "Yes. And his name is Clint Perkins. He's an unknown. Have you ever seen him?"

"No. Few people have over the years. Or at least, if they have, they aren't talking. But I can tell you that many still look upon him as some sort of Robin Hood."

"But you don't."

Argood snorted in disgust. "He's no better than a common outlaw. And personally, from what I know about him, I think he's insane."

"Is he headquartered in this area?"

"No one knows. He's a mystery man. And a master of disguises." He looked at the most famous gunfighter in the West. "You think he'll show up here?"

"I think so. This is just too good for him to miss." He didn't know how much the editor knew, so he chose his words carefully. "I think there is a lot of hate in the man; all bottled up and ready to explode. When it does, it's going to get very interesting."

"That, young man," Argood said drily, "is one way of putting it."

Chapter 7

Smoke took the bank draft from the cattle buyer and tucked it safely away in a money belt around his waist. He had a letter from Walt giving him the authority to endorse the draft and deposit it in the bank over in Malad City, a wild, rip-roaring town with a history of murder, lynchings, and stage holdups. But the Overland Stage Company—whose run stopped at Malad City—had a good record of foiling holdups, so Walt's money would be reasonably safe after being deposited.

Smoke told Dolittle and Harrison to keep the boys close until he got back.

He crossed the Bear and headed for the wide-open town of Malad City. The town was named by French trappers, who, after becoming sick from gorging on beaver meat, named the town Malade, thinking the area unhealthy.

Smoke had a hunch that with the news of Jud Vale's hiring of gun hands now so widespread, Malad City would be crawling with guns for hire stopping for liquid refreshments—and a fling with the hurdy-gurdy girls—as they made their way to the Bar V. And he also wondered if the ante on his head had been upped past the five thousand dollar mark.

It wouldn't surprise him a bit.

As he rode, Smoke tried to put some more reason behind what Jud Vale was doing. Or was what Walt had told him the sum total of it all? Smoke concluded that Walt was probably right in his assessment of the situation. If Vale could get his hands on the Box T, he would then have the largest spread in the state, and would certainly be a powerful man, a man to reckon with.

On this trip, Smoke stayed with the main road leading to Malad City, and a sorry road it was.

He met several groups of men, riding in twos and threes, all looking like hardcases, and all heading east. They either did not recognize him, or did not want to brace him with such short backup.

Since he had been late getting away from the railhead, Smoke made camp just to the south of Oxford Peak, the snow-capped mountain thrusting up more than a mile and a half into the air. He was boiling his coffee and frying his bacon when he heard the faint sounds of hooves approaching his camp from out of the fast falling dusk, the rider coming from the north.

"Hello, the fire! I'm friendly."

"Then come on in and light and sit. Coffee's almost fit to drink."

Smoke saw the young man's hair sticking out from under his hat before he saw anything else. Flame red. He'd bet the young rider was called Rusty. The man's outfit was old, but well-cared for, and Smoke liked the way the young rider saw to his horse's needs before he took care of his own. He carefully rubbed the animal down with handfuls of grass and saw that it was watered and picketed on good graze. Smoke also noticed that the redhead's gun was tied down—which might not mean anything, or everything.

As he approached the fire, tin cup and plate in his left hand, his grin was genuine and his handshake firm and quick.

"Sure am glad to see a friendly face. Most of the hombres I been seein' the past couple of days all looked like they could eat a porcupine and not feel the quills!"

Smoke filled his coffee cup without comment.

"My folks dubbed me Clarence, but nobody calls me that. Just Rusty."

"I guessed right at first glance." Smoke speared some bacon out of the pan and handed a hunk of bread to Rusty.

"Much obliged." He let his eyes drift over Smoke's rig, noting the two guns, one butt-forward.

"You ridin' east like all them others?" Smoke asked.

"West for a day, then I'll do a turnaround back to the Bear. Any work over yonder?"

"I'm lookin' for hands."

"You shore found one. My poke's as flat as a sit-on pancake."

"Might be dangerous signin' on with me."

Rusty's eyes narrowed. "What kind of work you got in mind, mister-whatever-your-name-is?"

"Punching cows. Fixing fence. Cleaning out waterholes. Cowboy work. You up to it?"

"Shore! That's what I been doin' since I was big enough to sit a saddle. What's the danger you talkin' about?"

Smoke sipped his coffee before replying. "Big rancher who is about half nuts is trying to run the old man and woman who own the spread off their land. They hit us the other night. We emptied seven saddles."

"How many is us?"

"You talking about hands?"

"Yep."

"Three old men who are about seventy and a handful of kids, average age twelve."

Rusty looked dead at him. "Are you serious?"

"As a crutch."

"What're you payin'?"

"A hundred a month and found."

"A hundred a month! Shoot, man! You just hired yourself a hand."

"Those are fighting wages, Rusty."

"I kinda figured they was. But I got to tell you, I ain't never hired out my gun."

"Can you use it?"

"Oh, yeah. I reckon I'm as good as the next man. I've drug iron a time or two."

"Any family?"

"Ma and Pa died years back. I got some cousins somewhere that I ain't never seen."

"Just curious. I want to know who to notify if you catch one."

"Just plant me where I fall, I reckon. And make sure my horse is taken care of. He's a good one."

"I'm heading over to Malad City. Then we'll head back to the Box T."

"Sounds good to me. You got a name?"

"Doesn't everyone?"

"You are a most exasperatin' feller! You 'shamed of your handle?"

"No."

Rusty cussed and then ate his bacon, mopping the grease out of his tin plate with bread. He poured another cup of coffee, rolled a cigarette, and leaned back. "You a gunfighter?"

"Some say I am."

"You look familiar to me. I seen you somewheres before. On a wanted poster, maybe?"

"No. I'm not wanted. I own a ranch down Colorado way. The Sugarloaf. I'm just helping out an old couple. I don't like to see folks shoved around."

"Right nice of you. I kinda get riled up some myself when somebody tries to roll over other folks. You gonna tell me your name?"

Smoke smiled faintly. "I tell you my name, you might not come to work."

"For a hundred a month and found? You could tell me your name was Satan and I wouldn't back away."

"All right," Smoke replied. "Come to think of it, you just might be riding into a corner of Hell after all." He left it at that.

Smoke and Rusty reached Malad City at mid-morning, just as the town was catching its breath after a wild and raucous night. Things had been reasonably quiet the previous night, with only one killing.

"Don't never ask nobody for directions in this place," Rusty told him. "When they laid out these streets, they just tossed a handful of sticks on the ground for a blueprint . . . and then followed it."

They stabled their horses and Smoke pointed out a cafe, telling Rusty he'd meet him there in a few minutes. He took care of Walt's bank draft and walked the boardwalk to the cafe. He saw several gunslicks he knew by name and a dozen more who had the hardcase brand stamped all over them. And a half-dozen punks who were looking for a reputation, but more than likely would find a grave to hold their swagger long before they found a reputation.

Smoke Jensen had been elusive for over a decade, surfacing outside of his ranch in Colorado only briefly. Many people knew his name but could not put a face to it, unless they had memorized the covers of the many penny dreadfuls, most of which were rarely accurate.

He received many a furtive glance as he walked toward the cafe, for danger clung to him; it was an aura that made many strong and brave men step aside until he had passed.

Smoke was scarcely into his thirties, just now approaching the prime years of his life, but he was already a living legend, and not just west of the Mississippi. Had he elected to cut notches into the handles of his Colts after each kill, he would have gone through half a dozen sets and still not have any handles left. But only tinhorns did that.

He opened the door to the cafe and stepped in, the good smells of cooking making him realize how hungry he was. Rusty was already working on his first plate of bacon and eggs and fried potatoes—and the first of several pots of coffee.

The redhead pushed out a chair with his boot and Smoke sat down.

"Been several folks wonderin' who you are," the newly hired puncher said. "Most I heard come to the conclusion that you was a lawman of some sort."

"I've worn a badge a time or two," Smoke admitted, then called out his order to the counterman. He picked up his cup and allowed the waitress to fill it.

She met his eyes. "I seen you two or three years back," she spoke the words softly. "You be careful in this town. It's filled up with hired guns, all of them just burnin' to kill you."

"I appreciate that."

She nodded and walked back into the kitchen.

Rusty's freckled face screwed up with disgust. "Seems like ever'body knows who you are but me!"

Smoke sugared his coffee and stirred. "The name is Jensen."

The redhead's fork froze midway to his mouth. *"Smoke Jensen?"* he finally managed to say.

"That's it. Now close your mouth before a bug decides to fly in there."

Rusty filled his mouth with food and then closed it. "Boy, I sure know how to pick 'em," he muttered. "I'm beginnin' to wonder if a hundred a month is enough."

"And found," Smoke reminded him.

"Food ain't too tasty with a bellyful of lead," the puncher said mournfully. But there was a definite twinkle in his eyes.

"You didn't sign a contract," Smoke reminded him. "Feel free to ride."

"Naw! Hell, I'll stick around. I ain't never ridden with such highfalutin' company before. Might be interestin'."

"I'm not looking for trouble, Rusty. After we eat our meal, I plan on saddling up and riding out."

"That must be why you walk around with them hammer thongs off your guns."

Smoke grinned. "I just believe in being a very cautious man, that's all."

"Right. With your name, you damn well better be."

The two men cleaned their plates, Rusty eating two plates of food without apology, then finished off another pot of coffee. Not as strong as they liked it, but it would do. Then they leaned back, rolled cigarettes, and lit up. The cafe was gradually filling with the lunch crowd, all of the diners giving the two men short and cautious looks as they took their seats.

Then the door opened and four hardcases stepped inside.

Bob Garner and Montana Slim were the only two that Smoke recognized. The other two were unknown to him.

But Garner and Montana Slim were quite enough to face on a full stomach.

Or an empty belly for that matter.

Slim's eyes widened as they settled on Smoke and recognition set in. Then he grinned, his hands close to the butts of his guns.

But the humor—if that's what it was—did not reach his killer eyes.

"We done got the hotshot all bottled up, boys," Slim announced, in a too-loud voice. "And some funny lookin' pup with him."

"This dog's got teeth, partner," Rusty told him. "An' I ain't been a pup in a long time."

"Little puppy dog done got up on his hind legs, boys," Gamer said with a nasty grin. "I just might have to find me a stick and whup his tail back between his legs. What'd you boys think about that?"

"I wouldn't try it," the redhead warned. His quietly spoken words had steel behind them. "You just might find that stick stickin' out of a part of you that you didn't figure on."

Several of the men in the cafe laughed at that.

Several more men in the cafe softly pushed back their chairs and took their leave before the lead they knew was coming started flying.

And a stray bullet doesn't give a damn who it hits.

"You got a fat mouth, red on the head," Slim told Rusty.

"You wearin' a gun, ugly face?" Rusty popped right back at him.

Slim's face turned as red as Rusty's hair. "In here or outside?" He challenged the soft-voiced but hard-talking puncher.

"It don't make a damn to me."

The counterman came up with a sawed-off shotgun, pointed right at Slim's belly. "You hardcases ain't gonna shoot up this place," he informed them, earing back both hammers. "So this is my way of tellin' you to take your guns and your big mouths and your quarrel out into the street. And I mean lak raht now!"

Slim nodded then looked at Smoke and Rusty. "We'll meet you boys at the south edge of town. That is, if you've got the belly for it."

"We'll be there," Smoke told him, finishing his cigarette and stubbing it out. "Watching our backs all the way."

Bob Garner spun around, red from the neck up and his ugly face turning even uglier. "What the hell does that mean, Jensen?"

"It means, Garner, that I think you're all a bunch of back-shooting cowards!"

"Git outta here!" the counterman hollered. "Afore I turn loose both of these barrels!"

The four hired guns and bounty hunters stomped out of the cafe. Smoke poured another cup of coffee and Rusty did the same. They sugared and stirred and sipped.

"How do we handle this?" Rusty asked, his voice low so that only Smoke could hear. "And what's this about them bein' back-shooters?"

"They're not back-shooters. I just said that to make sure they wouldn't try it. It's a matter of pride for them now. Some of their own kind would shoot them if they tried to set up an ambush."

They both looked up as the waitress set two thick slices of apple pie on the table before them.

"On the house, boys," the counterman said. "I ain't never had nobody as famous as Smoke Jensen come in my place afore."

The men nodded their thanks and fell to eating the pie, chasing it down with gulps of coffee. Around them, men were beginning to place wagers on the outcome of the impending gunfight. Most of the bets went to Smoke and the red-headed cowboy with him.

Their pie and coffee finished, Smoke and Rusty pushed back their chairs, settled their hats on their heads, and stood up, hitching at their gunbelts.

"Good luck, boys!" the waitress called, as they were stepping out the door and onto the boardwalk.

The street that had been bustling with people when Smoke entered the cafe was now barren of human life as the two men began their lonely walk toward the edge of town. The word had been quickly passed among the townspeople that lead was about to fly.

A dog looked up from its midday doze and wagged its tail, its eyes seeming to say: you leave me alone and I'll do the same for you.

They walked past the animal, their spurs softly jingling. They stayed in the shadows of the buildings until coming to the very edge of town.

"I got a hunch that Slim and Bob will stay together," Smoke said. "So we play it like that. I'll take Montana Slim and Bob Garner. You handle the other two. I don't know them; they might be fast as lightning."

"I ain't all that fast," Rusty conceded. "But I don't hardly ever miss."

"That's the main thing. Many so-called fast guns usually put the first bullet into the dirt. There they are, Rusty. I got a hunch they'll want to jaw a little first; work up some courage. We'll let them. You ready?"

"As I'll ever be."

The men stepped off into the dirt of the street and began the short walk toward destiny.

Chapter 8

The hired guns and bounty hunters had positioned themselves by a falling-down old barn, obviously one of the first structures to be built in the town. And it was just as obvious that the men had done so with a plan in mind. Smart, Smoke thought.

"After the first rounds are fired," Smoke told Rusty, "any left standing are going to dive for the protection of that old barn. You hit the ground behind that log pile and I'll take the back of the building." His words were spoken low, so only Rusty could hear.

But the hired guns could see his lips moving. "What the hell are you two whisperin' about?" Montana called. "You workin' up some sort of sneaky play?"

"Neither one of us need sneaky plays to deal with scum like you," Smoke called, his voice easily carrying the distance.

Montana Slim cursed them both, loud and long.

All four of the men Smoke and Rusty faced were wearing two six guns, low and tied down.

"Most men can't use but one gun at a time. And some of them can't use that one very well," Smoke pointed out as the gunfighter and the cowboy continued their shortening the distance to death.

"And you . . . ?"

"I'm the exception," Smoke said without a single note of bragging. He was simply telling the truth.

There was about fifty feet between them when Smoke halted the parade.

"All right, Montana," Smoke called. "You made your brags back at the cafe. Now let's see if you've got the sand to back it up."

"Ten thousand on your head, Jensen!" Bob Garner called out. "We'll live nice on that money."

"You have to collect it first, Garner," Smoke tossed that reminder out to him.

Garner's laugh was full of confidence.

Ten thousand, Smoke mused. Surely it can't go much higher than that.

But then, after a second's thought, he changed his mind, realizing that perhaps there was no limit to Jud Vale's obsessions with being king.

"Ten thousand!" Rusty muttered. "Man, I am choppin' in some high cotton, Smoke. Somebody is shore scared of you."

Smoke did not reply, nor did his eyes leave Montana Slim. It was as he had thought, Slim and Garner were partners and were staying together. Rusty would have to deal with the two bounty hunters—if that's what they were.

Smoke could hear faint rustlings on the boardwalks behind them. He knew that the crowds were gathering to watch the show. It was a dangerous sport for spectators, and many an onlooker had caught a stray bullet. But entertainment was scarce in western towns; many folks packed picnic lunches and would drive a wagon for a hundred miles, bringing the entire family to make an all-day event out of a public hanging.

"I'm tired of all this jawing, Slim," Smoke told him. "And I really don't want a killing. Why don't you boys just get on your horses and ride out of here?"

There was something unnerving about Smoke, something that shook even a hardened gunfighter like Montana Slim. He was just so damned sure of himself. Maybe he ought to be, Montana admitted silently. He's put more than a hundred men in the ground and there he stands, lookin' at me.

But Montana Slim knew he had backed himself into a corner with only two ways out: either walk away victorious, or be propped up in front of the undertaking parlor on a board for all the folks to see.

"And I'm just damn tarred of your mouth, Jensen," Montana yelled. "Grab iron!" His hands flashed to his guns.

Montana thought he heard Smoke say, "All right, Slim." Then he felt twin hammer-blows slam into his chest as his knees began to buckle. Out of the corner of his eyes, the light fading fast, he saw Bob Garner run into the old barn. Montana Slim, the veteran and victor of half a hundred gunfights, lifted his hands and looked at them.

They were empty! Jensen had been so fast he hadn't even grabbed iron. But that was . . . impossible! That thought was his last as he pitched forward into the dust, dead.

Rusty had taken his time and placed his shots well. One bounty hunter was down on his belly, his blood staining the dirt from two bullet holes in his belly, and the other so-called gunfighter was holding up his one good arm in surrender; his other arm, his shooting arm, was broken at the elbow and hanging at a very queer angle.

Smoke was off and running between the old barn and another building which looked to be in just as bad a shape as the barn. He quickly reloaded as he ran.

A bullet whammed into a corral post and Smoke dropped to his belly, scooting behind an old watering trough. He caught a glimpse of a red and white checkered shirt and snapped off a shot. He didn't think he hit Garner, but the slug came close enough to bring a yelp of surprise from the man.

Smoke triggered off five more rounds then holstered that Colt, drawing his left-hand pistol just as Garner ran briefly into view.

Smoke dusted him from side to side, spinning the man around and holding him there long enough for Smoke to take careful aim and put another slug into the man's chest. Bob Garner went down slowly and didn't get up.

It was over.

For this go-around anyway.

Smoke reloaded both guns and walked over to where he'd seen Garner fall. The gunny was lying on his back, very close to death.

It was not a pretty sight. Of course, Garner hadn't been very pretty to start with.

Smoke squatted down beside the man. There was not much life left in him.

And much of what life remained was spent in cussing Smoke.

Smoke waited until the dying man coughed up blood and tried to catch his breath. "Anybody you want me to write, Bob?"

A funny look came into the gunfighter's eyes. He shook his head. "Best . . . if the wife . . . just don't never see me agin. I ain't . . . been much of a husband or . . . father."

"Any money you got you want me to send them?"

"Spent it last . . . night on the . . . whoors."

Rusty walked up and stood listening.

"I'll swap your guns for a buryin', Bob," Smoke assured him.

"Right kind . . . of you. See you . . . boys in Hell!" Bob Garner closed his eyes and died.

Rusty was quiet as they rode out of Malad City that afternoon. The dead gunman had, for the moment, taken the fight out of those remaining in the town. They stood on the boardwalk and watched Smoke and Rusty clear town. Most would continue on toward the Bar V. But there were some, mostly older and wiser, who would elect to seek another trouble spot where they could ply their deadly trade. It was not that they were cowards, far from it. They simply knew Smoke Jensen's reputation and their own capabilities and limitations.

"Mean right up to the end," Rusty finally broke his silence.

"What are you talking about?"

"Garner. What makes a man like that, Smoke?"

"Some folks back East and in the cities are claiming it comes from bad rearing."

"Huh!" Rusty summed up his opinion of that. "I ain't disputin' your word, Smoke, but I just don't believe in that at all. I been on my own for years. And my pa was a mighty mean man. He liked to whup up us boys and girls. Didn't make no difference to him. My older sister run off when I was just a little shaver. I heard she was doin' good out in California. My other brother died from a beatin' Pa give him. Hell, Pa knocked me unconscious with his fists or with a chunk of stovewood more'un once. And I ain't never stole nothin' in my life, or rode the hootowl trail or done nothin' much that was ag'in the law. And nobody could have had a worser home life than me. So them folks that think what you just said don't know a pot of beans from a pile of cow droppin's."

Smoke grinned. "I had to be a man grown just after my thirteenth birthday, working a hardscrabble farm back in Missouri and looking after my sick mother. Wasn't ever enough food; just enough to keep body and soul together. So I know what you mean, Rusty. And no, I don't believe those so-called experts either.

"What makes men like Montana Slim and Bob Garner and all the rest be what they are?" He shook his head. "I think they were born to it, Rusty. They could have had all the advantages in the world and they would have turned out bad. A different kind of bad, maybe, but bad just the same."

"What do you mean, a different kind of bad?"

"Oh, they might have been bankers cheating old ladies or grocers cheating people and being mean-spirited folks. That type of thing."

Rusty thought about that for a mile or so. "You know, Smoke. You're right. There sure are a lot of mean-minded and mean-spirited people in this world. Why, I know a few people who was born into money, and come from nice parents. Kind parents. But their kids would steal the pennies off'n a dead man's eyes."

"That's what I mean, Rusty. Born to it. I call it the bad seed theory."

Rusty settled into the bunkhouse with the old men and the kids. Smoke had taken to sleeping in a room out in the barn.

And Doreen stopped batting her eyes at Smoke and seemed to be quite taken with Rusty—much to the relief of Smoke. She got to getting all gussied up and swishing around him until it was embarrassing for all the others around them. Rusty, he just grinned like an egg-suckin' dog and stood around in sort of a daze.

There had been no trouble from Jud Vale or his men during the time Smoke had been gone.

But gunfighters kept drifting into the area, in groups of twos and threes. Pretty soon, Smoke thought, Jud Vale was going to have his own private army. And he was going to have to make his move pretty quick, for he was paying out a lot of money for all his hired guns to sit around and do nothing. While many of the bounty hunters and hired guns could work cattle, Smoke had a hunch that damn few were going to. Most of them were just downright lazy.

On a bright, sunshiny morning, Smoke lined the boys up and laid it on the line to them, telling them what their parents had said, and leaving the final decision up to the young cowpunchers.

The boys huddled together for a time, and then Jamie stepped out of the group and faced Smoke.

"I allow as to how we'll stay, Mr. Smoke," the boy said. "We got to have the money to help out at home. And it ain't as if we never faced outlaws and the likes of Jud Vale before, 'cause we all have. I figure it like this, and you tell me if it don't meet with your approval and we'll work something else out."

Smoke waited, as did the other adults.

Jamie took a deep breath. "You see, sir, me and Alan and Cecil and two or three of the others, well, we know more about Jud Vale than you do, we think. We know it won't make no difference to him whether it's a grown man or a boy—not when it comes to standing in his way when he's a-goin' after something he wants. Like this ranch and Miss Doreen. So we went ag'in your orders and each of us stuck a pistol in our saddlebags."

Smoke sighed. He couldn't really blame the boys. He would have done the same thing had he been in their position. Smoke had been toting a pistol since he was thirteen. A Navy .36 caliber that had been given him back in '63 by the as yet unknown Confederate guerrilla fighter name of Jesse James.

"'Way we all figure it, Mr. Smoke, it's gonna be comin' down to the nut-cuttin' right shortly. And it ain't fair for no one to ask us to ride unarmed when we might catch a bullet at any moment. I reckon that's all I got to say, Mr. Smoke."

Smoke towered over the boy, staring down at him. Finally, and with a sigh, Smoke nodded his head. "All right, Jamie. I fear for your lives, but I can't ask you to disarm yourselves. I been packing a pistol since I was just a boy. But I have to ask you all to show me that you know how to use those guns."

"That's fair, sir," Jamie agreed. "When do you want us to do that?"

"Nothing like right now."

Cheyenne took one group of boys, Rusty took another, and Smoke took the third.

But damned if Smoke was going to have ten-year-olds packing pistols. Any boy under the age of twelve would stay close to the house and work in the yard or in the barn or corral. The boys packing iron would be Jamie, Matthew, Ralph, Leroy, Cecil, Alan, Rolly, Pat, and Oscar.

The frail Matthew, thick glasses and all, surprised Smoke. The boy was a born gun hand, the pistol seeming to be a natural extension of his arm. And his aim was deadly true. Even Jamie took a backseat to Matthew. Smoke had held the very strong suspicion that Matt had been secretly practicing his draw and firing for some time. He asked him about it.

"Yes, sir," the boy said, blushing. "Whenever I could scrape up a few pennies to buy ammo, I been ridin' out far from the house and workin' at my draw."

"It's a natural talent you have, Matt. But it's not one your ma and pa will look upon with favor. You know that, don't you?"

"Yes, sir. I reckon that's right. But if a feller's got a knack for something, he ought to polish on it, shouldn't he?"

Should he? Smoke silently pondered, staring down at the frail boy packing the short-barreled sheriff's model Peacemaker. Should he? What would I be doing now if I had not discovered and polished my talent for weapons? How many graves have I filled because of my quickness with a gun? And did this boy have enough sand in him to live with a gun by his side and not use it recklessly?

But can I stop him? Should I stop him? This was still the frontier, and it was filled with hard, tough, and often cruel men. Men like Jud Vale and his hired guns.

"Yes, Matt," Smoke said slowly. "Yes. Conditions being what they are, I guess you should polish it. As long as there are men like Jud Vale around, and with us being miles from the nearest law, I guess you should. But use that gun wisely, boy. If the law can handle it, let them. If you're pushed into a corner, then it's all up to you. I reckon that's the way it's always been and I suppose that's the way it's always going to be."

"I ain't smart like no grown-up," Matt said. "But that's the way I think, too."

Matt turned, drew, cocked, and fired. All in one smooth quiet motion, the bullet striking true. Smoke experienced a hard push of memory, winging him back in years. Back to when he was a boy, traveling with Preacher. Back to his first real gunfight with white men.

Preacher and the boy, Smoke, had stopped in a rip-roaring mining camp just west of the Needle Mountains. It would soon be named Rico.

They had bought their supplies and were just about to leave when two rough-looking and unshaven men stepped into the combination trading post and barroom.

"Who owns that horse out yonder?" one demanded, trouble plain in his voice. "The one with the SJ brand?"

The boy Smoke laid his purchases on the counter and slowly turned. "I do."

"Which way'd you ride in from, boy?"

Preacher had slipped to his right, his left hand covering the hammer of his Henry rifle, concealing the click as he thumbed the hammer back.

Smoke's hands were at his sides; his left hand just inches from his left hand gun. "Who wants to know—and why?"

No one in the room said a word.

"Don't sass me, boy!" the bigger and uglier of the two said. "My name's Pike, and I say you come through my camp yesterday and stole my dust!"

Smoke smiled grimly. "You're a damn liar!"

Pike grinned, an ugly peeling back of the lips, exposing blackened rotting stumps of teeth. His right hand was hovering close to the butt of his pistol. "Why you smart-mouthed little punk. I think I'll just shoot your damned ears off."

"Why don't you try. I'm sure tired of hearing you shoot off your mouth," Smoke told him, no fear in his voice.

Pike looked confused for a moment. This kid didn't seem to be at all afraid of him. Odd. Pike was as big and strong as he was ugly. And he had been a loud-mouth bully all his life. People just didn't talk to him like this kid was doing. "I think I'll just kill you for that, kid."

Smoke laughed at him.

Pike and partner reached for their guns.

Four shots thundered in the low-ceilinged room. Four

shots so closely spaced they seemed as one thunderous roaring. Dust and bird's nest droppings fell from the ceiling. Pike and friend were slammed out through the open doorway. One fell off the rough porch, dying in the dirt street. Pike, with two holes in his chest, died with his back against a support post, his eyes wide staring in disbelief that the kid, any kid, could be so fast. Neither man had managed to clear leather before the death blows hammered them into the hot, yawning, smoking gates of Hell.

All eyes in the black powder–filled and dusty barroom moved to the young man standing by the bar, a Colt in each hand.

"Good God!" a man whispered the words in awe. "I never even seen the draw!"

Preacher had moved the muzzle of his Henry to cover the men at the tables. The bartender put his hands slowly on the bar, indicating that he wanted no trouble.

"We'll be leaving now," Smoke said, holstering his Colts and picking up his purchases from the counter. He walked out the door without looking back.

Outside, Smoke stepped over the sprawled, dead legs of Pike and walked past his dead friend.

"What are we 'posed to do with the bodies?" a man asked Preacher.

"Bury 'em."

"What's that kid's name?" another called.

"Smoke Jensen."

Smoke brought himself back to the present, standing and watching Matt shoot. The boy turned with a smile on his lips, waiting for approval from the most famous gunfighter in all the West.

"You'll do to ride the river with, Matt," Smoke told him.

Chapter 9

Smoke walked back to his room in the barn, his thoughts still lingering back over the years—long and bloody years. He tried to recall the year he'd killed that trash over at Rico—1868, he thought it was.

He'd have to watch Matt, and watch him carefully.

He looked up as Cheyenne entered the room, his wise old eyes still startled at the speed of the young boy.

"Cheyenne, take the boy under your wing, just like Preacher did me. Teach him what Preacher taught me. He's going to need all the help he can get, I'm thinking."

Cheyenne nodded. "First time one of them so-called gun-slicks of Jud Vale tries to draw down on that boy and gets plugged in the brisket, the boy is gonna be legend. Like another young man I do seem to recall from some years back."

Smoke nodded. "Yeah, I've been recalling it myself. Matthew's sure got the speed and the eye, Cheyenne. But I don't think it's God-given. I think it's passed up from Hell!"

"Mayhaps you be right. I have thought the same thing myself more'un a time or two. Now then, Jamie ain't real fast, but he's shore enuff a good shot. And Leroy is a fine rifle shot but ain't worth a puma's pool with a short gun. Damn near shot hisself in the foot awhile ago."

"How about the others?"

Rusty walked in, hearing the last. "They'll do, Smoke. They ain't no burnin' firebrands with short guns, but they generally hit what they aim at. I been teachin' them to take their time and aim, even though the lead might be flyin' around them."

"Good advice. Sometimes hard to follow though," he said the last with a grin.

"I heard that." Rusty returned the grin. "Been there myself a time or two."

Cheyenne poured a cup of coffee from the ever-present battered old pot and squatted down on the rough board floor. "I been doin' some head-figurin' whilst you was gone, Smoke. Jud's got hisself a regular army now. I figure he's got nearabouts thirty gunslicks recent hired on the payroll. That ain't countin' his regular hands, which is about fifteen on any given day. That comes to about fifty men ag'in us. And that ain't countin' the bounty hunters snoopin' and a-salivatin' around the countryside, lookin' for a shot at you."

"Yeah, we were lucky the other night. Jud won't be fool enough to try that move again. But it bothers me about the boys carrying guns."

"They've had 'em in they saddlebags all along. And you can bet that whilst they was out of our sight, they was haulin' 'em out and showin' 'em around. Bet, too, that Jud Vale's had snoopers out lookin' us over through spy glasses and seen them boys with the guns."

"I hadn't thought of that, Cheyenne. You're right." He

glanced at Rusty. "Think you can do a day's work without your mind on Doreen?"

Rusty grinned. "That woman can walk into a room and raise the temperature fifteen degrees."

"Do we have to tell you what to do to cool it off?" Cheyenne grinned at him.

The flush on Rusty's face was a pretty fair match with his hair. He mumbled something about having to see to his horse and left the room while Cheyenne and Smoke had a good laugh at his expense.

The days began to drift together, each one bringing with it the promise of full summer. And still Jud Vale made no more moves against the ranch. Smoke couldn't figure out what he was waiting on. Then an idea came to him.

"Is Mr. Argood Mormon?" he asked Walt.

"Big time Mormon. Big worker in the church. It's just about time for him to take his annual trip down into Utah. Church meeting of some sort."

"That's what I figured," Smoke said.

"Figured what?" Cheyenne asked.

"That's what he's waiting on. For the editor of the paper to be gone. No news would be reported if Argood was not around to cover it. And you can bet that Vale will create some incident around Montpelier to keep that young reporter busy while he's striking at the ranch."

"You may be right," Walt said, touching a match to the tobacco in his pipe. "He's sorry, but smart."

"It's time for another run into the village for supplies. I'll take two of the boys with me. I want to leave as many defenders behind as possible. We'll pull out in the morning."

Leroy drove the wagon; Smoke and Matthew rode beside the wagon as it bumped and bounced along the narrow, rutted road toward the trading post. Smoke knew he was taking a chance bringing Matt along, but the boy needed some personal things for himself and wanted to buy his ma a present with money he'd earned himself. Smoke had not asked Matthew to stow his pistol in the saddlebags. The gun had become a natural part of the boy—a feeling that Smoke knew only too well.

But Smoke had talked hard to the boy just before leaving. "Matt, I want you to realize that out here, once you strap a gun on, there are those who won't give a damn how young you are. The only thing they're going to see is that hogleg on your hip. If any of Jud Vale's hired guns are at the post, they're going to taunt you; try to pull you into a fight. And because the West is what it is, I won't interfere unless they gang up on you."

"I understand, Mr. Smoke," the boy had replied solemnly.

"You won't reconsider and stay at the ranch?"

"I reckon not, sir."

"Very well."

Smoke breathed a sigh of relief as they approached the post. Only a couple of horses were tied at the hitchrail, and he recognized them as belonging to some area cattlemen, men whose holdings were so far to the west of Jud Vale's spread that they really had little to fear from the man and his obsessions—so far.

Smoke felt that they might be able to pick up the supplies and get away safely. At least he hoped so. But he wasn't going to put any money on it. Once again, doubts assailed him. He could have ordered Matt to stay behind at the ranch. But the boy had earned his money and had a right to spend it. Matt was not a slave to the Box T; he could come and go as he pleased.

Smoke swung down from the saddle and looped the reins around the hitchrail, Matt doing the same. Out of the corner of his eyes, Smoke watched the boy slip the hammer thong from his pistol. Cheyenne had drilled that into the boy's head. With a sigh, Smoke stepped up onto the porch. He handed Leroy the supply list and told Matt to stay with his friend. Smoke turned away and stepped into the saloon for a cool beer.

The barkeep eyeballed him dubiously as he pushed open the batwings.

"You agin! My stars and garters. I was in the hopes you'd left the country!"

Smoke grinned at the man. "It's me in the flesh. Pull me a cool one."

Drawing the brew, the barkeep said, "Did my eyes deceive me or did I really see that four-eyed kid wearing a gun?"

"You saw it."

The barkeep snorted in disgust. "Some of Jud Vale's men is liable to take that thing off'n him and spank his butt with it!"

"I'd hate to be the one who tried it," Smoke told the man.

"They might decide to do it in a bunch."

"Then if that happens I reckon I'll just have to step in."

"Naturally," the barkeep said mournfully. "And I just had new tables and benches built."

Smoke sipped his beer and kept his eyes on the outside, as best he could through the dirty, dusty, and fly-specked window.

One of the two cattlemen broke the short silence. "Why don't you just ride on outta here, Jensen? Jud Vale will settle down if you was to leave."

"You really believe that?" Smoke had turned, his back to the plank that served as a bar.

"That's what he told us," the other cattleman said. He had noticed that the hammer thongs had been slipped from Smoke's Colts.

Matt was sitting quietly on a bench in front of the store, minding his own business and sipping a bottle of sarsaparilla. Leroy was still inside the store, picking out the supplies from the list Alice and Doreen had given him. Smoke wished that Matt had stayed inside the store. He reflected sourly that people in Hell wished for ice water, for all the good it did them.

"Jud Vale is a good decent man," the cattleman said. "He's gonna bring changes to this area. Good changes. Progress and all that."

Smoke smiled grimly. He wondered if these men really believed that or had Jud bought them off with more than just words?

"Yeah," the other rancher said. "And if that little snip Doreen had any sense, she'd grab ahold of the offer Jud's handed her. She could live like a queen in that big mansion of hisn."

"She doesn't love him."

"Love!" the other said contemptuously. "Hell's fire, man! What's that got to do with anything?"

"Yeah," his drinking buddy agreed. "Love ain't got nothin' to do with livin' well. All a woman's got to do is perform her wifely duties when the lantern is turned off and keep her mouth shut 'cept when she's told to talk. And I'll tell you something else, gunfighter: you best get shut of them snot-nosed squatters' brats you hired to work on the Box T."

His buddy gave him a dark look and the cattleman shut his mouth.

"Is that a threat or a warning?" Smoke asked.

"Tain't no threat, gunfighter," the man said, his mind quickly working through the murk the alcohol had caused, as he realized just who he was talking to. "Jist a fact, is all. Jist lak 'at four-eyed little turd rode in with you with a man's iron strapped on. I've a good notion to go out there and take it away from him. But you'd stick up for him, wouldn't you?"

"No," Smoke surprised them both by stating. "Not as long as it stayed one on one. But I'd leave that boy alone if I was you."

The cattleman muttered something that Smoke could not make out. His buddy said, "He ain't gonna bother that boy, Jensen. That's just whiskey talk."

"Why did he say to get rid of the boys?"

"I don't know," the man said, then fell silent.

Smoke sipped his beer and ignored the drunk and near drunk cattlemen. He had thought all along that the age of the boys would make no difference to Jud Vale—when the man decided to make his move. In a way, he was glad the boys had taken to carrying guns.

He walked to the door that opened into the store, looking in. Leroy was still buying supplies. The boy caught his eye.

"It's gonna be a few more minutes, Mr. Smoke. Miss Alice and Miss Doreen really gave me a long list."

"Take your time, Leroy. I'll have another beer."

"Yes, sir."

Smoke walked back to the bar and ordered a refill. "And pull it from a new barrel," he told the barkeep. "That last one was flat."

The barkeep grinned. "Cain't blame a man for tryin' to drain the barrel, now, can you?" He pulled a fresh brew. "This one's on the house, Mr. Jensen."

Smoke nodded his thanks and leaned against the plank. He had a bad feeling about this day. One he just could not shake. At the sounds of hard-ridden horses he knew his premonition was about to turn into reality.

Four Bar V riders came to a halt in an unnecessary cloud

of dust, fogging everybody and everything in a brief dust storm. Smoke silently cursed as he recognized one of the riders as a man called Śmith. Smith had a shallow-made reputation as a gunslinger; but Smoke knew there wasn't much to the man. He was a bully who picked his fights, fists, and guns very carefully.

"Wal, lookie here!" Smith hollered, spotting Matt sitting on the bench, a disgusted look on his young face as he brushed the dust from his clothing. "Would you boys just take a look at that little piss-ant with the big iron strapped on!"

Smoke forced himself to stay put. He had warned Matt. Warned him several times. Smoke would not interfere unless the Bar V riders tried something in a bunch. As long as it was one on one, with both parties armed, it was an unwritten code that the fight was fair. It was not always a fair code, but that was the way it was.

Leroy heard the commotion and went out the back door to the wagon, getting his Winchester and jacking a round in the chamber of the carbine, easing down the hammer. He reentered the store and moved to the open doorway, staying concealed from the Bar V riders.

He had been getting something extra for Miss Alice. Some candles. She was going to surprise Matthew with a birthday cake. Tomorrow was his birthday. His fourteenth.

If he lives through this, Leroy added that to his thoughts.

Then his thoughts turned grim as he gripped the Winchester. Matthew would live through it. One way or the other. It was time for everybody in this section of the state to stand up to Mr. Jud Vale. And if it had to begin right here and now? . . . Well, let it come.

The Winchester he carried was a hand-me-down from somebody. His dad never said where he'd got it. It was a .44-40 that some owner had sawed the barrel off to make into a saddle gun. It was several inches shorter than the short .44 carbine. It kicked something fierce, but when that bullet hit, it packed a wallop, especially at short range.

Leroy had never shot a man before—and didn't especially want to now, but if his friend Matt got into it with that trash from the Bar V . . . well, there was a first time for everything. He wished he could have had his first time with a girl before having to kill a man. But if wishes were horses then nobody would have to walk, would they? He inched closer to the door and settled down, waiting.

"Yes, siree!" Smith said. "I think we ought to get us a bottle of whiskey and hold the little craphead down and pour it in him. Since he's totin' a man's gun, he ought to have hisself a man's drink."

Matt wisely ignored the bully's comments. He had finished brushing himself off and then calmly wiped the neck of his soda pop bottle on his shirt sleeve and proceeded to take a big swig.

"Hey, piss-ant!" Smith hollered. "I'm talkin' to you, pig farmer's boy!"

"I'm not deaf," Matthew said softly. "Do you eat bacon, mister?"

"Haw?"

"I said do you eat bacon?"

"Why . . . hell, yes, I eat bacon. Don't ever'body?"

"Where do you think it comes from—grown on trees?"

"Are you gettin' sassy with me, punk?"

"No, sir," Matthew replied respectfully. "I was just curious. If you enjoy eating bacon, why do you make fun of those people who raise the hogs?"

Smith—no mental giant anyway one wanted to view it—wore a look of bewilderment on his face. "I don't think I lak you very much, four-eyes. As a matter of fact, I *know* I don't lak you."

"That's a shame. I have nothing against you, mister."

"Let's take his pants down and make him ride back home buck-assed nekkid!" another Bar V hand suggested.

The four men all agreed that would be a great idea. They made some crude remarks about what they might find when they shucked Matt's jeans. And what they might do if one of them could find a corncob.

"No way," Smoke muttered, as he stepped away from the bar.

The two cattlemen suddenly looked very sorry, sober, and sick.

The barkeep shook his head in disgust at the Bar V hand's suggestion.

Leroy eared back the hammer on the .44-.40.

Matt set his soda pop bottle on the bench and stood up, his right hand hanging by his side.

"Well, now!" Smith said, surprise in his voice. "The little piggy's done gone and thought hisself to be all growed up."

"I'll get the corncob, Smith," a Bar V hand said.

"You'll get a bullet," Matt told him, his quiet words stopping the man and turning him around.

"You threatenin' me, pig-boy?" the hand challenged.

"Aren't you threatening me?" Matt countered.

Leroy stepped to a dusty window and pulled the Winchester to his shoulder, sighting in one of the V hands.

Smoke moved closer to the batwings.

"Why, you little turd-faced punk!" the Bar V hand hissed at the boy. "I think I'll just kill you!"

"You have it to do," Matt said softly.

The Bar V riders spread out, all of them grinning, seconds away from a killing.

Chapter 10

Smoke pushed open the batwings and stepped out onto the porch. "I'll take these two so-called gunslicks on the right, Matthew."

"And I've got that ugly, skinny, bow-legged one on the far left in rifle sights!" Leroy called from inside the store.

"I guess that leaves you and me, doesn't it?" Matt told Smith.

The Bar V riders looked sick at the appearance of Smoke Jensen. This was not something they had counted on.

"You got no call to interfere in this, Jensen!" Smith hollered. "This ain't none of your concern."

"It is when four of you gang up on one boy, you sorry piece of buffalo droppings." Smoke then proceeded to hang a cussing on the Bar V riders, and having been jerked up, so to speak, by the old mountain man, Preacher, Smoke could let the cuss words fly when he had a mind to. And today was one of those days.

The riders took it for a time, and then pride got the best of them.

"I've had it, Jensen!" one yelled at him. "You don't cuss me like some saddle bum!"

"Then make your play, damn you!" Smoke lost his temper and started to push.

The puncher held his hands away from his side. "No way, Jensen. I ain't no match for you with guns. But I'll tear your damned head off with my fists if you've got the belly for it."

"I'll take you up on that, partner. Whatever your name is."

"Larry Noonan."

"Oh, yeah!" Smoke said, his voice filled with scorn. "I know enough about you to know you're a yellow little two-bit punk. You killed an unarmed sheepherder. Shot him in the back, so I recall reading on the dodger."

Noonan flushed but did not deny the damning charges.

"I still got something to settle with this loud-mouthed, sassy pig-farmer's kid!" Smith said. "You gonna interfere with that, Jensen?"

"No. I'm as aware as you concerning a fair shoot out between two armed men. In this case a man and a boy. But I'll kill any of your buddies who try to step in."

"You ready, punk?" Smith sneered at the boy.

Matt had stepped to the edge of the porch. Smoke glanced at him. There was no fear to be seen about the boy. His face was impassive and his hands were steady. He stared at Smith through his thick spectacles.

"Too bad, boy," Smith tried to rattle Matt. "You got about ten seconds left to live."

"I have a whole lifetime ahead of me, Mr. Smith. Let's just say this is payback time for you."

"Huh?"

"Don't you remember that time you and those other hooligans rode your horses over my mother's garden? Ruined it. We didn't eat very good that winter, Mr. Smith. It was too late to replant. I remember it very well."

"You gonna bawl about it, kid?" Smith sneered at him.

"No, sir. But I am going to kill you."

Smith stared at the boy while something crawled slowly across his face. He wanted to brush away the invisible sensation, for he knew what it was. Fear.

"My baby sister died that winter, Mr. Smith. I won't say it was all because of what you done, even though you did kill our milk cow. She needed milk bad. You had a hand in her dying."

Smith said nothing. There wasn't very much left to say.

"Goddamn nesters should have stayed out this area," Smoke heard one of the cattlemen in the bar say.

Smoke ignored him for the time being. The man had his own conscience to live with. Providing he had one at all.

"Are you ready, Mr. Smith?" Matthew asked, very politely.

"Smith," one of the Bar V hands spoke softly. "Back away. I don't like this. The kid's too damn sure of hisself."

"I ain't backin' up for no damn snot-nose pig farmer's whelp!" He stared at Matt. "All right, boy. You've made your brags. Now do something 'sides talk!"

"After you, Mr. Smith."

Smith hesitated. Something was terribly, awfully wrong here. He'd seen any number of two-bit, show-off, would-be gunhands in his time. At the last minute, they always backed down. And even before they backed down, they were nervous, their voices shrill, faces shiny with the sweat of fear. But not this kid. Kid, hell! He was just a *boy*—barely in his teens.

"My little sister suffered, Mr. Smith. I don't think I'll ever forget that."

"Shut your mouth, damn you!" Smith screamed. "Draw, you punk!"

Matt waited, waited in his worn-out, low-heeled farmer's boots. In his faded and patched old jeans and carefully mother-mended shirt. His eyes were calm behind his thick glasses.

Smith jerked iron. He just managed to clear leather as Matt's pistol belched and roared smoke and sparks. The first slug hit him in the belly, spinning him around in the dirt. The second slug struck him in the side and knocked him down to one knee. The expression on his face was one of utter disbelief that this could be happening to him. The third slug hit him in the face, entering between nose and upper lip and making one god-awful mess. Smith trembled once and died.

The three remaining Bar V hands stood in open-mouthed shock, all of them knowing they were not nearly as fast as this fresh-faced, as-yet-to-shave farmer's kid standing on the porch of the store, and all of them so very, very glad they had not tried to brace him.

Leroy stepped out of the store, his short-barreled .44-.40, hammer back, in his hands. The barrel of the carbine was pointed straight and rock-steady at the belly of a Bar V hand.

"I'm out of this, kid!" the hand said quickly.

"You interfere in the fight between Mr. Smoke and Noonan and you'll be out of it forever," Leroy told him, his young voice holding hard steel.

Matt had quickly reloaded and holstered the Peacemaker. His calm eyes, magnified behind the thick glasses, looked at the other Bar V hand.

"That goes for me, too, kid!" the hand said.

"Mr. Smoke?" Matt said.

"Matt?"

"If you'll excuse me for a minute, I got to go behind the building and throw up!"

"Go on, Matt."

The boy ran from the porch.

"I done the same thing my first man," a Bar V rider admitted. "It ain't nothin' to be 'shamed of." He didn't know what else to do with his hands—only wanting to keep them as far away from his pistol as possible—so he stuck them into the back pockets of his jeans.

Noonan looked at the bulk of Smoke Jensen and swallowed hard. "Come on, boys!" he urged, panic in his voice. "They's three of us. We can take them two."

The Bar V rider with his hands in his back pockets told Noonan what he could do with his suggestion, together with the same corncob they had originally had in mind for Matthew.

"That goes double for me," the remaining Bar V rider added. "You wanted to fight Jensen, you just go right ahead, Noonan." He removed his gunbelt and hung it on his saddle horn.

The other hand thought that was a dandy idea, and did the same. Leroy shifted the muzzle of the .44-.40 to Noonan's belly and the man let his gunbelt fall.

The shopkeeper, his wife, the barkeep, and the two cattlemen had walked out on the porch, to stand and stare. The body of Smith was, for the moment, being ignored. Matt walked around from behind the building, wiping his mouth with his shirt sleeve.

Smoke took off his guns and laid them on the bench. He stepped off the porch, walked up to Noonan, and knocked the puncher down in the dirt with one very quick and unexpected hard left hook.

Noonan rolled and came to his boots, the side of his jaw beginning to bruise from the blow. He shook his head, clearing it of stars and chirping birdies, and backed up, lifting his fists.

He swung at Smoke. Smoke ducked the punch and busted the cowboy in the belly with a hard right. Noonan whoofed out air just as Smoke came around with another left which connected on the man's ear, spinning him around and seriously impairing his hearing for a few moments.

Just as Noonan regained his balance, Smoke stepped in and blasted him in the mouth with another straight right punch. Noonan's boots left the dirt and he sat down hard on his butt, his mouth bloody.

Smoke backed up. He wasn't even breathing hard; hadn't even worked up a sweat yet.

Noonan wisely sat on the ground. He took another good long look at the gunfighter who stood above him, his fists balled, hanging at his sides, waiting. Smoke looked awesome. A big man, six feet or more, with a massive barrel chest and shoulders and arms that were packed with hard muscle.

Noonan came off the ground in a rush, a long-bladed knife in his right hand.

Smoke slipped the first swing of the knife, bending down as he parried the thrust, his left hand scooping up dust from the road. When Noonan closed with him, Smoke tossed the dirt into the man's eyes, momentarily blinding the man.

Smoke kicked the man on the knee, bringing a howl of pain. Smoke hit the man twice in the face, a left and a right. The knife dropped from his hand just as Smoke's right hand clamped down on the man's fingers. Smoke bore down, using all his strength. Noonan began screaming as the bones in his fingers were crushed, the crunching sounds causing all the spectators to wince.

Still holding onto Noonan's now ruined hand, Smoke began battering the man's face with short, hard, chopping blows from his left fist. Within a minute, the man's face had been turned into a bloody, misshapen mask. His nose was flattened, his lips smashed into bloody pulp, several teeth knocked out of his mouth. Both eyes were beaten closed.

Smoke let him drop to the dirt. Noonan was unconscious.

Smoke walked to the horse trough and washed his face and hands and buckled his gunbelt around his lean waist. He looked up at Leroy.

"All the supplies loaded, Leroy?"

"Just about, sir."

"I'll get right on that, Mr. Jensen!" the store owner said. He and his wife rushed back into the store.

Smoke looked at the now completely sober cattlemen. They were standing on the porch, faces pale under the tan, staring at the crippled Noonan.

Smoke pointed first at Smith, then to Noonan. "When you men decide to take a stand in this issue," Smoke told them, "I would suggest that both of you keep this sight fresh in your minds."

Smoke turned and swung into the saddle.

The news of the gunfight between the seasoned Smith and the nester's kid, and the short but brutally crippling fight between Smoke and Noonan spread like unchecked wildfire throughout the southeastern corner of Idaho. Noonan would never regain the use of his right hand. The so-called badman drifted out of the country, sucking on a bottle of laudanum to ease the pain. He would drift far away, change his name, and work the remainder of his life as a cowboy with a crippled hand, his true identity hidden forever, even to the grave.

Jud Vale had been oddly silent after the shooting and the beating at the trading post. Smoke had a hunch all that would abruptly change as soon as Editor Argood left on his journey to Utah. And that was just about a week away.

At Smoke's suggestion, the ranch house and the bunkhouse had been fortified against both attack and against siege—Smoke suspected the latter would be tried, with Jud Vale's marksmen in carefully placed positions attempting to pick off the defenders one by one.

The remaining Box T herd had been moved to safer pastures; a huge valley with good grass and water, difficult for rustlers to get the cattle clear without being seen.

On a warm bright late spring morning, Smoke walked around the compound, inspecting the work that had been done. He could not think of anything else they could do.

And Smoke was growing restless. Edgy, might be a better word for it. Calm it might be—for now—but he knew their position was lousy, and if Jud would just do a little thinking and planning, logically instead of emotionally, and then turn his rabid dogs loose, there was no way that Smoke and the defenders could hold back a well-planned and well-executed attack against them.

So what to do?

Cutting down the odds would certainly help. Perhaps a little night work? Like headhunting?

Smoke smiled a warrior's smile, thinking: Why not?

He remembered Preacher's words: "You'll always be a fighter, boy—a warrior. You'll take the quiet home life for a time, then the itch will git to where you cain't jist sit at home and scratch it. And then you'll head for the high lonesome, lookin' for trouble. And knowin' you, boy, you'll find it."

Smoke rounded up Cheyenne and Rusty and took them to one side. "I'll be gone for a couple of days, maybe longer. I don't like the odds, so I think I'll do something about them."

"You crave some company?" Cheyenne asked.

Smoke shook his head. "No. This is something that's best left to one man. I'll be pulling out at dusk."

"You going to tell Walt and the wimmin what you're up to?" the old gunfighter asked.

"I'll tell Walt. If he wants to let the women in on it, that's up to him."

"If anybody can pull it off, you can, son. You had the best teacher in the world in Preacher."

Smoke certainly agreed with that last sentence. There had been no finer night fighter in the world than Preacher. "I'll start getting my gear together. Rusty, fix me up with a packet of food enough to last two days."

The cowboy nodded and walked away. Smoke turned back to Cheyenne. "My horse is too well known. Put a rope on that steeldust for me, will you? He's mean as hell but he's mountain bred and quick as lightning and can go all day and still have bottom left."

"He's a good one. I'll doh him for you."

Smoke filled up all the loops in his gunbelt and filled up a bandoleer, slinging that around his shoulder. He slipped another box of .44's into his saddlebags and made sure his moccasins were tucked into the leather. He would soon slip out of his boots and into the moccasins when it was time for the night stalking to begin. He sat down on his bunk and began putting a finer edge on his Bowie knife. That done, he walked to a stone building behind the barn and opened the locked door with a key he had found in a cabinet in the store-room. He had a hunch what he would find, and his hunch was correct.

He filled a small sack with sticks of dynamite and caps and fuses. He might not be able to cut the head off the snake, but he was sure intending to tweak its tail.

Chapter 11

Smoke talked to Jamie and Matthew before he pulled out into the night.

"Tell the boys to ride carefully and keep a sharp eye out. I'm going into the lion's den, and there is no telling what Jud Vale will have his men do in retaliation after I'm through."

"There used to be a lot more farmers in this area than there is now, Mr. Smoke," Jamie said. "Women and girls has been tooken and misused by Vale and his riders. Men has been tarred and feathered and horsewhipped and killed. Killed outright if they was lucky. A deputy sheriff come in here once. He just disappeared. There ain't been no more lawmen come around the Bear. Jud Vale is pure trash, Mr. Smoke. Trash livin' in a big fancy house, with servants and such as that. When he can get them to stay, that is. He fancies young women all around, to wait on him. And he abuses them in ways we heard that would make you sick to your stomach, so they leave as soon as they can get a way out.

You cain't tell us nothin' about Jud Vale and what he might decide to do."

"The more I hear about this man the more I think the best thing to do would be to just go in and chop his head off, so to speak," Smoke said.

"Ain't gonna be that easy, Mr. Smoke. Not even for you. Jud ain't never alone. He's got half a dozen bodyguards with him all the time. Men that have been with him for years, my pa says."

"We'll see, boys. We'll see. I might not be able to do much more than rattle the bars on his cage this time around. But, by God, he will know that his territory has been violated."

Walt came out to the barn just moments before Smoke was to pull out. "Clint Perkins is in the area, Smoke. Don't ask me how I know—I can't explain the feelings I get when he's close. I just know. You be careful."

"Whose side is he on, Walt?"

"His own," the old rancher said bluntly. "He's like a goose; wakes up in a new world every day. I always knew he was about half nuts. Now I think he's gone slap dab crazy."

Smoke led the steeldust out of the barn and swung into the saddle. "I'll see you in two or three days, Walt."

"Be careful, boy."

Smoke rode slowly away from the ranch and into the night. He fought shy of the roads and well-traveled trails as he worked his way toward the range of the Bar V. Editor Argood had told him that there was not one single person on the Bar V payroll that was worth the gunpowder it would take to blow their brains out. To a man, Argood said, they were bullies and trash and petty criminals and all wanted by the law somewhere. The people in the area put up with them because Jud Vale kept them all on a tight leash. Jud had forbidden them to enter Montpelier, restricting their carousing to a few small towns and trading posts in the area around the Bar V range.

All in all, Smoke concluded as he rode through the night, a snake pit could best describe the Bar V . . . and that included the owner.

With a tight smile on his face, Smoke thought that the next couple of days and nights should prove to be quite interesting.

Before leaving the Box T, Smoke had taken tape and silenced anything that might jingle. Only the clop of the steeldust's hooves and the occasional creak of saddle leather could be heard. By midnight, he was on Bar V range. He would ride for a while, then dismount and stand listening for several moments. He began passing bunched and sleeping cattle and slipped his rope free, knowing he would soon make contact with a night herder. If his luck held, the night herder would think him one of the Bar V riders—at least long enough for Smoke to dab a loop over the man and cause a little mischief.

He rode parallel to a series of ridges for a few moments, before finding a pass that would, hopefully, take them to the flats on the other side. He let the steeldust set his own pace and pick his way through the night. On the flats, reined up in the opening of the draw, Smoke spotted the night herder as the man worked his way around the herd, riding slowly so as not to spook the cattle, which was an easily done job. The cattle had, as usual, risen about midnight, grazed for a few moments, and then settled back down.

As the night herder passed Smoke's position, the gunfighter let the loop fly and jerked the rider out of the saddle. The man hit the ground hard, knocking the wind out of him. Smoke was off and running as the loop settled and he further silenced the herder by a hard right fist to the side of the man's jaw. He then tied him up, using cut-off sections from the Bar V rider's own rope. He gagged the man with a dirty bandana taken from the man's equally dirty neck and then squatted down beside him, waiting for him to regain consciousness.

The man's eyes opened and widened as he recognized who he was looking at.

"You want to live?" Smoke asked softly.

The man nodded his head up and down vigorously.

"You know who I am?"

The rider nodded.

Smoke took out his long-bladed knife and laid the cold sharp steel against the man's throat. "I've a good notion to cut your throat and just have done with it."

The Bar V man made desperate choking sounds behind the gag, being careful not to move his head for fear the sharp blade would slice him.

"On second thought," Smoke told him, "I think I'll just strip you and tie you between two steers and then stampede the herd."

More frantic choking sounds.

"Unless you agree to ride out and never show your face in this part of the state again."

The muffled sounds from behind the gag were definitely in agreement with Smoke's last remarks.

Smoke very slowly moved the knife point, just scraping the man's unshaven jaw, and the Bar V night herder looked like he was developing the first stages of a heart attack. With one flick of his wrist, Smoke cut the gag from the man's mouth.

"Oh, Jesus!" the rider softly moaned.

Smoke grabbed him by the hair and jerked his head back, exposing the softness of the rider's throat. He laid the blade against the man's skin and the sharp odor of urine filled the night.

"If I see you again, I'll kill you," Smoke told him.

"Mr. Jensen, if you was to cut me loose, I'll be two counties away come the dawn."

Smoke cut his bonds and stood up. "Ride. Ride like you've never ridden before. Forget your warbag hack at the bunkhouse. Just get clear of this area."

"I'm gone, mister!"

The cowboy staggered to his boots and ran to his horse and swung into the saddle, wet drawers and all, and was gone into the night, heading west. Smoke had not disarmed the cowboy, but the man made no moves toward his six gun. The night became quiet as the rider got the hell gone from Smoke Jensen.

Smoke removed his spurs and stashed them in a saddlebag. Back in the saddle, he guided the steeldust out to the edge of the herd and began making the night herder's rounds, working in a slow, rough circle. He soon spotted another night rider.

Smoke rode up to the man and just as the rider realized he was not looking at a Bar V hand, Smoke leaned over and knocked him clear out of the saddle. He was on the ground and standing over the man as the cowboy came up, fighting mad and cussing to beat sixty. He reached for his gun and Smoke knocked it out of his hand then proceeded to beat the man to an unconscious bloody pulp. Smoke tossed him belly-down across the man's saddle, tied him securely, and slapped the horse on the rump, knowing the animal would head straight for the corral.

Smiling, Smoke swung back into the saddle and went in search of more night herders.

Long before first light, he had cleared the Bar V range of nighthawks. He had sent three packing, riding hell-bent for leather toward a more hospitable climate, and had either whipped with his fists or clubbed over the head four more, tying them across their saddles and sending the horses racing back to the corral, jumping and bucking under the strange load.

Smoke headed for the high country and some food and sleep. He was still smiling as he plopped his hat over his eyes and leaned back, his saddle for a pillow. The sun was just coming up. He was less than a mile from Jud Vale's mansion.

Jud Vale threw his hat on the ground and stomped around, cussing and hollering. "Get him!" he finally screamed, his face beet-red, spittle spraying over his lips. "Put a rope on him and drag that bastard back here! Ten thousand dollars to the man who brings him in, dead or alive! *Ride,* damnit!"

Forty riders hit their saddles and left the ranch complex in a cloud of dust, which was exactly what Smoke planned on them doing. He knew they would not expect him to be within ten miles of Jud Vale's mansion, much less standing on a brush-covered ridge overlooking the estate.

Smoke had carefully picketed the steeldust over good graze and a small pool of collected water—water enough for a couple of days. If Smoke did not return, the steeldust could break free with little trouble and head back to Box T range.

Smoke took his time studying the ranch layout through field glasses, including ways to reach it and ways to get out once there. Jud had chosen his building site carefully, including a little creek that ran some three hundred yards behind the out of place mansion.

Smoke removed his boots and slipped on moccasins. He carefully checked his guns, wiping them free of any dust they might have collected. He removed his Winchester from the boot and checked it, making sure it was loaded full up. He patted the steeldust on the neck and spoke to it for a moment, then he started to move out.

Movement on the other side of the creek halted him. He squatted down and watched. He was sure he had seen movement. Or had he? He waited. There! He'd been right. Somebody, or something, was sure enough down there. He went back to his saddlebags and got his field glasses.

He moved several hundred yards closer to the mansion, adjusted the glasses for range and once more settled down to wait. Then he picked out the shape of a man. It startled him as the face of the man came into view. It was almost like looking into a mirror. There was some difference, of course, but the facial features of the man were startlingly similar to Smoke's own.

Clint Perkins. It had to be. But what the devil was he up to?

He watched as the man left the creek and ran to one of several privies behind the house. The privies surprised Smoke. He thought Jud would have installed some of those new fangled indoor water closets he'd seen back East.

Clint began working his way closer to the mansion, finally ducking into a shed not far from the back porch. The call of a meadowlark drifted to Smoke, and Smoke could tell the call was not real. Within a moment, a young woman stepped out onto the porch, shaking out a small rug.

Someone must have said something from inside the house, for the girl turned her head. Smoke could see her lips move in reply. She had an angry expression on her face. Her reply must have satisfied the questioner for she moved off the porch and walked toward an outhouse.

She angled toward the privy just behind the shed; that move would effectively block the view of anyone watching from the house, but not from the ridge and Smoke's magnified eyes.

The girl did not go into the outhouse. But she did disappear from view. So the shed either had a back door or a couple of loosened boards. Clint Perkins, the so-called Robin Hood of the West, either had him a girlfriend, or was planning to rescue the lady from the sweaty evil clutches of Jud Vale. Probably a combination of both, Smoke thought. This Clint Perkins, as it was turning out, was quite the ladies' man.

Smoke wondered just how many starry-eyed women Clint had loved and left and how many woods' colts this dubious Robin Hood had in his back trail?

After only a few moments, a man wearing two guns belted around his waist stepped onto the porch and, judging from the expression on his face, started yelling. The girl appeared, seeming to come from out of the privy. And from the expression on her face, she seemed to be yelling at the man. When she reached the porch, the man slapped her, staggering her, only the railing preventing her from falling off the porch. He grabbed her by the arm and hurried her into the house, slamming the door behind them.

Interesting, Smoke thought. Then he wondered how many more young ladies Jud Vale was keeping against their will in the huge mansion?

Smoke settled back in a more comfortable position, his back to a tree, his hat on the ground beside him and waited and watched. This might prove to be a very interesting morning.

And Smoke might not have to do anything for a change.

Except enjoy the show.

Chapter 12

Smoke shifted his attentions to the front of the mansion as Jud Vale stepped out onto the porch with a cup of coffee in his hand and took a chair. Smoke envied him that cup of coffee, for a fact. His had been a cold camp the night before, and he sorely missed his usual full pot of hot, strong, black cowboy coffee upon waking up.

He contended himself by chewing on a biscuit sandwich made with fried salt pork and chasing it down with sips of water from his canteen.

The girl Smoke had seen meeting with Clint Perkins came out onto the porch and began talking to Jud, gesturing with her hands.

Jud shook his head a couple of times and then, with an angry expression on his face, pointed toward the door. The girl, her shoulders slumped in defeat, walked back inside the house.

Jud stood up and hollered something; Smoke could see his lips move but could not make out the words. Three men stepped out of a bunkhouse and walked toward the house. Three more men, with the girl in tow, quite unwillingly, Smoke noted, by the way one held onto her arm, came out of the mansion to stand by Jud on the porch.

The man holding onto the girl nodded his head and the three went back into the mansion. Shifting his glasses, Smoke watched as Clint ran the short distance from shed to back porch and then disappeared into the mansion.

Gong to get interesting very soon, Smoke thought.

Jud's horse was saddled and led to the porch, and Jud and three of his bodyguards rode off. Smoke finished his biscuit and salt meat and waited for something to start popping.

It wasn't long in coming.

One man was suddenly hurled through a side window, the side of his head bloody. Gunfire shattered the early morning quiet and one of Jud's bodyguards came staggering out onto the back porch. He fell over the railing and lay still.

More gunfire came from within the house and the third bodyguard fell out of the front door, on his back, on the porch. The front of his shirt was bloody.

Wisps of smoke began leaking out of an open window in the rear of the house as Clint and the girl ran out the back door and toward the creek. Several moments later, Smoke watched as two horses pounded away, the girl riding astride. They topped a hill and were gone.

"Robin Hood strikes again," Smoke muttered, as he took out another biscuit and settled back, just as Jud Vale and his bodyguards came galloping back to the ranch.

The fire had been confined to the kitchen and had been extinguished in a few minutes Jud was talking to the man who had been bashed on the noggin and tossed out the side window.

"So it wasn't Jensen all along," Jud said, standing up, his face tight with anger. "It was that damn Clint Perkins!"

"They look enough alike to be brothers," Jason reminded his boss. "Be easy to mistake them in the dark."

"Maybe they're brothers?" a hand suggested. "And Smoke Jensen come in here to help him out?"

But Jud Vale rejected that on the spot. He'd been in the West for some years when the stories about Smoke Jensen first began surfacing. Jud knew that Jensen's father had died and the mountain man, Preacher, took care of the boy's raising after that. Smoke had always been a loner, with no family to speak of, certainly no brother.

He shook his head. "No. He doesn't have a brother. Not anymore. His brother was killed in the war. Tortured and killed by a group headed by three men who later moved into Idaho. Jensen killed them all and detroyed the town."

"Then what's he doin' here, Boss?" Jason asked.

"Exactly what he said he was dong," Jud replied, bitterness in his voice. "He was just seeing the country when we braced him. That got his back up, and he stayed." Jud shrugged. "We brought it on ourselves."

"And we do what about it?" a gunslinger asked.

"Kill him."

A Bar V hand had gotten close to Smoke's hiding place while taking a shortcut to a search area. He now found himself flat on the ground looking up into the cold eyes of Smoke Jensen, with a knife blade across his throat. There were any number of questions he wanted to ask, but wisely kept his mouth shut, figuring if Jensen wanted him to talk, he'd tell him so.

"Who is in the house besides Jud Vale and his men?" Smoke asked.

"Nobody! I swear it!"

"The girl who got away—who is she?"

"Susie somebody-or-another. Nester's kid from over Wyoming Territory."

"She was the only servant?" Smoke moved the razor-sharp knife blade and the man cringed in fear.

"If that's what you want to call what she done. Yeah. She cain't cook and don't clean house. It's like a boar's nest in that house. There was two more girls. One run off—never seen her agin, and Jud kilt the other. But it was an accident, Jud said. He broke her neck whilst they were messin' around. You know."

"Sounds like a nice gentle fellow, this Jud Vale does."

The hand didn't know how to respond to that, so he kept his mouth closed.

"What's Clint Perkins's beef with Jud?"

"Lord, man, I don't know! 'Ceptin' that Perkins is crazy, I reckon. He hates rich folks, I do know that."

Smoke stared hard at the man. The Bar V hand was scared and sweating, even though the day was cloudy and cool, threatening rain. "Where are you wanted?"

The hand hesitated. Smoke moved the big blade. That loosened his mouth. "Kansas!" he blurted out.

"What for?"

"I robbed a store. I was down on my luck and needed some cash."

Smoke grabbed him by the hair and jerked his head back, exposing his throat even more. "Tell it all!"

"Nebraska! I robbed a bank, kilt a teller! You gonna turn me in?"

"Not if you level with me."

"Anything you want. Jist anything at all, Mr. Jensen. You want me to git down and howl lak a dog, you jist say so."

"Is there any puncher on Vale's payroll who isn't wanted by the law?"

"Lord, no! Jud laks to hire people on the hoot-owl trail. He's got more control over 'em. They's more outlaws down yonder than at Robber's Roost."

"And Jud Vale wants to be king of this part of the state?"

"Mister Jensen, he *is* king!"

"Uneasy lies the head that wears a crown."

"Huh?"

"Shakespeare wrote that."

"I ain't never heard of him. What outfit does he ride for?"

"Forget it." Smoke stuffed a gag into the man's mouth and tied him to a tree. He picked up his rifle and began making his way toward the creek that ran behind the mansion of Jud Vale. He wasn't worried about being spotted by any ranch hands; there weren't any hands left on the ranch, except those gunslingers and bodyguards in the house with Jud. Every hand, including the cook, was out looking for Clint Perkins and the girl. According to the tied-up and gagged BarV hand, no one believed Smoke was within thirty miles of the mansion. And by this time, there wouldn't be a puncher, bounty hunter, or hired gun within ten miles of the ranch.

The day had turned cloudy along with the coolness, and any gunfire would be muffled by the humidity, not carrying nearly as far as on a fair, sunshiny day.

Smoke followed the creek to the rear of the house and then made his way to a pile of wood stacked behind the great two-story mansion. He poked his rifle through a good-sized crack in the stack and let a few shots bang.

The first shot tore through the kitchen wall and ricocheted upward, shattering a chandelier in the fancy dining room and sending bits of glass and coal oil from the expensive lamps spraying. Jud Vale and his men hit the floor, yelling and cussing. The second .44 round whined off the polished wood of the dining room table and stopped in the china hutch, destroying several plates and cups. The third round bounced off a kettle in the kitchen and whined wickedly around the stove before rolling across the floor and coming to rest about three inches from Jud Vale's nose.

The men began crawling across the floor, toward the rear of the house. Smoke anticipated that move, and lowered the muzzle of the Winchester, letting it bang.

"Somebody get around to the side of the house!" Jud yelled. "Try to get him in a crossfire."

But Smoke was off and running, coming to rest behind the gazebo in the side yard. He saw the bodyguard come chugging around the corner and knocked a leg out from under him. Dragging his limb, the man crawled back around to the front of the mansion.

Jud and his men moved to the side of the house, but by this time, Smoke had again changed locations, back to the rear of the house. He decided he'd pressed his luck enough for this day, and took a stick of dynamite out of his pocket, capping and fusing the thunder stick. He lit it and let it fly and was heading for the creek before the sputtering stick landed.

The charge landed on the ground and rolled under the porch. When it blew, it tore the whole porch off the rear of the house and busted most of the windows in the back of the mansion.

Smoke stopped at the creek bank long enough to empty his rifle into the back of the house and then ran toward the ridge and his horse.

Inside the mansion, their hearing momentarily impaired from the booming of the giant stick, Jud and his men hugged the floor until the rifle fire stopped. Their ears ringing, the men crawled to their knees.

"That wasn't Clint Perkins," Jud said, his voice seeming to come out of a well. "That was Smoke Jensen. Bet on it!"

Chuckling, Smoke cut the Bar V hand loose, laid the barrel of his pistol on the back of the man's head, insuring that he would be out for some time to come, and mounted up, riding off.

He had a full day of headhunting to do.

The hand Smoke had busted on the noggin finally found his horse and rode back to the mansion, a lump on his noggin the size of a hen's egg.

"Jensen," he told Jud.

"Which way did he ride out?"

"Don't know. He busted me on the head. I just now come to my senses. I don't know how long I've been out."

Jud cussed and stomped and paced up and down behind the mansion and the ruined porch. He fought to keep his anger under control and managed it.

"Get the boys in," he told Jason. "Jensen was raised by Preacher. Probably the best Injun fighter the West ever seen. He's gone headhunting, bet on it. If the boys stay out, he'll do us some more damage. Get them back here, pronto."

Jason looked confused. "Jesus, Boss. How? They're scattered all forty miles."

Jud Vale sat down on a stump and cussed. Smoke Jensen planned all this, he concluded. He didn't know how, or even the why of it, but it was all Smoke Jensen's fault. He convinced himself of that. Damn Smoke Jensen to the pits of Hellfire!

Jud again calmed himself and did a little mental figuring. As of last evening, he had 18 hands on the payroll. He had hired 25 men at fighting wages—God knows they hadn't earned a penny of it—and he was giving another 15 or 20 men—he forgot the exact number—money just to hang around. Three riders had deserted him last night, thanks to that damn Clint Perkins; or had it been Perkins? And two more had been so badly beaten they were out of it for several days. Maybe a week. So savagely mauled that they hadn't even been able to leave the bunkhouse when Perkins and then Jensen attacked the house. He had lost two of his most trusted men to the guns of Perkins. Jensen had busted the leg of another. And a third had his head busted open.

"Damn!" he muttered. He looked up at Jason. "You boys stick close to home. I reckon them forty-odd men out in the field can deal with Smoke Jensen."

A gunslick whose Christian name was Wilber Hammersmith—his friends called him Hammer—thought a damn puma had done jumped onto his back, knocking him from the saddle. Then he looked up into the eyes of Smoke Jensen, sitting on top of him, and suddenly felt an urgent need to relieve his bladder.

He cut his eyes as Jensen balled his right hand into a huge fist. "Aw, hell, man!" he managed to say before his whole head exploded in pain.

And speaking of his head . . . when he finally awakened, he had a whale of a headache, his whole world was upside down, and his head was unnaturally cold.

Hammer figured out why his world was upside down. It wasn't the world—it was him! Jensen had taken Hammer's rope and strung him upside down from a tall limb. After stripping him down to his long handles and taking his boots and socks and guns.

But how come his head was so cold? He had always been

right proud of his blond hair. He finally managed to get his hands free and to his head.

He screamed as if he'd been mortally wounded, the sound echoing around the hills and ridges.

That damn Smoke Jensen had taken his knife and shaved his head!

"Halp!" Hammersmith started hollering as he swayed in the breeze at the end of the rope. His own rope. "I'm a-gonna kill you, Jensen!" Hammersmith squalled. "Damn your eyes, you heathen! This ain't right. Halp!"

Buck Wall thought he heard someone hollering. He pulled up and listened. Yep. Someone was sure hollering all right. Coming from over that next ridge, he thought. He eased over that way and found the source of all the noise.

"Boy," he said to Hammer. "How come you got yourself all tied up like that there?"

"Cut me down, damnit!" Hammer squalled.

"All right, all right." Buck was in the process of dismounting when the loop settled over his shoulders and he felt himself jerked from the stirrups. He landed heavily on the rocky ground.

Then Smoke Jensen was all over him, fists flying. The last thing Buck recalled, for a few moments, was that getting the living hell beat out of you was not a very pleasant experience.

When he woke up, his world was also upside down. And his clothes were gone, right down to his socks and boots and guns. And there was not a horse to be seen anywhere.

"Hammer," he managed to speak through battered lips. "The next time you get in trouble, I wish you would please keep your mouth shet!"

"Halp!" Hammer hollered.

"Will you stop that! You're makin' my head hurt!"

"Halp!"

"Who said that?" Hammer asked.

"Well, it damn shore wasn't me!"

By twisting around, they could just see a newly hired gunny name of Ben Lewis. Someone—Jensen for sure—had peeled him buck naked and tied him backwards in the saddle. And from the looks of him, he'd been sitting in that saddle for some time. Looked worn to a frazzle.

"I'm a-gonna kill that crummy Smoke Jensen!" Ben hollered.

"Yeah," Buck said drily. "Right. Shore you are. Me, too. But furst I'd like to get shut of this damn tree limb!"

Chapter 13

The hired guns and bounty hunters and would-be toughs began drifting back to the ranch one by one, and they were a sorry sight to behold. Jud Vale sat on the front porch sipping whiskey and viewed the unfolding scene with disgust in his eyes.

Glen Regan, the punk who fancied himself fast with a gun, was the first back. Hoofing it. Naked, except for his fancy silver conchoed gunbelt, all the shells shucked out of the loops. He wore his empty holsters in strategic locations.

"Plumb pitiful," Jud said mournfully.

"What do you want done with him, Boss?" Jason asked.

"Get him out of my sight. And, Jason? Get ready for a lot more of the same. Jensen's playing games."

Barstow, the no-good from Colorado way, was the next to come limping in. Barefoot and clad only in a bush he had uprooted. Jensen hadn't even left him his guns. Jud just pointed to the bunkhouse and poured another drink.

Three of Jud's own regular hands came staggering in about fifteen minutes later. They were drawerless and had been tied together in such a way so they had to move in a circle to get anywhere. They were so dizzy they fell down in a heap in the front yard.

Jud looked at the pile of struggling flesh in his front yard. "Jason?"

"Boss?"

"Get me a headache powder, will you?"

"I believe I'll join you," the foreman said. "But it cain't get much worse than this."

"Don't bet on it."

Jaeger, the German gunhand, came in riding his own horse and wearing clothes. But he had a bloody bandage tied around his big head and a very grim expression on his broad face. "Jensen shoot ear off," he said, and rode on toward the bunkhouse.

"Least he left you your britches," Jud told him.

"I vould ratter have mein ear!" the German called.

The bounty hunter, John Wills, came riding in without his clothes, his hands tied to the saddle horn. But Smoke had neatly wrapped him up, from neck to waist and both his legs, in poison ivy. He was already breaking out and swelling.

Jud pointed to the bunkhouse. "Ointment in the cabinet over yonder," he said with a sigh.

Hammersmith and Buck had found their horses and came riding in with Ben Lewis, the last two in their birthday suits. No guns or rifles. Jensen was going to have quite a collection before this was over.

Of course, Jud knew what he was doing: arming the kids to the teeth.

"I don't want to hear it," Jud told the three, and pointed to the bunkhouse.

It just got worse. But the numbers were fewer. Hazelhurst

came in draped over his saddle. His partner explained. "He wanted to make a fight of it. Stupid thing to do with Jensen. I figured my life was worth more than my britches and guns. Jensen said the shirts and jeans was gonna have to be altered some—and shore washed—but the kids would have work clothes a-plenty."

"Get a shovel and some boys and plant Hazelhurst," Jud told him, a weary note to his voice.

Vale got up and walked into the house, closing the door behind him. He just did not want to see any more of this.

Smoke stampeded the Bar V horses that night. He jerked down the corral bars and tossed a stick of dynamite outside the corral so no horses would be hurt—just scared half to death.

It was a move that no one expected. After the damage he had done all that day, all thought he would head back to the Box T.

Smoke put an end to those thoughts by emptying his six guns into the bunkhouse, then grabbing two more hung on the saddle horn and blasting away at the mansion, sending Jud Vale jumping out of bed, skinning his knee, banging his big toe on the chiffonier and ultimately falling down his own fancy curving stairs. In his long handles.

"You son of a bitch!" Jud hollered, holding his aching head where he'd banged it on his way down the stairs, head over butt. "I'll get you, Jensen. I swear by my mother's grave—I'll kill you for this!"

But Smoke was smiling as he crossed over the series of ridges that would lead him out of Bar V range, leading a Bar V pack horse carrying clothes and guns.

* * *

"Don't you look like the cat who licked the cream," Cheyenne told him when Smoke rolled out of bed and walked outside to wash and shave.

When Smoke had finished telling him what he'd done, the old mountain man and gunfighter was cackling and slapping his knee.

"By God, I'll just bet that was some sight to see! I'd have give a month's wages to seen 'er."

"Well, it was fun," Smoke admitted with a smile. "Most of it. But there is no telling what Jud will do in retaliation."

"And Clint Perkins come up and stole the girl away, huh?"

"Yes." Walt and Rusty had walked up, to stand listening. "He's a tough one. Don't ever sell him short on courage. He's got his share and more of that."

Smoke had collected thirty pistols and fifteen rifles and more than five hundred rounds of .44 and .45 caliber ammunition. He distributed the weapons and ammo and gave Alice and Doreen the clothes to wash and alter for the boys. He had tossed the boots in a pile in the barn for the boys to prowl through.

"Argood has gone to Utah," Walt told him. "Be gone for a month or more."

"Then Jud will throw everything he's got at us," Smoke said. "It'll be open warfare from this point on." He smiled. "And after what I did to the Bar V, I sure can't blame them."

With little else to do, Chuckie, Ed, Eli, Jimmy, Clark, and Buster busied themselves at the creek, picking up and carefully selecting rocks for the weapons they had been working on. The rocks they picked up were just the perfect size, round and smooth, flawless. They would fit well in the pockets of their slingshots. Maybe they couldn't carry guns around, but they could sure use those slingshots with deadly accuracy.

And the youngsters had just as carefully picked out the spots from which they would launch their small war when Jud Vale's men attacked the ranch. And it was there they stashed their carefully chosen hoard of rocks and spare slingshots, telling no one else about it.

But Cheyenne, wise and watchful old man that he was, had seen the boys scurrying about and became curious as to what they were up to. When he had satisfied his curiosity, he sat down and chuckled.

"Brave little lads," he muttered. And he knew just how deadly a slingshot could be in the hands of a boy with a steady eye. They might not kill anybody with those propelled little rocks, but they could spook some horses and cause some fearful bumps and dents in the head and some painful bruises in the flesh of any attacker.

"I do believe it's gonna get right interestin' around here," he quietly said to himself.

Matthew had been practicing daily with his Peacemaker. One hour a day, faithfully, every day, he practiced his draw. And with lots of ammo available, he could also practice his marksmanship.

The boy was a natural. Better than good, he was awesome in his ability with a short gun.

"I hate to see it," Smoke said to Cheyenne, after watching Matt practice.

"He'd a done it with or without us, Smoke," the old gunfighter said. "I allow as to how it was best that we was here to hep him along."

"Maybe you're right. But the West is slowly changing, Cheyenne. Perhaps not all for the better, but law and order is coming and fast guns will be a thing of the past before we know it."

"I'll never live to see it," the old man said flatly. "And for all the lawyers and judges with their fancy words, and hand-sewn duds, it's gonna be years afore all the West is tamed—maybe never. Matthew will be a growed-up man afore he'll be able to hang up his guns. And who knows, Smoke? Maybe he'll go on to become a fine lawman. There ain't a bad bone in the lad."

"I'm going to encourage him to do just that."

"I already been doin' that," Cheyenne said. "He seems interested in it, for a fact."

Smoke's eyes came open out of sleep. Something, or somebody, was in the barn. He looked out the open window without moving from his bunk. About three o'clock, he guessed.

He lay still, his right hand around the butt of a Colt. When the sound came again, Smoke eared back the hammer.

A soft chuckle came out of the darkness, just outside the open door to his room. "I didn't think I'd be able toget this far without you hearing me," the voice spoke.

"Perkins?" Smoke returned the whisper.

"Oh, my, yes. I've come to lend whatever assistance I can to this little war."

"I watched you the other day. From the ridges."

"Careless on my part, not seeing you. You're very, very good. As good as your reputation makes you out to be, I must admit."

Smoke felt that Perkins was not alone. All his senses were working overtime. "The girl with you?"

"Good guess, *compañero*."

With that correct usage, Smoke knew the man had spent some time below the border. "Going to leave her here?"

"I really have no choice in the matter. She'll be much safer with Walt and Alice."

"Why do you hate them so? They seem like good people to me."

"Oh, I don't hate them. Not at all. I know they think that, but it isn't true. There is a medical term for my mental condition, but I shan't bore you with ten-dollar words when a single word can sum it all up rather well. I'm crazy."

"You have good days and you have bad days."

"Umm. Gunfighter you may be, but you are not overcome with ignorance. Yes. That is correct."

"Have you sought help?"

"Oh, my, yes. But unfortunately, the field of psychiatry is still in its infancy, and the methods they use are really quite primitive. And they don't work," he added the last with a note of bitterness.

"There ought to be some coffee left in the pot. Help yourself."

"Thank you, but I'm afraid I must decline your kind offer. How is Micky?"

"He's a fine boy."

"Ah, good. Doreen thinks I deserted her out of pure callousness. That was not the case. When these twilight moods strike me, I can kill anybody who stands in my way, who speaks to me in a cross manner, or simply because of a wrong word. I would be sorry for it immediately afterward, but apologizing to a corpse is a rather futile gesture, don't you agree, Mr. Jensen?"

"I would think so, yes."

"Should our paths cross again, Mr. Jensen, and I have a rather obvious wild-eyed look about me, leave me alone. Depart the area immediately. It's for your own good, I assure you."

"I'll remember that."

Silence.

"Clint?"

But he was speaking to shadows. Clint Perkins had vanished as softly and silently as he had arrived.

"Susie?"

"I'm right here, Mr. Jensen."

Smoke rose from his bunk and dressed. Then he lit the lamp. Susie was perhaps eighteen—no more than that. A very pretty girl, she had a wide-eyed scared look on her pale face.

"You don't have to be afraid of me, Susie," Smoke told her. "Come on. Let's go wake up the house and get you settled in."

Over coffee and bear sign, the story Susie told was one of horror, dearly indicating that Jud Vale was as nutty as a tree full of squirrels. She told of beatings, of being forced into Jud's bed—and into the bed of Jason when Jud was feeling magnanimous. And of being forced to do things, things about which no decent person should know. Walt looked sick and Alice and Doreen almost had an attack of the swooning vapors, both of them fanning themselves vigorously.

Cheyenne wore a very uncomfortable look on his leathery face. Rusty's face was red as a beet. Smoke had heard the boys gather around the windows, outside the house, but said nothing about it. They were getting an earful, no doubt about that. Dolittle and Harrison had not been awakened.

"Have you seen Jud kill other . . . slaves?" Smoke asked her.

"One. But half a dozen have just disappeared. I know where they're buried, though."

"Your parents?"

"Dead. I was on my way to California to stay with my

uncle and aunt when outlaws robbed the train. They took me and sold me to Jud. If he finds out I'm here, he'll attack this ranch."

"He's going to do that anyway, girl," Walt told her. "Just relax. You'll be safe here with us. When this is over, we'll get you to California."

"How did Clint find out you were at the Bar V?" Smoke asked.

"How does he find out anything?" she countered. "He's like a ghost." She looked at Doreen. "And no, there was never anything between us. He's just been a good friend."

The look Doreen gave her silently stated that she believed that about as much as she believed elephants wore pink tights and danced the can-can.

Susie met Doreen's eyes and accurately read the other woman's expression. She shrugged indifferently.

"Micky can sleep in with his mother," Alice said, stepping between the hot looks. "Susie, you take the boy's bedroom until we can fix up the other bedroom. Go on, dear. Walt's put fresh water in the basin and the towels are on the rack and the bedpan's clean. You get some sleep. We'll talk more in the morning."

"Good idea," Walt said, knocking the ashes from the bowl of his pipe and standing up. His wife joined him and they left the kitchen, Doreen and Susie following.

Smoke, Cheyenne, and Rusty sat around the table for a few more minutes, with Rusty and Cheyenne eating up every doughnut they could find.

"Near four thirty," Smoke said, refilling his coffee cup. He was almost forced to break Rusty's hand as he reached for the last bear sign. "No point in going back to bed."

Rusty looked frantically around for another platter of doughnuts.

He found a fresh chocolate cake and his smile almost added new light to the room as he whacked off a hunk that would choke a bull.

"Growin' boy still," Cheyenne said with a grin. "Cut me a piece of that, too, Rusty."

"Smoke?"

"I'll pass, Rusty, thanks. I'm fixing to rustle me up some bacon and eggs before long."

"Fix some for me, too," the young puncher spoke around a mouthful of cake.

"Yeah. Me, too," Cheyenne said.

Smoke grinned and shook his head at the two characters. Then he sobered when he thought of what Jud Vale might do in retaliation. And another matter had been nagging at him off and on for a week or so.

"What you ruminatin' about?" Cheyenne asked.

"Jud Vale, for one thing."

"Just ride over and call him out and kill him. Me and Rusty and Walt will go with you."

"The odd thing is, Cheyenne, I don't want to kill him. He's not right in the head, and therefore he isn't responsible for what he's doing. It might come to a killing, but I hope it isn't me who has to do it."

Cheyenne thought about that for a moment. "And the other thing?"

Smoke sighed and finished his coffee. He nodded his head toward the outside. Rusty cut the lamps low and followed them. They walked over to the corral and Smoke pulled out the makings and built himself a cigarette.

"Walt has confided in me that he is a wealthy man," Smoke said. "Why doesn't he hire guns and let them bang it out with Jud's men?"

"I've pondered over that my very own self," Cheyenne admitted. "I can't come up with no firm answer."

Rusty looked startled for a moment. Then he shook his head in disbelief. He threw down his own cigarette and stomped it out, his spurs jingling with the movement. "I can't believe you two guys!" he finally blurted.

"What do you mean, you red-headed pup?" Cheyenne looked at him.

Rusty just laughed at him.

"I'll bust you up side your punkin head," Cheyenne told him, balling a hand into a fist and drawing it hack.

"Whoa!" Rusty stepped back.

"You better explain yourself, Rusty. If you know something we need to know, spit it out."

"I didn't mean to laugh at neither of you. I just figured that you both knew."

"Knew what, you knothead?" Cheyenne growled at him.

Rusty looked at Smoke. "Soon as you told me I was workin' for the Box T, I figured the fire had done reached the grease. But it never dawned on me that Mr. Walt hadn't leveled with you. Hell . . ." He paused. "Well, maybe the old bunch has died out and the new bunch of folks in this area don't know. Jud Vale is Walt's kid brother!"

Chapter 14

After recovering from his shock, Cheyenne said, "I been in and out of here for the last fifty years, Rusty. I ain't never heard that story."

"Rancher up in Montana told me some five or six years ago. Sorry, boys, I just figured you knew."

"So Clint is really Walt's nephew," Smoke spoke the words softly. "I wonder what surprises Doreen has in store for us?"

Rusty blushed.

"Not those surprises, Rusty! I wonder if she's kin to Walt and Alice?"

"Beats me. I done told you all I know."

"You shore this rancher wasn't just pullin' your leg?" Cheyenne questioned.

"I don't think so. We was sittin' around the fire one night during roundup, passin' a bottle around. Lemmie see if I can remember all, or most, of what was said." He rolled another cigarette, deep in thought while he was shaping and licking and lighting the tube. "Mr. Randolph—that was the rancher I was workin' for at the time—he said that Walt come out to this part of Idaho 'way back. The first white-man to settle in this part of the territory."

"That much jibes with what Walt told me," Smoke confirmed.

"Mr. Randolph said that Walt had left a baby brother behind. I believe he said Ill-o-noise or O-hi-o or some of them faraway places like that. Said that Walt never really knew the kid all that good. He was in diapers when Walt left. The kid started gettin' into trouble right off the mark. Then as the kid got older, the trouble got worser. He's supposed to have raped and kilt a woman when he was 'bout fourteen or fifteen and had to flee, two steps ahead of the law."

"And Walt didn't know what was going on back home?"

"No way he could have. A thousand miles away like he was. Sure wasn't no letters bein' posted to this part of the territory. Mr. Randolph said that the kid turned to a life of crime—bad stuff. Robbin' and murderin' folks and abusin' women. He robbed a U.S. gold shipment, hundreds of thousands of dollars and him and his gang come out this aways. Jason's been with him from the git-go, 'way Mr. Randolph told it. That gold was what set him up in the ranchin' business.

"Walt went to see the rancher one day, and was shook right down to his boots when Jud Vale—that's the name he took—started talkin' about where he was from. Walt started writin' letters to folks he figured was still alive back to home. He started puttin' two and two together and soon realized that Jud Vale was his baby brother.

"But he never let on to Jud. Not until about ten years ago, I reckon, maybe more than that. Mr. Randolph never did say; or if he did, I forgot. 'Way Mr. Randolph told it, Jud went into a screaming rage for some reason, and told Walt he would destroy him and take all the gold that Walt had found. Walt tried to tell his brother that there wasn't no more gold on the Box T, that the strike had been a fluke and had played out. But Jud wasn't havin' none of that."

"I wonder why Editor Argood didn't tell me all this?" Smoke questioned, his voice soft in the night.

"Well, he probably figured you knew already. Just like I done."

"And now you know it all," Walt's voice came from behind them.

The trio turned around to face the rancher.

"I wish you had told me," Smoke said.

"Shame. It was shame that prevented me from telling you."

Smoke swore an ugly streak. "You're lying, Walt. You've lied to me right from the start and I'm telling you now: clear the damned air and level with us!"

Walt came to the corral and hung his arms over the railing. He lit his pipe and sighed. "There isn't much else to clear. He's my brother, boys. Our blood is the same. I had him in rifle sights once and couldn't pull the trigger. I just couldn't kill him. Even knowing what trash he is—what he had turned into. I just couldn't do it. That's why, until recently, at least, I was just letting him run all over me. Then I got mad. I sent out word that I was hiring gunfighters." He laughed sourly. "But if I paid a hundred a month, Jud would pay two hundred. And so on. I had half a dozen. They left me and went to work for Jud. I hired some straight punchers. Jud and his men drove them off or killed them. I finally reached the point where I just didn't know what to do. I was confused, alone with the wife and Doreen and Micky. Scared for them and for myself. I'm not a young man. There is more than twenty years' difference between me and Jud Vale. His real name is Paul Burden. Then, Smoke, you showed up."

For the first time since arriving at the Box T, Smoke believed the man. "Doreen is no kin to you? No blood kin?"

"No."

"Walt, I've told Cheyenne that I don't want to kill Jud. He needs killing, I'll be the first to admit that. He's a vile, loathsome person, for a fact. But I don't want to be the one to pull the trigger on him. And I won't unless he pushes me to it or gets caught up in gunfire while attacking this ranch. The man is insane. He needs to be confined in an asylum. For the rest of his life."

Walt's laugh was bitter. "You think I haven't tried to do that. I personally called on the territorial governor and informed him of Jud—without telling him that Jud was my brother. He sent people in to talk with Jud. Jud charmed them. He has that ability. Just like his son, Clint. And just like Clint, he can go off the beam into a raging, killing darkness at the smallest slight or word. Smoke, I don't know what else I can do. I have reached my wit's end in this matter."

Smoke felt an intense sorrow for the man. A grandson that wasn't his, and a blood brother who was a raging lunatic and invariably would have to be destroyed like a rabid dog was enough to fell all but the strongest of men.

"We'll work it out, Walt," Smoke assured him.

After Walt had returned to the house, Cheyenne asked, "Just how do you figure we're gonna work it out, Smoke?"

"I don't have any idea," Smoke admitted.

Susie slept late, it being almost noon when she walked out into the front yard. When the weather was good, the boys took their meals at a long setup table in the yard. When the weather was bad, they had to take shifts eating in the house.

Susie was amazed at the youth of the hands, and equally amazed at the ages of the old men. No one asked her to lend a hand with the cleaning up, she just fell to it as one by one the boys finished their nooning and got up, going back to work.

"Rider comin'," Cheyenne said, squinting his eyes.

"Who is it?" Rusty asked.

"Blackjack Morgan," Smoke told them. "You never know about Blackjack. Or Jackson, for that matter. They operate under a strange code."

Matthew had moved over from the table, to stand by the rose bushes planted in front of the house. The hammer thong was off his Peacemaker.

"You just steady down, boy," Smoke said. "Blackjack's not looking for trouble."

Blackjack reined up at the hitchrail and waited for an invite to dismount.

"Coffee's hot, Blackjack," Smoke told him. "You're welcome to a cup and something to eat if you're hungry."

Blackjack swung out of the saddle. "Neighborly of you, Smoke. Coffee sounds good." His eyes widened and he smiled. "Is them bear sign I spy?"

"Yes. Help yourself, Mr. . . . ah, Blackjack," Alice said.

"Thank you kindly, ma'am." He poured coffee and got a couple of doughnuts. He looked at Smoke. "But I got to say that this ain't what you'd call a social visit. At least not right off, it ain't."

"I didn't figure it was." Smoke moved to the table and sat down.

Blackjack munched on a doughnut and sipped his coffee. "That editor feller is gone to Utah. Won't be back for a month or more. And that youngster he hired to cover the news has recently got hisself a bad case of jitters. Didn't take much; just a little talkin' to, is all. He won't be comin' around here no more."

"We expected that."

Blackjack's eyes held a visible light of amusement as he looked around at the boys and the old men. "Damnedest outfit I ever did see. Pardon my language, ladies. These boys doin' a man's work. Drove that herd all the way to the railhead without a bobble. You boys is all right in my book. I brung a message from the Bar V," he said abruptly.

Smoke took a bite from a doughnut and waited.

"Jud Vale has done declared war on anybody ridin' for the Box T. Man, woman, or child. That don't set too well for a few of us. Me and Jackson, most especially. I don't believe in mistreatin' women or hurtin' no kid or dog. So, I ain't a-gonna do it. Neither is Jackson."

He finished his bear sign and wiped his mouth with the back of his hand. He drained his coffee cup and thanked Susie as she refilled it.

"But that's just two out of about forty-five . . . with more comin' in shortly. The odds is too high, Smoke. You can't win this one."

"These folks have no place else to go, Blackjack. So we have to win it."

"Figured you'd say that. You bein' who you is and all that."

Blackjack sipped his coffee. "Now I ain't got nothin' personal ag'in you, Smoke. But that ten thousand dollars that Jud's done hung on your scalp is just too good for me to walk away from. That money would get me a right nice spread down in Texas and I can hang these guns up."

"You ain't never gonna hang them guns up, Blackjack," Cheyenne told him. "You been around too long. You're one of the old breed. There's always gonna be some punk kid who wants to make hisself a rep."

"Not me, Cheyenne. I'm a-gonna change my name and bury myself down near the Barrillas. Me and Lassiter. We done talked it over. So me and Lassiter will be waitin' for you over at Preston, Smoke. That's the way it's got to be, and you know it."

Smoke nodded.

Blackjack cut his eyes to Matthew. "Git shut of that gun, boy. It ain't nothing but grief. You already got the stamp on you, but it ain't too late to shake it off. As young as you is, you kill another man, you're gonna be marked."

"I plan on becoming a lawman," Matt told him.

"Huh! That's even worse. Puttin' up with drunks and whoors and tinhorns and gamblers. It ain't no life." He smiled sadly. "O' course, my life ain't been all that great, neither." He stood up and smiled at the women. "Much obliged for the coffee and bear sign, ladies." Turning, he looked at Smoke. "Lassiter's just over the ridge. We're headin' for Preston. I 'spect we'll see you there, Smoke."

Blackjack Morgan walked to his horse and swung into the saddle. He rode off without looking back.

"Now that is interesting!" Walt said.

"Not really." Smoke began rolling a cigarette. "They're setting me up, that's all."

"You can bet on that!" Cheyenne agreed. "Blackjack and Lassiter will prob'ly have four or five men with them. Their plan is being the only ones standin' after the battle."

"That's the way I read it at first. Now I'm not so sure."

"What do you mean, son?" Walt asked.

"Jud wants me away from the ranch, probably figuring I'll take someone with me."

"And he'll hit the ranch when you're gone," Alice stated, a sick expression on her face.

"That's the way I see it."

"And if you don't go into Preston, Blackjack and them others will spread the word that Smoke Jensen has turned yeller," Cheyenne added that.

Smoke shrugged that off. "That kind of talk never bothered me, Cheyenne."

"Son, you can't face seven or eight men alone," Walt told him.

Smoke smiled. "I faced eighteen alone one time. I did take some lead. But I put them all down. Don't worry, Walt. I have no intention of riding into a setup. If I just stay put, that will probably make Blackjack and the others so mad they'll do something rash."

"Like what?" Rusty asked.

"Oh . . . like moving their ambush a lot closer than Preston. Like over to the trading post."

"And you'd ride over there to face them?" Susie asked. "One man against seven or eight gunslingers?"

"I'd give it some serious thought," Smoke told her, pouring another cup of coffee.

"That man said that more gunfighters would be coming in shortly," Doreen said.

"I'm fresh out of ideas, Doreen. What do you want me to do, girl?"

"You could put the ranch up for sale. Advertise it in the paper, in papers all over the state. That would draw a lot of attention to our situation and maybe make Jud Vale back off."

"She's got a point, Walt," Smoke told him.

But the old rancher shook his head. "I been out here goin' on fifty years. Me and Alice fought Indians and outlaws, blizzards and droughts. We come close to packin' it in several times. This ain't one of them times. If you all was to leave—and I wouldn't blame you none if you was to pull out—I'm stayin'."

His wife moved to his side. "*We're* staying, Walt."

He put his arm around her waist and pulled her close.

The younger of the boys looked at each other, all thinking they had best head back to the creek as quickly as possible and gather up some more stones for their slingshots.

Matthew hitched up his gunbelt.

"This here is a right good job of work," Dolittle said. "So me and Harrison is stayin' put. If I'm gonna die, I'd druther it be with food in my belly and some coins to jingle in my jeans."

"I'm stayin'," Cheyenne said.

"So are we!" the boys shouted as a unit.

Rusty shrugged his shoulders. "Count me in, too."

"That's settled," Smoke said. "Let's get back to work."

Chapter 15

The sheriff rode out to the ranch two days after Blackjack Morgan had tossed down the challenge. He had three tough-looking deputies with him.

He told Walt to get his crew together. His adult crew.

Only Smoke, Cheyenne, and the women were close to the house. They sat at the long table in the front yard and talked.

"Lines bein' what they are," the sheriff said, "I ain't rightly sure this place is even in my jurisdiction. But I know damn well that Preston is. Excuse my language, ladies. And I ain't a-gonna have no gunfights in my town." He looked at Smoke. "I thank you for not ridin' in."

"I'm waiting for them to move it closer to the ranch."

The sheriff nodded his head. He waved his hand at the three deputies. "This is it, folks. You're lookin' at the law enforcement in this county . . . providing, that is, the Box T is even in my county. New lines was drawn up last year and it's still all confused. But that ain't the point. The point is that Jud Vale's done hired himself about sixty men, all drawin' fightin' wages, and there ain't a damn thing I can do about it. Oh, I could ride over to the Bar V and try to throw my badge around. But you all know how much good that would do. Jud's a charmer. He'd just tell me he was gettin' ready for roundup and hired all them men to punch cows."

He sighed. "Walt, there may still be warrants out on Jud back East. I know the story. And I've sent telegrams to them folks back yonder. The parents of the girl that Jud was supposed to have killed is dead. The lawmen who were in charge when it happened are gone. So that's a dead end. No help there."

"What you're trying to say, Sheriff," Smoke said, "is that we're on our own here."

"That's blunt put, Jensen. But yeah, that's just about it. You say that Jud attacked your ranch. Can you prove it in a court of law?"

"I doubt it," Walt admitted.

"There still ain't no laws about two growed-up men facin' each other over gun barrels. There will be someday, but that time ain't here yet. I talked to a man from the governor's office. The governor ain't got the manpower to step in and settle every dispute between ranchers. Territory is just too big. I've said what I come to say, Walt. I wanted to tell it to you face to face."

"I appreciate that."

"You've told us, Sheriff," Smoke said. "Now let me tell you."

The sheriff cut his eyes to the gunfighter.

"Just stay out of it," Smoke said flatly. "I roughed up a few and killed one the last time out. The next time I go head-hunting, I'm going to leave bodies all over the range."

The sheriff flushed, but wisely kept his mouth shut.

"And that goes for me, too," Cheyenne said. "In spades.

I'm gettin' tarred of all this dilly-dallyin' around. I'm an old man; I ain't got many years left me. So it don't make a damn to me if I check out now, just so long as I take a few, or a bunch, with me. And I plan on doing just that."

The sheriff stood up and his deputies followed suit. "I wish you luck." The lawmen walked to their horses and rode away.

"He's a good man, the sheriff is," Walt said. "I ain't takin' what he said nearabouts as hard as you boys. Maybe I just understand the feelin's around here better than you."

Smoke stared at the man. "What do you mean, Walt?"

"I've tried to tell you time and again, boy: folks around here is scared of Jud Vale. He's had them buffaloed for years, and it ain't got much better—if any better—since you come along. Man told me last time we went to the post that most of the bettin' money was with Jud and against you."

"You should have told him he was a fool."

"I did. Problem was, I don't know how convincing I sounded."

Walt and Alice, with Doreen and Susie right behind them, went back into the house. Smoke and Cheyenne walked to the corral and stood in silence for a few minutes.

"You changed your mind any 'bout just ridin' up to Jud and pluggin' him?" Cheyenne asked.

"No."

"Didn't figure so. Still think that would be the smart thing to do."

"You're probably right, Cheyenne. But it just isn't my style."

"You want me to do it? He ain't nothin' but a rattle-snake."

"No." Smoke looked off into the distance. "But it worries me about him declaring war on the women and the boys."

"It don't surprise me none," the old gunfighter said with a snort. "A rattlesnake don't give a damn who he strikes. Sometimes they'll just lay there on the trail still as death and watch you go past without even a short rattle. Next time you come by, they'll hit you. Jud Vale ain't got no more sense than a rattler. And is just about as useless. Come to think of it, a rattler might be worth more. Least they kill rats and mice."

The old rounder limped off, toward the bunkhouse and a cup of coffee.

Smoke stood for a time by the corral, deep in thought. Maybe Cheyenne was right. Maybe he should just ride over to the Bar V, line up Jud Vale in rifle sights, and end it.

But Smoke knew he wouldn't do that. At least not yet.

But if one of the boys got hurt . . . ?

He shook his head. He didn't even like to think about that.

With his back to the corral rails, he watched the boys ride out, heading back to work; a gutsy bunch of kids.

Smoke wondered where Clint Perkins had gotten off to. The so-called Robin Hood of the West had not been heard from since he had rescued Susie from the Bar V. But Smoke had no doubts about his being near, waiting for that invisible trigger in his brain—always on half-cock—to fire his unstable mind into action.

Smoke went into the house, told Doreen to fix him a bait of food, and with the food-packet in his hand, went to the barn, saddling Dagger. Rusty had ridden in and was seeing to his horse.

"You headin' out?"

"Yes. Is the herd bunched?"

"And boxed."

"I want you and the others to stick close to the ranch. I don't know how long I'm going to be gone. Three days;

maybe a week. However long it takes me to cut the odds down some."

"You goin' to face Blackjack and them others?"

"Probably. But it will be on my terms, not on theirs. Nobody has to leave the ranch. We're well-stocked with food; God knows we have enough guns and ammo to stand off a dozen attacks. Keep an eye on the boys, Rusty." He swung into the saddle.

"I'll do it. You watch your back trail, Smoke."

"I've been doing that since I was fifteen years old," Smoke said with a smile.

He rode for the Bar V range, keeping to the timber and the brush, riding slow and stopping often to sit his saddle and listen. He marveled at the size of Jud's herds. The man was worth a fortune in beef alone; there wasn't a rancher anywhere who wouldn't be satisfied with these herds. Only Jud Vale wanted more. But then, Smoke concluded, Jud wanted everything.

Especially Doreen.

Smoke had warned her to stick very close to the ranch, and to stop wandering out into the meadows to pick wildflowers. Jud had made his brags that he would have Doreen, one way or the other. But whether Smoke's warnings had gotten through to the girl was something only time would prove out.

Smoke steered clear of Jud's mansion. What he wanted to see was whether anyone was working Jud's cattle, and after spending most of the afternoon carefully watching from the hills and ridges, he concluded that the cattle had been pretty much left on their own.

So Jud had pulled in all his hands. For what? An attack on the ranch? Maybe. But somehow he doubted that.

He had tried that once, with disastrous results. So if not an attack against the Box T . . . then what?

Smoke could come up with no reason for leaving the herd unguarded. Of course, Jud probably felt—and rightly so—that no one would have the nerve to rustle cattle from him, so his herds were safe.

So what was going on? And why had he not run into any of the Bar V hands this day? Odd. Very odd.

With about three hours of good light left and guessing that he was a good ten miles—maybe more—from Jud's mansion, Smoke rode to near the top of a high ridge. Keeping in the timber, Smoke dismounted and took his field glasses, making his way to the top of the hill. There, on his belly and under cover, he began carefully sweeping the area.

Far in the distance, he picked up the small figures of men, some on foot, some on horseback. They were making a meticulous sweep of the area. Looking for what? Smoke silently questioned. Or for whom? Certainly not him. Jud knew he was at the Box T . . . or had been for days.

Had to be looking for Clint. That was all that Smoke could come up with. Had Clint pulled something over the past few days that Smoke did not know about? It was certainly possible.

Smoke studied the tiny figures of searching men through his field glasses. At least twenty-five or thirty. And that brought yet another thought to Smoke's mind: where were Jud's other hands and hired guns? That question made him uncomfortable.

He decided to get the hell gone from there.

He mounted up and rode toward the deep timber that lay to the east of the mansion, but still well on Bar V range. As he rode, he began seeing signs that this area had been searched and searched thoroughly. He reined up suddenly, knowing then where the other Bar V men were.

All around him, waiting to see if Clint—if that's who they were searching for—would double back.

Smoke found a place which offered deep cover and a good two days' graze and water for Dagger, picketed him, and slipped into moccasins. He filled any empty loops with .44's and taking his rifle, began Injuning his way through the brush and timber.

Smoke was under no illusions: these were dangerous men he was surrounded by, and after Smoke's initial attack against the ranch, and his making fools of the men, they would be doubly alert, with more than one of them mad as hell and looking for blood.

Smoke's blood.

Making about as much noise as a drifting ghost, Smoke wormed his way under a pile of blown down brush and dead limbs—hoping that a rattlesnake had not made this spot his home—and settled in for a time.

As he waited, Smoke ran some questions through his mind: Why the systematic search for Clint? Had the man staged another raid, or had Jud just decided to take out his enemies one at a time? Then Smoke rejected both ideas as another thought came to him.

Clint Perkins was a wanted man, a fugitive from justice. So what better way for Jud to show the people that he was a straight-up, honest, and law-abiding citizen than by killing or capturing the most wanted man in Southern Idaho. That would certainly swing public opinion in his favor.

And there was something else, too: after Clint was taken—and Smoke felt the man would not be taken alive, Jud simply could not risk that—Vale could, and probably would, charge that Walt and Alice and Doreen had been hiding the outlaw. That would further erode Walt's credibility with his neighbors.

Slick! Smoke thought, as his eyes continued to sweep the

terrain from his hiding place. Jud Vale was beginning to think in a more rational way.

And that, Smoke reflected bitterly, was something he had not even considered Jud doing. He had been counting on the man to continue behaving in his usual emotional and irrational manner.

A stick popped not far from Smoke's hiding place. Smoke cut his eyes, not moving his head. That was no animal, for animals seldom stepped on sticks unless they were running in fear. And Smoke heard no follow-up sounds of any animal in panic.

He waited, motionless, his breathing very shallow and through his mouth to cut down even the slightest sound.

He saw the man move; a fatal mistake on the man's part, for movement attracts attention much faster than sound in any deadly game of hide or be killed.

The man was dressed in earth tones, blending in well with his surroundings. Smoke concluded that the man was a skilled woodsman, and the stick was the only mistake he had made.

It just took one mistake in this game, and the man had made his.

The manhunter moved closer, moving stealthily through the timber. As he drew closer, Smoke could make out his features. It was one of those he had seen stepping off the train some days before. A bounty hunter.

The man carried a Winchester in his hand, a bandoleer of cartridges slung over one shoulder. The manhunter stopped, tensed, and suddenly dropped to the ground.

Smoke watched through a small space in the pile of brush and dead limbs. What had the man seen? Or had his hunter's sixth sense alerted him of the unseen danger?

Probably the latter.

Now it was a game of wait and see.

Smoke waited. Several minutes passed. He could detect no other men, so the bounty hunter was probably working alone. But Smoke couldn't be certain of that, although he believed it to be true.

A bird flew into the timber, started to settle on a branch, then abruptly took once more to the air, its wings flapping furiously.

Smoke's smile was a grim one. Thank you, bird, he thought. Have a long and happy life.

He had yet to move his head. Only his cold hunter's eyes had shifted. Now they remained fixed on the dangerous brush where the bounty hunter lay.

The top of the brush moved ever so slightly, the movement indicating the man was coming toward Smoke's location, making his way very cautiously.

Had he been spotted? Smoke didn't think so.

Smoke waited for several minutes, watching the slow movement of the man. He wanted him much closer; close enough to use his knife. He did not want to risk a shot; not knowing how many others were within earshot of his location.

Then the bounty hunter rose, all in one fluid motion. He was so close that Smoke could see the hard cruelty in his eyes.

The bounty hunter moved closer, pausing a few feet from the brush pile where Smoke lay.

Smoke exploded out of the brush, his knife in his hand.

Chapter 16

The bounty hunter wheeled around, his eyes wide with panic, the rifle in his hands coming up. But Smoke's forward charge knocked the man sprawling, loosening his grip on the Winchester. The man opened his mouth to yell a warning. With one hard swing of the long-bladed knife, Smoke ended the life of the hunter.

He took the man's rifle, pistol, and ammo, and then dragged the body into the pile of brush. Smoke made his way back to Dagger, using a different route, stashed the weapons, patted the big stallion on the neck, and once more headed out into the woods.

This time out, he was going to show Jud Vale what he thought of a man who would declare war on women and young boys.

And he would write the message in blood.

Smoke stayed near the top of a ridge, working his way along, keeping to the brush and timber, not skylining himself. At the highest point of the ridge, Smoke bellied down and made his way to the crest.

A Bar V hand chose that time to stick his head up and look Smoke right in the eyes. Smoke recovered from his shock before the puncher and clobbered the cowboy right between the eyes with the butt of his Winchester, sending the man sprawling backward, his forehead bleeding.

Smoke was over the crest and on top of the hand before the man could recover. Smoke busted the man on the side of the jaw with the butt of the rifle and the hand's eyes rolled back in his head. He was out for a long time, with a broken jaw.

Smoke tossed the man's pistol into the brush and smashed the man's rifle useless against a tree trunk. He moved down the ridge, mad and on the warpath. A Bar V gunny spotted him and raised his rifle to fire. Smoke leveled his Winchester and shot the man in the belly, doubling him over and bringing a scream of pain.

Now the fire had reached the hot grease and the war was on.

The landscape seemed to erupt with ugly and very hostile gun hands as Smoke dived for cover just as unfriendly fire began zinging and popping and ricocheting all around him.

Jumping behind a fallen log, Smoke wriggled his way to the other end and rolled into a small depression in the earth. Below him, the Bar V gunnies were shouting and cussing.

Smoke leveled his Winchester and put an abrupt and permanent halt to one gunfighter's swearing. The .44 slug caught the man in the chest. The hand's rifle went flying as blood stained the front of his shirt.

Smoke lunged out of the depression and made the timber before the others could get him in gun sights; shooting uphill was just as tricky as shooting downhill.

On the crest of the ridge, in deep timber, Smoke settled in

for the siege. He dusted one Bar V gunny's position, sending the man hugging the earth and losing his hat. Just for spite, knowing what value Western men put on their hats, Smoke lifted his rifle and knocked the hat spinning, ventilating the Stetson.

The gunny cussed Smoke, loud and long.

Smoke ducked down as the lead began whining wickedly all around him, bringing the thought to his mind that now would be just a dandy time to haul his ashes out of that particular location.

During a break in the firing, Smoke eased back, clearing the crest of the ridge, and began making his way west, working in a slow, careful semicircle until coming to a better, if temporary, area in which to work.

He lifted his Winchester, sighted in a foot sticking out from behind a large rock, and squeezed the trigger. The yowl of pain that followed told him he had taken another gunny out of the fight. The man was screaming in pain from his bullet-shattered ankle.

Another gunny, with more guts than sense, left his safe position to move to what he felt was a better one.

Smoke shot him, the bullet going in his left side and tearing out the right side, spinning the man like an out-of-balance top and dropping him to the hard, rocky ground. He did not move.

Smoke punched more .44's into his Winchester and made life miserable for a gunhand who was crouched behind a tree. The man decided to seek better cover and made a run for it. Smoke knocked a leg out from under him and the man rolled down the hill, hollering and cussing. He finally managed to break his downhill rolling by grabbing onto a small tree and painfully work his way behind it. Smoke let him be, and concentrated on the others.

But the fight was gone from this bunch. Smoke watched without firing as they began working their way down the hill, staying in cover, carrying and helping the wounded back out of range of Smoke's deadly rifle fire.

He left his position and worked his way back into deep timber, paralleling the gunnies' retreat, sensing from their urgency and the direction of their travel that they were heading for their horses. He was waiting for them when they reached the picket line.

Smoke shot one badman in the belly and dusted another gunhand before they all left in a confusing and disorderly retreat, some of them losing their weapons as they stumbled and ran away.

Smoke ran into the camp, grabbed up the fallen weapons, and stuck them in empty saddle boots. He grasped as many reins as he could, swung into a saddle, and led the horses back to where he had left Dagger. There, he tied and grouped the horses and headed back for Box T range.

All in all, it had been quite a profitable day.

It was late night before Smoke reached the ranch house. He put the horses into the corral, told the boys to strip the gear from them and clean and store the weapons. He switched horses and then filled a sack with dynamite and caps and fuses, and was back in the saddle, heading once more for Bar V range.

He made a cold camp, slept for a few hours, and was up about three in the morning. He checked his guns and then saddled up. With a grim smile on his lips, Smoke went head-hunting under the stars.

About two miles from the main house, and not running into a single Bar V hand, Smoke moved several hundred head of cattle toward the direction of Jud's mansion and then tossed two sputtering sticks of dynamite near the bunched-up herd of Bar V cattle. The explosions sent them into a snorting, wild-eyed stampede heading straight for the mansion.

Smoke tagged along to see what other mischief he could get into this fine night.

The hard-running cattle hit the mansion grounds at full speed, demolishing several outhouses and destroying one corral. Smoke drove half a dozen of the frightened cattle into the mansion and then circled, tossing a stick of dynamite into a bunkhouse.

The charge of giant powder blew out one entire end of the bunkhouse and sent gun hands—in various stages of undress—rolling and running and crawling in all directions.

The dust kicked up from the wildly stampeding herd only added to the confusion, limiting visibility to only a few yards in any direction. Smoke's horse ran into one long handle–clad gun hand, knocking the man to the ground. The gun hand screamed as the horse's steel-shod hooves ripped flesh and cracked bone.

Jud Vale appeared on the balcony of the second floor of the mansion, clad only in his underwear. He was jumping up and down and screaming almost incoherently. "Somebody come up here and get this goddamn cow out of my bedroom!" he finally managed to squall.

With his six gun, Smoke put several slugs around Jud's bare feet. The man did a frantic little dance, and hollering to beat sixty, leaped back into the bedroom, obviously preferring the company of a smelly wild-eyed cow to the lead that was sending splinters into his tootsies.

A puncher grabbed onto Smoke's leg, trying to pull him out of the saddle. Smoke laid the barrel of his Colt against the man's head, splitting it wide open and dropping the man to the ground.

Hot lead came awfully close to Smoke's cheek and that

convinced him that it was time to move. Riding bent low over his horse's neck, Smoke galloped around to the back of the house. Jud had just rebuilt the back porch and replaced all the windows at the rear of the house.

Smoke lit another fuse with the small can of burning punk and tossed the stick under the back porch.

Jud's wild cussing could just be heard over the confusion.

Smoke had cleared the creek and was heading into the starry darkness as the porch blew. The giant powder demolished the newly rebuilt porch and once more broke all the windows from the rear of the mighty mansion.

"Goddamn you, Jensen!" Jud's voice rang out over the dusty night. "I'll get you for this. I swear I'll get you! I'll stake you out over an anthill and let them eat your eyes. I'll . . ."

Laughing as Jud's voice faded, Smoke headed for the deep timber.

Dawn found him cutting fence wire and scattering Jud's cattle all to hell and gone. An hour later he had blown two dams and torn down several line shacks.

He looked up at the sounds of pounding hooves and cut his horse toward a long-deserted cabin and barn about half a mile away. The story was that the cabin and barn had belonged to a rancher and his wife. Jud had moved in and moved them out, after killing the rancher's son and badly wounding the rancher.

Smoke chanced a glance over his shoulder. There were ten or twelve riders coming hard at him, but still too far away for accurate shooting on their part.

As he rode toward the cabin, Smoke made his plans as he bent over the horse's neck, keeping a very low target. The cabin was built into a hill. The sod roof had long since become a living thing as the grass from the hill caught life and flourished.

Smoke dismounted at a run and threw open the door, leading the horse inside. He knelt in the open doorway and leveled his Winchester, clearing one saddle of a hired gun. The horse trotted on toward the cabin as the other gun hands veered off, left and right, seeking some sort of cover. They all knew how deadly Smoke was with any type of weapon.

Smoke grabbed the reins of the spooked pony, pulled the rifle from its hoot, tore loose the canteen—that would give him three full canteens—and jerked off the saddlebags. He slapped the pony on the rump, sending it on its way.

Smoke slammed the door and dropped the old bar across it just as rifle shots began slugging into the logs of the cabin. He led the horse into the rear part of the house, as far out of harm's way as possible, gave it a hatful of water, and returned to the front of the cabin. If worse came to worst, he could pull grass from off the roof and feed the animal.

He smiled when he saw the kitchen. Luck was with him. Some of the Bar V hands had used the cabin as a line shack, and used it recently. Staying low, Smoke closed the still sturdy inside shutters—put there long ago against Indian attack—and tried the pump in the kitchen. Cold clear water gushed forth. He opened the cabinet. Cans of beans and peaches looked back at him. He selected a can of peaches and opened it with his knife, then ate the peaches and drank the juice.

"All the comforts of home," he muttered, then checked the Winchester he'd jerked from the boot of the riderless horse. It was full up.

He looked into the saddlebags of the hired gun who now rested facedown on the ground. Several biscuits with salt meat, three boxes of .44's and a spare pistol and holster under one flap. Dirty underwear under the other flap. He kept the biscuits, the pistol, and the .44's.

Smoke moved to a gun port and looked out. He could see

a man slowly working his way toward the house, but still too far off for a shot. Smoke let him come on.

He moved to the other side of the house just in time to see a man run from tree to tree. This one was well within range. Smoke eared the hammer back on his Winchester and waited. The gun hand broke cover and made a run for the corral. Smoke stopped him at midpoint, the .44 slug turning him around as it hit his side. Smoke didn't finish the man, choosing instead to let him lie on the ground and scream in pain. That would work on his buddies much more than a death shot.

Smoke sat down on the floor, his back to an overturned table as the lead really began to fly in his direction. He ate one of the salt meat biscuits and sipped water from his canteen and let the attackers expel all the ammunition they wanted to.

After a time, the hostile fire slacked off and then died. Smoke smiled a grim curving of the lips and moved to the window. He let out a long groan. He waited, and then groaned again.

"We got him!" a man shouted. "We really got the bastard this time!"

"Oh, yeah?" came the sarcasm-filled question. "And who wants to be the one to walk up and look inside the cabin to be sure?"

No one replied.

"That's what I figured," the man said.

Smoke removed the bar from the door and moved back to the overturned table, laying his rifle on the floor, pulling his Colts and easing back the hammers. He waited. When they opened that door—and he figured they would come all bunched up for moral support—more than a few of them were going to be in for a very nasty surprise.

Once more, the outside air was filled with lead. Smoke waited.

"Hell, he's had it," a man called. "I'm goin' in."

"I'll go with you," another called, and several more added their agreement to that.

Smoke waited.

He heard the jingle of spurs as the hired guns and bounty hunters approached the cabin. Smoke had removed his boots and arranged them behind the table, placing them so it appeared he was lying dead, his body concealed behind the table. He slipped on moccasins and then stepped back into the shadows of another room.

The front door was pushed open with the barrel of a rifle.

"See anything?" a man asked.

"Hell, are you crazy? I ain't stickin' my head in yonder!"

"I see his boots," another said, looking through a gun slit. "He's all sprawled out and stone cold dead behind a table."

The room crowded with men.

Smoke opened fire, the Colts belching sparks and flame and death. He pulled the pistol he'd taken from the saddlebags and ended the lopsided gunfight. One lone gun hand tried to rise up and shoot him. Smoke shot him between the eyes. "Your mamma should have told you there'd be days like this," Smoke said.

He then counted the bodies. Six. He figured maybe three were left on the outside still alive, and that included the badly wounded man by the corral.

He reloaded and moved toward the open door, staying close to the log wall. "Come on, boys!" he shouted. "Come join the party."

"Hell with you, Jensen!" a man shouted. "They's always another day. We're gone!"

"Then ride, scumbag!"

The man cursed him. A moment later, the sounds of horses galloping away reached Smoke.

Smoke gathered up all the weapons and tied the rifles together. He found a bounty hunter's horse and stuffed the saddlebags full of pistols and gunbelts, looping some over the saddle horn. He secured the rifles to the saddle and led the horse to the cabin. Shoving the dead out of the doorway, Smoke led his own horse outside and mounted up. He walked his horse over to the corral and looked down at the man lying on the ground. The man was dead. He left him there and rode out into the plain. The first man he'd shot out of the saddle was lying on the ground, on his back, his eyes open and staring at Smoke. His shirt front was covered with blood.

"You're a devil!" the man gasped.

"I've been called worse," Smoke acknowledged from the saddle.

"I ain't gonna make it, am I?"

"Not likely."

The man cussed him but made no attempt to reach for the pistol still in leather.

Smoke waited until the man stopped cussing and tried to catch his breath. "Anything you want me to do for you?"

"Fall out of the saddle dead!"

Jud Vale had hired hardcases, for sure. No give in them. "Would you really have shot one of those little boys over at the Box T?"

"Just as fast as I'd shoot you, Jensen."

"Then I don't think I'll turn my back to you."

"It wouldn't be a smart thing to do, for a fact."

Smoke sat his saddle for a few minutes. The gunny began to cough up blood. Twice he tried to pull his pistol. But the thong covered the hammer and he could not clear leather. The gunny died with a curse on his lips.

Smoke turned his horse and slowly rode toward Box T range.

Chapter 17

Jud Vale pulled in his horns, so to speak. Even with his monumental ego and glaring arrogance, he was shocked to the bone at the havoc and carnage that Smoke Jensen had wreaked upon his possessions and hired guns. He had not believed it possible that one man could do so much.

A half dozen of his older and wiser hardcases drew their time and drifted out of Southeastern Idaho, wanting no more of Smoke Jensen. Had most of those who left known Jensen was involved in this matter, they would not have signed on in the first place.

Jud spent a lot of time on his front porch—while his back porch was being rebuilt, again—drinking coffee and wallowing in his festering anger. He had sent out the word that he was still hiring men at fighting wages, and men were drifting in. But even Jud Vale could see that most of them were trash and scum. That made no difference; he hired them anyway.

And then the gunfighter Barry Almond and his four brothers came riding up to the mansion. They were dressed in long dusters and were unshaven, with cruel eyes their hat brims could not conceal.

Jud sat on the porch staring at the men while Barry sat his saddle and met the man's eyes.

"I'm Barry Almond," the gun slick finally broke the silence.

"I know who you are."

"That ten thousand dollars still on Smoke Jensen's head?"

"It's still there."

"Me and my brothers come to claim it."

"I've heard that from fifty other men over the weeks," Jud snorted.

"This is the first time you've heard it from me, though."

Jud nodded his head in agreement with that. "All right, you're all on the payroll."

"I ain't punchin' no gawddamn cows," Barry bluntly told him.

The rancher laughed, but the short bark was void of humor. "Nobody else is either," Jud replied, the bitterness thick on his tongue. Ranch was going to hell in a bucket. "So what else is new?"

"We'll just drift around some."

"You do that." Jud poured another cup of coffee and watched the gunfighter brothers head for the long new bunkhouse which Jud had been forced to build because of the overflow of hired guns and because Jensen had destroyed one end of the other bunkhouse.

Jud silently cursed Smoke Jensen. It made him feel better. But not much.

* * *

On the day that Smoke accompanied the supply wagon to the trading post, Blackjack Morgan, Lassiter, and four bounty hunters headed for the post for a drink of whiskey. The men were in a bad mood and ready for a killing. Especially if it was Smoke Jensen or some of those snot-nosed brats on the Box T payroll. . . .

Clint Perkins lay on his ground sheet in his hidden camp and tried with all his might to fight the madness that once more began to slowly muddle his brain. He lost the battle. Clint stood up, pulled on his boots and buckled his gunbelt around his waist. With a strange smile on his lips and an odd look in his eyes, he saddled up and went looking for trouble. . . .

Matthew and Cheyenne were moving some strays toward the huge box canyon that was the home for what was left of Walt's herds. The old gunfighter and the young boy had become good friends in a short time. . . .

Doreen slipped out the back door of the ranch house to go walking toward a meadow about a mile back of the house. She had seen some lovely wildflowers there and felt that a bunch of them would look very nice on the kitchen table. She didn't think Jud would be foolish enough to try anything in the daylight. . . .

Jud Vale and Jason and Jud's bodyguards chose that time to make a daylight foray into Box T country. They were heavily armed and one of Jud's men had a gunnysack filled with dynamite and caps and fuses. If they could get close enough to Walt's place, they intended to return in kind what Smoke had given them. Twice. And if some of those snot-nosed nester brats got killed . . . ? Big deal. It would serve them right and send a message to the rest of the nesters in what Jud considered to be his territory. . . .

Don Draper and Davy Street and half a dozen other Bar V hired guns had left the bunkhouse to see if they could cause some trouble for the nester brats working the Box T herd. They headed straight for the area where Matthew and Cheyenne were working. . . .

Rusty was about a mile from the box canyon, working alone. . . .

It was ten o'clock in the morning when all the ingredients that were needed to bring to a full boil what would turn out to be the bloodiest range war in all of Idaho Territory's history were dropped into the cauldron.

Smoke stepped down from the saddle in front of the trading post/barroom, and slipped the leather thongs from the hammers of his guns. Walt went into the store to give the shopkeeper his order for supplies.

Doreen sat amid a wild profusion of flowers and began carefully picking out the most lovely and putting them into her basket.

Susie stepped out of the ranch house at Alice's request to go looking for Doreen. She waved Alan over and asked him if he'd seen her. The boy pointed to the meadow rising in wild and beautiful colors above the ranch, a good mile and a half away, he figured.

"She hadn't oughta get that far from the ranch alone," he added. "You want me to go fetch her, Miss Susie?"

"We'll both go, Alan." She looked at the gun belted around the boy's waist. "You really know how to use that thing?"

"Yes, ma'am. I sure do."

Susie hesitated for a moment. "Get a rifle, Alan. Just in case."

"Yes, ma'am. I'll be back in a couple of minutes."

Susie looked toward the meadow. She suddenly had a very bad feeling about this lovely day.

"Riders comin'," Cheyenne said, twisting in the saddle.

Matt turned and spotted the riders. He slipped the leather from the hammer of his six gun.

The movement did not escape the eyes of Cheyenne. "You just stay out of this, boy."

Rusty had seen Cheyenne and the boy working the strays. Then he saw a bunch of strays moving toward a coulee and went after them. Cheyenne and Matt were quickly lost from his sight as he followed the strays down into the deep coolness of the ravine.

"Boss!" one of Jud's bodyguards said, pulling up and pointing to the tiny figure sitting amid the wildflowers in the meadow.

Jud squinted his eyes and an evil smile turned his mouth. His lips were suddenly dry and he licked them as all sorts of wild, lustful and immoral thoughts, all involving Doreen and himself, raced feverishly around in his brain.

"Get her!" Jud ordered. "I'll have that woman. She'll come around. She'll learn to love me. I'll make her my queen!"

The bodyguards spurred their horses.

Doreen looked up at the sounds of pounding hooves, fear in her eyes. She jumped to her feet, her heart racing. She dropped the basket of wildflowers and began running just as Susie and Alan were beginning the long walk to the meadow.

Alan took stock of the situation quickly. He jerked Susie to the ground, knowing that he could not shoot—the distance was far too great. And there was no point in them being spotted and taken prisoner—or worse. At least for Susie.

All they could do was lie amid the flowers and watch.

Doreen ran for her life, screaming as she ran. Strong and hard hands jerked her off the ground and swung her across a saddle. She felt the horse turn and gallop back across the meadow. The horse slowed, then stopped, and she was dumped to the ground. She looked up into the hard eyes of Jud Vale.

"My queen," the rancher said. "You'll be my queen; you'll reign by my side. Together we'll rule this whole country."

"You're crazy!" Doreen hissed at him. "You're plumb loco!"

Jud laughed at her as his eyes roamed over her young body. "Hoist her up here, boys. I want me a handful of that woman."

Doreen began screaming.

Cheyenne had wheeled his horse to face the Bar V gun hands. The old gunfighter's face was hard, his eyes narrowed to obsidian slits. He looked straight at Don Draper. "What the hell are you and this bag of crap ridin' with you doin' on Box T range, Draper?"

"For a skinny old man, Cheyenne, you got a big fat mouth, you know that?"

"And for a punk, Draper, you're 'way over your head and outclassed facin' me, you know that?"

Draper flushed. "Anytime you're ready, Cheyenne. Then me and the boys will take that kid and have some fun with him."

"You'll visit the privy ever' day if you eat regular," Cheyenne popped back. "And you ought to, 'cause you're shore full of it."

Draper's face darkened further at that remark. But still he hesitated, as did Davy Street. Cheyenne was known throughout the West as an old He-Coon who had never backed down from anybody or anything at anytime. If the truth be known. Cheyenne had killed as many men, or more, as Smoke Jensen or John Wesley or Rowdy Joe or Tom Horn—and maybe as many as all of them combined.

Old he might be, but Cheyenne was still a man not to be taken lightly.

It was an old man and a young lad that faced the eight Bar V gun hands that hot morning, but the smell of fear was coming from the so-called gun slicks, not from Cheyenne or Matthew.

"You're a fool, Cheyenne!" Draper spoke, stalling for time.

"Naw," the old gunfighter said, amused at the man's reluctance to drag iron, but at the same time worried about Matthew. "I'm just an old man who's lived a long, long time, that's all. Now I'm ready to see the varmint and rest for a time."

"We gonna kill you and this snot-nosed brat!" a gun hand sneered at him, cutting his shifty eyes to the bespectacled Matthew.

The boy waited, his right hand close to his six gun.

"You might," Cheyenne admitted. "But they's gonna be a fearful toll taken on you boys whilst doin' it."

"You say!" the gun slick said.

"I say," Cheyenne replied calmly. He had faced this a hundred or more times, and he knew the time was now. This was the entire world. No one else existed. This little pocket was all there was. Time had stopped. Eternity was looking them all in the eyes.

"Now!" Davy yelled, grabbing for his gun.

Cheyenne drew, cocked, and fired, all in one smooth and practiced motion, blowing Davy out of the saddle, the slug taking the man in the center of the chest and knocking him backward.

Don jerked iron and fired, the slug striking Cheyenne in the side. Cheyenne leveled his long-barreled pistol and fired just as Matthew's Peacemaker barked. One slug struck Don in the belly, the other one took him in the chest, the bullet nicking his heart. He stayed in the saddle, one dead hand still holding onto the reins.

A Bar V gun blasted the smoky air, the bullet passing through Cheyenne's lungs. Cheyenne grinned a bloody smile and put a slug between the man's eyes as he was sliding from the saddle. The old gunfighter fell to the ground, on his knees just as Matthew put hot lead into the Bar V hand's stomach.

Cheyenne managed to lift his six gun and drill another hired gun before that pale rider came galloping up to touch him on the shoulder.

The old mountain man and gunfighter died on his knees, still wearing his hat and boots and holding onto his six gun.

Matthew was knocked out of the saddle by a slug that hit his left shoulder and tore out his back. But he held on to his Peacemaker, and even though he had lost his glasses he could still see well enough to shoot. The boy leveled the Colt and shot the gun slick in the throat just as Rusty came galloping up, the reins in his teeth and both hands filled with guns.

When Rusty had emptied his Colts, only one Bar V man was left in the saddle and he was hard hit and fogging it back to more friendly range, just barely managing to stay in the saddle.

Rusty took one look at Cheyenne and cursed at the loss of a friend and another man who had helped in the uneasy settling of the West. Rusty hoisted Matthew back into the saddle, found his glasses for him, and tied Cheyenne across his saddle.

"All hell is gonna break loose now, boy," the redhead told the boy. He had inspected the boy's wound and found it to be very painful but not too serious. The bleeding was slow, indicating that no major artery or vein had been hit. Rusty plugged the holes with a torn handkerchief and stabilized the arm in a sling.

"Feels like to me it has broke loose," Matthew said, his voice grim and old for his age. He looked at Cheyenne. "He was my friend."

"He was my friend, too, boy. Let's ride."

* * *

Both Alan and Susie had raced back to the ranch compound, yelling as they ran. Alice started crying and Micky joined her.

The boys wanted to ride after the kidnappers and shoot it out and rescue Miss Doreen. Jamie yelled them into silence and literally had to slap some sense into a couple of them. They would wait for Mr. Smoke and that was that. There wasn't no point in going off half-cocked and getting killed.

"Oh hell!" the barkeep moaned as Smoke stepped into the saloon. "Not you agin!"

"If this keeps up I'm going to get the feeling that you don't like me," Smoke said with a grin. "But of course," he added, "you would be at the end of a very long list, I reckon."

Bendel shook his head. "That don't seem to worry you much." He returned the smile. "One thing about it, Mr. Jensen—with you around I don't never have to worry about bein' bored." He drew Smoke a mug of beer and set it down on the bar.

"I had hoped this place would not be filled up with Bar V riders."

"Stick around," the barkeep said mournfully. "It will be."

"We won't be here long. Just long enough to get supplies."

"I'm glad you didn't bring that four-eyed kid with you. That youngster is so calm he spooks me."

"He'll do to ride the river with, for sure." Smoke sipped his beer while he waited for Walt to finish with his supply ordering. They were making a trip a week to resupply, for with fifteen growing boys to feed, the food went fast. And Rusty was no slouch when it came to grub. He could eat up a whole apple pie all by himself if the girls didn't keep a good eye on him.

Smoke heard the sounds of horses coming up to the post and inwardly he tensed.

The barkeep cursed.

"What's the matter, Bendel?"

"Some of Jud Vale's hired guns ridin' up. A whole passel of 'em."

Smoke sighed. "One of these days I'm going to get to finish a beer in peace."

Chapter 18

Doreen had been dumped into an upstairs bedroom. It wasn't long before Jud opened the door, his arms filled with boxes and a big grin on his broad face. He dumped the boxes on the bed.

"Them's the finest gowns and underthings all the way from Paris, France," he boasted. "Silks and satins and the like. And in that little box, they's a diamond and ruby thing you wear in your hair. I forget what it's called."

"Tiara?" she asked.

"Yeah! That's it, all right. I bought it all just for you, Doreen."

"But I don't want any of these things!"

Jud ignored that. Waved it away. Then he began to pout. "But I bought them just for you," he said, a sulky tone in his voice.

Doreen looked at the bulk of the man, lifting her eyes to his. She could plainly see the madness in his eyes; the same kind of madness she had refused—at first—to see in Clint's eyes. Clint Perkins, Jud Vale's own flesh and blood. And in that instant, she realized something else: that if she was going to survive, she had best humor Jud.

But that thought, or warning, flew right out the window as Jud opened more boxes. Grinning at her, he laid the gold and jewel-encrusted headpiece on the bed and shook out the garment. "See what I bought for myself, Queen Doreen. My, oh, my, won't we both look fine!"

Doreen couldn't help it. She burst out laughing and laughed until the tears were running down her cheeks.

"You stop that this minute!" Jud screamed like a petulant child.

But Doreen could not stop laughing. And her laughter became uncontrollable when Jud stamped his boot on the floor and began to jump up and down, behaving very much like a naughty boy caught with his hand in the cookie jar.

Her laughter almost put her on the floor. Where it failed, Jud's fist succeeded. "You're really not going to wear that on your head, are you?" she questioned, just as Jud swung a big fist.

Doreen got her reply as her head exploded in pain and she lost consciousness.

When Rusty brought Matthew in, the hysteria of the women vanished and they took over the doctoring of the boy while Rusty solemnly cut the body of Cheyenne loose and told Jamie and Leroy to get shovels and start digging. They'd wait and have the funeral in the morning. The body would keep that long.

What to do about Doreen?

Rusty didn't know. He looked at Alan. "Boy, could you positive say in a court of law that Jud took her?"

The boy looked at Susie. Both of them shook their heads. "No, sir," the boy replied. "We was too far off to say positive it was him."

"What are you getting at, Rusty?" Alice asked.

"He'll hide her if anybody gets within ten miles of that ranch. You can bet he'll have lookouts posted ever'where. He may be crazy, but he ain't stupid."

"So we wait for Smoke to come back?" Susie asked.

"That's all I know to do." Rusty would have liked to go charging into the mansion, both hands filled with Colts. But he was forced to put his anger and his feelings for Doreen aside and do his best to think logically, knowing that even if he should manage to reach the mansion without catching a slug, he would never breach the big house—not alive, and he would certainly be no good to Doreen dead. Or anybody else for that matter.

He would wait for Smoke to return.

Bendel looked out the dusty window. "Six of them, Mr. Jensen. I know two of them by name."

"Who are they?"

"Blackjack Morgan and Lassiter. But them others look just as tough."

Smoke signaled for another beer with his right hand as his left hand touched the butt of his left-hand Colt. Of late, he had been loading the Colts up full. You never knew when that extra round might save your life.

Boots and jingling spurs sounded on the porch of the trading post. The batwings squeaked open. Smoke did not turn around.

Blackjack paused at the bar and spoke to Smoke's back. "Well, well, boys. Look what we done come up on here. The famous gunfighter, Smoke Jensen. You reckon we ought to bow down or something like that?"

His friends laughed. Smoke did not acknowledge the presence of any of them. He sipped at his beer and spoke to Bendel. "I thought I just heard a jackass bray, Bendel. You certainly do have a very strange clientele."

Bendel got a sudden case of the jumps and moved to the end of the bar, carrying a couple of bottles of whiskey with him. He knew the drinking habits of Blackjack and Lassiter and could guess at the tastes of those with them. A tray of shot glasses were bottom's up on a towel near the end of the bar.

"You callin' me a jackass?" Blackjack demanded in a loud voice.

Smoke slowly turned to face the man. "Why . . . it isn't a jackass, after all. It's Blackjack. Excuse me, Morgan. I must have been mistaken."

"That's the damnedest apology I ever heard," Lassiter said.

"Who said I was apologizing." Smoke cut his eyes to the gunfighter.

"What'll it be, boys?" Bendel hollered.

"We ain't deef," one of the bounty hunters said sourly. "Whiskey."

Blackjack still stood by the bar, facing Smoke. Smoke had noted that all the men wore their guns loose in leather, free of hammer thongs. And Blackjack wanted to try Smoke something awful; Smoke could read the challenge in the man's dark eyes.

"Don't do it, Blackjack," Smoke spoke the words softly, so softly that only Morgan could hear them. "It isn't worth it, friend."

"Don't give me orders, Jensen." Blackjack's returning

words were equally soft, less than a whisper; a scant moving of the lips. "I want you before the Almond Brothers find you."

Smoke had heard of the Almond Brothers. A trashy bunch of no-goods that had drifted out of the Midwest some years back. A pack of back-shooting scum who would steal the pennies off a dead man's eyes. Jud was certainly scraping the bottom of the barrel by hiring that bunch.

"If they take me, Blackjack, it won't be facing me."

"They'll still have the ten thousand and you'll still be just as dead."

Smoke smiled and turned his back to the man.

"Don't you turn your backside to me!" Blackjack snarled, putting out his hand and dropping it to Smoke's shoulder, spinning the man around.

Smoke hit him with a left to the belly and followed that with a beer mug to the side of Blackjack's head, knocking the man to the floor.

Blackjack was up like a rubber ball, blood streaming down his cheek from the gash on his head. He swung a fist and Smoke ducked under it, again popping the man in the gut and bringing a grunt of pain.

Blackjack connected with a left to Smoke's head that backed him up. Blackjack was no stranger to brawls and he could punch.

Smoke faked him with a left and Blackjack took the bait, grinning and dropping his guard. Smoke punched through the hole and erased the grin, as he connected with a right to the mouth that smashed Blackjack's lips and loosened some teeth. Blackjack shook his head and came in swinging.

Smoke sidestepped and stuck out a boot, sending the man to the floor, clubbing him on the back of the neck as he went down.

With a curse, Blackjack got to his boots just in time to receive a left and right combination to both sides of his jaw that staggered and stunned the man. He fell back against the bar planking.

Smoke pinned him there and went to work, smashing at the man with big work-hardened fists. Smoke flattened Blackjack's nose and ruined his mouth. One of the man's ears was swollen and pulpy and the gunfighter's eyes were glazing over.

Smoke stepped back and let Blackjack fall to the floor. The man did not move.

Lassiter chose that time to stand up. "By God, Jensen, you'll not do that to another good man," and went for his piece.

Smoke shot him.

He drew, cocked, and fired in less than a heartbeat, his slug striking Lassiter in the belly and knocking him back against a table, splitting the wood right down the middle. Lassiter was drawing iron as he was falling and managed to get off one shot, which dead-centered the painting of a nude female hanging on the wall behind the bar.

"Why, you sorry son!" Bendel hollered. "I paid good money for that." He came up with a shotgun just as one of the bounty hunters was dragging iron.

Lassiter lifted his six gun as blood was leaking from his mouth.

Smoke shot him between the eyes just as Bendel's shotgun roared, the buckshot creating a terrible mess at close range. The torn-apart bounty hunter was literally lifted off his boots and flung across the room. He bounced off a wall and fell to the floor, lying still in a bloody mess. Two of his buddies cursed and then tossed good sense and caution to the gods of fate as they grabbed for their six guns.

Bendel gave one the other barrel just as Smoke shifted the muzzle of his Colt and let the .44 bang, the slug taking the second man in the chest and dropping him to his knees.

The lone bounty hunter left alive lifted his hands out from his body and held them wide apart to show that he was out of this affair.

Walt stuck his gray head into the gunsmoke-filled barroom. He held a six gun in his hand, the hammer eared back.

"It's over," Smoke told him, just as Blackjack moaned on the floor and tried to sit up.

Smoke jerked the man to his boots and spun him around, so he could see the carnage in the saloon.

Blackjack's eyes were swollen from the beating he'd just received, but he could see well enough to know that the best thing he could do would be to keep his mouth closed.

"Get on your horse and ride, Blackjack," Smoke told him. "And if you have any sense at all you'll keep going and not look back until you've cleared a couple of counties."

Blackjack broke his silence. "Lassiter was a pal of mine, Jensen."

"Was is right."

"I'll not let his death go unavenged."

"Then you're a fool. As crazy as Jud Vale." Smoke shoved him toward the batwings. "Get out of here, Blackjack. If you're in my sight ten seconds from now I'll kill you."

"And stay out of my saloon!" Bendel hollered. "All of you trash that work for the Bar V. I'm tellin' you now; pass the word: I'll kill the first one of you that pass through those batwings. I'm tired of this." He leveled his reloaded double-barrel, sawed-off express gun. "Move, damn you!"

Blackjack moved.

Smoke glanced at Walt. "Supplies loaded?"

"All on the wagon."

"Let's get back to the ranch. I suddenly got a bad feeling about this day."

Jackson took one look at Jud Vale and struggled to contain his laughter. At the same time he was fighting to keep from busting out laughing, he was making up his mind about the Bear Lake Fight, as it was being called by some.

Jackson was switching sides.

Jackson was a gunfighter, and a good one, but he had had a bad taste in his mouth about this fight right from the git-go. He just didn't think it was right to fight women and kids and old men. And now he had heard that Jud Vale and Old Walt were really brothers, and that didn't set well with him at all. He didn't have any trouble understanding how brothers could hate each other; he'd seen that many times before. But in this situation, there wasn't any reason for it. Come to think of it, there wasn't any reason for any of this, and there damn sure wasn't even one ounce of reason roaming around in Jud's crazy head.

And where in the hell did Jud come up with that costume he was struttin' around in?

Man looked like the fool he really was.

Time to go, Jackson concluded, just about the time the lone hand came staggering in from the gunfight with Cheyenne and the kid.

Jackson listened, then slowly walked to the bunkhouse to get his kit together. He rode out without being noticed. He headed for Box T range, but in a very roundabout way, going by the way of the trading post and stopping in for a drink of whiskey.

That longing for a drink of whiskey just about cost him his life: when he stepped into the saloon he was looking down the barrels of a sawed-off shotgun.

"Whoa!" Jackson said. "I'm friendly, Bendel!"

"Not if you're ridin' for the Bar V, you ain't."

"I quit 'um. Jud Vale is as crazy as a bessy-bug. All the wrappin' done come plumb off him." He grimaced, remembering the sight of Jud all dressed up in that silly-lookin' outfit. "In a manner of speakin', that is. I figured I'd toss my saddle on a Box T horse."

Bendel lowered the express gun. "They need some help, for a fact. Have a whiskey, on the house."

"Don't mind if I do. Smells like gunsmoke in here, Bendel."

Bendel told him what had gone down.

Jackson sipped his whiskey and mulled over that bit of information. He would have liked to seen Blackjack get the snot whipped out of him. If ever a man deserved a good butt-whippin', Morgan did. Him and Lassiter and those others with that grand plan to ambush Jensen. That hadn't set well with Jackson either, but by the time he'd learned of it, it had all blown over.

Jackson thanked Bendel for the whiskey, stepped into the general store for some tobacco and cartridges, then headed out for the Box T.

He was feeling better with every mile he put behind him.

Chapter 19

"And I seen Jud sendin' men out in all directions," Jackson was wrapping it up for Smoke and Rusty and the others. "Ain't no way we're gonna bust Miss Doreen out of there with just two or three men and a handful of kids. I don't think her life is in no danger. Don't you ladies take this the wrong way now, 'cause I think a man doin' what Jud is gonna do against her will is wrong, but at least she'll be alive."

"And you say Jud has really gone around the bend?" Walt asked.

"Gone around the bend! Man, he is total loco. Walks around that big house with a gold crown on his head, all done up in diamonds and rubies and the like. And he wears a robe."

"You mean he's wearing something like a dressing gown?" Smoke asked.

"Hell, no! Excuse me, ladies. I mean one of them ear-mine robes that he had handsewn and all made up for him over in Russia."

"Ear-mine?" Alice questioned. "You mean ermine fur?"

"Yes'um. That's it. A white one. Comes all the way down to his ankles. He looks real stupid stompin' around the house in that robe, wearing a crown on his head, and cowboy boots on his feet. I'm tellin' y'all, it's gettin' to be awful weird around that place. Plumb spooky."

"Are the men laughing at him?" Walt asked.

"Not to his face. He's still totin' a gun strapped around his waist. And that makes him look even dumber."

"But still dangerous," Rusty added.

"Even more dangerous," Jackson told them. " 'Cause you don't never know what a crazy man is goin' to do."

They all agreed with that.

Walt leaned back and scratched his head. "Well, let's come up with some way to get Doreen out of that nuthouse. Anybody want to start?"

Those seated around the table fell silent as they looked at one another. Smoke finally broke the silence.

"I'll gear up and leave tonight. We've got to know just where in the house she's located and how many men Jud has on guard and where they are. I'll find that out and then we can make some plans. But first we have to bury Cheyenne. Let's do it at sunset. That was his favorite time of day."

They all agreed that was a good suggestion.

"I just wish I knew if Doreen was all right," Alice sighed the words.

"She ain't all right, ma'am," Jackson said, a grim note to his statement. "But she ain't dead either."

They buried Cheyenne just as the sun was going down, with Walt reading from the Good Book. Alice and Susie and

Micky cried, and some of the other boys looked like they were having a tough time of it keeping the tears back. All but Matthew. The boy stood with a grim look on his face. Smoke knew the look well. He could read revenge clear on the boy's face.

Smoke knew just how Matt felt. He'd been down that rocky path many times in his life.

After the words were read, one by one, they filed past the dark hole and tossed a handful of earth into the pit. The clods rattled against the rough pine box that Young Eli had built for Cheyenne that afternoon. Then each one of the other boys had solemnly driven a single nail into the coffin.

Moments after the funeral, Smoke saddled up and rode off into the gathering darkness. There was a hard look on his face. He was getting more than a little weary of Jud Vale and his hired guns.

Deep into Bar V range, about three miles from the mansion, he guessed, Smoke picketed his horse and slipped into moccasins, leaving his hat and taking his rifle. He had swung wide getting to the location where he had left his horse, taking a route that if he were in Jud's place, would post the least number of guards.

He worked his way toward the mansion, hoping to find the location of just one of the guards. He wanted to talk to one of Jud's men. Smoke didn't think it would take him long to get what information he needed . . . and it didn't.

The guard woke up with a raging headache from where Smoke had clubbed him on the back of the head. There was a bandana tied over his mouth and he was very cold from the waist down. He couldn't understand that. Then he realized his britches were gone. He cut his eyes and felt even colder fear clutch at his heart as he looked at Smoke Jensen, squatting a few feet away, clear in the moonlight, a big-bladed knife in his hand.

"I'm going to ask you a few questions," Smoke said, in a voice that made the hired gun want to go to the bushes to relieve himself something fierce. "And you're going to give me correct answers. You know who I am?"

The man nodded his head.

"You've heard the story about what I did to one of the men who raped my first wife and then killed her and our baby son?"

The hired gun almost came unhinged. *Everybody* knew what Smoke Jensen had done to the gunfighter Canning. He had taken a knife—maybe the same damn knife Smoke was now holding—and turned Canning into a gelding—then cauterized the wound with a hot running iron.

The hired gun nodded his head vigorously.

"You wouldn't want me to do that to you, would you?"

The man made strangling, choking noises behind the bandana.

"I didn't think so." Smoke reached out with the point of the blade and the man almost had heart failure. He breathed a little easier as Smoke cut the gag loose.

"You yell, and it will be the last sound you'll ever make on this earth," Smoke warned him.

The hired gun nodded.

"What's your name?"

"Johns."

"I want the locations of all the guards. Quickly."

Johns told him. Quickly.

"What room is Doreen being held in?"

"Top floor. The room facin' the crick back of the house. The winders is all nailed shut so's she can't get out."

"Has any harm come to her?"

"No, sir. Jud hit her once, but that's all. He ain't messed

with her in no way. He says he's savin' all that for when they get hitched up proper."

"And when is that going to be?"

"Don't know. And that's the truth."

"How many men does Jud have on his payroll?"

"I'd have to say close to a hundred now. He's got a regular army. But a lot of them is trash. They ain't gonna stand when it starts gettin' hot. I'd say he's got near 'bouts seventy fighters. And hirin' more."

"Jud can't afford to pay that many men."

Johns sighed. "He can afford it. I'll tell you all I know. Then if you'll let me go, I'm gone to see the Pacific Ocean."

"You level with me and you can ride."

"Deal."

Smoke cut his bonds and told him to put his pants back on. And to wash his long handles the first chance he got. Smoke built a cigarette and tossed Johns the makings. The man lit up and inhaled, then started to talk.

"The ranch is just a front for Jud's other doings. He's into all sorts of things. Got hisself four or five gangs workin' all over two or three states, robbin' trains and stagecoaches and stealin' gold and cattle and you name it. I don't know all that he's got goin' for him, but I do know that he's a rich man, and that he's gone plumb crazy. A lot of his own men—not none of the ones that's been with him for years—is beginning to talk about doin' him in and takin' over. I been thinkin' about driftin'. So far I ain't kilt nobody that wasn't facin' me with a gun, and I ain't never stole much of nothin' in my life. A beef ever' now and then for something to eat, is all."

"Is he going to call his gangs in to help in this range war?"

Johns snubbed out his cigarette. "Smoke, there ain't no way of tellin' what that man is gonna do. He might have done sent for them for all I know. I'm tellin' you the man is crazy as a lizard."

"Anything else you can tell me?"

Johns thought for a moment. Then slowly shook his head. "I reckon not. Except for maybe to warn you to expect anything. Jud Vale has done turned crazy."

After Johns had ridden away, Smoke said, "All right, Clint, you can come in now."

A chuckle from the darkness. "You are very, very good, Mr. Smoke Jensen. But I fear I must decline your kind invitation. I am in one of my moods and there is no telling what I might do."

"Jud has Doreen."

"I know. But now is not the time to attempt to mount a rescue. We are too few and Jud has too many. We will have to devise some sort of diversion to pull as many men as possible away from the ranch, and then no more than two or three go in to get her."

"Have you a plan?"

"Unfortunately, no. But I know Doreen very well. She is very, very bright. I am certain she has guessed that the key to her survival lies in her keeping a cool head about her. If Jud Vale wants her to be his queen, to parade about in fine gowns from Paris, France, that's what she'll do if that's what it takes to stay alive."

"Jud's own men—some of them—are talking mutiny. That might turn out bad for Doreen."

"Yes. I thought about that. I think we have a week or so before anything like that happens. Probably longer. It will take that long for Jud to pull in his various and far-flung gangs."

"If that's what he has in mind."

"He does. I've been on these ridges since early afternoon. He's sent riders out in all directions. I'm guessing that some of them are riding for the gangs."

"Then we'd damn well better do something before the odds against us get ridiculous."

"I'll let you know when I have a plan."

Smoke heard a whisper of cloth against brush, and knew that Clint Perkins was gone, slipping into the night.

Smoke sighed and shook his head. This had turned into one great big mess. The next time you think about a vacation, he thought sourly, try riding east instead of west.

Then he felt guilty for thinking that. His own children would be grown some day, and if they got into a jam that was not of their own doing, he hoped someone would be around to help them.

Someone like Smoke Jensen.

He rose to his moccasins and started back to his horse. This was one of the few times in his life that he felt helpless, and he had a hunch the feeling was going to get much worse until it bettered out.

If it ever did.

Matthew remained in bed, embarrassed by all the fuss being made over him, but enjoying it nonetheless. There were no signs of infection in his wound, and he seemed to be healing nicely and quickly.

Walt had ordered all the boys to stay close to the ranch. What cattle remained were bunched in the box canyon with plenty of graze and water and could take care of themselves for a time. The boys worked at turning the ranch compound into a fort.

Everybody knew that an attack, and it would be a big one, was inevitable. It was just a question of when.

Smoke and Rusty and Jackson went over everything they could think of.

"As far as weapons and ammo goes, we got enough to outfit a battalion of army," Jackson pointed out. He grinned. "I recognize a whole lot of them rifles and pistols from the Bar V boys."

"We've filled ever' water barrel we could tote in," Rusty said. "The house and barn and bunkhouse is fortified like none I ever seen. That was a good idea Jamie had about haulin' up big rocks and stackin' them window high around the house and bunkhouse. It'd take a lot of giant powder to do any damage."

Jackson rolled a cigarette, licked, and lit up. He glanced at Smoke. "You in deep thought, Smoke." He passed him the makings.

"Three reasonably young men—that's us. Three old men. Two women. One little boy, and fifteen young boys. That's all that's standing between maybe a hundred or more hired guns, bounty hunters, outlaws, and a crazy man who walks around his mansion in an ermine robe with a jeweled crown on his head proclaiming himself to be king. I've been in some strange situations in my time, but this one has got to take the cake."

"How about ridin' into town and sendin' a wire to the governor?" Rusty suggested.

Smoke shook his head. "I discussed that with Walt. We both agreed we'd be wasting our time. The governor has made it clear that he doesn't have the manpower to do us any good down here. Reading between the lines of that remark, I'd have to say that the governor is not going to get involved. Why, is anybody's guess."

Jackson was thoughtful for a moment. "I know maybe half a dozen men I could get to come in here. If I could find them, that is."

"Yeah, that's my problem, too," Smoke said. "Louis Longmont would come in here in a flash, but I have no idea where to find him. For all I know, he might be in Europe. I have a hunch that all this is going to be over before any of us could locate and bring people in. Jud's got the jump on us in that respect."

"If we could just get Doreen free of that nuthouse of Jud's, we could sit back here and wait Jud out," Rusty reflected. "I think even if Jud sent all his men over here, we stand a pretty good chance of holding them off."

"Attacking us here will come," Smoke said. "I believe that. But only as a last resort. Jud's got Doreen; that's what he wanted most of all. His main concern now will be in keeping her."

"The thing to do, the way I see it," Jackson said, "is to try to think like Jud. But how in the blue blazes could anyone think like a crazy man?"

"You can't," Smoke nixed that. "I think his moods change, or could change, every day, maybe every hour. I believe he's so far around the bend that he's become totally unpredictable."

Rusty glanced at him. "You're sayin' that even Jud don't know what he's gonna do next?"

"That's right. And if you ever get a chance, look into the eyes of Clint Perkins. His and Jud's eyes are identical. They're both madmen."

"Then it's true that Jud is Clint's father?" Jackson asked.

"Yes. And Clint can be just as whacky as Jud. No telling what he'll do next. He doesn't even know."

"You think he still cares for Doreen?"

Smoke shrugged. "In a way, I suppose. But I think he's driven more out of hate for Jud than concern for Doreen. And that could get Doreen in trouble if Clint tries something on his own."

"How about contactin' the Army and seein' if they'll do something?" Rusty grabbed at straws.

Smoke shook his head. "There again, we'd have to go through the governor to get them. And for some reason, the governor, or more likely, someone in his office, is blocking all requests for help."

"Nearest Army unit is stationed up near that little ol' town some folks have taken to callin' Pocatello," Jackson said. "And there ain't no more than a handful of soldier boys garrisoned there."

"We seem to be just goin' around in circles," Rusty said bitterly. "Gettin' nowheres in a hurry."

Jackson allowed as to how that was the truth.

"Did you know that Matthew has Cheyenne's old Colt?" Rusty asked Smoke.

"No, I didn't. But it doesn't surprise me. The boy loved that old man. And every time I look into his eyes I see revenge."

"I do know that feelin'," Jackson said. "The boy's a natural gun hand, Smoke. And there ain't nothin' none of us can do to slow him down. I knowed that the first time I seen him. I don't have to tell you that it's in the walk, the bearing, the eyes. He's gonna be hell on wheels, you mark my words."

Smoke slowly nodded his head. "I know. I saw it, too. It was like looking into a mirror and seeing myself years ago."

"I do know that feelin' myself," Jackson said drily. "I sometimes wish my daddy had taken the gun away from me and beat me over the head with it when I was a young'un. But it wouldn't have done no good. I had a fortune teller read my palm once. She told me I was a gunfighter. I was fourteen years old at the time. Rememberin' that still spooks me." Jackson touched the butts of his guns. "I think, Smoke, that when it's all said and done, we're gonna have to go in and fetch Miss Doreen."

"So do I, Jackson. But for now, all we can do is wait."

Rusty looked toward the direction of Bar V range. "I sure miss that girl. I surely do. I reckon I've been smitten, and she feels the same way." He looked into the eyes of Smoke Jensen. "And I ain't waitin' very long."

Chapter 20

Jud pounded the end of his staff on the floor and bellowed at his "subjects," as he had recently begun calling the assorted riffraff he had on his payroll.

"Bring the queen to my side!" he squalled.

Several of his bodyguards—he now had a dozen around him at all times—went upstairs to fetch the most unwilling Queen Doreen.

Jud had ordered all the furniture removed from one downstairs room in the mansion. All the furniture except for two huge padded chairs that were placed in the center of the room: his throne and Doreen's slightly smaller throne. Jud's "staff" was a thick piece of oak, about four feet long and weighing about twenty pounds, long enough and stout enough to fell a buffalo. Jud had read several books about how royalty dressed and behaved. Since he didn't have a goblet from which to drink his wine—wine being something royalty drank—he had found a quart jar, so he used that in place of a jewel-encrusted goblet. It was kind of hard to hold, but it was either that or a bucket, and a bucket wasn't very dignified. Jud had also stopped shaving and was growing a beard; that was something else that all male royalty of the time did. Or so he had read.

He had been informed that the sole survivor of the gunfight with Cheyenne, Matthew, and Rusty had died of his wounds. Jud waved that off with a mutter about serfs and the like. Since the gun slick who delivered the message had no idea what a serf was he couldn't take umbrage. He did think his boss looked like a plumb idiot; but as long as the good money kept coming, the gun hand didn't really care how Jud dressed. But he did figure that damn fur coat Jud wore was kind of hot for this time of the year.

Doreen was ushered in, all silks and satins and fancy shoes, with a jeweled crown on her head.

Jud pounded his staff on the floor and bellowed, "All rise for Queen Doreen!"

Since there weren't any chairs in the room except for the two thrones, that was an unnecessary command, but Jud thought it sounded regal so he did it anyway.

Highpockets left the "Crown Room" and walked up to Gimpy Bonner on the front porch. "The son of a bitch is crazy, Gimp!"

"I allow as to how you're right, Highpockets. But as long as the money keeps comin', I don't care if he walks around bare-butt nekkid and rides a camel."

"Now that would be a sight to see!"

King Jud and Queen Doreen held court for a few minutes, but since there was nobody with any complaints for Jud to hear and rule on it got sort of boring after a few moments.

"Would you like to stroll about the estate, my queen?" Jud asked.

"But of course," Doreen said with a smile. I might find a chance to cut and run away from you, you ninny! she was thinking behind her smile.

It was quite a sight to see. Jud in his cowboy boots and spurs, his six guns belted around his middle, wore a ankle-length ermine robe and toted his twenty-pound staff. Doreen had on a gown that would have been the envy of the Queen of England. As they strolled around the "estate," both were careful not to step in the many piles of horse droppings that littered the grounds.

"I wish you would do something about this . . . unpleasantness," Doreen said, pointing to a fresh pile of road apples.

"You're absolutely right, my queen." Jud told one of his bodyguards to order the mess cleaned up and keep it clean.

It did not take Doreen long to conclude that while Jud certainly was as crazy as a road lizard, he wasn't stupid. The bodyguards flanked them as they strolled, and there were guards in the front of them and in the back. Jud summed it all up with a strange smile on his face.

"There is no way you are going to escape, my queen. So put it out of your pretty head and just enjoy all the privileges you are being accorded. This is your home, for now and for always."

"Very well," Doreen spoke through tight lips. "I want my room redone and I want it done immediately. I hate the colors!"

"Uh . . . yes, dear."

"And I want satin or silk sheets. Those cotton sheets are just so shabby!"

"Right, my queen."

"I want my breakfast served to me in bed."

"Uh . . . of course, dear." Jud was beginning to wonder if having a woman around on a permanent basis was going to be worth all the trouble. He wondered if other kings had the same problem.

"And I want a party."

"A party!"

"Yes. A great big fancy ball." She was doing some fast thinking and hoping it would work. "And I want everybody in southeastern Idaho invited. We'll announce our engagement there."

Jud fell to his knees; unfortunately, one knee landed squarely in a fresh pile of horse manure, but Jud appeared not to notice. "Oh, Doreen—do you really mean that?"

"Of course, I do. I'll start working on the invitation list immediately."

Jud kissed her hand. "I'm so happy, my queen!"

You won't be so happy when you see the guest list, Doreen thought. And on the night the ball is held, that's when I turn back into a pumpkin and get the hell away from you and this outhouse!

"Bar V rider comin'," Jackson said. "And he's comin' up holdin' a white flag."

Jud had reluctantly agreed to invite Walt and Alice and Smoke and Rusty. He had done so after Doreen had pointed out that he had a hundred or so men on the ranch; what could Smoke do with all those guns around him?

Scott Johnson, the Arizona gun hand, handed Smoke several envelopes. "You lose, Jensen," he said with a nasty grin. "Miss Doreen and Jud is gonna announce their weddin' plans at this here shindig. And she said to tell you that that Shakyspear feller said it best when he was talkin' about friends, romans, and countrymen. Whatever the hell that means."

Scott turned his horse and rode off.

Smoke smiled, thankful that he had wintered that time with Preacher and all those books. He remembered the line well. I come to bury Caesar, not to praise him!

"Wipe that hound dog look off your face, Rusty," he told the man. "She's telling us to get her out of there and giving us a way to do it."

"Damned if I see how."

"Jud'll probably have men at the door friskin' certain people before they enter the mansion," Jackson said. "We won't be able to carry guns inside." He paused. "We, hell, I wasn't even invited!"

"You'll be going though," Smoke told him. "At least part of the way." He looked at the date on the invitation. "We've got a week to plan things out. First thing I've got to do is see who all was invited and who is planning to attend. I'm going to send Jamie and Leroy to poke around some." He looked at Rusty's long face. "Relax, Rusty. We'll get your sweetie back."

The governor was invited to the party. He sent word that he would not be able to attend. So did the general in charge of all federal troops in Idaho Territory. But Sheriff Brady said he wouldn't miss it for the world. And the young reporter from the Montpelier newspaper would attend. Most of the ranchers and a few of the farmers—Doreen had insisted the nesters be invited—agreed to attend the party.

Smoke had decided he would go in unarmed. When the time came to grab Doreen, he would bust a guard over the noggin with something—maybe the punchbowl if it came to that—take his guns and really liven up the party.

Smoke was going to stay close to the ranch until the night of the big event. He didn't want to put Doreen's rescue in jeopardy by running into any of the bounty hunters who were out looking for him. That could come later.

At the Bar V, Doreen had everybody there, from the cooks to the cowboys, running around the lower half of the territory, driving them about half-crazy, picking up this, that, and the other thing for the ball. She wanted them to be so tired come the night of the event that all they would want to do is lie down and sleep and to hell with the party. She didn't know if that would be the case, but it was worth a try.

Jud had ordered cases of champagne sent in, and as many different types of "finger foods," as Doreen called them, as could be found within three days' ride of the Bar V. Since no one in their right mind would work for Jud Vale, he was forced to use some of his own hired guns and cowboys to act as waiters. He bought them all brand new black suits, with white shirts and black string ties, and low quarter shoes and white gloves. There was a lot of bitching going on about that, but Jud told them either do it or haul their ashes.

Doreen had insisted upon a band, so Jud managed to round up a guitar player, a fiddle player, and someone to toot on a bugle. It was the best he could do on such short notice.

Jud was undecided as to what to wear to the gala event. Doreen said she would clean up his ermine robe—it had a few food and wine spots on it—and he could polish his crown and shine his boots and spurs. He would look so nice.

She wanted him to look like the fool he was so everyone there could see the real Jud Vale.

"Can I wear my guns, Doreen?" Jud asked.

"Oh, but of course, darling!" She had overheard him telling his men to frisk everyone. She hoped Smoke and Rusty would be able to arm themselves once inside the outhouse.

Time was running out.

*   *   *

Smoke laid down the ground rules.

"Walt, when you get the signal from me, you take Alice and get gone from Jud's place. I'll wait about forty-five minutes before making my play. That'll give you time to get Alice to the west side of the creek. You wait there."

The rancher nodded his head in agreement.

"Jackson, you and Dolittle and Harrison will be stationed at the creek, our side of it, with rifles. Just as soon as we drop Doreen off, Alice and Doreen can take the buggy and hightail for the ranch. We'll hold off the men Jud is sure to send after us."

"Sounds good to me," Dolittle said. "I been cravin' some action."

"Yeah, me, too," Harrison agreed. "I may not be good for too much else, but I can damn sure still pull a trigger."

"And you can bet that Jud will have everybody that can ride a horse after you," Jackson warned. "He'll be killin' mad."

"We'll have a good fifteen to thirty minutes' start on him though," Smoke said. "After Doreen makes her little speech about being kidnapped, and me with a Colt stuck up Jud's nose, the sheriff will have to make some noises about law and order and all that. Of course, once I turn Jud loose and he hoofs it back to the mansion, he'll ignore anything the sheriff might have to say and come fogging after us."

"We might get some more people on our side by doing this," Walt mused aloud. "Maybe this will give some of the smaller ranchers and farmers the backbone to join us in fighting my brother."

"If this don't, nothing will," Rusty added. He looked at Smoke. "You got another plan if this one don't work?"

"No," Smoke admitted. "But I'm thinking this will work because it's so simple and it's something that Jud won't even suspect any of us trying. For a handful of us to kidnap the man right in front of all his men, at his very own engagement party is something that has to be unthinkable to him. At least that's what I'm hoping."

"I have to tell you, Smoke," Walt said. "Matthew says he's going to be a part of the action come the night of the party, whether we want him to be, or not."

Smoke took that news without even so much as a blink. "It doesn't surprise me, Walt. The boy has shed his youth and left it behind him. We've both seen it happen out here many times. It's a hard time in a hard land that's filled up with hard men. I was only about a year older than Matthew when I teamed up with Preacher. About two years older than him when I killed my first man, with a pistol that Jesse James gave me back on that hard-scrabble farm in Missouri. Matthew will make it, and I'd not be a bit leery of him standing alongside me in any gunfight."

"I wanted you to know," the rancher closed the subject.

Smoke nodded his head. "Stash fully loaded rifles and pistols in the buggy, Walt. Cover them with a blanket. We're not going to have time for reloading once the fight gets to the creek."

"We have enough weapons, for sure," Walt said with a grin, his eyes twinkling. Then he sobered. "I'm going to lay the rules down to the boys. They are to remain on this ranch come the night of the party. Anyone who disobeys that order loses his job."

"Good. I think they'll stay put." Smoke met the eyes of the men. "We're only going to have one chance at pulling this off, people. So let's do it right the first time. That's it."

Chapter 21

"My, my, what a grand place," Rusty remarked, as the huge mansion of Jud Vale came into view. "Looks like a palace for sure."

Smoke's Colts were hanging from his saddle horn, as were Rusty's guns. Both men felt naked without the weight of the pistols. The buggy was loaded with rifles and pistols, the arms covered with a blanket.

"Well, we're certainly not the first to arrive," Alice pointed out. "Even though it is early."

Susie had stayed at the Box T to look after Micky and the boys.

Smoke looked at Walt and saw that the old rancher's eyes were sad.

"My brother had it all," Walt said. "But he couldn't stay away from crime. And now he's as crazy as a loon, surrounded by men on his own payroll who plot to kill him. It's tragic."

Smoke disagreed with that summation, but then, it wasn't his brother in question. He kneed Dagger forward, moving toward the mansion.

They were conscious of many eyes on them as they entered the ranch grounds. Hostile, murderous eyes—everyone thinking about that ten thousand dollars on the head of Smoke, and wishing that Jud hadn't lifted it for this event.

Smoke swung down from the saddle and looped the reins around a hitchrail, with Rusty doing the same, and looked up at the sky. He read the sun at about half-past five. The invitation had read from six to ten. Smoke figured to start his own party at seven.

"Mr. Vale said that all hosses was to be put in the corral," a surly puncher told Smoke.

Smoke turned and grinned at the man. "His name is Dagger. He killed the last man who tried to do anything with him. But you're welcome to try."

The Bar V hand eyeballed the walleyed stallion. Dagger showed the man his big teeth and the puncher made up his mind.

"Hell with that hoss." He looked at Rusty. "What about yourn?"

"They're brothers," Rusty told him.

"Hell with him, too!" The puncher walked off.

Walt and Alice were already climbing up the steps to the porch. Shorty DePaul was there, standing by the door, collecting invitations, looking very uncomfortable in his stiff new black suit.

Smoke grinned at him. "You do look awfully cute, Shorty."

Shorty told Smoke where to go, how to get there, and what to do with his comment along the way.

"Feller's plumb testy, ain't he?" Rusty said.

Shorty had a few words for Rusty, too.

Smoke and Rusty followed Walt and Alice inside the mansion.

It was a grand place, Smoke noted, no doubt at all about that. Imported chandeliers and French furniture and all sorts of knickknacks and assorted gewgaws scattered all over the place.

"What's all this stuff good for anyways?" Rusty questioned.

"For people to look at and admire," Smoke told him.

"Looks junky and sissy to me."

Smoke grinned at him. "Your mind will change after you're married." Rusty blushed at the thought.

The punk gunfighter who called himself the Pecos Kid walked up, carrying a tray of little crackers and a bowl of dark-looking stuff. "Gentlemen," he said, speaking the word as if it hurt his mouth. "Some whore-derves?"

"What the hell is a whore-derve!" Rusty said, leaning over to take a sniff.

"That is Russian caviar," Smoke told him. "Louis Longmont used to keep some on hand at all times. Try it, it's good."

"How do you eat it?"

"Take a cracker and use that little spoon to dab some caviar on the cracker."

Rusty spooned a glob on a cracker. "Well, ain't I the fancy one, though? My, my." Rusty took a nibble and grimaced. "You got any ketchup, Pecos?"

Smoke thought Rusty and Pecos were going to tie up right then and there, and if they had, Rusty would have shoved that whole bowl of caviar up the nose of the Pecos Kid. He pulled Rusty away and told him to behave himself; they had a more important mission that came first.

One of the ranchers who had been in the trading post when Matthew shot it out with Smith walked up to him. His face was ashen.

"What's the matter with you?" Smoke asked.

"Have you seen Jud?"

"No."

"He's walking around with a crown on his head and all dressed in a fur robe. He's carryin' a stick that looks like a good-sized saplin'. The man is insane!"

"That's what some folks have been trying to tell you people for months. Don't you people even care that he took Doreen by force and is holding her here against her will?"

"I heard that but I didn't believe it." He sighed. "All right, gunfighter. I believed it. But what could I have done?"

"Join in the fight against Jud?"

But the man shook his head. "No. He has too many hired guns on the payroll. He'd roll over us like stepping on a bug."

There was contempt in his eyes and scorn in his voice when Smoke replied. "Do you look under the bed at night for ghosts and goblins before you blow out the lamp?"

The rancher flushed but wisely contained his sudden anger and kept his mouth closed.

Smoke turned his back to the man and then stopped short when he spotted Jud. Rusty was standing with his mouth open, staring at the man as if he was sure his eyes were deceiving him.

Jud was quite a sight. He looked to Smoke like he'd just stepped out of a Russian opera. Jud cut his eyes to Smoke and hate filled them. He snarled at Smoke and walked away.

"You seen Doreen, Smoke?" Rusty said.

"No. I expect she'll be making her entrance just a tad after six. That's the way the fashionable ladies do it, so I been told."

"Why? Hell, she can tell time, cain't she? She ain't stupid."

"No. I mean, yes, she can tell time. No, she isn't stupid.

Ladies do that so all the people will be present to look at them when they make their entrance."

"I shore don't know much about wimmen."

"Rusty, after you've been married for five or six years, you'll discover something."

"What?"

"That you don't know any more about women after all those years than you did when you got married."

"Well, ain't that just something to look forward to?"

Smoke laughed at him and moved on, walking through the lower part of the mansion. He spoke to several of the farmers that he knew. Ralph's father took his arm.

"I don't know what you got planned in the way of gettin' Miss Doreen out of this place, Smoke. But I'm with you all the way. Me, and about a half dozen other men."

Smoke started to tell him to stay out of it, then changed his mind. Somebody had to be the first ones to stand up to Jud and his army of hired guns. If the cattlemen in the area wouldn't, then maybe the farmers would shame them into joining them.

"All right, Chester. Here's what you do: when you see Walt and Alice leave, you and the others follow them. I'll tell Walt that you boys are with us."

Chester smiled. "I put rifles in the wagon. The wife can shoot nearabouts as good as I can."

"Good man!" Smoke gripped his arm and walked on. They stood a chance if he could just get Doreen out.

Smoke declined a glass of champagne being offered by the German gunfighter, Jaeger, who was minus the top part of an ear, thanks to Smoke. The German glared pure hate at Smoke.

"I ought to take off the other ear, Jaeger," Smoke told him. "So you'd have a matched set. But then you'd have a hell of a time wearing a hat, wouldn't you?"

Jaeger growled something at Smoke in German and moved on, toting his tray of drinks.

Smoke moved over to stand by Sheriff Brady's side. The sheriff gave him a curious look.

"Have you decided whether this is in your county, or not, Sheriff?"

"I don't know. I didn't come here to arrest anyone. I didn't bring any men with me. Why? Are you planning on starting something?"

"Me?" Smoke managed a shocked look. "Heavens no, Sheriff. I'm just here to have a good time."

"Right," the lawman's reply was drily given. "Sure, you are."

"Have you seen Jud, Sheriff?"

A pained look passed over the sheriff's face. "Yes, unfortunately. But there is no law against a man wearing a fur robe and a jeweled crown."

"Oh, I never said there was, Sheriff. But it might make a person question Jud's sanity—right?"

"Like I said, Jensen: I'm not here in any official capacity."

"Enjoy yourself, Sheriff." Smoke moved on, snaking his way through the growing crowd. Somewhere in the house, a clock chimed six o'clock.

He caught the eyes of several farmers; they gave him a slight nod and a wink. Chester had done his part; the men were with him. Smoke returned the nods and found a place next to a wall. Rusty soon joined him and with their backs to the wall, they waited.

At ten after the hour, the bugler started tooting, the guitar player started strumming, and the fiddler started sawing.

"Sounds like a cat fight to me," Rusty said.

Then Doreen made her entrance, and the crowd oohhed and aahhed. She was dressed to the nines, all done up in silks and satins. She was playing her part to the hilt, acting like a queen as she moved through the crowd, smiling and offering her hand to the folks.

Jud stood to one side, a big grin on his big face. He looked like a damned idiot.

Walt and Alice offered their congratulations to Doreen and then Walt glanced at Smoke. Smoke nodded his head. The old rancher and his wife slipped unnoticed out the front door and climbed into their buggy, heading back toward Box T range.

In pairs, the farmers and their wives began slipping out of the mansion. At a quarter to the hour, all those who were on Smoke's side had left. Smoke found Rusty.

"Start staying close to the Pecos Kid, Rusty. When I make my move, you grab his guns and watch my back."

The cowboy nodded and moved off into the milling crowds.

The band was doing their best to play a tune that Smoke could but vaguely recognize. Sounded to him like they were all in different keys.

Smoke moved over to a table near the hallway where the grandfather clock was located and took a glass of champagne just as the chimes donged out seven o'clock. He finished the glass then walked up to Jud and Doreen, jerked both Jud's guns out of leather and placed the muzzle of one in the man's ear. Jud's bodyguards froze, not knowing what to do.

The band stopped playing; the milling crowds were still as the word spread throughout the ground floor of the mansion.

Rusty had clobbered the Pecos Kid with a silver platter of fried chicken and grabbed his guns. The Kid lay on the floor, his head on a pile of chicken.

Smoke said, "Tell your men to start tossing their guns out

the windows, Jud. If just one of them tries anything, I'll kill you where you stand."

"See that they do it, Jason," Jud managed the words out of his fricasseed brain and past his anger.

Six guns began sailing out the open windows.

"Get horses out front for Doreen and King Vale," Smoke ordered.

Jason nodded at one of the bodyguards.

"Make your speech, Doreen," Smoke told her.

Doreen spun around to face the crowd. "Jud Vale kidnapped me and brought me here against my will. I've been a prisoner in this house." She looked straight at Sheriff Brady. "Do you hear me, Sheriff?"

"I hear you, girl."

"I hate this man," Doreen said, pointing to Jud. "I would sooner marry a grizzly bear. I planned this whole party so's Smoke and the man I really love, Rusty, would come and rescue me."

Rusty was grinning and blushing. He looked like a lit railroad lantern.

"I'm ashamed of you people!" Doreen yelled at the crowd of men and women. "Not a one of you would help Walt and Alice or Smoke and Rusty stand up to this nitwit!" She glared at Jud, standing with his crown tilted to one side of his big head. "To hell with you all!" Doreen shouted.

"Let's go!" Smoke said, shoving Jud toward the door.

Outside, Doreen hiked up her expensive gown and showed Rusty bare legs as she stepped into the stirrup and mounted up. The cowboy did his best to look away, but the sight was just too tempting. One eye was going one way and the other was on a shapely leg.

"Settle down, Rusty," Doreen whispered. "Your time is coming. I promise."

"Have mercy!" Rusty said.

Smoke prodded Jud into the saddle. Jud hiked up his robe and showed some leg, too; but it was definitely not a scintillating experience for anyone. Especially the horse, who swung his head and tried to figure out what it was on his back.

Smoke stepped into the saddle. "Jud dies if anyone follows," he warned the crowd. "Tell them, King Vale," Smoke said sarcastically.

Some lucidity had returned to Jud. Having the muzzle of a .44 laid against one's ear can do that. He twisted in the saddle. "Stay back. Our time will come. Just stay back."

"Let's go, King," Smoke said. "Your royal procession is about to parade."

The Pecos Kid woke up with a chicken leg stuck in one ear, wondering why the band had stopped playing.

Chapter 22

"You'll die hard for this," Jud warned them all, as they clip-clopped along, Jud's crown bouncing from one side of his head to the other. "Especially you, Doreen. I'll turn you over to my men and let them have their way with you. And that's a promise."

Doreen turned in the saddle, balled her right hand into a fist, and busted Jud square on the nose. His crown flew off his head as the blood began to trickle, leaking down into his beard.

"You can pick your crown up on the way back," Smoke told him.

Jud cursed them all.

Smoke turned at the sounds of a single horse coming up fast behind them. It was the young reporter from the paper at Montpelier.

"I'm on my way to get this story written," he shouted at them. "I'll see that this is printed all over the state."

He galloped on past and then cut north, toward the town.

"He's dead, too," Jud growled.

"Give it up, Jud," Smoke advised the man. "Send your gun hands packing, break up your outlaw gangs, and settle down."

Jud mouthed a few choice words at Smoke, none of them the least bit complimentary.

Smoke rode on for another mile and then twisted in the saddle and knocked Jud sprawling, on his butt, in the road. Smoke grabbed the reins of the riderless horse and shouted, "Let's go, people!"

Jud sat in the dirt and squalled at them, shaking his fists and cussing.

"They'll be coming after us now!" Doreen yelled over the pounding of hooves.

"We'll make the crick," Rusty told her.

Jud jumped to his feet and began loping up the road, back to his ranch. He reached the spot where his crown lay in the dust, the jewels twinkling under the starry light. Jud plopped his crown back on his head and stomped on, his anger and hate growing with each dusty step. A mile farther on, he met a large force of his men, hanging back a couple of miles.

"They're heading for the creek!" Jud shouted, pointing. "Get them. Kill them! Kill them all."

Jason rode up, leading a horse. "I figured they'd set you afoot, Boss." He handed Jud a brace of six guns.

Jud swung into the saddle. "Somebody give me a piece of rawhide," he ordered.

A piece of thin rawhide was found and handed him.

Jud made a chinstrap for his crown, tying it tightly under his square jaw. He rode to the head of the group and paused, looking back. At least sixty riders. He lifted his hand into the air. "Forward!" he shouted. "Slay the infidels!"

"What the hell's an infidel?" Gimpy asked.

"Beats me," Jake Hube told him. "Must be something like a Injun, maybe."

The riders surged forward, with King Vale in the lead waving a six gun and shouting curses.

But many of the smarter gunfighters had either stayed back at the ranch or were bringing up the rear of the force. They were too wise in the ways of Smoke Jensen to think Smoke would not have a backup plan in Doreen's escape. Probably he had set up an ambush.

John Wills, who had been wrapped up in poison ivy by Smoke, and his buddies, Dave and Shorty and Lefty, trailed a good mile behind the main force. Jaeger and Chato Di Peso and Hammer, along with Blackjack and Highpockets and DePaul and about a dozen others had not even left the ranch area. They sat on the long front porch of the mansion, eating fried chicken dunked in caviar and drinking champagne. All of them had a very strong hunch that many of those chasing after Smoke this starry night would not come back at all. The rest would come straggling back in, all shot to hell and gone.

But that would be all right with them. They were professionals in this business, and hardened to the ways of their chosen profession. This night would probably see the end of many of the punks and two-bit gunslingers who had hired on, looking for a cheap and fast buck and a few quick thrills to take back home and boast about. What they would get is a shallow grave. If they were lucky.

The crowds had quickly departed after Smoke had made his move. All but the bugler; he was now drunk as a cooter and blowing cavalry calls into the night. Some of the gunslingers had dumped him, bugle and all, into a horse trough. But that had only slowed him down for a few moments. He had shaken the water out of his bugle and kept right on tooting.

Jaeger spread some caviar on a cracker and nibbled. "Only ting de damn Russians ever did dat vas any gut vas make caviar," he growled.

"What's this stuff made of anyways?" Pike asked.

"Vish eggs."

"What the hell's a vish?" Highpockets paused in the lifting of a caviar-spread cracker to his mouth.

"A vish is a vish. Swim in wassar."

About half of the men threw the caviar to the porch floor and stayed with the fried chicken.

"Here they come," Jackson announced.

Smoke, Rusty, and Doreen had just made the creek in time to dismount and take positions. Alice and Doreen had told Walt and the others they were staying and to shut up about it. They had taken rifles and squatted down behind logs with the other farmer women.

Matthew stood by a cottonwood, Cheyenne's long-barreled Colt in his right hand. The boy was calm as death, and his hand was steady.

Smoke eared back the hammer on his Winchester; he heard the sounds of others doing the same. As the charging riders came into range, Smoke lifted his rifle and took aim at Jud's crown. He squeezed off a round and drilled the arch of the crown, blowing off the arms and the dangling pearls.

"Huugghh!" Jud croaked, as the chin strap momentarily tighted, cutting off air due to the force of the impacting slug.

Those on the Box T side of the creek began filling the night air with hot lead. The first volley cleared half a dozen saddles and wounded that many more.

Spooked horses began bucking and jumping, sending another half-dozen riders to the hard ground. One gunslinger, afoot, his hands filled with Colts, tried to ford the creek.

Young Matt took careful aim and squeezed the trigger, dead-centering the man, putting the slug right between his eyes. The gunny pitched face-forward into the creek.

Rusty shot the punk Glen Regan just as the kid was turning. The rifle slug went right through both cheeks of Glen's buttocks. Glen dropped squalling and crying to the creek bank, losing his guns, both hands holding onto his injured backside.

"Fall back, men!" Jud yelled. "Regroup but don't lose courage. They are but riffraff and swine who face us. You have the power of royalty on your side."

Jackson put another dent in Jud's crown, knocking it down to one side of the man's head, giving the man a thunderous headache. Jud's horse spooked and tossed him into a thorn bush and royalty's bare legs and backside took the full brunt of long thorns.

"Yowee!" Jud hollered, jumping to his feet. Holding his ermine robe waist high, he beat a hasty retreat up the bank and jumped over the crest.

"Let's get gone from here!" Cisco Webster shouted, just as Walt put a slug into the man's saddle horn, tearing the horn from the saddle and knocking it spinning. Cisco's horse panicked and went snorting and racing into the night. Unfortunately for Cisco, the horse stampeded the wrong way, taking him right across the creek. "Whoa, goddamnit!" Cisco yelled.

Rusty reversed his Winchester and knocked Cisco slap out of the saddle, the butt of the rifle catching the man on the jaw. Cisco was unconscious before he hit the ground, landing amid what was left of his broken teeth.

The fight was gone from Jud and his men. Jud screamed in pain as he was lifted into a saddle. He was still yelling and cussing and waving his arms as what was left of his army rode back toward the mansion.

The night fell quiet, broken only by the moaning of the wounded.

"What do we do with them?" Alice asked, listening to the pleadings for help.

"Leave them!" Chester's wife said, bitterness making her voice hard. "Would they help us if the situation was the other way around?"

Smoke booted his Winchester and swung into the saddle. He turned his horse's head toward the Box T ranch house and his back to the wounded bounty hunters.

That ended any further discussion as to the fate of those who chose to take fighting wages from Jud Vale.

Smoke stepped out of his room the next morning and stood in the pre-dawn quiet, drinking his first cup of coffee. He had an odd feeling, a premonition, that matters would be coming to a head very soon. Why that jumped into his mind, he didn't know—only that he felt it to be true.

Jackson walked out of the bunkhouse, a mug of coffee in his hand. He joined Smoke on the bench by the side of the barn and built him a cigarette, passing the makings to Smoke.

"I got a funny feelin'," Jackson said. "Come on me sudden-like; woke me up."

"That Jud Vale is going to bring this war to a head real soon?"

"Huh? You been readin' my mind. Yeah. Reckon why we both come up with that?"

"We've made a fool out of him too many times, Jackson. Last night was probably that much-talked about straw that broke the camel's back. Now he knows that people are laughing at him. With his ego, he won't be able to tolerate that.

He'll have to do something to reinstill the fear that people once had for him."

"By killing us." Jackson's words were offered in a flat tone.

"That's it. Or part of it, at least."

"He ain't gonna get it done."

"I believe that. I just don't want to see the women or the kids get hurt."

They drank coffee and smoked their cigarettes in silence for a time. "What are you gonna do when this mess is over?" Jackson asked.

"Head south. My wife and kids are down in Arizona. The youngest took a lung infection. Had to go there for health reasons. You?"

Jackson took a moment before replying. "Walt's asked me to stay on. Says he'll give me a working interest in the ranch if I do. And . . . well, me and Susie been eyeballin' each other. I might do it. I backed into gunfightin' like a lot of other men. Never set out to hunt me no reputation. It just come on me. One day I looked up—I'd been punchin' cows for a man over in Nevada Territory—and these two men 'bout my age come into the saloon where I was havin' a beer and braced me. Said they was gonna kill me. I asked them why? They said 'cause of who I was. Surprised the hell out of me that I was anyone special. They grabbed for iron and I was faster. The boss said he didn't want no gun slicks on his payroll and paid me off the next day. I drifted. Hooked up with some men headin' for Utah to draw fightin' wages. I reckon the rest is history."

Rusty had walked up, to stand quietly and listen. When Jackson fell silent, Rusty said, "You ought to stay, Jackson. Me and Doreen is gonna get hitched up soon as the trouble is over. The ranch is damn sure big enough for the both of us."

"I been thinkin' on it for sure."

"Light's on in the kitchen," Smoke said. "Breakfast pretty soon."

"Dolittle's up. He'll wake the boys," Rusty told him. "What's up for today?"

"Going over every inch of this ranch compound and making sure we can stand off a heavy attack. It's got to come. Jackson, I want you to take some of the boys and start clearing off all the brush from the hills and ridges around this place. Make damn sure we can't be burnt out. That'll also cut down on the risk of any riflemen slipping in on us."

"Good move," Jackson agreed.

"I'm hungry," Rusty said, one eye on the light coming from the kitchen window.

"I've never seen you when you weren't," Smoke said with a smile. "When you and Doreen get married, you best plant a big garden."

"You do know how to use a hoe, don't you?" Jackson kidded him.

"I 'spect, the way you and Susie is calf-eyin' each other, you'll be hoein' right along 'side me," Rusty fired back.

Jackson laughed. "Yeah, if it all works out. Be a welcome relief from gunfightin'."

"Don't ever pack those guns too far out of sight, Jackson," Smoke warned him. "It doesn't work. I know. I changed my name and tried it for a time. You'll always have to keep a sharp eye on your backtrail."

"I know," Jackson's words came after a sigh. "But I do wish that some of us could get that message through to young Matt."

"Could anybody tell you anything when you were his age?"

Jackson smiled ruefully. "Nope. I heard all the words, but they never sunk in."

"Matt will have to find his own way," Smoke said, standing up from the bench. "Just like we did. But I think Old Cheyenne—in the time he had to spend with him—taught Matt a thing or two."

"Walt is talkin' about hirin' the boy on as a full-time puncher," Rusty said. "Matt says he's through with schoolin'."

"That's a good idea. I imagine Matt will stay for a year or two. Then he'll get ants in his pants and drift. All we can do is wish him well."

Rusty looked toward the ranch house and the lighted kitchen window. "Damn, I'm hungry!"

Chapter 23

Jud Vale lay on his belly in bed, while a doctor from Montpelier probed and dug and pulled out thorns, some of them more than three inches long. Jud hollered and squalled and carried on all through the procedure.

But the pain seemed to have done one thing: it had cleared Jud's mind, at least for the moment. His ermine robe and crown had been tossed to the floor. He was still as nutty as a pecan pie but some lucidity had crept through the madness.

Through the open window of his bedroom, Jud could see men digging graves to bury the recent dead. He cursed Smoke Jensen, his brother, his bastard son, and everyone else he could think of.

Especially Doreen. He cussed Doreen for playing him for a fool until he was breathless. Long after the doctor had left, doing his best to hide a grin, Jud was still cussing.

Jason came to his room and waited until his boss and

long-time partner in murder, rape, and robbery had calmed down some. "What do you want me to do with them royal duds and that bent crown?"

"Put them in the closet. I might decide to wear them again."

"Jesus, I hope not!"

"I lost it for a while, didn't I, Jas?"

"You were off your trolley for a fact. I thought I was going to have to shoot you there for a time. You was becomin' unbearable."

"Was I that bad?"

"You turned into a plumb idiot."

"It's so hazy. I don't remember much of it."

"Be thankful for that." Jason pulled out a chair and sat down. "You think you're all right now?"

"Yes. For a time. But I don't know when I might go off again. Or for how long. It's frightening, Jas. It really scares me."

"You want me to bring one of them newfangled head doctors in to take a look at you? I could have it done on the sly."

Jud thought about that. It was tempting. Finally he shook his head. "No. Let's see if I can't lick this thing on my own. Did Luddy and his boys come in?"

"Early this mornin'. Phil and Perry and Rim is on the way. Be about thirty more men."

"How many did we lose last night?"

"Six dead. A dozen wounded. A couple of them ain't gonna make it." Jason was beginning to feel better; Jud was starting to talk like he had good sense.

"How many quit us?"

"That's surprisin'. Nobody. Yet."

"I figure it's gonna be a week before I can sit a saddle. Then we're going to wipe out the Box T. We're going to kill everyone there, bury the bodies deep, and burn all the buildings. Scatter the ashes with rakes; carry off the stones. Level the well and fill it up with rocks, cover that with dirt. Plant some trees and bushes. Not a sign is to remain that anyone ever lived there. I am Walt's only living relative. And I can prove that in a court of law. Everything will go to me. The land, cattle, money, and all that gold that's over there."

"Sounds good to me." He grinned at Jud. "Good to have you back, Boss."

"It's good to be back, Jas." He moved and grimaced, his southern exposure throbbing with pain. "Pass me that bottle of laudanum."

The hills and ridges around the ranch complex of the Box T were cleared of brush for a half mile in any direction. In heavily timbered areas, the timber was thinned and cut up for firewood. Wagons were put into use to haul dirt from far out in Box T range, the dirt used to fill up any depressions in the earth for five hundred yards from the complex. It kept the boys busy and Smoke and the others close to the ranch.

But when the week was drawing to near a close, Smoke was told by Walt they had to make another supply run to the post for food.

"Let's do it," Smoke told him. "We have time to do it now and get back before dark. I'll tell Jackson to stay here at the ranch. We'll take Rusty. If we run into any of Jud's men, they might try to prod Jackson into a fight for changing sides."

"And you don't think they'll prod you, Smoke?"

"They'll die if they do," he replied simply.

"Any trouble?" Smoke asked Bendel.

The owner of the trading post shook his head. "I ain't

seen hide nor hair of any Bar V hand all week and I have been expectin' them. I got the word that they was gonna come in and bust up my place." He smiled. "But I understand King Jud Vale is havin' to sleep on his stomach of late."

"Oh?"

"Yeah. Seems like his horse throwed him and he landed in a thorn bush. He was wearing that silly-lookin' robe. Doc Evans from over Montpelier way spread the tale, to use his words."

Smoke and Rusty and Walt—the rancher was having a rare drink of whiskey while the shopkeeper filled the order—all had a good laugh, at Jud's expense.

Walt wiped his eyes with a bandana and smiled. "I guess any feeling I might have been carrying around for Jud has finally left me. God might punish me for the way I feel, but I can't feel anything except contempt for the man now."

"He doesn't deserve anything else, Mr. Burden," Bendel told him. "He's made life miserable for everyone around here for years."

Rusty had taken his beer to the batwings. "Riders pullin' up outside," he announced. "'Bout a half dozen of them. I don't know none of these old boys. Don't look like I'd really care to get to know them all that good, neither. Damn, but they is *ugly!*"

Smoke walked to the batwings. "The Almond Brothers. Killers. Call themselves bounty hunters. Barry, that's the oldest, he's got a few brains. The rest of them are close to being morons." Smoke finished his beer and set the mug on the plank. "I'm going outside. No point in having your place shot up."

Rusty stepped back into the store, exited that way, and pulled a rifle from his saddle boot, jacking in a round. At the sound of the cartridge being shucked into the chamber, Barry Almond looked over the saddle at him.

"You huntin' trouble, cowboy?" the bounty hunter asked.

"Naw," Rusty told him. "I just seen me five big rats. I like to shoot rats."

"Rats? Where'd you see five rats?"

"I'm lookin' at one of them," Rusty told him, just as Smoke pushed open the batwings and stepped out on the porch. Walt was right behind him, holding Bendel's double-barreled express gun.

Barry smiled, a slight cruel movement of his lips. His eyes did not leave Smoke. "I seen you work once, Jensen. You're fast, all right. I'll give you that much. So I reckon some of us, including me, will probably take some lead. But they's five of us ag'in you, that ugly redhead, and one stove-up old man."

"Ugly!" Rusty blurted. "Me! Why, you so ugly you ought to wear a sack over your head! And I ain't real sure them brothers of yours is even human. I've seen bears that was better lookin' than them."

"I'm a-gonna kill that freckle-faced puncher, Barry," an Almond brother said.

"You can sure have him, Race," Barry said. "But Jensen is all mine."

Smoke had stepped off the porch to stand in the street. He didn't want Dagger to catch a bullet. And there was something else: the stallion was alert to trouble, and he had sensed the situation building. If Cal Almond, who was standing next to the big horse, put a hand on him, Dagger was going to kick him into the next county.

Cal shoved roughly at Dagger. "Git the hale outta the way, horse!" he said, stepping around to Dagger's rear.

Dagger let him have it. Both rear hooves lashed out, one

steel-shod hoof catching the killer in the groin, the other in the belly. Cal went sailing out into the middle of the street, screaming in agony.

"One down," Walt said.

Leo drew on the old man. But Leo never really knew the mettle of the men who came to the West when it was really raw. And he had failed to notice that Walt had eared back both hammers of the 12 gauge.

Walt shot the bounty hunter in the belly. Really, he shot him all over the place as rusty nails and ballbearings and other assorted bits of hand-loaded metal tore his body apart.

Rusty stepped out and leveled the Winchester just as Max turned, drawing. Max caught a slug in the belly that bent him double and swung him around. Max pulled the trigger and shot himself in the knee. He tumbled to the street, screaming rage and hate and pain.

Smoke palmed both Colts and began putting lead into Barry and Race. The .44 slugs dotted the trail-dusty dusters, pocking them with blood as the slugs tore into flesh.

Race went down first, sinking to his knees in the dirt, dropping his guns as life left him.

Smoke felt a bullet tear his cheek and another slug rip a narrow gouge on the outside of his left thigh. Smoke and Barry Almond faced each other, guns belching fire and death. Smoke had known that Barry was going to be hard to put down, and the bounty hunter was livng up to his reputation.

As the fourth slug from Smoke's .44's hit Barry, the man went down to one knee, cursing as he slumped to the dusty and rutted road. Using all his strength, he lifted his left hand .44.

Smoke shot him between the eyes just as Cal managed to work his way past his terrible pain to lift his guns. Smoke turned and fired twice just as Rusty's Winchester barked and Walt's express gun roared. The last of the Almond Brothers died on his belly in the dirt, torn to bloody bits by the three guns.

The silence was shatteringly loud for a moment. Then Smoke broke the stillness as he ejected empty brass and began reloading. The spent brass tinkled as it struck small rocks in the road. Loaded up, Smoke holstered his Colts and turned to face Walt, still standing on the porch of the trading post.

"Thanks, Walt."

"Felt good," the old rancher said. "In more ways than one. I knew that night back at the crick I'd misplaced my backbone for too long."

Max groaned and cursed as he lay in the dirt, his blood staining the earth under him.

Rusty walked over to the killer and kicked his guns out of the dying man's reach. "He ain't got long," the puncher said, glancing at Smoke.

Max looked up at him and cussed the redhead.

"If I was a-goin' where you're goin', partner," Rusty told him, "I believe I'd try to clean up my mouth some."

The last words to pass the bounty hunter's lips were curses.

"You boys put them down," Bendel said, coming out of his saloon with several shovels. "You can damn well help me plant them."

They looked up at the sounds of hooves clip-clopping up the road. Several gun hands from the Bar V were riding out, bedrolls tied behind the saddle and their saddlebags bulging full.

"We ain't huntin' no trouble," one told Smoke, eyeballing the carnage sprawled in the dirt. "We're pullin' out."

Smoke knew the man and knew he was no coward.

Something had happened at the Bar V. "What's the problem, Jake?"

"The mainest thing is you, Smoke. This here poker game has done got too rich for my blood. I'll hire my guns out to whoever pays the price, and you know that. But I ain't no thief. I ain't never stole nothin' in my life." That curious moral streak possessed by so many men who lived by the gun surfaced in Jake. "That damn Luddy Morgan and his bunch of no-goods come in. Rim Reynolds and Perry Simmons and that crazy Phil What's-His-Name is due in anytime. I ain't havin' no truck with that trash."

"If we're lucky, Jake, we'll never see each other again," Smoke told him.

"You're gonna have to ride clear over to Oregon if you want to see me, Smoke. And since I ain't on Vale's payroll no more, I can tell you this much without betrayin' no confidence: Jud's gonna attack the Box T—I don't know when or I'd tell you. He's gonna burn the place to the ground, kill ever'body there, and then bury the bodies deep . . ."

Walt's lips tightened at that.

"He's gonna remove all sign that there was ever a building on the place," Jake continued, "and he ain't prancin' around wearin' that stupid robe and crown no more, neither. He's come to his senses . . . for a while, at least. But the fool is liable to go off agin any time. He's worser than any cow who ever et loco weed when he drops off the deep end."

A hired gun pulling out with Jake spat a stream of tobacco juice into the dirt and said, "Them ol' boys that's comin' in is all bad, Smoke. And the ones that's stayin' is just as bad. Jud's gonna take this here fight right down to the killin' end." He noted the thin trickle of blood oozing down Smoke's cheek. "You lucked out agin, Smoke. An inch over and somebody would be plantin' petunias on your grave."

Smoke nodded in agreement. His leg hurt but he knew it

was not a serious wound. He'd had enough lead dug out of him to fill a good-sized gunnysack. "How many men does Jud have?"

"I'd say nearabouts a hundred," Jake told him. "Maybe more. He's promisin' them the moon and the stars and wimmin and apple pie and ever'thang else 'ceptin' his drawers iffen they'll stay with him and see this thing through. I reckon most of them will do that. Me and the boys here just couldn't see to do that. I never did like the idea of fightin' wimmin and kids." He looked at Rusty. "You got yourself a good woman with that Doreen. She'll stand by a man when the goin' gets rough. Wish I could find one like that. See you boys." He lifted the reins and Jake and his buddies rode on.

"Well," Rusty said. "Let's plant these ol' boys and get back to the ranch. Looks like we're in for some excitement. Lord knows," he added drily, "we been so bored of late."

Chapter 24

Walt had doubled the supplies and borrowed packhorses to bring the additional staples to the ranch. There, Smoke made a slow walking inspection of the area surrounding the complex. There could be nothing else done to make the place any more secure.

After supper, he called a meeting in the lantern-lit barn.

"Here's the way it's going to be, people. No one leaves this area. No one. Not for any reason. Jud is going to hit us, and he's going to hit us hard. When? Very soon, I'm thinking. He should be able to sit a saddle most anytime." He noticed the smiles at that and had to join them in the rough humor. But his smile faded quickly. "I thought that after the so-called party at the Bar V the other night, and what happened afterward, that Sheriff Brady would do something—anything! But that doesn't appear to be the case. I don't know whether Jud has bought him off, or what. Maybe the sheriff just doesn't want to get involved. Whatever the reason, it looks like we're in this thing all by ourselves. We can handle it. But it's going to get rough and dirty. Any of Jud's hired guns with an ounce of mercy in them have pulled out. What's left is the crud. That's what's going to be hitting us. Be ready for it. That's it."

Smoke looked at the young kids, kids that were growing up fast. Too fast, probably, for he saw no fear in their eyes. Did they really know the danger that faced them, or was this just kid excitement? Probably a combination of both, he thought.

"I'll stand the first watch," Walt said. "Then Smoke and Rusty and Jackson can divide up the rest. We're going to have to do this every night. Three-hour pulls for each of us until it's over."

"Anybody seen or heard anything from Clint?" Alice asked. No one had.

"The last time I spoke with him," Smoke said, "he said he was having one of his spells—one of his moods is what he called it. He wouldn't come close to me."

"That's probably good for you," Doreen said. "He gets murderous when those things take hold of him. He thinks everybody is his enemy."

There was nothing else to say, so Walt broke up the meeting by telling everyone to go to bed. He got his rifle and took up a position by the corral, taking the first watch.

Smoke slept a few hours and then went out to relieve the rancher. It was one of those Idaho nights that inspire poets to write the loftiest and most eloquent of verses. The heavens were filled with stars that clung so close to earth one could almost feel they were touchable.

"Quiet," Walt said, standing up and stretching. "Everything is at peace with the other, I reckon. Well, almost. Even the birds stopped calling a few minutes ago."

Smoke tensed. "No birds are calling?"

Walt was silent for only a few seconds, then he cursed himself for being an old fool! "Damnit! What's the matter with me? I'll alert the others." The old rancher took off in a bowlegged lope.

Smoke ran toward the bunkhouse, catching up with Walt and telling him to get to the house and get Little Micky into the root cellar; he'd alert the others.

Smoke knew better than to bust into the bunkhouse with everyone on the alert. That would be a good way to catch a bullet. He paused at a window.

"They're here, boys!" he called softly. "Get to your positions and keep the lights out doing it."

He rousted Jackson and Rusty and they ran to preset positions around the compound. None of them saw the youngest of the kids leave the bunkhouse and race across the area, stopping by the side of the barn for a moment, and then slip into the darkness of the huge barn.

Chuckie and Clark and Jimmy and Buster grinned at each other. They'd had the very devil of a time getting just the rocks for their slingshots; but they'd finally found some with just the right texture and their weapons were strongly made, their pockets bulging with smooth little stones.

They knelt down in the darkness and waited. They could hear Smoke up in the loft on one end of the barn, talking to Jackson who was up in the loft on the other end.

The boys waited in silence, slingshots in their hands.

Smoke searched the darkness of his perimeter but could see nothing out of the ordinary. If Jud and his men were out there—and that was still iffy—they were on foot and staying very quiet.

Chuckie thought he heard something behind him, at the far end of the barn. He looked at the others. Their eyes were wide; they had heard it, too. Then the very faint sound came again, but this time it was closer.

Someone was in the barn with them, and it wasn't anyone from the Box T. The boys knew all the positions of those friendly.

Chuckie slipped a rock into the pocket of his slingshot and ever so slightly shifted positions. Then he saw the clearly outlined figure of a man. And the shape of the hat told him it was no one from the Box T. Chuckie lifted his slingshot, pulled the rubber taut, and took aim. He let the rock fly and his aim was true. The rock struck the man in the center of his forehead and knocked him off his boots. The man made one grunt of pain as the rock hit him and then lay still on the barn floor.

Smoke was down the loft ladder in seconds. He looked at the slingshot-armed boys and sighed. It was too late to send them back to the house. But he couldn't help but feel proud of them. They were a gutsy bunch.

Smoke moved to the fallen man. He didn't know him.

"What's goin' on down there?" Jackson whispered from the hayloft.

"One of Jud's men," Smoke returned the whisper. "The boys dropped him with a slingshot."

Jackson chuckled softly.

"That means they've infiltrated us. Look sharp, Jackson."

Smoke cut several lengths of binder twine and securely tied the hired gun. He stuck the man's guns behind his belt and took his rifle. He looked at the boys looking at him. "I ought to spank you," he whispered. "But I feel too proud of you to do that. Now, damnit, boys, stay down and out of sight! This is not a game."

"Yes, sir," Buster said, as Smoke headed for the ladder.

Smoke had just cleared the landing when Rusty's rifle barked from his position in the bunkhouse. A man cried out in pain as the bullet struck true. Smoke ran to the hay door as gunfire began pouring in from all sides of the ranch complex.

Below him, the boys readied their slingshots as they crouched down behind bales of hay.

Jackson sighted a running figure, fired, missed, and fired again. The second slug dusted the man and sent him sprawling to the ground, side-shot and out of it.

Then the compound was filled with running men as they left their positions on the near-barren hills and ridges around the ranch and charged. Smoke could hear, over the gunfire, the sounds of horses coming hard.

The first wave of running men were cut down by the savage fire from the house, the barn, and the bunkhouse. Their bodies lay sprawled under the starry sky. One man, only slightly wounded, tried to make the barn. He was knocked to his knees by slingshot-propelled rocks and then knocked unconscious as a rock fired by Buster hit him on the side of the head and dropped him to the ground.

The boys grinned at each other.

Doreen sighted in a man and pulled the trigger, the Winchester slamming her shoulder. The slug caught the hired gun in the chest and ended his career.

Susie turned one around with a rifle shot and Alice finished him with a pistol. The rancher's wife was calm and steady, this being nothing new to her. She'd fought Indians for years before this.

One of Jud's men reached the outside bunkhouse wall. Jamie shot him between the eyes as he carelessly poked his head up just a tad too far.

Then the hard-running horses came into view, the riders carrying burning torches. The first half-dozen to reach the compound were blown out of their saddles by rifle fire. The boys in the lower level of the barn then went to work, sending rocks which impacted with horses' butts.

One man was knocked out of the saddle as a rock struck him on the jaw. He fell on his torch and quickly became a living firebrand. He rose screaming to his feet, his clothing ignited, and tried to run. Walt ended his agony with a bullet to the head.

The horses went into a panic as the rocks pelted them, stinging and confusing and angering them. The horses began bucking and jumping, trying to escape the hurting stones. Riders were tossed to the ground and shot down by rifle and pistol fire.

One managed to reach the house and jumped in through a window. Doreen picked up a pot of coffee from the stove and tossed the contents on the man, the scalding coffee catching him flush in the face. He dropped his guns and began screaming in agony, running around the room, crashing into furniture in his frantic rush to get away from the awful pain.

Alice shot him in the head and permanently ended the wailing.

A bounty hunter ran into the barn as rocks from slingshots pelted him, stinging but not stopping his charge for cover.

Little Chuckie grabbed up a pitchfork, tines out, and braced himself against the impact. The gun hand ran right into the pitchfork, knocking Chuckie down as the tines tore into his belly. Screaming in pain, the gunny ran toward the other end of the barn. The handle of the pitchfork, sticking several feet out of his belly, hit a wall and stuck there. The gunny screamed his life away, unable to pull the handle from the crack in the stable wall or free himself of the tines.

Chuckie got sick.

A torch hit the roof of the bunkhouse and lodged there, soon catching the roof on fire.

Smoke lit the fuse on a stick of dynamite and tossed the

bomb into the milling and panicked scene below him. The explosion knocked several horses to the ground, busting a couple of riders' legs and creating even more confusion in the fire-lanced night.

Smoke began tossing stick after stick of dynamite from loft to the ground, as his eyes spotted Rusty and the boys running from the bunkhouse to a storage shed. A Bar V rider turned his horse as he spotted the boys, lifting his pistol. Smoke shot him out of the saddle. His boot hung in the stirrup and the frightened horse took off at a gallop, dragging the screaming, flopping, and helpless man.

All the steam seemed to leave the Bar V men at once. Those still mounted wheeled and raced from the fire-lit ranch. Those on foot ran away into the darkness.

"Cease firing!" Smoke yelled. "Hold your positions!"

The crackling flames from the bunkhouse became the only sounds in the bloody night.

"I'm gonna let it burn itself out!" Walt yelled from the house.

"You all right, Jackson?" Smoke called.

"I'm okay. How about the boys down below?"

"We're all right," one called. "Chuckie got sick, is all."

Smoke climbed down the ladder. He stopped as his eyes saw the pitchfork-impaled gun hand, the man's hands still gripping the handle in death.

"I had to do it, Mr. Smoke," Chuckie said. "I didn't have no choice."

"You did fine, Chuckie," Smoke assured him. "You boys stay down behind those bales of hay."

Smoke found a sack and then eased his way out of the barn. Staying close to whatever cover he could find, he began working his way to the storage shed. On the way, he passed men who were moaning and twisting in pain. He took their guns from them and dropped them into the sack. Rusty saw what he was doing and stepped out to begin calming and corralling the milling Bar V horses. Jackson stayed where he was, keeping a sharp eye out for any return raiders.

But Jud's hired guns had apparently had enough for one night. No more hostile fire came.

Susie and Doreen rolled the dead man out of the living room and off the porch. A couple of the boys dragged the man out of the front yard.

"Rusty, at first light, I want you to ride for Montpelier and get that reporter and then find Sheriff Brady. Bring them both here. If Sheriff Brady won't come, send a wire to the governor's office and one to the Army up at Fort Hall. But I think Brady will come."

"Right. What do we do with the bodies?"

"Lay them over by the side of the barn and cover them with whatever you can find. Use their own bedrolls and ground sheets if they were carrying any. We'll put the wounded in the barn."

Walt walked up. "I count twenty dead and twelve wounded. Some of them ain't gonna make it."

"I guess you better bring Doctor . . . what's his name, Walt?"

"Evans. He's a good man. He'll come." Walt looked up at the sky. "I hope they come quick. It's gonna be a warm day and these bodies'll start to bloat in a hurry. Flies will be awful."

Chapter 25

Sheriff Brady took one look at the lined-up bodies and paled under his tan. Doctor Evans and his assistant began working on the wounded.

"I'm filing charges against all these men," Walt told the sheriff. "And I'm filing charges against Jud Vale. They worked for him, they acted under his orders."

"Can you prove that in a court of law?" Brady challenged. "And I ain't tryin' to be a horse's butt about it, Walt. Just askin' what the judge will ask."

"I understand. We can prove it if some of these men will talk."

"Fat chance of that," Brady said. "But we'll give it a try. Walt, I'm going to call in the U.S. Marshals. It'll take them about two days to get in here by train. I just don't have the men to handle this by myself."

"Then why not deputize all the farmers and such around

here?" the rancher suggested. "Form a posse. We'll go in and arrest Jud and his men."

"First I got to find a judge to sign them papers authorizing such a move. I think it's best if we let the marshals handle it. And I ain't tryin' to back out of my duty, neither."

"I understand. All right, Sheriff. We'll play it your way."

Brady looked around him at the carnage, the burned-out bunkhouse. "This has got to end. I just ain't gonna tolerate it no more. I'll be back with the marshals, Walt. And that's a promise." He looked at the doctor. "You need some help with these wounded, Doc?"

"A few of them can sit a saddle. Walt's lending us a wagon to transport the rest. Help me load them up and we'll be on our way."

The wounded bounty hunters and hired guns were loaded into a wagon, and not too gently either. With Sheriff Brady leading the way, the wagon rolled out, those sitting saddles doing so with their hands tied to the saddle horn. Smoke didn't hold out much hope of any of the hired guns talking.

And as for the U.S. Marshals coming in . . . Smoke didn't think they'd be coming in anytime soon, although he believed that Sheriff Brady would certainly try to get them in. The U.S. Marshals' force was a small one, with a lot to do. They would probably look at the sheriff's request as just another flare-up between ranchers over water or graze, and promptly forget it.

The reporter had indeed written his story about the kidnapping of Doreen and her rescue, but nothing had come of that report. This was still the raw West, with lawmen few and far between. Communities were still expected to handle their own problems without crying for outside help.

Smoke said as much to Walt and the others.

Jackson was the first to agree. "I've seen this happen time and again. In the end, it's all gonna boil down to men facin' men with guns. That's the way it's always been, and that's the way it's gonna be . . . for a while yet."

"I'll cling to a small hope that the marshals will come in," Walt said.

"Cling to a gun with your other hand," Smoke told him.

Chuckie and other smaller boys went down to the creek, looking for more small stones for their slingshots. None of them had ever seen a U.S. Marshal and didn't expect to see one anytime soon.

Jud Vale took his afternoon coffee on the front porch of his mansion. He was feeling much better—physically and mentally. But he had enough sense to know that his mind could flip him back into madness at any moment, without warning.

He sucked at his coffee cup, with some of the hot brew trickling out of his mouth and dribbling onto his shirt front. Jud didn't pay it any attention. He hadn't gone on the past night's raid against his brother; Blackjack and Molino had assured him they could handle it. They handled it, all right. Came straggling back in with half their men either dead or wounded and captured, talking about kids with slingshots— *slingshots,* for Christ's sake—and dynamite and all kinds of other excuses for having failed.

Jud shook his big head. Slingshots!

He mentally laid aside his burning hate for his brother and forced himself to think rationally.

A frontal attack, a mass attack of the Box T had failed for the second time, so Jud had to discard any further thoughts along that line. He knew that at one time, and not that long ago, a couple of weeks back, maybe a month, he'd had several plans in mind. Now he couldn't think of a single one, and that scared him. Was he losing his marbles again?

He thought hard; sweat broke out on his forehead. Then it

came to him. Burn the damn nesters out. Yeah, that had been one of them. There had been other plans, but the burning out of the nesters was the only one he could think of at the moment. Pretty good plan. Instead of striking at the head of the beast, the head being his brother and Smoke Jensen, start chopping away at the arms and legs.

He called for Jason and told him of the plan. Jason thought that it might work.

"No one will be expecting any trouble this soon after the raid on the ranch. Send some boys out this afternoon. Start with that damn interferin' Chester and his old woman. He was one of them at the creek, wasn't he?"

"Sure was."

"Kill them and burn them out."

"We won't even have to send any of the top guns to do this," Jason pointed out. "I'll send them three punks that come in on the train with some of Perry's bunch."

"Sounds good. Do it."

The six hired guns were in good spirits as they rode out of the Bar V range, heading for Chester's farm. This was going to be good fun. And maybe the nester had a good-lookin' daughter . . . that would be even more fun. They'd hogtie the farmer and his old woman and make them watch while they had their way with the girl.

The punk kid who called himself Tucson Bob vocalized his plan.

The outlaw known as Cline grinned, exposing a mouthful of rotted teeth. "I like that idea, Tucson. You all right." Then he sobered. "But what if they ain't no young girl?"

"Then we'll hang the nester slow; make it last and watch him kick and choke."

"I'd druther have me a young girl who don't want to give

it up, but the second idea is a right good one. How far did Jud say this pig farm was?"

"It's just up ahead. Do we ride through the garden first and tear it up?"

"Might as well. They'll get 'em so scared they won't know what to do."

The six hired guns hit the small farm at a gallop, whooping and hollering and firing into the house, riding right through the neat garden.

Chester's wife stuck a shotgun out of a window and blew the would-be gunfighter called Randy out of the saddle just as Chester came out of the barn with a Winchester and emptied another saddle, ending the life and career of the outlaw called Fox. The farmer's wife let loose with the other side of the double-barrel and the punk who should have stayed home and learned his father's dairy business back in Wisconsin hit the ground, landing hard amid the green beans and cabbage, half of his left arm torn off from the buckshot.

Cline leveled his pistol at Chester just as the farmer pulled the trigger. Cline felt a hard blow to his chest and slipped from the saddle, his world dimming just as neighbors galloped up, all armed.

"Don't shoot!" Tucson Bob yelled, his eyes wild with fear.

A neighbor knocked him out of the saddle with the butt of his shotgun just as a gun hand tried to jump the fence and get away.

A half-dozen guns barked and the outlaw hit the ground, right into the pigpen. The hogs moved toward him.

Chester walked up, his eyes hard and his face grim. He stood over the scared punk. "Somebody shoo them hogs away from the body 'fore they eat him. And then get a rope," Chester added.

Tucson Bob started screaming.

*   *   *

"Where'd you hang him?" Walt asked.

Chester and a few of his neighbors had ridden over to the Box T with the news of the attack, after they had returned from the creek.

"Down at the line separating your range from Jud's. Right at the crick so's he can be found. We dumped all the bodies there, too."

"Kinda bothered me hangin' that kid," a farmer said. "He sure blubbered and hollered and begged, callin' for his ma. But then I had to think about what he told us they was gonna do if Chester's girl had been found. Then it didn't bother me so bad."

"How about the kid with his arm shot off?" Jackson asked.

"He didn't make it to the crick 'fore he died."

"After he died," Chester said, "the other kid started talkin' his head off, tellin' us 'bout what they had in mind to do with any girl they found at farmers' homes they was plannin' to raid. He said that's what Jud's men was goin' to do from now on out. I guess he thought by tellin' us ever'thing he knew we would spare him from the rope. He thought wrong."

Walt told the men about Sheriff Brady's try to get U.S. Marshals in.

Chester shook his head negatively. "You been out of touch too long, Walt. And I ain't sayin' that it's all your fault. Brady is a good man, and he'll make his request for help. But it ain't gonna come in. Somebody higher up will block it. We done tried to do what you're tryin' early last year. We sent Jim Martin to see the governor. He didn't get in to see him and was ambushed on his way back home."

"I remember," Walt said, shaking his head. "Another good idea shot all to hell."

Smoke cut his eyes to Jackson, remembering the gun-fighter's words: "In the end, it's all gonna boil down to men facin' men with guns. That's the way it's always been, and that's the way it's gonna be . . . for a while yet."

Smoke couldn't agree more.

Several days drifted by, and it was as Chester had predicted: nothing was heard from Sheriff Brady. One week after the night raid by the gunmen, Brady rode slowly up to the Box T. He looked like a man with the weight of the world on his shoulders.

Walt waved him onto the porch, where the rancher was sitting with Smoke, Jackson, and Rusty. Brady took a chair and the cup of coffee that Susie brought out to him.

"You look like a man whose best horse just died," the rancher remarked. "What's the matter, Sheriff?"

"It's worse than that, I'm here to tell you. There ain't gonna be any help comin' in from the government, Walt. And that's just the beginning of it." He sighed and took a sip of coffee. "I been ridin' all over this county. I can't find a judge who'll sign papers against Jud. One of them outright laughed at me. And I had to turn all them gun hands loose. Judge's orders. He says that since you didn't personal come in and swear to the truth of the raid, I can't hold them."

"Judge Monroe?" Walt asked.

"You got it."

"I always knew he was takin' money from my brother."

"I don't think it would have made a whit of difference if you had come in and signed them papers," the sheriff said. "I've had to open my eyes these past few days and look at things I guess I been avoiding over the years." He sighed. "The mainest thing being that Jud Vale's got a lot of people with their hands in his pockets . . . and some of them hands has been there for a long time. I'm finding out, really finding out, what it means to butt your head up against a stone wall."

"I hate to be the one to ask you this, Sheriff," Walt said, "but how about your deputies?"

"Can they be trusted? Yes. They been with me for a long time and they'll stand. I've bet my life on that too many times not to be totally sure of them." He looked at Smoke and Rusty and Jackson. "You boys want a badge?"

Smoke shook his head. "Not me. Too many restrictions go with a badge."

Rusty and Jackson also declined the offer of being deputized.

Brady said, "I'm about to do something that I ain't never done in all my years of totin' a star around." He was thoughtful for a moment, then drained his coffee and stood up, hitching at his gunbelt. "You boys handle this anyway you see fit. I won't interfere in no way. If Jud starts squallin' for the law to come in, I'll tell him I'll get to it as soon as possible. Then I'll toss his complaint into the trash can. If the judges get on me about my foot-draggin', I'll tell them the people elected me, not them, and if the people don't like the way I'm doin' things, then come election time, they can vote me out of office as easy as they voted me in."

Brady stepped off the porch and walked to his horse. After swinging into the saddle, he looked at the men on the porch. "Good luck, boys. If you need help, holler, and I'll come a-foggin'."

Brady turned his horse and rode out of the ranch without looking back.

Smoke took out the Colts, one at a time, and filled up the empty chamber under the hammer. Rusty and Jackson did the same. Walt rose from his chair and walked into the house. When he returned, he had his gunbelt in one hand and a box of .44's in the other. He sat down and began filling up the loops in the belt.

"I fought for this land," the old rancher spoke. "Fought hard for it. But until you boys come along, I reckon I'd misplaced my backbone. I'd turned into a scared old man. That scared old man ain't no more. Maybe it takes me a little longer to get goin' in the mornings, but there ain't nothin' wrong with my eyes nor my trigger finger. And I made up my mind about something else: my brother can go right straight to Hell! And if it has to be me who sends him there, so be it."

Chapter 26

Days after the disastrous attack against the nesters, Jud was still having trouble accepting the fact that most people, from the territorial line west to the Little Malad River were no longer going to bow and scrape to him. Jud had not only lost his power base, but now he felt his mind going again. He struggled to maintain control. He managed to hold on, but it was becoming increasingly difficult to make rational thoughts work their way through the fog that clouded his brain.

Jason was talking to him, but Jud was having a hard time understanding the words.

"Jud!" Jason shouted at him.

Jud turned his head. Blinked his eyes. "Yes, Jas. I hear you."

"Can you understand me, Jud?"

"Yes. Now, I can. What were you saying?"

"It's time to pull in our horns. We got enough money to

last us ten lifetimes. It's time to quit. Break up the gangs and send them packing. Stick with ranchin'. The people has turned ag'in us. It can't do nothin' 'cept get worser."

Jud didn't believe the words he was hearing. This wasn't like Jas. Jas had been his strong friend and supporter for years—long, bloody, murderous, and savage years. Together they had raped and murdered and stolen and savaged from Illinois to Idaho. Now the man was telling him it all had to come to an end. Jud shook his head. "No way, Jas. It's too late for that." Lucidity was returning to Jud's darkened brain. "Far too late. We are what we are. We can't change. The people won't let us. We've got to stay strong, and we've got to show the people that we're still the kingpins of this area."

"For God's sake, Jud—how? You haven't ridden around the area like I have. Every move I make, they's anywhere from five to fifteen guns on me. The people have had it, Jud. We've come to the end of our string."

Jud looked at the man. "You want to ride, Jas?"

"You mean leave?"

Jud nodded.

"No. You know me better than that. We been together since we was young bucks, full of piss and vinegar. If you say we're gonna stand and fight this out, then I'll be right beside you."

"How many men are still on the payroll, drawing fighting wages?"

"Seventy."

Jud's eyes were hard and savage. "Then tell them to start earning it."

The riders struck at night, wearing masks and dusters. They struck a small farmhouse near the Wyoming line and burned it to the ground, killing the farmer and abusing his wife and oldest daughter before tying them naked to a tree and leaving them. Then they vanished into the night, scattering, leaving no trail that Sheriff Brady and his men could follow. The raiders did the same thing the next night, miles away from the first scene of horror and degradation.

The third night the raiders struck, Sheriff Brady and his men were at the extreme south end of the county while the raiders were working the northern tip of the county. It was the same operation: a farm was burned, the man was killed, the women abused.

But what Jud didn't know was that after the first raid, Smoke had been absent from the Box T, roaming mostly at night, looking for tracks, and holed up during the day. Just before dawn on the morning of the fourth day, he watched the raiders return to the Bar V, still wearing their dusters. He waited until he was certain that all who were coming in were in, then began slowly and carefully backtracking the trail.

By eight o'clock, he had found where all the raiders came together after scattering. It was on the Bear River Range, but he wasn't certain it was on Bar V holdings. He felt this might be public range.

He began following the main body of the raiders, finally discovering where they had built a hidden corral to keep their spare horses. Smoke backed off a good half-mile, rubbed down Dagger, and cooked himself a meal. He stretched out on the ground to sleep for a few hours. This night, the raiders would be in for a surprise when they came for their horses. A very deadly surprise.

When he opened his eyes, he guessed the time to be about four o'clock. Smoke built a small fire and made coffee, frying some bacon to go with the last of his bread. After eating, he leaned back against his saddle and rolled a cigarette, enjoying his coffee and the peace and quiet. Come the night, it would not be a bit peaceful, and it sure as hell wouldn't be quiet.

Before dusk settled over the land, Smoke put out his small fire and saddled up, moving closer to the hidden corral. He dismounted and carefully picketed Dagger, hopefully out of the line of fire. Taking his rifle, he moved to well within throwing distance of the corral and found himself a good position. He chambered a round and eased the hammer down, then Smoke settled in to wait for the first of the raiders to arrive.

He didn't think they would come all in a bunch, but instead come drifting in by two's and three's. The first bunch of outlaws would wait until the last had arrived, then take off to do their dirty work.

But Smoke had some dirty work of his own in mind, and he was confident that the number of raiders who rode out would be considerably less than the number who rode in this night.

The first bunch rode in almost carelessly, certain that no unfriendly eyes were upon them.

Smoke waited and watched through the gathering gloom as the assorted scum on Jud's payroll checked the corrral to see if their spare mounts were still there. One man busied himself building a fire and making coffee.

Then the damning evidence showed itself as the men began unrolling white dusters from behind their saddles and shaking out the black bandanas they would use to cover the lower half of their faces.

More men began drifting in until the number had reached twenty. They drank coffee and began slipping into their dusters. The talk was rough as the conversation drifted to where Smoke lay hidden. The Bar V hired guns laughed as they casually talked of murder, rape, and torture. Another man tossed more wood on the fire.

Smoke had carefully gauged the distance between his location and the main body of men. With a grim smile on his lips, he lit the fuses and tossed two sticks of giant powder into the group.

It took a couple of seconds for the men to react, and a couple of seconds was all it needed for the short fuses to burn down. When the dynamite blew, the din was enormous in the night.

Outlaws were hurled off their boots, some landing hard and breaking bones, others with the wind knocked from them. Horses reared up, screaming their panic, breaking loose and galloping off into the darkness. Those hired guns who were still on their feet were stumbling around, cursing and disoriented and momentarily deafened from the huge explosion.

Smoke knocked half a dozen men sprawling with fast but well-placed rifle shots, then shifted locations, reloading as he made his way toward the corral. The outlaws began pouring lead into the area Smoke had just vacated.

Smoke jerked the rawhide string holding the gate to the post and fired into the air, stampeding the remuda. The frightened horses ran right into and through the milling gun hands, knocking a few screaming to the earth before the steel-shod hooves mangled flesh and broke bones.

Smoke took that time of painful confusion to run back to where he had picketed Dagger and swing into the saddle. Smoke got himself gone from that area, feeling very confident that the raiders would not strike against women and children this night.

He did not head for the Box T, instead pointing Dagger's nose toward the Bar V. He had not gone a mile before a horseman rode onto the trail and waved at him.

Clint Perkins. Smoke reined up and looked at the man.

"Heading for the Bar V to do some mischief, Smoke?"

"That was my plan."

"I'll ride along with you."

"Your funeral."

Clint laughed in the night. "Oh, not just yet, Smoke. Oh, my, no! I have that auspicious but final event all worked out in my mind. And the time is close, but not this night."

"Whatever you say."

"Your plan for the Bar V?"

"Lay up on the ridges and put about a hundred rounds into the house and bunkhouse. Just let Jud know that I haven't forgotten him."

Clint laughed. "Let's ride!"

They rode hard for a couple of miles, then slowed to a walk, sparing their horses but still covering the distance swiftly. They did not talk until they were about two miles from the mansion.

"I'll take this side, Clint," Smoke told him. "The other side is all yours."

"That's fair. How long do we keep it up?"

"Oh, ten or fifteen minutes. We'll wait about half an hour before we start. That'll give our horses time to catch their breath and for some of those behind us to make the ranch and spread the news. There'll be lots of lanterns and lamps lit when they return. That'll give us better targets."

Clint smiled. "See you around, Smoke Jensen." Then he was gone into the night.

Smoke angled off into the timber and carefully made his way to a ridge overlooking the great mansion. He picketed Dagger and settled in behind a tree, just at the crest of the hill.

The minutes ticked by, turning into half an hour. What was left of Jud's raiders began trickling back to the ranch complex, about half of them belly-down over a saddle, tied in place. Smoke brought his Winchester to his shoulder, compensated for the downhill shooting, and sighted in a man, squeezing the trigger.

The slug went high and knocked the man's hat from his head, sending the hired gun to the ground. Smoke's second shot was true. The gun hand tried to rise up on one elbow, then fell face-forward, neck-shot.

From across the way, Clint opened up, the outlaws clearly visible under the light of the moon and the starry night. Smoke joined in, concentrating his fire into the mansion.

Jud, Jason, and the bodyguards hit the floor as .44 slugs began tearing through the walls and windows of the mansion.

A slug shattered the knee of a bodyguard, bringing a howl of pain. Clint was pouring rifle fire into the running men in the yard. He quickly punched more cartridges into his rifle and began peppering the bunkhouse. Smoke shifted the muzzle of his rifle and put two fast rounds into one of the newly built outhouses. A man came rushing out, trying to run while holding his britches up with one hand. One knee caught in his dangling suspenders and sent him sprawling to the ground.

Smoke tried for a lamp in the mansion, his third shot finally striking true, sending coal oil and flames worming across the floor like a flaming snake. Jud and Jason and the bodyguards began stomping at the flames before they caught and burned the place down.

There was little the men around the mansion could do except curse the birth of Smoke Jensen; they knew it was Smoke on one of the ridges. And probably Clint on the other ridge.

Smoke decided he'd pressed his luck to the maximum for this night, and began working his way back to Dagger. It would take Clint only a couple of minutes to understand that Smoke was gone.

Inside the mansion, hopping mad, jumping around like a huge frog, his eyes bugged out, cursing at the top of his lungs, and just barely hanging onto what little sanity was left him, Jud began screaming orders to get Smoke Jensen, declare war on everybody, burn down Montpelier, assassinate President Arthur; do whatever needs to be done . . . just kill that damned Smoke Jensen!

Clint fired one more round before he pulled out, putting his shot into the living room and plugging a suit of armor Jud had imported from England.

"Another day, Father," Clint muttered, slipping back to where he'd tied his horse. "Soon."

Smoke slept soundly the remainder of that night, in his room in the barn at the Box T. He had stopped at several small farms, telling the people what had gone down and also that he doubted Jud's raiders would be out doing their dirty work that night. But keep a guard posted just in case.

He slept late; it was nearly six o'clock when he awakened and put on his hat, then his pants and boots and shirt, slinging his gunbelt around his waist, and stepping outside.

"What went down last night?" Jackson asked, handing him a cup of coffee.

Smoke took a sip of coffee before replying. Jackson was smiling when Smoke finished.

"Wish you had invited me along," he said wistfully.

"I didn't know what I was going to do until the last minute. But it will be interesting to see what Jud does next."

"Interesting is one way of puttin' it, for sure."

Chapter 27

"Jud's sellin' his herds," the farmer said, dismounting in front of the ranch house. Walt led him to the porch and offered the man coffee, as Smoke and Jackson and Rusty joined them.

It was just past dawn and three days after Smoke and Clint had assaulted the mansion.

"He's pulling out?" Walt asked, a hopeful note to the question.

"No," Smoke said. "I'd say he's gearing up for a long and expensive war. Putting his hands on as much hard cash as possible." He glanced at the farmer. "When did you find out about this?"

"Late yesterday evenin'. My neighbor, Jim Morris, had been up to Montpelier. Stopped in for a drink and heard cattle buyers talkin' about it. Them buyers done sent men in to move the cattle."

"Knowing we wouldn't harm any innocent party," Smoke

mused aloud. "Good move on Jud's part. Then they've begun moving the cattle out?"

"Oh, yeah. Job's might near half done, I reckon." He cut his eyes to Smoke. "Them bounty hunters—Wills is one of them?"

Smoke nodded. "I know them."

"I heard some talk, Mr. Jensen; heard it this mornin'. Word is they're pullin' out on Jud's orders. Goin' down to Arizony, lookin' for your wife and family."

"It would be something Jud would do," Walt said. "That would be one way to get you away from here."

Smoke stepped from the porch, his face tight and his eyes hard. He walked to the barn and saddled Dagger. The road by the trading post would be the one they would be most likely to take. Smoke would be waiting for them. It was time to bring this boil to a head. Crazy or not, when Jud Vale started threatening Smoke's wife and family, Jud Vale was a dead man.

Doreen had a poke of food waiting for him when he rode up to the ranch house. Smoke stowed it in his saddlebags. There was a gunnysack filled with dynamite tied onto the saddle horn. One side of his saddlebags was stuffed with ammunition and spare pistols. Smoke looked at Rusty and Jackson.

"Jud may be doing this trying to pull us all away from the Box T. Well, it isn't going to work that way. You boys stay here. This is my show. I'll be back."

The farmer grabbed hold of the reins. "No, sir," he said firmly. "That ain't the way it is and it ain't the way it's gonna be. This is *our* show. They's men comin' here right now. Farmers and hired hands and shopkeepers and such from all over; as far away as Montpelier. Sheriff Brady and his men is comin' in, too."

"Riders comin' for a fact," Rusty said. "Horses and wagons. Looks like a regular parade."

Smoke cut his eyes. It did look like a parade. He picked out Chester and his wife, and a dozen other farmers and family. He smiled as he saw Doc Evans's buggy. Right behind it was the editor of the Montpelier paper, Mr. Argood. Coming up to intersect the line of horses and wagons and buggies, was Sheriff Brady and his men. Chester whoaed his team and stepped down, helping his wife to the ground.

The farmer had a gunbelt around his waist and his wife carried a rifle. He walked to Smoke and looked up at him. "We ain't no good as gunfighters, Mr. Smoke. But we can damn sure defend this ranch while you boys is gone."

"I can't interfere or condone this, Smoke," Sheriff Brady said. "But I can stay right here and then sort out the pieces when it's over."

"And I'll be here to patch up the wounded," Doc Evans told him.

"I'll get my guns." Walt turned toward the house.

"Walt!" Alice said.

"Hush, woman," the old rancher told her. "A man's got to do what he's got to do. You just keep the coffee hot. I'll be back."

Rusty and Jackson were walking toward the barn to saddle up.

Matt walked his horse toward Smoke. There was a grim look on Smoke's face as he noticed the way the boy was wearing his guns. He carried his Peacemaker on his right side, and Cheyenne's old Colt on his left side, butt-forward for a cross draw.

It was like looking into a mirror that reflected years back. Like looking at himself as a boy.

"I'll be comin' with you," Matt told him.

"I can't stop you."

"That is correct, sir," Matt said politely.

They waited and watched for a few moments, as the farmers took up positions around the ranch and the women gathered on the porch. Rusty and Jackson rode up, leading Walt's horse. The rancher stepped out of his house, kissed Alice on the cheek, and swung into the saddle, booting his Winchester. The four men and the boy headed out, Smoke in the lead.

It was to be the start of the bloodiest day in that part of Idaho Territory.

They reached the trading post, coming in from the back of the long building, dismounting and tying their horses in the rear of the store. Jackson had pointed out the bounty hunters' horses in front of the saloon.

"Jackson and me will handle this," Smoke said. "The rest of you stay here."

The shopkeeper's wife rushed out the back door. "They got my husband and Bendel all trussed up like hogs," she whispered hoarsely. "They're waitin' on you, Mr. Jensen. And there's eight or ten more gun hands just over that ridge," she said, pointing.

"Thank you. Hunt some cover, ma'am." He looked at Jackson. "First things first," he said, then pushed open the back door and stepped into the gloom of the storage room.

Smoke had made up his mind that this battle and as many others as he could arrange would not be stand up, face, and draw. The odds were just too high.

He had both hands full of Colts, hammers back, when he kicked in the door to the saloon and went in shooting, Jackson right behind him, doing the same.

Lefty went down with the front of his shirt stained with blood and smoking holes. Smoke dropped to one knee, partly to give Jackson better shooting room and partly to show a smaller target, and put two slugs into the head of Shorty

Watson. Jackson had knocked John Wills and Dave Bennett spinning. Bennett went down to the floor, blood leaking from his mouth, dying and cursing as Wills staggered out the batwings and fell off the porch, landing on his back.

Smoke stepped outside just as Wills was lifting his guns. Smoke shot him between the eyes just as the sounds of galloping horses reached him.

Walt, Rusty, and Matt stepped around the corner of the building, rifles in their hands, and emptied some saddles. The charging gun hands did not slack up.

Smoke lifted his Colts and let the hammers down just as a hired gun galloped past the trading post. The .44's knocked the man from the saddle. Jackson was beside him on the porch, guns blazing. The badman turned good man emptied two more saddles.

The early morning became eerily quiet as Smoke and Jackson began punching out empties and reloading. The shopkeeper's wife untied her husband and Bendel. The saloonkeeper was furious as he joined Smoke on the porch.

"By God, I've had it!" he yelled. "I'll not tolerate anymore of Jud Vale's highhandedness."

"Nor will I," the shopkeeper said, taking the shotgun his wife offered him. "From now on, I see a Bar V brand, I blow the rider out of the saddle."

"That goes double for me," Bendel said, stripping the guns from Wills and loading them full.

Matt led the horses around front.

"Let's ride!" Walt said.

Three miles from the trading post, Smoke and his little force rode right into a group of Bar V riders. There was nothing gentlemanly or honorable about the fight. Smoke just dragged iron and started shooting, Walt and the others doing the same.

They looked up from the body-littered road as Clint

Perkins rode up, a wild glint in his eyes. "It is time, is it?" he called. "Very well. I recall an Indian saying: It is a good day to die." He turned his horse's head and rode off toward the Bar V.

"I didn't know we was just gonna ride up to Jud's front door and start shootin'," Rusty said.

"I didn't either," Smoke said. "But maybe that's the way it's got to be." He put Dagger into a gallop and the others followed, leaving the bodies in the road without a second glance.

One hired gun groaned and rolled over in the road. Finally he sat up, his head bloody and throbbing. He gingerly touched the wound and winced. It was painful, but not serious. He got to his boots, found his horse, and crawled into the saddle.

"Hell with this!" he said. "It's gone sour." He reined up when the trading post came into view, and watched Bendel and the shopkeeper and wife digging holes in the back. The gun hand wisely changed his mind about having a drink and carefully skirted the trading post. He thought California ought to be a real good spot to head for.

He knew there had been four or five men at the trading post, about ten more lying in ambush out from the post, and five with him. That was twenty men dead or dying at the hands of Smoke and them others, all in one morning—and the morning wasn't even half over! Yeah, California sounded real good.

"Move, horse. Jud Vale's number is comin' up this day, I'm thinkin'."

Cisco Webster, the Texas gun hand whose teeth had been knocked out by Rusty back at the crick, looked up at the road, just at the point where it crested the hill. He felt a touch of fear clutch at his belly.

Six men sat their saddles, looking down at the mansion, and Cisco didn't need a crystal ball to know who they were.

Highpockets noticed the direction the man's eyes were taking and looked up. Like Cisco, the gunfighter felt a slight lash of dread touch him at the sight.

The yard crowded with bounty hunters and gunslingers, all looking at the crest of the hill.

Smoke urged Dagger forward, riding with the reins in his teeth and his hands filled with Colts.

"What the hell are they goin' to do?" Hammer asked.

"It's over," Buck Wall told him. "I woke up with a bad feelin' about this day."

"You quittin'?" Chato Di Peso asked.

"I shore am." Buck walked toward the bunkhouse just as Jud appeared on the front porch.

"Where the hell do you think you're going?" Jud yelled at him.

"I'm quittin'," Buck called over his shoulder. "Like right now."

Jason had appeared on the porch beside his boss. "The hell you are!" he said, and shot Buck in the back.

The gunfighter pitched forward, dead before he hit the ground.

Smoke picked that time to charge. They split up, with Smoke and Clint riding right into the front yard, the reins in their teeth and hands full of Colts.

Matt and Walt went to the right, Jackson and Rusty to the left.

Hammer grabbed for his guns. Smoke shot him down, the slug taking him in the chest. Hammer died sitting on his butt in the road, his hands by his sides. After a few seconds, he slowly toppled over.

Shorty DePaul came out of the bunkhouse just as Walt and Matt were galloping past. Shorty sighted in Walt. Matt's gun crashed and Shorty felt the sledgehammer blow take him in the belly, about an inch above his belt. Matt fired again, his second slug striking the gunfighter in the chest and knocking him down.

"Kilt by a punk kid," were Shorty's last words.

Rusty and Jackson rode right into a knot of startled gun slicks. Pike and Becket went down under bullets fired at almost pointblank range. Molino stepped out of the barn and put a slug into Rusty's shoulder. Rusty border-rolled his Colt and shot the man in the throat. Molino hit the ground, coughing and gurgling.

Jaeger and Chato Di Peso saw very quickly the outcome of the fight and slipped through the dust and confusion to the bunkhouse, quickly gathering up their possessions. They grabbed horses—neither one of them giving a damn whose horse it was—and pulled out.

Cisco Webster watched as Smoke jumped from the saddle, and ran behind a building, reloading as he ran. Dagger trotted to the corrral and began harassing the mares.

Cisco ran to the storage shed, flattening out against a wall. He stuck his head around the corner just in time to catch a bullet right between the eyes. He sank to the ground, a very curious expression on his dead face.

Clint, out of the saddle and down on one knee, doubled over the Colorado gun hand, Barstow, with two .44 rounds to the belly, then shifted his Colt and ended the career of Highpockets.

Jackson had helped Rusty out of the saddle and left him behind good cover with a half-dozen Colts taken from the dead and dying. Jackson went headhunting. He walked right up to Rim Reynolds and several of his men and began shooting as fast as he could cock and fire. Rim went down screaming in pain with two slugs in his belly. Jackson was burned on one arm and took the loss of part of one ear but he was still standing when the others were down. He calmly and swiftly reloaded, shook the blood from his face and stepped back out in the fracas.

Walt and Matt were standing side by side, the old and the young, their guns taking a terrible toll. Crazy Phil was down on his knees, with four of his men on the ground with him. Old Walt winked at young Matt as they reloaded.

Clint was working his way closer to the house. He had but one thought in his demented mind.

The Pecos Kid and Glen Regan—Glen was walking slow due to the gunshot wounds in his butt from back at the creek—tried to make the corral and get away. Rusty dropped them both midway.

Blackjack Morgan stood with legs spread wide, his hands over the butts of his guns, facing Smoke, who still held his Colts in his hands. "I'm faster, Jensen!" he called over the din of battle.

"No. You're just dead," Smoke told him. He lifted his right hand and shot the gunfighter. There was a time for discretion and a time for valor, but at no time was there a moment to be wasted on fools.

Smoke stepped over the dying man and walked on.

A searing pain in Smoke's left leg turned him around and slammed him up against a wall. Gimpy Bonner and Scott Johnson faced him. Smoke lifted his Colts and let them bang. When the dust and gunsmoke cleared, Smoke was bloody but still standing.

Smoke reloaded, checked his wounds, and bound a bandana around the leg wound. He walked on as the sounds of galloping horses came to him over the shooting. About a dozen men were hauling their ashes away from the ranch. Smoke lifted his right-hand Colt and ended life for Ben Lewis who had lined up Jackson with a rifle. Ben danced for a moment, his spurs jingling his death chant, then slumped to the ground.

"Jensen!" the voice turned Smoke around to face Luddy.

Smoke didn't hesitate. Just lifted both guns and began firing and walking toward the man. He stood over the bloody outlaw, their eyes meeting.

"I thought you'd give me a fair chance, Jensen!" Luddy gasped.

"Did you ever give anyone a fair chance, Luddy?"

Luddy laughed humorlessly. "Can't say that I ever did, come to think of it." He shivered once. "Cold. Mighty cold all of a sudden." He closed his eyes and died.

Smoke turned away.

The gunfire had all but faded away. The grounds around the great mansion were littered with bodies. Jason was sitting on the steps, his shirt front bloody, but he was holding on to life long enough to see the outcome of what was about to take place in front of him.

Clint and Jud faced each other, both of them with the same wild light in their eyes.

"Hello, Daddy!" Clint said sarcastically.

"You son of a bitch!" Jud snarled at him.

"You sure got that right," the son told the father, then grabbed iron.

Father and son stood ten feet apart and put lead in each other. Both went to the ground on their knees at the same time. Both continued firing. Jud toppled over and Clint was only about one second behind him.

Walt walked up, one arm dangling useless from a .45 slug. He looked at the scene in front of him then lifted his eyes to Jason.

"I reckon it's over and done, ain't it, Walt?" the man gasped.

"I reckon it is, Jason."

"I reckon Jud just tried to toss too big a loop. Is that the way you see it?"

"Why did you and Jud kill my son?"

Jason laughed, a nasty bark of dark humor. "'Cause we wanted to, you old bastard!" Jason closed his eyes as the pale rider came closer.

Walt lifted his Colt and eared the hammer back. Then he slowly lowered the weapon as Jason tumbled down the steps to lie on the ground.

"Ride for Doc Evans and the sheriff, Matt," Smoke told the boy.

"They're comin' up the road now, Smoke," Matt told him, pointing. "And it looks like the Army is with them."

Chapter 28

Smoke had to hang around for the hearings—both state and federal government, since the Army had finally gotten involved—but that was all right, his wounds needed the time to heal. He watched as Rusty and Doreen, then Jackson and Susie got married. Since Walt was Jud's sole living survivor, Walt took possession of the Bar V. He signed over the Box T to Rusty and Doreen and gave the Bar V to Jackson and Susie. Matt stayed on as a hand for Rusty. Walt and Alice were going to build a little place on Bear Lake and retire.

Jackson was having the great mansion torn down on the day Smoke rode out. The couple planned to build a smaller, much more practical ranch house.

Smoke stopped by the trading post for a beer and to say good-bye to Bendel.

He was halfway through his beer when Jaeger and Di

Peso pushed open the batwings. Smoke sighed and set the mug down.

"Your time to die, Jensen," Di Peso told him.

"I don't think so," Smoke replied, turning and drawing both guns.

Smoke stepped over the bodies and walked to Dagger, swinging into the saddle and pointing Dagger's head south, toward Arizona and Sally and the kids. Bendel's voice stopped him.

"Smoke!"

He twisted in the saddle.

"If you ever plan a return visit, do me a favor, will you?" Bendel yelled.

"What's that?"

"Please bring a damn shovel!"

WAR OF THE
MOUNTAIN MAN

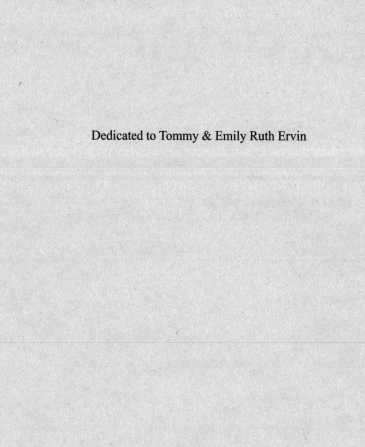

Dedicated to Tommy & Emily Ruth Ervin

What man was ever content with one crime?

Juvenal

I had rather live with the woman I love in a world
full of trouble, than to live in heaven with nobody
but men.

Robert G. Ingersoll

Chapter 1

"I don't like the idea of the kids on the ocean," Smoke said. "By God, I just don't."

Sally faced him from across the table in the house in the high-up country of Colorado. "Smoke, there is a new treatment available in France, and Louis Arthur has got to have it. We've been to the finest doctors on this continent. They all say the same thing."

"Sally, I'm not arguing that. I want what is best for Baby Arthur. But why do all the children have to go? My God, they'll be gone for more than a year."

She smiled at him. Smoke Jensen and Sally never had the hard, deadly quarrels that so many couples suffered. They were both reasonable people of high intelligence, and each loved the other. "The exposure to a more genteel climate—and I'm not talking about the weather—will be good for the older children. They need to broaden their horizons."

Smoke laughed as he picked up his coffee mug, holding it

in one big, flat-knuckled hand. The laughter was full of good humor and did not contain a bit of anger or scorn. He stuck out his little finger. "They gonna learn how to hold a coffee cup dainty-like, with their little pinkies all poked out to one side?"

Sally laughed at him. "Yes. You heathen."

Smoke chuckled and rose from the table, picking up Sally's cup as well as his own. He walked to the stove, a big man, well over six feet, with broad shoulders, huge, heavily muscled arms, and a lean waist. He walked like a cat. His presence in a room, any room, usually brought the crowd to silence. His eyes were brown and could turn as cold as the Arctic. He was a ruggedly handsome man, turning the heads of ladies wherever he traveled.

He was Smoke Jensen. The man some called the last mountain man.

Smoke was the hero in dozens of dime novels. Plays had been written and were still being performed about his exploits. Smoke, himself, had never seen one. He was, without dispute, the fastest gun in the West. He had never wanted the title of gunfighter; but he had it.

There was no accurate count of how many would-be toughs, punks, thugs, thieves, and killers had fallen under the .44's of Smoke Jensen. Some say fifty; others said it was closer to two hundred. Smoke didn't know. As a young man, scarcely out of his teens, he had ridden into a mining camp taken over by the men who had killed his wife and baby son and had wiped it out to the last man.

His reputation had then been carved in solid granite. Smoke had become a living legend.

He had met Sally, who was working as a schoolteacher, and they had fallen in love. Together, working side by side— even though she was enormously wealthy, something Smoke didn't find out until well after they were married—they carved out a ranch in Colorado and named it the Sugarloaf.

For three years Smoke dropped out of sight, living a normal, peaceful life. Then he had to surface and once more strap on his guns in a fight for survival. He stayed surfaced. He would not hunt out a fight, but God help those who came to him trouble-hunting. As the western saying goes: Smoke could point out dozens of his graveyards.

Their coffee mugs refilled, Smoke sat back down at the table and they both sugared and stirred. Sally laid her hand on his. "Roundup is all over and the cattle sold, right, honey?"

"Yes. And it was a good one. We made money. Now we're rebuilding the herds, introducing a stronger breed, mixing in some Herefords. What'd you have on your mind, Sally?"

"I'd like to go with the children . . ." She put a finger on his lips to stop his protests before they got started. "But I'm not. I know what the doctors said. And I'm never going to set foot on a ship again. But if we stay here, rattling around in this house, we'll both go crazy with worry. Let's wait until we receive the wire that the ship has steamed out, and then take a trip. Just the two of us."

"That's a good idea. The boys can run the spread; no worries there. You got some special place in mind?"

"Yes. It's a friend I went to college with. She and her husband just moved to Montana. They live near a small town about thirty miles from Kalispell. She's married to a doctor and they have a small ranch. I'd like to see her. She was my best friend."

"Suits me. We'll take a trip up there. It'll do us both good to get away, see some country, and meet new people. We'll take the train as far as it goes and then catch a stage."

"No," Sally shook her head. "Let's put the horses in a car

and ride in, Smoke. It'll be worth it to see the expressions on their faces when we ride in."

"Sidesaddle?" he kidded her, knowing better.

"You have to be kidding!"

Smoke was with her. "All right, honey. But we're going to be heading into some rough country. I've been there. Cousin Fae lives not too far from there. We can take the train probably to Butte. That's wild country, Sally. Some ol' boys up there still have the bark on. And that's Big Max Huggins's country."

She smiled, but the curving of her pretty lips held no humor. "That's one of the reasons we're going, Smoke."

He laughed. "I was wondering if you were going to get around to leveling with me."

"You know this Max Huggins?"

"Only by name. We've never crossed trails."

She stared into her coffee cup.

"Sally, this town your friends have settled near . . . it wouldn't be Hell's Creek, would it?"

"Yes."

Smoke sighed and leaned back in his chair. "Then they didn't show a lot of sense. Hell's Creek is owned—lock, stock, and outhouse—by Big Max Huggins. It's filled with gunfighters, whores, gamblers, killers. . . . You name it bad, and you'll find it there. Why did they settle there?"

"Robert—that's Vicky's husband—befriended an old man who took sick while visiting back East. Robert was just setting up his practice. Years later, he got a letter from an attorney telling him the old man had died and left him his ranch."

"And Big Max wanted the ranch?"

"Yes. But mostly he wants Victoria."

* * *

The next morning, Smoke rode into town and checked with Sheriff Monte Carson.

"What can you get me on Hell's Creek and a man named Big Max Huggins?"

Monte snorted. "I can tell you all about Big Max, Smoke. We got lead in each other about ten years ago."

"Over near the Bitterroot?"

Monte nodded his head.

"I remember that shoot-out. Is there any kind of law in Hell's Creek?"

"Only what Big Max says. Oh, there's a sheriff up there. But he's crooked as a snake's track and so are his deputies. I hear the governor keeps threatening to send men in to clean up the town, but he hasn't done it yet. Why the interest in Hell's Creek?"

"Sally has some friends who live near there. We're going to visit them. I'd sort of like to know what I'm riding into."

"You're riding into trouble, Smoke. Hell's Creek is a haven for outlaw gangs. In addition to Big Max's gang—and he's got forty or fifty men who ride for him—there's Alex Bell and his boys. Dave Poe, Warner Frigo, and Val Singer all run outlaw gangs out of Hell's Creek. The only way that town is ever going to be cleaned up is for the Army to go in and do it."

"Damn, Monte, it's 1883. The wild West is supposed to be calming down."

Monte shifted his chaw. "But you and me, Smoke, we know better, don't we?"

Smoke nodded his head. "Yeah. There'll be pockets of crud in the West for years to come, I reckon."

"Any way you can talk your missus out of takin' this trip?"

Smoke just looked at him.

"I do know the feelin'," Monte said. "Women get a notion

in their heads, and a man's in trouble, for a fact. When are you and Sally pullin' out?"

"Probably in about a week. Who else do you know for sure is up there?"

"Ben Webster, Nelson Barlow, Vic Young, Dave Hall, Frank Norton, Lew Brooks, Sid Yorke, Pete Akins, and Larry Gayle. Is that enough?"

"Good God!" Smoke said, standing up. "You just named some of the randiest ol' boys in the country."

"Yeah. And believe you me, Smoke, they'll be plenty more up there just as good as them boys I just named. You're gonna be steppin' into a rattler's den."

"They do sell .44's up there, don't they?" Smoke asked dryly.

"Probably not to you." Monte's reply was just as dry.

Chapter 2

That night, lying in bed, Sally said, "We don't have to go up there, Smoke. I don't want you to think I'm pressuring you in any way. Because I'm not."

"You think a lot of this friend of yours, don't you?"

"Like a sister, Smoke. She's had a lot of grief in her life and I'd like for her to have some happiness. She's overdue."

"Want to explain that?"

"She lost two brothers in the Civil War. Her mother died when she was in high school. Then in her second year of college, her father died. She worked terribly hard to finish school. Took in ironing, mended clothes, worked as a maid; anything to put food in her mouth and clothes on her back. I'd help whenever I could, but Vicky is an awfully proud girl. She and Robert had one child . . . that lived. Two others died. She can't have any more. Their daughter Lisa is ten."

Smoke waited for a moment, his eyes on the dark ceiling. "Finish it, honey. Tell it all."

"This Max Huggins trash has threatened Lisa several times, to get to Vicky."

Smoke thought about that. For about five seconds. He turned his head, his gaze meeting Sally's eyes. "We'll start packing up some things in the morning."

On the day they received the telegram from Sally's father, informing them of the steamer's departure, Smoke rode around their ranch, checking things out and speaking to the hands. His crew was a well-paid and tough bunch, who to a man would die for the brand. Some of them had been outlaws, riding the hoot-owl trail for a time. Some were gunfighters who sought relative peace and found it at the Sugarloaf. All were cowboys, hardworking and loyal.

"I still think you ought to take some of the boys with you, Smoke," his foreman grumbled. "Them's a hard bunch up yonder."

Smoke rolled a cigarette and handed the makings to his foreman. "You boys are needed here. There are still lots of folks who would just love to burn me out if they got the chance."

"They won't," the foreman said quietly.

"You boys take care of the place. You know where I'll be and how to reach me. We'll see you when we get back."

Smoke and Sally pulled out the next morning, Smoke riding a midnight-black gelding he called Star, and Sally on a fancy-stepping mountain-bred mare who could go all day and still have bottom left. Smoke led a packhorse with their few pieces of luggage and supplies.

They headed east, toward Denver, where they would catch the train. Sally had much experience with trains; Smoke had ridden only a few of them, preferring to travel in the saddle.

The beautiful woman and the handsome man turned heads

when they boarded in Denver. And the whisper went from car to car: "That's Smoke Jensen! See them guns? He's killed a thousand men."

Smoke signed a half-dozen books about him and patiently answered the many questions that were asked of him, mostly by newcomers to the West, men and women making their first trip from the East.

One mouthy preacher lipped off one time too many about violent men who lived by the gun. Smoke finally told him to shut his mouth and mind his own business. The preacher's mouth opened and closed silently a few times, like a fish out of water. Then he sat back down and shut up.

They changed trains in Cheyenne and headed northwest, and Smoke had to endure yet another new bunch of pilgrims with a thousand questions.

"My, my," Sally said during a lull in the verbal bombardment. There was a twinkle in her eyes. "I didn't realize I was married to such a famous man."

"Bear it in mind," Smoke said with a straight face. "And the next time I ask for a cup of coffee, you quick step and fetch it."

Sally leaned over, putting her lips close to his ear, and whispered a terribly vulgar suggestion.

Smoke had to put his hat over his face to keep from busting out laughing. Sally was every bit the lady, but like so many western women, she could be quite blunt at times.

A fat drummer twisted in his seat and asked Smoke, "Will we see any Indians this trip? I've never seen an Indian."

"We might see a few," Smoke told him, aware that everyone within hearing range had their ears perked up. "But the tribes have pretty well been corralled. What we'll more than likely encounter—if anything—is outlaws working the trains."

"Outlaws!" a woman hollered. "You mean like . . . high-waymen?"

"Yes, ma'am. Once we cross over into Montana Territory, the odds of outlaws hitting trains really pick up. Especially this train," he added.

"What's so special about this train?" the lippy preacher asked.

"We're carrying gold."

"Now, how would someone such as you know that?" the preacher demanded.

Smoke ignored the scarcely concealed slur upon his character. "I saw them loading it, that's why."

"Well," the preacher huffed. "I'm certain the railroad has adequate security."

"They got an old man with a shotgun sitting in the car, if that's what you mean."

The preacher turned away and lifted his newspaper.

"Are we carrying gold, Smoke?" Sally asked.

"Yeah. And a lot of it. And not just gold. We're carrying several payrolls, too. For the miners."

"What are the chances of our getting held up?"

"Pretty good, I'd say. If I had to take a guess, I'd say we're carrying about a fifty-thousand-dollar payroll—all combined—and maybe twice that in gold. Be a juicy haul for those so inclined."

"They wouldn't dare attack this train," she kidded him. "Not with the famous Smoke Jensen on board." She punched him in the ribs.

"Your faith in me is touching." He rubbed the spot where she had punched him. "In more ways than one."

The day melted into dusk and then full dark, the train chugging on uneventfully through the night. The passengers slept fitfully, swaying back and forth in their seats to the rhythm of the drivers on the tracks.

Smoke sensed the train slowing and opened his eyes. Being careful not to rouse Sally, he stood up and stepped out into the aisle, making his weaving way to the door. He stepped outside and stretched, getting the kinks out of his muscles. On instinct, he slipped the leather thongs from the hammers of his six guns.

Smoke leaned over the side and saw the skeletal form of the water tower ahead, faintly illuminated by the dim light of a nearly cloud-covered moon.

Through the odor of smoke pouring from the stack of the locomotive, Jensen could almost taste the wetness in the air. A storm was brewing, and from the build-up of clouds, it was going to be a bad one.

He looked back at the lantern-lit interior of the car, the lamps turned down very low. The passengers, including Sally, were still sleeping.

The train gradually slowed and came to a gentle halt, something most experienced engineers tried to do late at night so the paying passengers wouldn't be disturbed.

Smoke caught the furtive movement out of the corner of his eyes. Men on the water tower. With rifles.

One big hand closed around the butt of a .44. He hesitated. Were they railroad men, posted there in case of a robbery attempt? He didn't think so. But he wasn't going to shoot until he knew for sure.

He saw the brakeman coming up the side of the coaches and Smoke called to him softly just as he dropped to the shoulder. "My name's Jensen, brakeman. Smoke Jensen. There are armed men on the water tower."

The man's head jerked up. "They damn sure ain't railroad men, Smoke. And we're carryin' a lot of gold and cash money."

"That's all I need to know," Smoke said. He leveled a .44 and knocked a leg out from under one gunman crouching on the water tower. The man fell, screaming, to the rocky ground.

Another gunman, hidden in the rocks alongside the tracks, opened fire, the slugs howling off the sides of the cars.

Smoke yelled, "Get these pilgrims down on the floor, Sally." To the brakeman, who had hauled out a pistol and was trying to find a target, he called, "How far to the next water stop?"

"Too far," the man said. "We got to water and fuel here or we don't make it."

"We'll make it," Smoke told him, pulling out his second .44 and jacking back the hammer.

One outlaw tried to run from the darkness to the locomotive. Either the engineer or the fireman shot him dead.

"How far is this payroll going?" Smoke asked, crouching down.

"All the way to the end of the line, up in Montana."

He knew the end of the line, at that time, was near Gold Creek. They would change trains before then. Smoke plugged a running outlaw and knocked him sprawling; but it wasn't a killing shot. The man jumped up and limped off. "Why in the hell doesn't the railroad put guards on these payroll shipments?"

"Beats me, Smoke. But I'm damn sure glad you decided to ride my train for this trip."

The pounding of horses' hooves punctuated the night. The outlaws had decided to give it up.

"Let's see what we got," Smoke said, shoving out empties and reloading as he walked over to the man he'd knocked off the water tower.

The man was dead. He'd landed on his head and broken his neck. He walked over to the man the engineer had shot. He was also dead. The third man Smoke had dropped was gut-shot and in bad shape, the slug blowing out his left side, taking part of the kidney with it. He looked up at Smoke.

"You played hell, mister. What's your name? I'd like to know who done me in."

"Smoke Jensen."

The man cussed. "Val sure picked the wrong train this time."

"Val Singer?" Smoke asked.

"Yeah. You know him?"

"I know him. Me and him . . ." Smoke broke it off as he looked down at the man. He was dead, his eyes wide open, staring at the cloudy sky. He looked over at the brakeman. "I winged another. Let's see if we can find him."

But he was gone. Smoke tracked a blood trail to where the outlaws had tied their horses. "He made the saddle. But as bad as he's bleeding, he won't last long. I must have hit the big vein in his leg."

The fireman walked up, his face all dark with soot. "Lem, you wanna toss them bodies in the baggage car and keep on haulin'?"

"I ain't having that crud in with me," the guard to the gold shipment said, walking up. He had not taken part in the fight because in case of an attempted robbery, he was under orders not to open the doors to anyone. "Toss 'em in with the wood and tote 'em that way."

Smoke shrugged his shoulders and helped wrap the men in blankets and carry them to the wood car. Back in his seat, Sally asked, "You suppose we'll have any more trouble?"

Smoke pulled his hat brim down over his eyes and settled down for a nap. "Not from that bunch," he said.

They changed trains in southern Idaho, staying with the Union Pacific line. This run would head straight north. End of track would put them about a hundred and fifty miles south of their destination.

The news had spread up and down the line that Smoke Jensen was on the train, and crowds gathered at every stop, hoping to get a glimpse of the West's most famous gunfighter. Smoke stayed in the car while the train was in station. He had never sought publicity and didn't want it now.

No more attempts were made to rob the train during the long pull north.

At the end of the track, Smoke off-loaded their horses while Sally changed from dress to jeans.

Packhorse loaded, they rode into the small town and purchased a side of bacon and some bread, a gaggle of kids and dogs right at their heels all the way.

"Right pleased to have you in town," the shopkeeper told them. "Sorry you can't stay longer. Things liven up quite a bit when you're around, I'd guess, Mr. Jensen. Be good for business."

"It usually is for the undertaker," Smoke told him, and that shut him up.

Smoke signed his name to a half-dozen penny dreadfuls, then he and Sally hit the trail, pointing their horses' noses north.

A young would-be tough, two guns tied down low, stepped out of the saloon and watched the Jensens ride out of town. He pulled his hat brim low, hitched at his guns, and said, "Huh! He don't look so tough to me. It's a good thing he didn't get in my way. I'd a called him out and left him in the street."

The town marshal looked at the kid, disgust in his eyes, then shoved the punk into a horse trough, guns and all, and walked away, leaving the big-mouth sputtering and cussing.

Smoke and Sally made their first camp alongside a fast-running and very clear and cold little creek. It didn't take either one of them very long to bathe. They knew it was time to exit the creek when they began turning blue.

They were up before dawn. After bacon and bread and coffee, Sally strapped on her short-barreled .44, and then they were in the saddle and heading north.

They were both ready for a hot bath and food they didn't have to cook over a campfire when they topped a ridge and looked down on a little town just south of Flathead Lake.

"Well," Sally said, straightening her back. "It has a hotel."

"Yeah," Smoke said with a grin. "And I'll bet they change the sheets at least once a month."

She smiled sweetly at him. "I'll bet they change them for me."

"Oh, yes, ma'am!" the desk clerk said, paling slightly as he checked the names on the register. "The feather ticks was just aired out and we'll get fresh linen on your bed pronto. You bet we will, Mrs. Jensen."

"And make sure the facilities are clean," Sally told him.

"Oh, yes, ma'am. I sure will."

The room was clean and it faced the street. Smoke laid out clean clothes and shook out and hung up one of Sally's dresses while she bathed. He looked out the window and was not surprised to see a crowd gathering on the boardwalks below their room. Neither was he surprised to see the sheriff and two deputies among the gawking people. The desk clerk had not been slow in running his mouth.

He bathed and shaved while Sally got herself all fixed up, then dressed in a dark suit, white shirt, and string tie. He strapped on his .44's and they went down to the dining room for an early supper.

Smoke got a shot of whiskey from the bar for himself and a glass of wine for Sally, then rejoined his wife in the dining room. The sheriff approached them.

"Mind if I join you for a moment?" the lawman asked respectfully, his hat in his hand.

Smoke pushed out a chair with one boot.

"Coffee, Marie," the sheriff ordered.

"Nice little town, Sheriff," Sally said, taking a sip of wine.

"Thank you, ma'am. And it's peaceful, too."

Smoke knew his cue when he heard it. "It'll stay peaceful, too, Sheriff. We're here to rest for the night and then we'll be moving on."

"Nothin' is peaceful around you for very long, Jensen," the sheriff said. "You attract trouble like honey does flies."

"We don't have any trouble in the town near where I live," Smoke rebutted. "Hasn't been a shot fired in anger in a long, long time."

"How do you manage that?"

"We get rid of the troublemakers, Sheriff. It's really very simple."

"You run them out of town, eh?"

"We usually bury them," Sally said.

The sheriff cut his eyes to her. Strong-willed woman, he reckoned. Man would be hard-pressed to hold the reins on this one, he figured.

He'd of course seen them riding into town, her astride that mare and packing a pistol. Way she carried it, the sheriff figured she knew how to use it. And, more importantly, would use it.

"There's some pretty randy ol' boys in this town, Smoke. Some of them would like to make a reputation. I thought I'd warn you."

"The only way they're going to get to me, Sheriff, is if they come into the lobby of this hotel and call me out while I'm reading the newspaper, come in here while I'm eating and call me out, or try to back-shoot me when I'm pulling out in the morning."

"And if they call you out . . . ?"

"Then I guess the local undertaker is going to get some business, Sheriff."

"The one that'll more than likely try to crowd you is called Chub. He's a bad one, I'll give him that. He's killed a couple of men and wounded a couple more in face-downs. He's quick, Jensen."

"I'll bear that in mind, Sheriff."

The sheriff drank his coffee and eyeballed Smoke. Wrists as big as some men's forearms. And his upper arms; Lord have mercy! The man had muscle on top of muscle. The sheriff had heard of Smoke Jensen for years, but this was the first time he'd ever seen him. And as far as the sheriff was concerned, it was a sight that he'd not soon forget.

The sheriff pushed back his chair and stood up. "See you, Jensen. Ma'am."

"See you around, Sheriff," Smoke told him just as the waitress put their dinner in front of them.

"Smells good," Smoke said.

"Then you'd better enjoy it, mister," a small boy said, walking up to the table. "'Cause Chub Morgan told me to tell you he was gonna kill you just as soon as you got done eatin'."

Chapter 3

Smoke looked at the boy. "You go tell Chub I said to calm down. When I finish eating and have my brandy, I'll step outside to smoke my cigar on the boardwalk. I get testy when people interrupt my dinner."

"Yes, sir."

Smoke gave the boy a coin. "Now get off the streets, boy."

"Yes, sir."

But Smoke knew he wouldn't. The boy would gather up all his friends and they'd find them a spot to watch. A shooting wasn't nearly the social event a good hanging was, but it would do. Things just got boring in small western towns. Folks had been known to pack lunches and dinners and drive or ride a hundred miles for a good hanging. And a double hanging was even better.

"Who is Chub Morgan, honey?" Sally asked.

"I have no idea, Sally. But I'll tell you what he's going to be as soon as I finish my food."

She looked at him. "What?"

"Dead."

Smoke had his coffee and a glass of brandy, then bought a cigar and stepped outside. Sally took a seat in the lobby and read the local paper.

It was near dusk and the wide street was deserted. All horses had been taken from the hitchrails and dogs had been called home. Smoke lit his cigar and leaned against an awning support.

He had played out this scene many times in his life, and Smoke knew he was not immortal. He'd taken a lot of lead in his life. And he would rather talk his way out of a gunfight than drag iron. But he was realist enough to have learned early that with some men, talking was useless. It just prolonged the inevitable. Smoke also knew—and had argued the belief many times with so-called learned people—that some men were just born bad, with a seed of evil in them.

And there was only one way to deal with those types of people.

Kill them.

Smoke puffed on his cigar and waited.

A cowboy rode into town and reined up at the saloon. He dismounted, looked around him, and spotted Smoke Jensen, all dressed in a black suit with the coat brushed back, exposing those deadly .44's.

The cowboy put it all together in a hurry and swung back into the saddle, riding down to the stable. He wanted his horse to be out of the line of fire.

After stabling his horse, the cowboy ran up the alley to the rear of the saloon and slipped inside. Everybody in the place, including the barkeep, was lined up by the windows.

"What's goin' on?" the cowboy called.

"Chub Morgan's made his brags about killin' Smoke Jensen for years. He's about to get his chance. That there's Smoke Jensen over yonder in the black suit."

The cowboy pulled his own beer and walked to the window. "You don't say? Damn, but he's a big one, ain't he? What's he doin' in this hick town?"

"Him and his wife rode in a couple hours ago. She's a pretty little thing. Right elegant once she got out of them men's britches and put on a proper dress. Packs a .44 like she knows how to use it."

"Jensen doesn't seem too worried about facin' Chub," the cowboy remarked.

"Jensen's faced hundreds of men in his time," an old rummy said. "He's probably thinkin' more about what he's gonna have for breakfast in the mornin' than worried about a two-bit punk like Chub."

"Chub's quick," the cowboy said. "You got to give him that. But he's a fool to face Jensen."

"Yonder's Chub," the barkeep said.

Smoke, still leaning against the post, cut his eyes as a man began the walk down the street. As the man drew nearer, Smoke straightened up. He held his cigar in his left hand, the thumb of his right hand hooked under his belt buckle.

"He's gonna use that left hand .44," the cowboy said. "Folks say he's wicked with either gun."

"Reckon where his wife is?"

"Foster from the store said she was sitting in the lobby, readin' the newspaper," the barkeep said.

"My, my," the cowboy said. "Would you look at Chub. He's done went home and changed into his fancy duds."

Smoke noticed the fancy clothes the punk was wearing. He'd blacked his boots and shined his spurs. Big rowels on them; looked like California spurs. His britches had been recently pressed. Chub's shirt was a bright red; looked like satin. Had him a purple bandana tied around his neck. Even his hat was new, with a silver band.

Smoke waited. He knew where Sally was sitting; he'd told her where to sit, with a solid wood second-floor support to her back to stop any stray bullet. Not that Smoke expected any stray bullets from Chub's gun. He doubted that Chub would even clear leather. But one never really knew for sure.

Smoke watched the man approach him and, for another of the countless times, wondered why a man would risk his life for the dubious reputation of a gunfighter.

"Jensen!" Chub called.

"Right here," Smoke said calmly.

"Your wife's a real looker," Chub said, a nasty edge to the words. "After I kill you, I'll take her."

Smoke laughed at the man. Chub's face grew red at the laughter. He cursed Smoke.

Smoke was suddenly tired of it. He wanted a good night's sleep, lying next to Sally. He hadn't ridden into town looking for trouble, and he resented trouble being pushed upon him. He was just damned tired of it.

"Make your play, punk!" Smoke called.

Chub's hands hovered over his pearl-handled guns. "Draw, Jensen!" he shouted.

"I don't draw on fools," Smoke told him. "You called me out, Chub, remember? Now, if you don't have the stomach for it, turn around and go on back home. I'd rather you did that."

"Then you a coward!"

Smoke waited, his eyes unblinking.

"You a coward, damn you!" Chub hollered. "Draw, damnit, draw!"

Smoke's cold, unwavering eyes bored into the man's gaze.

"How's it feel to be about to die?" Chub called, trying to steel himself for the draw.

"I wouldn't know, Chub," Smoke's voice was calm. "Why don't you ask yourself that question?"

The sheriff and his two deputies watched from the small office and jail.

"Now!" Chub yelled, and his hands closed around the butts of his guns.

Smoke drew, cocked, and fired with one fluid motion. A draw so fast that it was only a blur. Blink, and you missed it.

The .44 slug took Chub in the center of the chest, knocking him off his boots and down to his knees in the dusty street. His hands were still on the butts of his guns. The guns were still in leather.

"Good God!" the cowboy said. "I never even seen him draw."

The sheriff and his deputies stepped out of the office just as the boardwalks on both sides of the street filled with people.

Smoke stepped off the porch and walked to the dying Chub. He held a cocked .44 in his right hand.

Sally had risen from her seat to stand at the window, watching her man.

Chub raised his head. Blood had gathered on his lips. His eyes were full of anguish. "I . . . never even seen you draw," he managed to gasp.

"That's the way it goes, Chub," Smoke told him just as the lawman reached the bloody scene.

Chub tried to pull a pistol from leather. The sheriff reached down and blocked the move.

"Bastard!" Chub said. It was unclear whom he was cursing, Smoke or the sheriff.

A local minister ran up. "Are you saved, Chub?"

"Hell with you!" Chub said, then toppled over on his side. He closed his eyes and died.

The sheriff looked at Smoke. "Now what?"

Smoke shrugged his shoulders as he punched out the empty and reloaded. "Bury him."

Smoke and Sally rode out before dawn. The hotel's dining room had not even opened. They would stop along the way and make breakfast.

"Why do they do it, Smoke?" Sally broke the silence of the gray-lifting morning.

Smoke knew what she meant. "I've never understood it, Sally. Men like Chub must be very unhappy men. And very shallow men. Let's get off the trail and follow this creek for a ways," he changed the subject. "See where it goes."

The creek wound around and led them to the Swan River. There they stopped and cooked breakfast. "Fellow back at the hotel said the Swan would lead us right to Hell's Creek. We may as well stay with the river. There are two more little towns between here and Hell's Creek. He said it was right at a hundred miles."

"You've been in this country before?"

"Not right here. It's all new to me. But you can bet the news of the failed train robbery has reached Huggins by now."

"You think any of those men recognized you?"

"I doubt it. But the news of our heading north reached Huggins the day after we boarded the train in Denver. But I doubt he knows we're heading for Hell's Creek."

"I'm sorry I pushed this on you, Smoke."

"You didn't push anything on me, Sally. You want to visit an old friend who's in trouble. That's your right. And anybody who tries to prevent you from doing that is wrong. If they try to stop you, they'll answer to me. It's as simple as that."

She leaned over and kissed him on the cheek. "Everything will always be black and white to you, won't it, honey? No gray in the middle."

"I know what's right, and I know what's wrong. Lawyers want to make it complicated when it isn't. We'll see your friend and her husband and help them work out their problems."

"Legally?"

Smoke munched on a piece of crisp bacon. "Depends on whether you interpret legal by using common sense or what a lawyer would think, I reckon."

Smoke and Sally followed the river north. Two days later they crossed the river and rode into a small village located on the east side of the Swan. There was no hotel in the village but there was a lady who took in boarders. Smoke and Sally got them a room and cleaned up.

The town marshal was waiting on the front porch of the boarding house when Smoke stepped out for some fresh air while supper was being cooked.

"Mr. Jensen," the marshal said respectfully.

"Afternoon," Smoke replied, then waited.

"I got to ask," the marshal finally said. "You in town trouble-huntin'?"

"No. You can relax. I don't hunt trouble. Me and my wife are just passing through."

The marshal sighed. "That's a relief. I thought maybe you was on the prod for Jake Lewis."

"Who is Jake Lewis?"

The marshal looked startled. "One of the men who survived that shoot-out you had some years ago. Over to that minin' camp on the Uncompahgre."

It was Smoke's turn to look startled. "I didn't know there were any survivors."

"Only one that I know of. Jake Lewis. And you shot him all to hell and gone. There was fifteen men in that camp. You killed fourteen of them. Jake lived. He hid in a privy 'til you rode out."

"It's news to me, Marshal. I know he wasn't one of the men who raped and killed my wife and killed our baby. I know that for a fact."

"No, sir. He sure wasn't. He joined up with Canning and Felter later. Jake's brother was known as Lefty. You killed him in the shoot-out."

"I have no quarrel with Jake, Marshal. You can tell him that."

"Why don't you tell him, Mr. Jensen? It would sure set his mind to ease."

"Where is he?"

"Down at the saloon."

Smoke stared hard at the marshal, wondering if he were being set up.

The marshal picked his thoughts out of the air. "I run a clean town, Mr. Jensen. I don't take no payoffs from nobody and never will. This ain't no setup. But I got to warn you that Jake is armed, and he ain't drinkin'."

"What you're telling me is that you don't know what he might do, right?"

The marshal exhaled slowly. "That's about it, Mr. Jensen. He may throw down on you. I just don't know."

"But you want it settled one way or the other?"

"Yes. Jake's been livin' with this for a long time. Lately, it's been eatin' at him. When he heard you was on the rails, comin' north, he about went out of his mind with worry."

"Does he know Big Max Huggins?"

"I got to tell you that he does. He spends some time up in Hell's Creek."

"So he hasn't changed his ways much, right?"

"He ain't never caused no trouble around here. You know how it is, Mr. Jensen. I ain't got no warrants on him."

The marshal's authority ended at the edge of town.

Sally had stepped out on the porch to listen. Smoke turned and met her eyes. "Be careful," she said. "I'll save a plate for you."

Smoke nodded and slipped the hammer thongs from his .44's. He stepped off the porch and looked at the marshal. "You walk with me. If this is a setup, I'll take you out first."

"That's fair. If this is a trap, it ain't one of my doin'."

Smoke believed him, and he told him so as they walked up the street to the village's only saloon.

"Does Big Max ever get down this far south?"

"Not no more," the marshal said. "I killed one of his men several years ago and got lead in another one. I ain't the fastest man around with a gun, but I shoot straight."

"That's the most important thing. His men stay out of your town?"

"That's it. I allow any man one mistake. He leaves after the second one. Or he stays forever."

Smoke smiled, finding that he liked this blunt-talking marshal.

They stepped up onto the short boardwalk, walking past a dress shop, a gunsmith, and a large general store. The marshal pushed open the batwings and Smoke stepped into the saloon right behind him.

Jake Lewis stood alone at the bar. The other customers had taken tables. Smoke stared at the man, trying to place him. But the shoot-out at the old silver camp was years behind him, and he could not remember Jake Lewis.

Jake had brushed back his coat, exposing a pistol, the holster tied down. Smoke was curious about that. If the man wanted no trouble, why get set for it? Smoke concluded that Jake was wearing a hide-out gun. Maybe a sleeve gun. Shake his arm and the gun falls into his hand.

Smoke walked to the bar and ordered a beer. Jake turned mean little eyes on him. Jake was no lightweight. He'd hit a good two hundred pounds and looked to be in good shape. About forty years old, Smoke figured.

"You lookin' for me, Jensen?" Jake broke the silence.

"Nope."

"Just happened to ride into town and take a room, hey?"

"That's right."

"I wish I could believe that."

"Believe it. I got no quarrel with you, Jake."

"I wish I could believe that, too."

"You can. The silver camp was long ago. You weren't part of the bunch who killed Nicole and the baby. They're all dead. I know that for a fact."

"I damn near died, Jensen."

"That was your problem. You should have picked better company to run with."

"You sayin' my brother was no good?"

"You walk through a barnyard, you're going to get crap on your boots."

Someone in the seated crowd laughed at that.

Jake's face flushed. "Lefty was a good man."

"He wasn't good enough," Smoke told him.

Jake ordered a drink and sipped at the bourbon. He set the shot glass down and said, "I'm glad you showed up. We can settle this thing once and for all."

"There is nothing to settle, Jake. Nothing at all."

"I think there is. I sure do think that."

"I'm sorry to hear it."

Jake took another small sip of whiskey. "Momma took Lefty's dyin' pretty hard."

"I'm sorry for your mother. Not for Lefty. You keep walking around something, Jake. Get to it. I've got supper waiting at the boarding house."

"Don't crowd me, Jensen."

Smoke chuckled and Jake gave him a queer look. "I came in here to tell you that I wasn't trouble-hunting, and instead of being happy about it, you want to give me a bunch of lip. That shooting in the silver camp was ten years ago, Jake. I wouldn't have known you if you walked in my front door wearing pink tights and totin' a rose between your teeth."

All the men in the room had them a laugh at that. Jake's face tightened and flushed deeper.

"Big Max is waitin' for you up at Hell's Creek, Jensen," he said, grinding his teeth together in anger.

"Yeah? It figures that trash like you would end up rubbing elbows with trash like Huggins."

The crowd fell silent.

Jake slowly turned to face Smoke. "You know what I think, Jensen?"

"I'm not even sure you're capable of thinking, Jake. I think you're about as smart as a rock."

Jake curled one big hand around his glass and downed his whiskey. "You're a big man with them guns on, Jensen. What are you with them off? Can you bare-knuckle fight, gunfighter? Or do you have to let them .44's do your talkin' for you?"

"There's sure one way to find out, Jake. Providing you have the stomach for it." Smoke walked toward the man, stopping well within swinging distance.

"We take off our guns together?" Jake asked.

"Just as soon as you get rid of that hide-out pistol you're packing."

Jake grunted and nodded his head. "It's in my sleeve."

"I know it."

Jake shook his arm and the derringer fell out onto the bar. Together, they took off their gunbelts. They faced each other.

"I'm gonna stomp your face in, pretty-boy," Jake bragged.

"I doubt it," Smoke told him, pulling on a pair of leather gloves to protect his hands and to hit harder. He knocked the man down with a quick, hard right.

Smoke stepped back, took a sip of his beer, and said, "You going to lay on the floor all evening, Jake? Come on, hurry up. I have supper waiting for me."

With a roar of rage, Jake jumped to his boots and charged.

Chapter 4

Jake swung a big fist and Smoke ducked it, at the same time driving his right fist into Jake's gut and stopping him with the blow. Jake backed up and caught his wind.

With a curse, Jake came at Smoke, swinging both fists. Jake was a brawler, Smoke knew then, relying mostly on brute strength with little finesse about him. But he could be dangerous, Smoke reminded himself, if he landed one of those powerful fists.

Smoke danced back, forcing the big man to come after him, using up his wind swinging wildly and cussing.

Smoke saw a chance and took it, popping Jake smack in the mouth with a combination left and right. The blows brought blood and one tooth was knocked out, to roll and bounce on the sawdust floor.

With a howl of rage, Jake charged, both fists flailing, the blows catching Smoke on his arms and shoulders and doing no damage. Smoke back-heeled Jake and sent the man tumbling to the floor. He could have ended the fight right then, by kicking Jake in the mouth. But Smoke stepped back. He felt no anger toward Jake; but, then, he didn't especially feel sorry for him, either. He proved that by knocking Jake down just as soon as the man got to his boots.

It was another combination, both blows connecting to the jaw of Jake Lewis this time and knocking him back against the bar. Jake grabbed a bottle of whiskey and hurled it at Smoke. Smoke grabbed the bottle, popped the cork and, with a grin at Jake, took him a sip.

"You son of a . . ." Jake choked back the obscenity. He leaned against the bar, catching his breath.

"You want to quit, Jake?" Smoke asked. "You say so, and we'll have a drink together and call the fight over, with no hard feelings."

"Take him up on it, Jake!" the marshal said. "The man's bein' more than fair."

"You stay out of this," Jake yelled at the marshal. He looked at Smoke. "To hell with you, Jensen!"

Smoke shrugged his shoulders. "Whatever you say, Jake." Then he threw the bottle of whiskey at Jake, the bottle striking the man in the face and busting, spewing whiskey all over Jake and momentarily blinding him.

Smoke stepped up to him and began hitting Jake in the face, his big work-hardened fists like huge hammers as they pounded the man again and again. Jake's nose was broken, one eye closing, his lips smashed to pulp, and his jaw swelling. Smoke pounded the man with more than a dozen blows, then stepped back.

Jake wiped the blood and whiskey out of his eyes and reached down, pulling up his pants leg and jerking a knife out of his boot. "Now, Jensen, you get your guts spread all over the room."

The marshal jerked iron and jacked back the hammer.

300　　　　　　*William W. Johnstone*

"Drop the knife, Jake," he warned. "This is a fair fight and it's one that you wanted. You either drop the knife, or I'll kill you."

With a disgusted snarl, Jake tossed the knife to one side.

"Now you made me mad, Jake," Smoke told him. "Now you get what you've probably had coming to you for a long time." Smoke walked toward the man, his big hands clenched.

Jake lifted his fists and decided to use what boxing skills he had. He swung a roundhouse blow at Smoke, which would have knocked Jensen to the floor had it connected. Smoke grabbed the wrist with both hands, turned to one side, and Jake found himself flying through the air. He crashed through a front window and bounced off the board-walk.

Smoke stepped out the batwings and was all over Jake.

Smoke hit the man twice in the belly, doubling him over. He grabbed Jake behind the head and brought his face down and his knee up. The knee connected squarely, and what was left of Jake's nose was now spread all over his face.

Smoke backhanded Jake, knocking him off the board-walk and into the horse-crap by the hitchrail. One startled horse kicked Jake in the butt and sent him rolling and squalling into the middle of the street.

Smoke didn't let up. He had given the man a chance to not fight at all. Jake turned it down. Then Jake had shown his true colors by pulling a knife. To hell with him!

Jake staggered to his feet and feebly raised his fists. Smoke looked at the beaten man with blood dripping from his face and lowered his fists. He turned his back to Jake Lewis and walked back into the saloon. Jake sank to his knees in the street and tried to get up. He could not.

"Couple of you boys go out there and toss him into a horse trough," the marshal ordered. "Then I'll tell him to get the hell gone from town and don't come back." He looked at

Smoke. "You'll have to kill that man someday, Jensen. You know that, don't you?"

"I hope not," Smoke said, then ordered a mug of cool beer.

"You will," the marshal stated flatly. "You humiliated him, and men like Jake can't live with that. It eats on them like a cancer."

Smoke drank half his beer. "He'll have to come looking for me if he wants a killing. As far as I'm concerned, it's over."

Smoke drained his mug and walked back to the boarding house. He needed a hot bath.

The man and wife rode out of town before dawn the next morning and made camp at noon. Sally heated water for Smoke to soak his hands in to keep down the swelling.

They stayed in camp for two days, relaxing, fishing, and behaving like a couple of kids. They walked through the woods, went skinny-dipping in a creek, and loved every minute of it. The swelling went down in Smoke's hands, and they packed up and pulled out, heading north toward Hell's Creek, following the Swan.

Two days later they rode into a small town at the south end of a lake. They were a couple of hours' ride away from Hell's Creek. Their welcome in the town was slightly less than cordial. When they tried to check into the small hotel, they were told all the rooms were taken.

"Is there a boarding house?" Sally asked.

"It's full, too," the desk clerk at the hotel told them.

"Must be a convention in town," Smoke said dryly, looking around him at the deserted hotel lobby. "Sure are a lot of people stirring about."

Sally tugged at his sleeve. "Let's go, honey. We can camp outside of town."

"You don't know how the game is played, Sally," Smoke told her. "The word's gone out on us from Big Max. These people here are scared to death of him. I've seen a few western towns buffaloed before, but this one takes the prize for being full of cowards."

The desk clerk refused to meet Smoke's eyes.

Smoke spun the register book around and inspected it. The hotel was nearly empty.

Smoke dipped the pen and signed them in. He tossed money on the counter. "That's for your best room. Give me the damn key," he told the clerk.

The clerk hesitated, then with a slow exhalation of breath, he handed Smoke the room key.

"Thanks," Smoke told him. "Would you recommend the food in the dining room?"

"Yes, sir," the clerk said wearily. "I would. Dinner is served from five to eight."

"Thank you. You're a nice fellow."

Five minutes after checking in and finding their room, a knock came at the door. Two mean-eyed and unshaven men, both wearing deputy sheriff's badges, stood in the hall.

"You don't come into this town throwin' your weight around, Jensen," one told him. "You're goin' to jail."

"On what charge?"

"We'll think of something," the second deputy said. "And we'll see that your woman is taken care of, too."

Smoke hit him with a sneaky left. The blow snapped the man's head back and knocked him against the hall wall. Smoke backhanded the other deputy, spun, and knocked the second man down with a hard right to the mouth. He grabbed the stunned deputy he'd just slapped by the nape of the neck and the seat of his pants, propelled him down the hall, and threw him out the second-story window. The man landed on the awning, bounced once, and then rolled off, to land on the dusty street. He did not move. One leg was bent under him, broken.

Smoke ran back up the hall, jerked up the stunned and clearly frightened other so-called deputy sheriff, and gave him his exit-papers the same way. Smoke hurled him out the window, using all his strength, which was considerable. The man fell screaming, missing the awning and landing in the street on his belly, one arm bent under him. The sound of the arm breaking was nearly as loud as a pistol shot. Like his buddy, he did not move.

A crowd began gathering, looking at the two so-called lawmen and stealing glances up at Smoke, who was standing in the hall and glaring out the broken window.

"We do not wish to be disturbed," Smoke called down to the crowd. "I'll kill the next man who bothers us." He turned and walked back to the room. He smiled at Sally. "That's how you play the game, honey," he told her.

"My, my," she said with a grin. "The things I'm learning on this trip."

"Your education is just starting. It'll really get interesting in Hell's Creek. I'll order up some hot water and you can take your bath. You tell me which one, and I'll shake out and hang up your dress."

Smoke loaded up the usually empty cylinder he kept under the hammer and walked downstairs to the clerk. The lobby was filled with people.

"Send a boy upstairs with hot water," he told the room clerk. "Lots of it. My wife wishes to bathe. And she damn well better be left alone while she's doing it."

"Y . . . y . . . yes, sir," the clerk stammered.

"Who was that trash I threw out the window?"

"Big Max Huggins men," a portly man said, stepping up.

"Duly appointed deputies. By me. I'm Judge Garrison. And you're in a lot of trouble here, young man. We don't like ruffians coming into our town stirring up trouble."

Smoke slapped him. The blow knocked the man back, one side of his face reddening and blood leaking out of one corner of his mouth. The judge stumbled on a couch and fell down, landing heavily on his butt.

"So Max bought you, too, huh?" Smoke said, looking down at the scared judge, the sarcasm thick in the words. "Looks like he's got the whole damn town in his pocket."

"Not all of us," another man spoke up.

"You sure could have fooled me."

"You've brought us a lot of trouble, Mr. Jensen," another man said. "Come the morning, Big Max will be riding in here to settle up. Not just with you, but with all of us."

"Poor scared little sheep," Smoke said, looking at the knot of men. "Do you have to ask Big Max's permission to go to the bathroom?"

"Smoke," the citizen who first spoke said, "Max has got a hundred men up yonder in Hell's Creek. They's maybe thirty-five of us in town who'd stand up to them. Them ain't very good odds."

"Thirty-six," Smoke told him. "Thirty-seven counting my wife. And she's got more guts than any of you have shown me. How'd all this buffaloing come about?"

"Huggins killed our marshal and put in his own law," the citizen said. "Then he burned out or beat up anyone who tried to stand up to him. We used to have a paper here in town. The editor was killed. The minister over to the church was taken out one night and horsewhipped and tarred and feathered. Two of our women was molested by Max's men. A few of us stayed; most left."

"We're not cowards, Mr. Jensen," yet another citizen said. "We've all fought Indians and outlaws and scum. But

Max has threatened our children. He ain't never come right out and done it plain. But we all got the message."

"How do you mean?"

"My little girl come home with a sack of candy. Told her ma and me that a man give it to her. Said that next, if I didn't stop bad-mouthin' Max, they might take a little walk in the woods. We got the message."

Smoke said, "You all wait right here. I got an idea." He went back upstairs and peeked in the bathroom. Sally was up to her neck in suds. "Now there is a nice sight."

She made a face at him.

"You reckon Robert and Victoria have made it known that we're coming to see them?"

"Absolutely not. I told them not to say a word about it, and they won't."

"How about the letters you've sent them? The people at the post office will be on Max's payroll."

"They were sent to Kalispell. Robert goes there once a week to see patients."

Smoke winked at her. "Good girl."

"What's up, Smoke? I know that look in your eyes."

"We're going to stay here for a time. I got an idea."

"Suits me."

Smoke shut the door and let her finish her bath. He walked downstairs. He pointed to the judge, who was sitting on a couch, holding a wet cloth to his face. "Get up," he told him. The judge got up.

"One of you men go to the marshal's office and get me a marshal's badge."

Grinning, a man ran out the door and jogged across the street. The two deputies were still lying in the street, moaning and calling out for help.

Smoke faced the judge. "Are you a real judge? Commissioned by this territory?"

"I certainly am! And I'm going to swear out a warrant for your arrest . . . you hooligan!"

Smoke popped him again, staggering the man, rocking him back on his feet. This time the judge was really scared and his expression showed it.

"Oh, you're going to be issuing arrest warrants, Garrison," Smoke told him. "But probably for the first time in a long time, they're going to be legal warrants." He turned to a man. "Go outside and get me one of those deputy sheriff's badges from that crud in the street."

"Yes, sir!" the citizen said, not able to hide his grin.

The judge began to put it all together then, and his face became shiny with fear-sweat. "You won't get away with this, Jensen," he said.

Smoke smiled at him. "You wanna bet?"

"He did what?" Big Max Huggins yelled, rising from his chair behind the desk.

"He's the marshal down at Barlow," the gunhand repeated. "And it was all done legal. Judge Garrison signed the order creating a special election and the citizens voted him in. And that ain't all. The judge also swore him in as a deputy sheriff. That was done after Jensen whupped the hell out of Bridy and Long. Tossed 'em both out of a second story winder at the hotel. Bridy's got a busted leg and Long's right arm is broken. That's in addition to a bunch of bruises and cuts. They stove up for a long time."

Big Max Huggins nodded his big head, sat back down, and pondered these new events. Big Max did not get his name from the size of his feet, although they were large. He was large. Six six and two hundred eighty pounds. A handsome man, Max was also vain about his looks. He dressed carefully and neatly and never missed a day shaving. He was intelligent with a criminal's cunning. He was also a very cruel man.

And right now, he was a puzzled man. "What does Jensen want?" he mused aloud.

The gunhand who had brought him the news stood in silence and shook his head.

"Jensen's got him a big fine ranch down in Colorado. He married into old New England money; his wife's as rich as a king. Or queen," he added. "Supposed to be a real looker, too. The way I hear it, the only time Jensen leaves the ranch is when he takes a notion to stick his nose into someone else's business. He ruined Dooley Hanks a couple of years back. Just like he did Jud Vale last year. Right here in this territory. Now he's ten miles away and packin' a badge. That means he's come after me. But why?"

The gunhand knew that no reply was expected. He stood quiet.

Max leaned back in his chair. "Somebody sent for him," he finally said. "But who? Had to be somebody down in Barlow."

Max stood up and reached for his guns. "Get the boys. We're riding."

The gunhand grinned. "Down to Barlow, Boss?"

"Where else? I'm going to settle Smoke Jensen's hash once and for all."

Chapter 5

Big Max rode into Barlow at the head of a small army. He had fifty men behind him, all heavily armed. They kicked up enough dust riding into town to put a thin cover of dirt on every storefront.

Max dismounted and walked to the boardwalk in front of the marshal's office. He turned to face his men, and the instant his back was to the office, he felt the twin barrels of a sawed-off shotgun pressing into his back.

"Move, and I'll scatter your guts all over the street, Huggins," the voice told him.

Max froze. He knew what an express gun could do. A sawed-off shotgun could literally blow a man in two. "I'm froze," he told the voice. "You Smoke Jensen?"

"That's me. Now tell your men to drop their guns in the street. Every gun they've got. In the dirt."

"And if I don't?"

The muzzle of the shotgun nudged his back. That was all it took.

Max gave the order.

Men began appearing out of stores, all of them armed with rifles or shotguns, all of them with pistols belted around their waists.

Women came out after them, holding buckets of water and rags.

"What the hell? . . ." Max said.

"Your men created all this dust in town," Smoke told him. "So your men are going to clean it up. They're going to wash all the windows, sweep the boardwalks, and wipe down everything."

"I'll be goddamned if I will!" a gunny said, sitting his saddle.

Smoke stepped to one side and let one barrel of the express gun roar. It belched smoke and flame, and the mouthy gunhand was blown out of the saddle. He landed about ten feet behind his rearing and frightened horse, hitting the dirt in a bloody pile of torn flesh.

Holding the shotgun in his right hand, Smoke palmed one of his .44's and stuck the muzzle to Max's ear. "Give the order," Smoke told him, his voice very cold and deadly.

Max swallowed with an audible gulp. He was a hard man in a hard land and he'd known some salty ol' boys in his time. But none as hard as this man holding a .44 to his head. Smoke Jensen was death walking around.

"You boy's get to cleaning," he told his men. "I'm paying you and you take orders from me. Do it."

"And drag that trash out of the street and bury it," Smoke said. He looked at a citizen who'd introduced himself as Tom Johnson. "You get some boys and gather up their guns, Tom. All of them. And take their rifles from the saddle

boots. Bring them to me at the jail." He lowered and holstered his .44 and jerked Max's guns from leather. "In my
office, Max. Move."

Seated, Max studied Jensen. And he was impressed.
Smoke was about four inches shorter than him and probably
weighed sixty pounds less, but he was a hell of a man, Max
concluded. No doubt about that.

"You won the first little skirmish, Smoke," Max told him.
"But you can't win the war."

Smoke poured them both coffee and sat down behind the
desk. "What war, Max?" he asked innocently. "I did what I
did in this town because I don't like to see citizens bullied,
and I especially don't like to hear about children being
threatened."

Max grunted. "There . . . may have been some incidents
where my men got a little heavy-handed. But as far as I
know, no kids have been harmed."

"But if you continue, Max, they will be. The odds are
tilted that way."

"And you intend to do what about that?" Max challenged
the gunfighter.

"For the good of humanity, I ought to just stop it right
now."

"How?" Max smiled the question.

"By killing you," Smoke said bluntly.

Max studied Smoke Jensen carefully. He concluded that
Smoke meant what he'd just said. He also concluded that if
he was to leave this town alive, he'd better play his cards
close to the vest. Very close.

Max was a cold-blooded killer. But he was an intelligent
one. He knew he was sitting very close to the grave. He also
knew that like himself, Smoke Jensen had been born without
that one tiny cog in his psyche that prevented a man from
killing without remorse. But unlike Max, Smoke Jensen had

landed on the side of the law. He would always defend the underdog, the poor, the right and just causes.

"Are you?" Max asked softly.

"Am I what?"

"Going to kill me?"

"Probably."

Max felt the cold touch of fear grip his heart.

"Someday," Smoke added.

Max struggled with all his might to contain the emotion of relief that flooded him. He was not accustomed to the sensation of fear. It angered him that just by looking at Smoke Jensen such an emotion could be unleashed within him.

Big Max Huggins knew this, too: Smoke Jensen had to die. And soon.

"But for right now?" Max asked.

"I don't know," Smoke admitted. "But I wouldn't press it if I were you."

"I can't buy you off, can I?"

"No."

"Women?"

"I'm married to a beautiful woman. I have never been unfaithful to her and never will be."

"You're everything I am not, is that it?"

Smoke smiled. "Oh, we're somewhat alike, Max. We just took different paths, that's all."

And damned intelligent, too, Max thought. I'm not confronting some ignoramus. "What is it, specifically, that I do that offends you so?"

Smoke laughed softly. He turned his swivel chair and pecked on the window, pointing. "You missed a spot," he told the red-faced gunhand on the boardwalk with a wet rag in his hand. He turned his attention back to Max. "Everything about you, your type, offends me, Max. You're an intelligent man; could have been a success at anything you tried to do. But you chose to be an outlaw. You've probably been a bully and a thief all your life. You like to humiliate people. You like to grind them down under your boot heel. I'm going to play a game with you, Max. You like games?"

"I'm a gambler, you know that."

"But in my game, Max, if you cheat, you die."

Sweat broke out on Max's face. Goddamn this man! He's sitting there as cool as an icehouse and talking about my death. He glanced out the window. The body of Butch had been removed and another gunhand was sprinkling dirt over the blood-soaked spot on the street. He cut his eyes back to Smoke.

"You see, Max, I don't have to work. My ranch practically runs itself. My wife is very rich. And I have a lot of money personally. Do you have any idea how many thousands and thousands of dollars in reward money I've collected over the years just by shooting wanted men?"

Max personally knew of several dozen wanted men who had gone facedown in the dirt under Smoke's guns. And there were probably a hundred more that he didn't know about. "I know you're a wealthy man, Jensen," he said grudgingly. "What kind of game do you have in mind?"

"You're going to be a solid citizen, Max. You're going to run all the trash out of your town, build a new school, a new church, a new town hall, and be a credit to this territory."

"Are you out of your damned mind!" Max almost yelled the question. "If I ran all the scum out of Hell's Creek, there wouldn't be fifty people left."

"That is a fact," Smoke acknowledged.

"You're not going to shoot me now, are you, Jensen?"

"Not unless you push me to it."

"Don't worry, I'm not." The words were bitter on the big

man's tongue. He had never kowtowed to anyone in his life.
Until this moment. And he didn't like it one bit.

"You want to play the game or not, Max?"

"No." Max's courage was returning after standing on the
edge of death. He stood up slowly. "If you shoot me, Jensen,
you're going to have to shoot me in the back. And I don't
think you'll do that. I'm going to walk outside, gunfighter.
I'm going to sit on the bench just outside this office and
smoke me a cigar. I'm not going to bother a soul. When my
men have finished mopping and scrubbing this crappy little
town, we're going to ride out. We won't bother this town
again. I'll give my people orders to stay clear. But if you
ever come to Hell's Creek, I can't guarantee your safety.
Badge or not. That's my deal." He walked out the door and
sat down, pulling a cigar out of a breast pocket of his suit-
coat and lighting up.

Smoke stood up and stepped outside just as Tom Johnson
and several others came walking up, carrying sacks of guns
taken from the outlaws.

"Put the weapons in a cell and lock it," Smoke told them.

When that had been done, Smoke locked the front door to
his office and walked up the boardwalk, leaving Big Max
Huggins sitting quietly and smoking his stogie.

Smoke stopped to inspect the work of Larry Gayle, the
New Mexico gunslinger. Gayle turned mean eyes to him.

"I guess I'll have to kill you before long, Larry," Smoke
told him.

"You'll try." Larry growled the words at him.

Smoke chuckled and walked on a few yards, stopping at
the side of a gunny he didn't know.

"You ain't gonna kill me, Smoke," the man said. "'Cause
just as soon as I get done with this spit-polishin', I'm gone
like the wind."

Smoke patted him on the shoulder. "Good man. Find a job and settle down somewhere. Be a good citizen."

"I ain't promisin' that. But I will get gone from wherever you is."

Smoke walked on. He stopped when he spotted Pete Akins, a gunhand he had met down in Arizona about six months back. "You going to stay on Huggins's payroll, Pete?"

"Yep." Pete put the finishing touches on a windowpane. It was so clean it squeaked under the rag.

"There's going to be a lot of blood spilled before this is over, Pete."

"For shore."

"Sorry to hear you're staying. You've never done me a harm. But if you stay, you're my enemy. I just wanted you to know that, Pete."

"You could pull out, Jensen."

"Not likely. I never leave a job unfinished."

"Me neither. Now get on out of here and leave me alone. I got winders to wash."

Chuckling, Smoke walked on. He didn't really dislike Pete Akins. But that wouldn't prevent him from gunning Pete if push came to shove.

He crossed the wide street and stopped by the side of a young man probably still in his late teens. The boy still had a few pimples on his face.

"You better haul your ashes out of here, boy," Smoke told him. "Straighten up while you've got the time."

"I'll see you in Hell, Jensen," the punk told him.

"You'll be there long before I pass by, son," Smoke replied, and walked on.

He stopped by Ben Webster, who had finished his windows and was sitting on the boardwalk, smoking a cigarette. "You hire your guns, Ben, but I never knew of you working for someone as low as Big Max Huggins."

"He pays good, Smoke. 'Sides, the man who finally drops you can write his own ticket."

"You intend to be that man?"

"Yep."

"Make your will out. Ben. 'Cause when you pull iron on me, I'm gonna kill you."

Ben looked up at him. "That's a risk we take in this business, ain't it, Smoke?"

Smoke stared at the man hard. Ben finally dropped his eyes. "I don't hire my gun, Ben. Not for money."

Ben looked up. "Why then, Smoke? Why do you do it?"

"Because I have a conscience, Ben. And I've got to live with myself."

Ben spat in the street. "I don't have a bit of trouble sleepin' at night. Or in the daytime, for that matter."

"That'll make it easier when you decide to brace me, Ben."

Ben tossed his cigarette into the street and looked away.

Smoke walked on. "Sid," he spoke to Sid Yorke.

"Smoke. I ain't gonna forget this damn winder-washin'."

"Least it got your hands clean, Sid. That's probably the first time they've been clean since your mother stopped takin' a belt to your butt."

"There's always a day of reckonin', Jensen. My day's comin'."

Smoke crossed the street and sat on the bench beside Max. Now that he knew he'd live through this day, Max was beginning to see the humor in some of the toughest men in the territory washing windows and mopping up the boardwalk.

He saw Smoke watching him. "Yes, Jensen, I can see the humor in it. But have you thought about this: You've made some rough boys awfully angry at you. And they're going to be sore about this for a long time."

"They'll either get over it or come hunting me. If they come hunting me, they'll be over it permanently."

Max stared at him. "You're that sure of yourself, aren't you, Jensen?"

"I've put more than a hundred men in their graves, Max. I'm still standing."

"How many men have you killed, Jensen?"

"I honestly don't know. I would be very happy if I never had to kill another human being."

"Then quit."

"I can't."

"Why?"

"Because of people like you."

That stung the big man. His face darkened with color. He took several deep breaths, calming himself. "I never thought of myself as a bad person, Jensen. And that's the God's truth."

"You have any plans to change, Max?"

"No. And that's the truth, too. Why should I? You won't stay around here long. So I pull in my horns for a summer. So what? What have I lost? No, Jensen. Unless you kill me now, right now, in cold blood, I'll survive. Because you're going to have to come to my town to get me. And you won't last two minutes in Hell's Creek."

"You got it all figured out, huh, Max?"

"I believe so, yes."

"It promises to be an interesting summer, Max."

Max threw his smoked-down cigar into the street and rose from the bench. "I hope I don't see you again, Jensen," he said, with his back to Smoke.

"Oh, you will, Max. You will."

Smoke sat on the bench and watched as the sullen bunch of gunfighters rode slowly out of town, being very careful to kick up as little dust as possible. Only Pete Akins raised a hand in farewell.

With a grin on his face, he called, "See you around, Smoke."

"Take it easy, Pete."

The pimply-faced boy whose name Smoke had learned was Brewer, glared hate at him as he rode past.

"You bear in mind what I said, son," Smoke called to him. The young man gave Smoke an obscene gesture.

Bringing up the rear of the procession was a wagon, the two bone-broken deputies lying on hay in the bed, groaning as the wagon lurched along.

Tom Johnson crossed the street, leading a group of men and women, Judge Garrison among them.

"Tom, did you send those wires like I asked?" Smoke said.

"Yes, sir. Folks should start arriving in about a week. What about those people in town loyal to Huggins?"

"Tell them to hit the trail, Tom. You're the newly elected mayor."

"How about me?" Judge Garrison asked.

"You're staying, Judge. You and me, we're going to see to it that justice prevails in this part of the county. Tom has arranged for a man to come in and reopen the newspaper. He's got people coming in that include a schoolteacher, a preacher, and some shopkeepers. Barlow is going to boom again, Judge. Nice and legal."

"Young man," the judge said, sitting down on the edge of the boardwalk, "have you given any thought as to what will happen when you decide to leave?"

"Oh, yes."

They waited, but Smoke did not elaborate.

The judge sighed. "I must admit, it's a good feeling to be

free of Max Huggins." He cut his eyes to Smoke. "For as long as it lasts, that is."

"Trust me, Judge," Smoke told him, putting a finger to the side of his head. "I've got it all worked out up here." He pulled out his watch and clicked it open. "What times does the stage run?"

"It'll be here in about an hour," Tom told him.

"It turns around at Hell's Creek?"

"That's right."

Smoke smiled. "Well, then, I'll just make plans to meet the stage. Right now, I have to see about finding a deputy."

"That's not going to be easy, Smoke," the judge said. "I don't know of a single person who is qualified. Most of the ranches in this part of the county have only the hands they absolutely need to get by. There's about a dozen farmers in this area. Good people, but not gunslingers."

"Who is that prisoner in the jail? What's he being held for?"

The judge rolled his eyes. "His name is Dagonne. Jim Dagonne. He's not a bad sort; matter of fact, he's rather a likable fellow. He just likes to fight. The problem is, he never can win one. He's a good cowboy. Works hard. But when he starts drinking, he picks fights. And he always loses."

Smoke nodded his head, a smile on his face. "All right, folks, let's get to work. We've got a lot to do."

Chapter 6

Smoke unlocked the cell door and dragged the sleeping Jim Dagonne out of the bunk. He looked to be in his mid-twenties and in good shape, although not a big man.

"What the hell!" Dagonne hollered as Smoke dragged him across the floor and out the back door.

"Shut up, Jim," Smoke told him. He shoved him in a tub of cold water and tossed him a bar of soap. "Strip and scrub pink. I'll have your clothes washed and dried. Then we'll talk."

"Who the hell are you?" Jim hollered. "You let me out of this tub and I'll whup you all over this backyard."

"Smoke Jensen."

Jim sank into the tub and covered his head with water.

Twenty minutes later, sober and clean, wrapped in a blanket, Jim Dagonne sat in front of Smoke's desk and waited. He did not have a clue as to what Smoke wanted of him.

Smoke stared at the young man. Maybe five feet seven.

Not much meat on him, but wiry; rawhide tough. Hard to tell what he looked like, with his face all banged up and both eyes swollen nearly closed, but he appeared to be a rather nice-looking young man.

"You don't have a job, Jim," Smoke finally broke the silence. "The judge said you got fired from the Circle W."

"I probably did. Joe got tired of bailing me out of jail, I reckon."

"Joe who?"

"Joe Walsh. Owns the spread."

"Good man?"

"One of the best. Arrow straight. Are you really Smoke Jensen?"

"Yes." Smoke tapped the gunbelt on his desk. "This yours?"

"Yes, sir."

"Can you use it?"

"I'm not real fast, but I don't hardly ever miss."

"That's the most important thing. You wanted anywhere, Jim?"

"No, sir! I ain't never stole nothing in my life."

Smoke reached down on the floor and picked up a bulky package. He tossed it to Jim. "New jeans, shirts, socks, and drawers in there. Go get dressed. You're my new deputy."

Jim stared at him. "I'm a what?"

"My deputy. Your drinking days are over, Jim. You're now a full-fledged member of the temperance league. You take one drink, just one, and I'll stomp your guts into a greasy puddle in the middle of that street out there, and then I'll feed what's left to the hogs. You understand me?"

"Yes, sir!"

"Fine. Get dressed and go down to Judge Garrison's office. He'll swear you in as a deputy sheriff. Then you meet me back here." He looked at the clock. "Right now, I've got to meet a stage."

"Out," Smoke told the passengers before the stage had stopped rocking. Two hurdy-gurdy girls, a tinhorn gambler, one drummer selling corsets and assorted ladies' wear, and Al Martin, a gunfighter from down Utah way, stepped down.

"You stopping here or going on to Hell's Creek?" Smoke asked the drummer.

"Hell's Creek."

"Get back in the stage. The rest of you come with me."

"And if I don't?" the gambler challenged him.

Smoke laid the barrel of a .44 against the man's head, knocking him to the street. He handcuffed him to a hitchrail, then faced Al Martin.

"You got trouble in you, Al?"

"Probably. I know you, but I can't put a name to the face."

"Smoke Jensen."

Al eyeballed Smoke, his eyes flicking from the badge to his face. The hurdy-gurdy girls stood off to one side.

"Get moving," Smoke told the driver.

"Yes, sir. I'm gone!"

He hollered at the fresh team and rattled up the street.

"I'll just have me a drink and wait for the southbound stage," Al said.

"That's fine. Stay out of trouble." He looked at the saloon girls. "You ladies get you a room at the hotel and stay quiet. You're on the next stage south. It rolls through in the morning."

They wanted to protest. But the name Smoke Jensen shut their mouths. They twirled their parasols, picked up their baggage, shook their bustles, and sashayed down the board-walk.

"Off the street, Al," Smoke told the gunfighter.

Al tipped his hat, got his grip, and walked into the saloon.

Smoke dragged the gambler to the jail and tossed him in a cell.

"What's the charge, marshal?" the gambler called.

"Disobeying an officer of the law and littering."

"Littering?"

"You were lying in the street, weren't you?"

"Hell, man. You put me there."

"Tell it to the judge. He'll have court sometime this month."

Smoke stepped outside and rolled one of the few ciga-rettes he smoked a day. He lit up and smiled. It was going to be an interesting summer. He was looking forward to it.

Jim walked up, all decked out in his new clothes and with a shiny badge pinned to his shirt.

"What'd I miss?"

"Not much." Smoke brought him up to date.

"Littering?" Jim laughed. "Now that's a new one on me."

"We'll see what the judge has to say about it."

"Al Martin's a bad one. He's one of Big Max Huggins's boys. He'll try you, Smoke. Bet on that."

"He won't do it but once. Come on. I'll introduce you to my wife and we'll get something to eat."

They were halfway across the street when a dozen men came riding into town from the south, kicking up a lot of dust.

"That's Red Malone and his crew," Jim said. "He likes to ride roughshod over everybody. Owns the Lightning brand. I never worked for him 'cause I don't like him and he don't like me."

Smoke stood in the middle of the street and refused to move, forcing the horsemen to come to a stop.

"Get out of the damn street, idiot!" the lead rider yelled.

"You Malone?" Smoke asked.

"Yeah. If it's any of your business."

"There's a new law on the books, Malone. No galloping horses within the city limits."

Red laughed, and it was an ugly laugh. "I'd like to see the two-bit deputy who's gonna stop me." Then his smile faded. "Hey, you're new here. Didn't your boss tell you that me and the boys are to be left alone?" His face mirrored further confusion when he saw Jim and the badge pinned to his shirt. "What the hell's goin' on around here? You got stomped in a fight a couple of nights ago and got tossed in jail. Where is Bridy and Long?"

"Max come and got them this morning," Jim said with a grin. "They was all stove up after Smoke Jensen here tossed both of 'em out of that window up yonder yesterday." He pointed to the boarded-up window of the hotel.

Red Malone and all his men looked . . . first at the window and then back at Smoke.

"You asked what two-bit deputy was going to stop you, Red?" Smoke said. "You're looking at him."

"Lemme take him, Boss," a scar-faced man said. "I think I'm better than him."

Red Malone did not reply; he was studying Smoke carefully. "Heard about you for years, Jensen. You're supposed to be the fastest gun around. So what are you doing in this hick town?"

"Helping out the people, Malone. They had some bad law enforcement here. They asked me to take over."

"What'd Max have to say about that?"

"Not a whole lot, actually. And his men were too busy

washing windows and mopping up the boardwalk to say very much."

Malone silently chewed on that for a moment, not really sure what Smoke was talking about. For a fact, something big had gone down here in Barlow; something that had drastically changed the town.

And that something big and drastic had a name: Smoke Jensen.

"Come on, Red!" the scar-faced man insisted. "Lemme take him." He stepped out of the saddle, handing the reins to another man.

Malone looked at the man. He wasn't worth a tinker's damn as a cowboy, but he was fast with a gun. Malone nodded his head. "All right, Charlie. It's your show."

Red Malone and his crew lifted their reins and moved to the other side of the street.

"Watch my back, Jim," Smoke said.

"You got it."

"I been hearin' about you for fifteen years or more, Jensen," Charlie said. "I'm sick of hearin' about you. Makes me want to puke."

Red Malone cut his eyes to a rooftop. Tom Johnson stood there, a rifle in his hand. Marbly from the general store stepped out of his establishment, also with a rifle in his hands. Benson from the blacksmith shop appeared to Malone's right, a double-barrel shotgun in his hands. Toby from the hotel appeared on a rooftop, carrying a rifle.

The town was solidly behind Jensen, for sure.

Malone turned to his foreman. "John, we're out of this fight. Look around you. Pass the word."

John Steele looked. More townspeople had stepped out of their businesses and homes, all of them carrying weapons. John softly passed the word: Whatever happens between Jensen and Charlie, we're out of it.

Smoke stood relaxed in the center of the street. He had not taken his eyes off of Charlie.

The scar-faced gunny stood with his legs apart, body tensed for the draw. "You ready to die, Jensen?" he called.

"Not today, friend," Smoke said. "You got anything you want me to pass along after you're gone?"

Charlie cursed him.

"As a legally appointed deputy sheriff of this county, I am ordering you to surrender your guns, Charlie. There will be no charges filed against you if you do that."

Charlie laughed at him.

"You were warned," Smoke said softly.

"Draw!" Charlie yelled, and his right hand dipped down, the fingers closing around the butt of his pistol.

He felt something heavy and hard strike him in the chest. Charlie was on his back in the street, the sun-warmed dirt hot through his shirt. A shadow fell over him. Through the mist that had suddenly covered his eyes, he could see Smoke Jensen standing over him, a pistol in his hand, held by his side, the hammer back.

Charlie fumbled for his gun. He was astonished to find it was still in leather.

"I never seen anybody that fast," John Steele said to his boss. "It was like the wind."

"Yeah," Red reluctantly agreed.

The rest of Malone's bunch, all hardcases in their own right, sat their saddles quietly. They were all brave men, loyal to the brand, and all good with a gun. But they wanted no part of Smoke Jensen. Not face to face, anyway.

"You should have stayed in the bunkhouse today, Charlie," Smoke told the dying man.

"You! . . ." Charlie gasped the word. Then he closed his eyes and died.

Smoke holstered his .44 and walked over to Red Malone.

"No trouble in this town, Malone. No racing your horses and kicking up dust. No discharging of firearms. No foul language outside the saloon. Any of your crew gets drunk, you take them home, or me or Jim will put them in jail and the judge will fine them. Is all that understood?"

Hate leaped out of Red Malone's eyes. No one talked to him like that and got away with it.

He stepped out of the saddle without replying and turned his back to Smoke. A hard hand fell on his shoulder and spun him around, almost jerking him off his boots. Smoke Jensen stood staring at him, eyeball to eyeball.

"I asked you a question, Malone. I expect a reply."

Red noticed that Smoke had slipped on leather gloves. "I'll give you a reply, gunslinger," Red said. "and here it is."

Red swung a big fist. Had it connected, it would have knocked Smoke off his boots.

It didn't connect.

Smoke sidestepped and planted one big fist in Red's belly. The air whooshed out of the man as he stumbled back. Smoke stepped in and popped him on the jaw with a left, following that with a right. Red fell back against a hitchrail. He shook his big head and cussed Smoke.

"Anytime you've had enough, Red," Smoke told him, "you just holler quit and that's it."

"I run this end of the county, Jensen," he said, his lips peeled back in an animal-like snarl.

Smoke answered him with a sneaky left that snapped Red's head back and bloodied his mouth. Smoke stepped back and waited.

A thin middle-aged cowboy sat his saddle and cut his eyes to John Steele. He whispered, "The boss better uncle, Steele. Jensen's givin' him a chance. If he don't, Jensen'll beat him half to death."

"I got twenty dollars that says you're wrong, Sal," John replied.

"You're on."

Red faked with a left and connected against Smoke's jaw with a right. The punch hurt. Smoke stepped back and shook his head. Red pursued him out into the street, grinning through the blood on his mouth.

Smoke ducked a punch and hammered a right over Red's kidney, following that with an uppercut to the man's mouth. Blood leaked from Red's lips.

Red backhanded Smoke in the face and charged, trying to grab him in a bear hug. Smoke danced to one side and hit Red twice in the face with a left and a right.

Red slipped a fist through and busted Smoke on the jaw, but the punch had lost a lot of steam. Smoke hit him with another combination, belly and jaw, then tripped the man, sending him sprawling to the dirt.

Red came up with a fistful of dirt and hurled it at Smoke, trying to momentarily blind the gunfighter. But Smoke had been raised by mountain men, and he knew all the tricks and then some. He ducked under the dust cloud and rammed Red in the belly with his head, both hands around the man's hard waist. Smoke drove him into a hitchrail. The hitchrail broke under the impact and Smoke released the man just in time to see Red fall into a horse trough.

Smoke stood on the outside of the trough and hammered Red's face into a bloody mask. Red lost consciousness and slipped down into the water, bubbling.

Smoke stepped back, found his hat, and put it on just as John Steele and several others were frantically pulling their boss out of the trough before he drowned.

"Drag him over to the jail and dump him in a cell," Smoke ordered.

"I'll be damned if I will!" Steele shouted at Smoke.

Jim walked up and laid his pistol across the back of the foreman's head, and it was Steele's turn to fall into the trough, face first.

"Drag both of them to jail," Smoke ordered. This time, no objections were forthcoming. The Lightning brand crew dragged the boss and the foreman across the street and into the jail, depositing both of them in a cell.

John Steele opened his eyes and glared hate at everybody. Red Malone snored and bubbled on his bunk.

"Gimme my twenty dollars," Sal said.

John dug in his damp pockets and threw a double eagle at the man. "Here's your damn money. And here's something else: You're fired!"

"Suits me," Sal said, slipping the twenty-dollar gold piece into his vest pocket. "I'm tarred of listenin' to your big mouth a-flappin' anyways."

"The next time I see you, Sal, you better be ready to drag iron."

The thin bowlegged cowboy lifted his eyes and stared at the foreman. Smoke knew that look; he had worn it himself, many times: It was the look of a very dangerous and very confident man. Smoke smiled, thinking: I've found another deputy.

"You best think about that, John." Sal's words were softly spoken and ringed with tempered steel. "I've helped bury a lot better men than you."

John spat through the bars and cursed him.

Smoke caught Jim's eyes and tapped the star pinned to his shirt, pointing at Sal. Jim grinned and nodded his head in agreement.

Smoke stepped outside and faced the Lightning crew. "You boys can have your drinks at the saloon, buy your tobacco and needs, or whatever else legal you came to town to do. Make trouble, and you'll either join your bosses in there"—he jerked his thumb toward the jail—"or join Charlie in a pine box. The choice is yours."

"We're peaceful, Smoke," a hand said. "But this here is a friendly warnin' to you, and don't take it the wrong way. When you let Red outta there, he's gonna be on the prod for you. And right or wrong, we ride for the brand."

"That's your choice to make. Now, clear the street and drag Charlie off to the undertaker."

Jim and Sal stepped out onto the boardwalk. Smoke turned to the just-fired puncher and said, "You know anything about deputy sheriffing?"

"I've wore a badge a time or two."

"You want a job?"

"Might as well. Seein' as how I done been fired from cowboyin'."

"I have to warn you: It's going to get real interesting around here."

Sal hitched at his gunbelt. "I 'spect it will. Makes the time pass faster, though."

"Lemme out of here, you son of a bitch!" John Steele hollered.

Chapter 7

"I've had your suit pressed," Sally told him. "We're going to a party tonight."

"Oh?"

"Yes. The ladies of the town are giving us a party. They're all quite taken with you and want to meet you up close."

Smoke rolled his eyes. "I can hardly wait."

Red Malone had woken up and had joined John Steele in bellowing from their cell.

"What are you going to do about that?" Sally asked.

"I can either shoot them, hang them, or cut them loose. What do you suggest?"

"They probably deserve the former. The latter would certainly quiet the town considerably."

"Lay out my suit. I'll go speak with Judge Garrison."

"Oh, let's bond them out," the judge said. "All that

squalling is giving me a headache." He smiled. "We'll set the bond at a hundred dollars apiece."

"A hundred dollars!" John Steele recoiled from the bars and screamed like a wounded puma.

"Relax, John," Malone said. The man's face was horribly bruised, both eyes almost swollen shut, his lips puffy, and his nose looked like a big red beet that an elephant had stepped on. He took a wad of still-damp greenbacks from his pocket and carefully counted out two hundred dollars, passing the money through the bars.

Smoke took it and infuriated the man by counting it again.

"It's all there, you son of a . . ." He choked back the oath and stood gripping the bars, shaking with anger.

"Sure is," Smoke said cheerfully. He unlocked the door and waved the men out. "You boys take it easy now. And come back to Barlow anytime, now, you hear?"

The rancher and his foreman did not reply. They stomped out and slammed the door behind them. Smoke sat at his desk and chuckled.

Smoke suffered through the party given by the good ladies of Barlow. He answered the questions—from both men and women alike—as best he could, and ate fried chicken and potato salad until he felt that if he ate another piece, he'd start clacking and laying eggs.

Walking back to the hotel—they had now been moved to the best room in the place, the Presidential Suite, which included a private water closet—Sally said, "Max Huggins had pretty well beaten these people down, hadn't he, honey?"

"Yes. And that first day in town, I came down hard on

them—probably too hard. It's easy for someone ruthless to cut the heart out of people. It's ridiculously easy. Max is a smart man as well as a ruthless one. He went after the children of the townspeople. That shows me right there how low he is."

"You'll have to kill him, won't you, honey?"

"Me, or somebody. Yes."

Sal walked up, making his rounds, rattling doorknobs and looking up dark alleyways.

"Quiet, Smoke," the small man said. "I figure it'll be that way for three, maybe five days. Until Red gets back on his feet. And then he'll come gunnin' for you."

"I expect he will, Sal. I doubt if the man has ever received so thorough a beating as he got today."

"Smoke, he ain't never even been whipped before this day. And that's the God's truth."

"Walk along with us, Sal. Tell me about him."

"I ain't from this part of the country, Smoke. I was born in Missouri and come west with my parents in '50, I think it was. They settled in Nebraska and I drifted when I was seventeen. Most of my time I spent in Colorado and Idaho. That's how come it was I knowed who you was. I didn't come to this area until last year. I was fixin' to drift come the end of the month anyways. I just don't cotton to men like Red Malone and John Steele. I'll tell you what I know about him and about Max Huggins. I was told that Malone come into this area right after the Civil War. He was just a youngster, maybe nineteen or so. He carved him out a place for his ranch and defended it against Injuns and outlaws. Built it up right good. But he's always been on the shady side. Lie, cheat, steal, womanize. I was told his wife was a decent person. She bore him one son and one daughter, and then she took off when it got so Red was flauntin' his other women in her face. He's got women all over the country."

Smoke stopped them and they sat down on a long bench in front of the barber shop.

Sal pulled out the makings and asked Sally, "You object, ma'am?"

"Oh, no. Go right ahead. I'll take a puff or two off of Smoke's cigarette."

Sal almost dropped the sack at that. He kept any comments he had to himself. Strong-willed woman, he thought. Probably wants the vote, too. Lord help us all.

Sal rolled, shaped, licked, and lit up. "Red's daughter is a right comely lass. But Tessie is spoiled rotten, has the manners of a hog, and the morals of a billy goat. Melvin is crazy. Plumb loco. He likes to hurt people. And he's fast, Smoke. Have mercy, but the boy is quick. And a dead shot. But he's nuts. His eyes will scare you, make you back up. He's killed maybe half-a-dozen men, and they weren't none of them pilgrims, neither. Red's good with a short gun, but Melvin is nearabouts as fast as you, Smoke. And I ain't kiddin'.

"Naturally, just as soon as Big Max come into the area, him and Red struck a deal. Max would own the law enforcement of the county—and it's a sorry bunch—and control the north end of the county, and Red would control the south end. Red didn't have no interest in runnin' this town. He just wanted his share of the crooked games up in Hell's Creek, and his share of the gold and greenbacks taken in robberies. In return, he'd see that no one come in here with reform on their mind. So that means, Smoke, that you got to go. There ain't no other way for Red and Max to keep on doin' what they're doin'.

"Big Max, now, that's another story. Bad through and through. He's run crooked games and killed and robbed folks and run red-light houses from San Francisco to Fort Worth and north into Canada. He's a sorry excuse for a human being. I'd be happy to kill him if for no other reason than to clear the air for other folks."

"I can see why Max settled here," Smoke said.

"Sure. Wild country. One road runnin' north and south, one road runnin' east and west. No trains yet. Proper law ain't reached this part of the territory yet." He smiled, then added, "'Cepting in this little town, that is."

The next morning, Smoke escorted the gambler he'd jailed to the stagecoach office. Jim fetched the hurdy-gurdy girls from the hotel.

"You might eventually get to Hell's Creek," Smoke informed them all. "But it won't be by going through Barlow."

"This ain't legal," the gambler protested.

"Sue me," Smoke said, and shoved the tinhorn into the stage. He looked up at the driver. "Get them out of here."

"Yes, sir!" the driver grinned, and yelled at his team.

Smoke began his walk to the hotel to deal with Al Martin. The gunfighter had sent a boy to tell Smoke he wasn't about to be run out of town.

"How are you gonna deal with this guy?" Sal asked.

"He wants to stay in Barlow," Smoke replied. "So I'm going to let him stay."

"Huh?" Jim looked at Smoke.

"Forever," Smoke said tightly. "If that's the way he wants it."

Al Martin was lounging on the boardwalk in front of the hotel, having an after-breakfast cigar.

"He's quick," Sal told Smoke. "With either hand. I've seen him work."

Smoke had no comment about that.

Al Martin tossed his cigar into the dirt and stepped out into the street.

"You boys get out of the way," Smoke told his deputies. Sal and Jim stepped to one side.

Al brushed back his coat, exposing the butts of his .45's.

"One more chance, Al," Smoke called, never breaking his stride. "You can rent a horse at the livery and ride south."

"I'm headin' north," Al returned the call.

"Not through this town," Smoke told him.

"You don't have the right to do that."

"I'm doing it, Al."

Joe Walsh, the owner of the Circle W, had left his ranch early with two of his men, to buy supplies in Barlow. The men stood in front of Bonnie's Cafe and watched. Joe had heard of Smoke Jensen for years, but he had never seen him until now.

He was very impressed by this first sighting. He'd heard of what had happened to Red, and that amused him. If any man had a beating coming to him, it was Red. And Max Huggins. But Joe wondered if Smoke was hoss enough to take the huge Max Huggins.

"Last chance, Al," Smoke called. "I am ordering you to leave this town immediately."

Smoke stopped about forty feet from Al.

"You know where you can stick that order, Jensen."

"Then make your play, Al," Smoke said calmly.

Al went for his guns. He got both barrels of the .45's halfway out of leather before Smoke drew. Smoke shot him twice, in the belly and the chest, the slugs turning the man around and sitting him down in the street, on his butt.

"Holy Mother of Jesus!" Joe Walsh whispered the words. "He's so quick it was a blur."

His hands shook their heads in awe.

Smoke walked up to Al Martin. The gunfighter looked up at him. "Melvin's quicker, Jensen," he pushed the words past bloody lips. "You'll meet your match with the kid."

"Maybe. But you'll meet your Maker long before that happens."

Al fell over on his side. "Cold," he muttered. "Gimme a decent buryin'," he requested. "One fittin' a human being."

"I would," Smoke told him, his words carrying to both sides of the street, "if you were a decent human being."

"Bastard!" Al cursed him.

"That's a hard man yonder," Joe told his hands. "Probably the hardest man I ever seen."

Al Martin died cursing the name of Smoke Jensen.

Smoke punched out the empty brass and reloaded just as the combination barber/undertaker came walking up.

"What kind of funeral you want him to have, Sheriff?" he asked.

"Whatever his pockets will bear," Smoke told him. "Bring his guns and personal items to the office."

"Them's right nice boots he's wearin'," the man said. "Be a shame to waste that leather."

"Whatever," Smoke said. He walked over to the cafe and stepped up on the boardwalk.

The rancher stuck out his hand. "Joe Walsh," he introduced himself. "I own the Circle W."

Smoke took the hand.

"Good to have some decent law enforcement around here." He looked across the street at Jim Dagonne and grinned. "How'd you get him off the jug?"

"I told him I'd stomp his guts out and feed what was left to the hogs if he ever took another drink."

Joe laughed. "He's a good boy. I would have rehired him in a day or two, but I think he's better off in what you got him doing." He looked at Sal. "That's a good man, too."

"I think so."

"Watch your back when you ride out in the county. Red Malone don't forget or forgive. I'll tell the wife you're in town. You and your missus come out to the ranch anytime for dinner. We'd love the company."

"I'll do it."

Smoke had sized up the rancher and thought him to be a good, hard-working man. And one who would fight if pushed. Probably the reason Red and Max had left him alone. His hands wore their guns like they knew how to use them . . . and would.

Sal walked over. "The undertaker said Al had quite a wad on him. He's gonna hire some wailers and trot out his black shiny wagon for this one. He said the weather bein'as cool as it is, Al can probably stand two days. Ought to be a new preacher in town by that time."

Smoke nodded. "You and Jim watch the town. I'm going to lay in some supplies and take a ride. I'll be gone for a couple of days, getting the lay of the land."

"Watch yourself, Smoke. Red's probably sent the word out for gunhands."

Again, Smoke nodded. "You and Jim start totin' sawed-off shotguns, Sal. Any gunslicks that come in, either move them on or bury them."

"You got it."

"I'll see you in two or three days."

Smoke rode out of the valley and into the high country. The high lonesome, Old Preacher had called it. It pulled at a man, always luring him back to its beauty. The valley was surrounded by high snowcapped peaks, with the lower ridges providing good summer graze for the cattle.

Smoke had checked out the boundaries of the Lightning spread at the surveyor's office, and he carefully avoided Malone's range. Keeping Mt. Evans to his right, Smoke rode toward Hell's Creek. He wasn't concerned about Sally's friends being worried about their not showing up. By now, everyone in the county knew Smoke was in Barlow. He only hoped the doctor and his wife had sense enough to keep their mouths shut about their being friends with Sally.

He rode up to a farmhouse and gave a shout. A man in bib overalls came out of the barn and took a long look at Smoke. Then he went back in and returned carrying a rifle.

"If you be friendly, swing down and have some coffee," the farmer called. "If you've come to make trouble for us, my woman and my two boys have rifles on you from the house."

"I'm the new marshal at Barlow," Smoke called. "The name is Smoke Jensen."

"Lord have mercy!" the farmer said. "Come on in and put your boots under our table. The wife nearabouts got the noonin' ready to dish up."

"I'm obliged."

The fare was simple but well-cooked and plentiful, consisting of hearty stew made with beef and potatoes and carrots and onions, along with huge loaves of fresh-baked bread. Smoke did not have to be told twice to dive in.

Not much was said during the nooning, for in the West, eating was serious business. The farmer told Smoke his name was Brown, his wife was Ellie, and his boys were Ralph and Elias. And that was all he said during the meal.

After the meal, Ellie poured them all coffee and Smoke brought the family up to date on what had taken place in Barlow.

The farmer, his wife, and his sons sat bug-eyed and silent during the telling.

"Lord have mercy!" Brown finally exclaimed. "You whupped Red Malone. I'd give ten dollars to a seen that!"

Smoke imagined that ten dollars was a princely sum to Mr. Brown.

"I stopped going into Barlow because of the hoodlums and the trash, Mr. Jensen," Ellie said. "And I certainly wouldn't be caught dead in Hell's Creek."

"I can understand that, Mrs. Brown," Smoke said. "I surely can."

"I take the wagon and go into town about once every three months," Brown said. "We're pretty well set up here. I got me a mill down on the crick, and we grind our own corn and such. Haul my grain and taters into town come harvest, and we get by."

"You got neighbors?"

"Shore." He pointed out the back. "Right over the field yonder is Gatewood. Just south of him is Morrison. And beyond that is Cooter's place. Just north of me is Bolen and Carson. We done that deliberate when we come out. In twenty minutes of hard ridin', we can have twelve to fifteen guns at anybody's house."

"Smart," Smoke agreed. "Has Max Huggins given any of you any trouble?"

Man and wife cut their eyes to one another. The glance did not escape Smoke.

Ellie sighed and nodded her head.

"Yeah, he has, Mister Smoke," Brown said. "His damned ol' gunhands has ruint more than one garden and killed hogs and chickens. They killed the only milk cow Bolen had, and his baby girl needed that milk. His woman had dried up. The baby died."

Smoke drew one big hand into a huge fist. "Who led the gang that did it?"

"Vic, they called him."

"Vic Young," Smoke put the last name to it. "I know of him. He's poison mean. Rode into a farmyard down in Colorado and shot a girl's puppy dog for no reason. I haven't had any use for him since I heard that story."

"Man who would shoot a girl's puppy is low," Elias said.

"He's got him a widow woman he sees about five miles from here," Brown said softly.

Both boys grinned.

"Does he now?" Smoke said.

"Be fair and tell it all," his wife admonished him gently.

"You're right, mother," Brown said. "I'm not bein' fair to the woman." He looked at Smoke. "Martha Feckles—that's the wider's name—does sewin' for them painted ladies in Hell's Creek. She's a good woman; just got to make a livin' for her and her young'uns, that's all. This trash Vic, he come up to her place one night and—" he paused, "well, took advantage of her."

"He raped her, Mister Smoke," Ralph said.

"Hush your mouth," Ellie warned him.

"No, it's all right, ma," Brown said. "Let the boy tell it. Mister Smoke needs to know, and these young folks know more about it than we do."

"He beat her up bad, Mister Smoke," Ralph said. "Miss Martha, she's got her a daughter who's thirteen—Elias is sweet on her—"

"I am not neither!" Elias turned red.

"Shut up," the father warned him. "You are, too. Ever time you get around her you fall all over your big feet and bleat like a sheep. Tell it, Ralph."

"This Vic, he told Miss Martha that if she didn't go on . . . seein' him, he'd do the same to Aggie."

"I ought to kill him!" Elias said, considerable heat in his voice.

"Hush that kind of talk!" his mother told him. "The man's a gunfighter."

"Listen to your ma," Smoke told the boy, whom he guessed to be about fifteen at the most. "You have a right to defend hearth and home and kith and kin. You leave the gun-fighting to me. Is that understood, boy?"

"Yes, sir."

Smoke rose from the table and found his hat. "I'll be riding now. You all feel free to come shop in Barlow. We'll soon have us a newspaper and a schoolteacher and a preacher. I thank you for the meal." He reached into his pocket and pulled out a double eagle. Before Brown could protest, he said, "Buy some ammunition with that. It's going to get real salty in the valley before long."

Chapter 8

Smoke rode over to the Widow Feckles's house and made a slow circle of the grounds around the neat little home before riding up to the gate and swinging down from the saddle. A girl opened the front door and stepped out onto the porch. She looked to be about thirteen or fourteen, and Smoke pegged her as Aggie.

"Good morning," Smoke said. "I'm the new marshal over at Barlow. Don't be afraid of me. I'm here to help, not hurt you or your mother."

The girl's eyes widened. "Are you really Smoke Jensen?"

"Yes, I am. Is your name Aggie?"

"How'd you know that?"

"I nooned over at the Brown farm. Thought I'd come over and say hello to you and your ma. Is she home?"

"I'll fetch her for you."

Smoke waited by the gate. A very pretty woman stepped out onto the porch and smiled at him. "Mr. Jensen?"

"Yes, ma'am."

"I'm Martha Feckles. You wanted to see me?"

"If I may, yes."

"Please come in. I've just made a fresh pot of coffee."

The sitting room was small but neat, the furniture old and worn, but clean.

"You go look after your brother, Aggie," Martha said. "And don't stray from the house."

"Yes, Momma."

When the girl had closed the door behind her, Smoke said, "Are you expecting Vic Young?"

That shook the woman. Her hands trembled as she poured the coffee. "Brown spoke out of turn, sir."

"I don't think so. I think they spoke because they're worried about you. You're in a bad situation—not of your doing—and they'd like to see you clear of it."

"I'll never be free of Vic," she said with bitterness in her voice.

"Oh, you'll be free of him, Martha. You can write that down in your diary. When do you expect him again?"

"This evening."

Smoke sipped his coffee—mostly chicory—and studied the woman. She was under a strain; he could see that in her eyes and on her face. And he could also see the remnants of a bruise on her jaw. "Did Vic strike you, Martha?"

Her laugh held no humor. "Many times. He likes to beat up women."

Smoke waited.

With a sigh, she said, "Vic's killed women before, Mr. Jensen. He brags about it. I have to protect Aggie. I have to do his bidding for her sake."

"No longer, Martha. You'll not see Vic Young again. That's a promise."

"If you put him in jail, he'll come back when he gets out and really make it difficult for us."

"I don't intend to put him in jail, Martha. I intend to kill him."

His words did not shock her. She lifted her eyes to his. "I'm no shrinking summer rose, Mr. Jensen. I was born in the West. I don't hold with eastern views about crime and punishment. Some people—men and women—are just no good. They were born bad. I'll be much beholden to you if you saw to it that Vic did not come around here again. I can mend your shirts, and I do washing and ironing. I—"

Smoke held up a hand. "Enough, Martha. Do you have friends who would take you in for the night?"

"Why . . . certainly."

"I'll hitch up your buggy, and you take the children and go to your friends for the night. You come back in the morning. All right?"

"If you say so, Mr. Jensen."

After they had gone, Smoke put his horse up in the small barn, closed the door securely, and walked the grounds, getting the feel of the place. Back in the house, he read for a time. He dozed off and slept for half an hour, waking up refreshed. He made a pot of strong coffee and waited.

Just as dusk was settling around the high country, Smoke heard a horse approaching at a canter. He stood up and slipped the hammer-thong from his .44's. He worked the guns in and out of leather and walked softly to the front door.

"Git ready, baby," a man called from the outside. "And git that sweet little baby of yourn ready, too. It's time for her to git bred."

Smoke's face tightened. He felt rage well up inside him. He mentally calmed himself. Only his eyes showed what was boiling inside him.

"You hear me, you . . ." Vic spewed profanity, the filth rolling from his mouth like sewerage.

Smoke opened the door and stepped out onto the small porch. Vic crouched like a rabid animal when he spotted him.

"No more, Vic," Smoke told him. "You won't terrorize this good woman anymore."

"Who the hell are you?"

"The name is Jensen. Smoke Jensen."

Vic spat on the ground. "You rode a long ways to die, Jensen."

"You're trash, Vic. Pure crud. Just like the man you work for."

"No man calls me that and lives!"

"I just did, Vic. And I'm still living."

"Where's Martha and Aggie?"

"Safe. And I intend to see they remain safe."

"You got no call to come meddlin' in a man's personal business."

"I do when the man is trash like you."

"I'm tarred of all this jibber-jabber, Jensen. You tell me where my woman is at and then you hit the trail."

"You got any kin you want me to notify, Vic?"

"Notify about what?"

"Your death."

"Huh!" Vic looked puzzled for a moment. Then he laughed. "You may be a big shot where you come from, Jensen, but you don't spell horse crap to me."

"Then make your move, punk."

Vic was suddenly unsure of himself. He looked around him. "You alone, Jensen?"

"I don't need any help in dealing with scum like you, Vic."

"I'm warnin' you, Jensen, don't call me that no more."

"Or you'll do what, Vic? I'll tell you what you'll do. Nothing. You woman beaters are all alike. Cowards. Punks. Come on, Vic. Make your play."

All the bluster and brag left the man. His eyes began to jerk and the right side of his face developed a nervous tic. "I'll just ride on, Jensen."

"No, Vic. I won't allow that. You'd just find some other poor woman to terrorize. Some child to molest. It's over, Vic. You'll kill no more women."

"They had it comin' to them!" Vic shouted as the night began closing in. "All I wanted from them was what a woman was put on earth to give to a man."

Smoke waited.

Vic began cursing, working his courage back up to a fever. "Drag iron, Jensen!" he screamed.

"After you, punk."

Vic's hand dropped to his gun. Smoke drew, cocked, and fired as fast as a striking rattler, shooting him in the belly, the slug striking the child molester and rapist two inches above his belt buckle. Vic stumbled and went down on one knee. He managed to drag his pistol from leather and cock it. Smoke shot him again, the slug taking him in the side and blowing out the other side. Vic Young fell backward, cursing as life left him.

Smoke stood over him. Vic said, "You're dead, Jensen. Max has put money on your head. Big money. He . . ."

Vic jerked on the cooling ground and died staring at whatever faced him beyond the dark river.

Smoke took the man's gunbelt and tossed leather and pistol onto the porch. He fanned the man's pockets, finding a very respectable wad of greenbacks and about a hundred dollars in gold coins. Martha would put the money to good use. He put the money on the kitchen table, along with Vic's gun and gunbelt and the rifle taken from the saddle boot.

Smoke wrote a short note and left it on the table: HE WILL BOTHER YOU NO MORE.

He signed it Smoke.

He saddled up Star and rode around to the front of the house. Smoke tied Vic across the saddle of his suddenly skittish horse and locked up the house.

Leading the horse with its dead cargo, Smoke headed north, toward Big Max Huggins's town of Hell's Creek.

It was late when he arrived on the hill overlooking the bawdy town. Lights were blazing in nearly every building, wild laughter ripped the night, and rowdy songs could be heard coming from drunken throats.

Smoke slipped the lead rope and slapped the horse on the rump, sending it galloping into the town.

He sat his saddle and waited.

He didn't have to wait long.

"Vic's dead!" the faint shout came to him as the piano playing and singing and drunken laughter gradually fell away, leaving the town silent.

Smoke watched the shadowy figures untie the body of Vic Young and lower it to the ground. He couldn't hear what the men were saying, but he could make a good guess.

Every rowdy and punk and gunhandler in the town would have known that Vic was seeing Widow Feckles. And everyone would know that she was being forced into acts of passion with Vic. And since none of the sodbusters would have the nerve to face Vic—so the gunhandlers thought; whether that was true or not, only time would tell—it had to have been the Widow Feckles who did Vic in.

Smoke kneed Star forward, moving closer to the town.

"Let's burn her out!" the shout reached Smoke's ears.

"Yeah," another man yelled. "I'll get the kerosene."

Smoke swung onto the main street of Hell's Creek and reined up. Staying in the shadows, he shucked his Winchester from the saddle boot and eared back the hammer. He called, "Martha Feckles had nothing to do with killing Vic. I killed him."

"Well, who the hell are you?" came the shouted question.

"Smoke Jensen."

"Jensen! Let's get him, boys."

They came at a rush and it was like shooting clay ducks in a shooting gallery. Smoke leveled the Winchester and emptied it into the knot of men. A dozen of them fell to one side, hard hit and screaming. Smoke spun Star around and headed for the high country, leaving a trail a drunken city slicker could follow.

About five miles outside of town, Smoke found what he was looking for and reined up. He loosened the cinch strap and let the big horse blow. He took a drink of water from his canteen and filled up his hat, letting Star have a drink.

Smoke had reloaded his rifle on the run, and he took it and his saddlebags down to the rocks just below where he had tucked Star safely away in a narrow draw. He eared back the hammer when he heard the pounding of hooves. The men of Hell's Creek rounded a curve in the trail and Smoke knocked the first man out of the saddle. Shifting the muzzle, he got lead in two more before the scum started making a mad dash for safety.

Smoke deliberately held his fire, watching the men cautiously edge toward his position under a starry sky and moon-bright night. With a grin, he opened his saddlebags and took out a stick of dynamite. He had a dozen sticks in the bag. He capped the stick of giant powder and set a very short fuse. Striking a match, he lit the fuse and let it fly, sputtering and sparking through the air.

The dynamite blew and shook the ground as it exploded. Smoke saw one man blown away from behind a rock, half of an arm missing. Another man staggered to his boots and Smoke drilled him through the brisket. A third man tried to crawl away, dragging a broken leg. Smoke put him out of his misery.

Smoke put away the dynamite. Taking it along had been Sally's idea, and it had been a good one.

The trash below him cursed Smoke, calling him all sorts of names. But Smoke held his fire and eased away to a new position, which was some fifty feet higher than the old one. He now was able to see half-a-dozen men crouched behind whatever cover they could find in the night, some of that cover being mighty thin indeed.

Smoke dusted one man through and through. The man grunted once, then slowly rolled down the hill, dead. He shifted the muzzle and plugged another of Max's men through the throat. The man made a lot of horrible noises before he had the good grace to expire. Smoke had been aiming for the chest, but downhill shooting is tricky enough; couple that with night, and it gets doubly difficult.

The men of Hell's Creek decided they had had enough for this night. Smoke let them make their retreat, even though he could have easily dropped another two or three. He tightened the cinch strap, swung into the saddle, and headed south. He found a good place to camp and picketed Star. With his saddle for a pillow, he rolled into his blankets and went to sleep.

Two hours after dawn, he rode into the front yard of Martha Feckles. An idea had formed in his mind over coffee and bacon that morning, and he wanted to see how the widow received it.

"I think it's a grand idea!" she said.

Barlow had another resident.

* * *

Big Max Huggins sat in his office and stared at the wall. His thoughts were dark and violent. At this very moment, that drunken old preacher—he was all that passed for religion in Hell's Creek—was praying for the lost souls of three of those Jensen had shot in the main street of town last night. Those that had pursued him came back into town, dragging their butts in defeat. They had left six dead on the mountain. One of those had bled to death after the bomb Jensen had thrown tore off half of the man's arm.

"Goddamn you, Jensen!" Max cursed.

He leaned back in his chair—specially made due to his height and weight. He hated Smoke Jensen, but had to respect him—grudgingly—for his cold nerve. It would take either a crazy person or one with nerves of steel to ride smack into the middle of the enemy. And Smoke Jensen was no crazy person.

What to do about him?

Big Max didn't have the foggiest idea.

Smoke had put steel into the backbones of those in Barlow. A raid against the town now would be suicide. His men would be shot to pieces. There was no need to send for any outside gunfighters. He had some of the best guns in the West, either on his payroll or working out of the town on a percentage basis of their robberies.

Max's earlier boast that he would just wait Smoke out was proving to be a hollow brag. Jensen was bringing the fight to him.

Of course, Max mused, he could just pick up and move on. He'd done it many times in the past when things had gotten too hot for him.

But just the thought of that irritated him. In the past, dozens of cops or sheriffs and their deputies had been on his trail. Jensen was just one man. One man!

Max sighed, thinking: But, Jesus, what a man.

It was a good thing he'd invited those friends of his from Europe. A damn good thing. They would be arriving just in time.

The good ladies of Barlow welcomed Martha Feckles and her children with open arms. The mayor gave her a small building to use for her sewing. And Judge Garrison, now that he was free of the heavy hand of Max Huggins, was proving to be a decent sort of fellow. He staked Martha for a dress shop.

The preacher and schoolteacher had arrived in town. The newspaper man was due in at any time. Some of those who had left when Max first put on the pressure were returning. Barlow now had a population of nearly four hundred. And growing.

The jail was nearly full. Each time the stage ran north, Smoke jerked out any gamblers, gunfighters, and whores who might be on it and turned them around. If they kicked up a fuss, they were tossed in the clink, fined, and were usually more than happy to catch the next stage out—south.

A depty U.S. Marshal, on his way up to British Columbia to bring back a prisoner, was on the stage the morning a gunslick objected to being turned around.

"There ain't no warrants out on me, Jensen," the man protested. "You ain't got no right to turn me around. I can go anywheres I damn well please to go."

"That's right," Smoke told him. "Anywhere except Hell's Creek."

Amused, the U.S. Marshal leaned against a post and rolled himself a cigarette, listening to the exchange. He knew all about Hell's Creek and Big Max Huggins. But until somebody complained to the government, there was little they could do. He knew the sheriff, the city marshal, and all the deputies in Hell's Creek were crooked as a snake. But the outlaws working out of there never bothered anyone with a federal badge, and as far as he knew, there were no federal warrants on anyone in the town—at least not under the names they were going by now.

"Git out of my way, Jensen!" the gunny warned Smoke.

"Don't be a fool, man," Smoke told him. "You're in violation of the law by bracing me. I don't have any papers on you. So why don't you just go to the hotel, get you a room, and catch the next stage out?"

"South?"

"That's it."

"I'll rent me a horse and go to Hell's Creek."

"Sorry, friend," Smoke told him. "No one in this town will rent you a horse."

"Then I think I'll get back on the stage and ride up yonder like my ticket says."

Smoke hit him. The punch came out of the blue and caught the gunny on the side of the jaw. When he hit the ground, he was out cold.

Jim and Sal dragged him across the street to the jail.

"Slick," the U.S. Marshal said. "Against the law, but slick."

"You going to report what I'm doing?" Smoke asked.

"Hell, no, man! But I can tell you that the word's gone out up and down the line: You're a marked man. Huggins has put big money on your head. And I'm talkin' enough money to bring in some mercenaries from Europe."

"Are they in the country?"

"As near as the Secret Service can tell, yes. Two long-distance shooters, Henri Dubois and Paul Mittermaier, are on their way west right now. Our office has sent out flyers to you. Oh, yes. We know what you're doing here. We can't give you our blessings, but we can close our eyes."

"Thanks. Dubois and Mittermaier—Frenchman and a German?"

"Yep. And they're good."

"I don't like back-shooters. I'll tell you now, Marshal: If I see them, I'm going to kill them."

"Suits me, Smoke. Good hunting." He climbed back on board the stage and was gone.

Smoke turned to Jim and Sal, who had just returned from the jail. "You hear that?"

They had heard it.

"Pass the word to all the farmers and ranchers. Any strangers, especially those speaking with an accent, I want to know about. You boys watch your backs."

Sal spat on the ground. "I hate a damned back-shooter," he said. "These boys are gonna be totin' some fancy custom-made rifles. I see one, I'm gonna plug him on the spot and apologize later if I'm wrong."

"You know what this tells me?" Smoke asked. "It tells me that Max is in a bind. What we're doing is working. We can't legally stop and permanently block freight shipments to Hell's Creek. But we can hold them up and make them open up every box and crate for search. And I mean a very long and tedious search. It won't take long for freight companies to stop accepting orders from Hell's Creek."

Jim and Sal grinned. "Oh, you got a sneaky mind, Smoke," Sal said. "I like it!"

"The last freight wagons rolled through a week ago," Jim said. "There ought to be another convoy tomorrow, I figure."

"OK," Smoke said. He looked at Sal. "You get a couple of town boys. Give them a dollar apiece to stand watch about two miles south of town. As soon as they hear the wagons, one of them can come fogging back to town for us. Everything going north has got to pass through here." Smoke smiled. "This is going to give Max fits!"

The men grinned at each other. One sure way to kill a town was to dry up its supply line. Big Max was not going to like this.

Not one little bit.

Chapter 9

"Some of the boys is grumblin' about you puttin' up money on Jensen's head and then lettin' them foreigners come over here," one of Max's gunhands complained.

Max spread his hands. "I put up the money, Lew. Anybody who nails Jensen gets it. As far as Dubois and Mittermaier are concerned, they're old friends of mine. I sent for them long before Jensen entered the picture. Besides, they are much more subtle in their approach than most of those out there." He waved his hand. "You and I, of course, could handle it easily. I'm not too sure about the others."

The outlaw knew he was getting a line of buffalo chips fed him, but the flattery felt good anyway. "Right, Big Max. Sure. I understand. What do I tell the boys?"

"Tell them . . ." Max was thinking hard. "Tell them that we must be careful in disposing of Jensen. If we draw too much attention to us, the government might send troops in here and put us all out of business."

"Yeah," Lew said. "Yeah, you're right. They'll understand that, Max. I'll pass the word."

After Lew had left, Max leaned back in his chair. What next? he thought. What is Jensen going to do next?

"What are y'all lookin' for?" the teamster asked.

"Contraband," Smoke told him. "Unload your wagons."

The teamster paled under his stubble of beard and tanned skin. "All the wagons? Everything in them?"

"All the wagons, everything in them."

Griping and muttering under their breaths, the men unloaded the wagons, and Smoke and Jim and Sal went to work with pry-bars. With his back to the teamsters, Smoke pulled a small packet from under his shirt and dropped it in a box. "Check this box, Sal," he said. "I'll be opening some others."

"Right, Smoke."

After a moment, Sal called out, "Marshal, I got something that looks funny."

Smoke walked over. "The box says it's supposed to have whiskey in it. What's that in your hand?"

"Durned if I know." He handed the packet to Smoke.

Smoke had found the contents way in the back of the safe in the marshal's office. It was several thousand dollars of badly printed counterfeit greenbacks.

Smoke opened the packet. "Hey!" he said, holding one of the greenbacks up to the sunlight. "This looks phony to me."

A teamster walked over. "What is that?"

"Counterfeit money," Smoke told him. "This is real serious. You could be in a lot of trouble."

"Me!" the teamster shouted. "I ain't done nothin'."

"You're hauling this funny money," Smoke reminded him.

"Well, that's true. But that phony money sure as hell ain't mine."

"Oh, I believe you," Smoke eased his fears. "But this entire shipment is going to have to be seized and held for evidence."

"Marshal, you can have it all. Me and my boys work for a living. We're not printing no government money."

"Is this shipment prepaid?"

"Yes, sir. Everything sent to Hell's Creek is paid for in advance. That's the only way the boss would agree to do business with them thugs up yonder."

"So you and your men would prefer not to do business with those in Hell's Creek?"

"That's the gospel truth, Mr. Jensen. There ain't a one of us like the run past Barlow."

"All right, boys. You're free to turn around and head on back. We're sorry to have inconvenienced you."

After the wagons had gone, the men nearly broke up laughing as they stood amid the mounds of boxed supplies. Wiping his eyes, Smoke said, "Sal, go get some wagons and men from town. We've got to store all this stuff."

"Big Max is gonna toss himself a royal fit when he hears about this," Sal said. "This here is food and supplies for a month."

"Yeah. I figure they have probably a month's supplies left on the shelves. After that, things are going to get desperate in Hell's Creek."

Sal headed back to town and Jim said, "You know, Smoke, Max can't let you get away with this. His men would lose all respect for him."

"Yeah, I know. This may be the fuel to pop the lid off. What's the latest on Red Malone; have you heard?"

"Not a peep. I 'spect he's still recovering from that beatin' you gave him."

"He's got to have a meeting with Max. They'll get together and try to plan some way to get rid of me."

"No way to cover all the trails up to Hell's Creek. There must be a dozen, and probably a few more that I don't know about."

"Oh, I wouldn't try to do that. But I was thinking: Red has to buy supplies and he buys them in Barlow. It would be too time-consuming and costly to go anywhere else. Marbly hates Red. He never did knuckle under to him. He told me himself he still has the right to refuse service to anyone."

Jim smiled. "Oh, now that would tick Red off. He'd go right through the ceiling."

Smoke chuckled. "I'm counting on it, Jim. I am really counting on it."

"He did what?" Big Max roared, jumping up from his chair and pounding a fist on his desk.

The outlaw Val Singer repeated what he had heard.

"That's why the damn supplies didn't arrive yesterday," Max said, sitting down and doing his best to calm himself. "Jensen . . . that low-life, no-good, lousy . . ." He spent the next few moments calling Smoke every filthy name he could think of. And he thought of a lot of them.

Big Max shook himself like a bear with fleas and took several deep breaths. What to do? was the next thought that sprang into his angry mind.

Thing about it was, he didn't know.

"Burn the damn town down," Val suggested.

"They'd rebuild it," Max said glumly.

"Grab some of their kids, then."

"I have been giving that some thought, for a fact. But we'd have to be very careful doing it, Val. Very subtle."

Val smiled, a nasty glint in his eyes. "That daughter of Martha Feckles is prime. She could pleasure a lot of us."

Big Max had thought of Aggie a time or two. For a fact.

Something ugly and archaic reared up within him when he thought of Aggie.

He could envision all sorts of perversions, all with Aggie in the lead role . . . with him.

"I'll think about it," Max said, his voice husky.

Days passed and there was no retaliation from either Big Max or Red Malone. And that worried Smoke. To his mind, it meant that Max and Red were planning something very ugly and very sneaky. He warned everybody in town to keep a careful eye on their kids, to know where they were at all times. He warned the women to never walk alone, to plan shopping trips in groups. He visited everyone who lived just outside of town and warned them to be very, very careful.

He rode out into the county, visiting the small ranchers and farmers, repeating his message of caution at every stop.

"What do you think they're gonna do, Mr. Jensen?" Brown asked. Smoke had stopped in for coffee.

"I don't know, Brown. I wish I did so I could head it off. Whatever Max does, and probably Red Malone, too, is going to be dirty. Bet on that."

"Would the army come in if we was to ask them?"

"No. This is a civilian matter. I can't tell you who told me this, but I was told that the government is going to turn its back and let us handle it the way we see fit."

"That seems odd. I mean, why would they?"

"I've worn a U.S. Marshal's badge a time or two, Brown."

Smoke had worn a marshal's badge before, but that didn't

mean the government owed him any favors. He hoped Brown wouldn't push the matter, and the farmer didn't.

"If we got to go clean out that bunch at Hell's Creek, or if we got to ride agin' Malone and his bunch of trash, you can count me and all my neighbors in, Smoke."

Smoke smiled. "The word I got is that you farmers won't fight. That you're scared."

"You believe that?"

"Not for one second, Brown. I got a hunch you're all Civil War veterans."

"We are. Gatewood and Cooter fought on the side of the South, rest of us wore blue. But that's behind us now. We seldom ever talk about it no more. And when we do, it ain't with no rancor. Funny thing is, we never knowed each other during the war. We just met up on the trail and become friends. But don't never think we won't fight, Smoke. Some hoodlums along the trail thought that. We buried them."

They chatted for a while longer and then Smoke pulled out, heading back to Barlow. He had him a hunch that Max Huggins had already sounded out Brown and Cooter and the other farmers in that area. Max was no fool, far from it, and he had guessed—and guessed accurately—that tackling that bunch would be foolhardy. Like most men of his ilk, Max preferred the easy way over the hard.

He pulled up in front of his office and swung down, curious about the horses tied to the hitchrail. He did not recognize the brand.

He looped the reins around the rail and stepped up on the boardwalk. The door to his office opened and several men filed out, one of them wearing the badge of sheriff of the county.

"You Jensen?" the man asked, a hard edge to his voice.

"That's right."

The man held out his hand. "I'll take your badge, Jensen. I name my deputies."

"This badge is legal, partner. Judge Garrison swore me in and he has the power to do it. So that means that you can go right straight to Hell."

The sheriff shook a finger in Smoke's face. "Now let me tell you something . . ."

Smoke slapped the finger away and his hand returned a lot harder. He backhanded the crooked sheriff a blow that jarred the man and stepped him to one side.

"Don't you ever stick your finger in my face again," Smoke warned him. "The next time you do it, I'll break it off at the elbow and put it in a place that'll have you riding sidesaddle for a long time."

Sal and Jim had stepped out of the office, both of them carrying sawed-off shotguns. It made the sleazebag sheriff's deputies awfully nervous.

"Come on, Cart," one of his men said. "I told you this wouldn't work."

Smoke laughed. "You have to be Paul Cartwright. Sure. I remember reading about you. You served time in California for stealing while you were a lawman out there. Get out of this town, Cartwright."

"Come on, Cart," one of his men pulled at his sleeve.

"I'll be damned if I will!" Cart blustered. "I'm the sheriff of this county. And no two-bit gunslinger tells me what to do."

He took a swing at Smoke, who in turn grabbed him by the arm and tossed him off the boardwalk and into the street. Smoke jumped down just as Cart was grabbing for his gun. He kicked the .45 out of his hand and jerked the man to his boots.

Then he proceeded to beat the hell out of him.

Every time Cart would get up, Smoke would knock him

down again. The editor of the paper had grabbed his brand-new, up-to-date camera and rushed out of his office in time to see Smoke knock Cart down for the second time. He quickly set up and began taking action shots.

Cart was out of shape, and Smoke really didn't want to inflict any permanent injuries on the man. He just wanted to leave a lasting impression as to who was running things in Barlow and the south end of the county.

The editor, Henry Draper, got some great shots of Cart being busted in the mouth and landing in the dirt on his butt. Jim and Sal thought it very amusing. Cart's deputies failed to see the humor in it. But they stayed out of it mainly because of Jim and Sal and the express guns they carried.

Joe Walsh and several of his hands rode into town just as Smoke was knocking Cart down for about the seventh time. The rancher sat his saddle and watched, amusement on his face and in his eyes.

The county sheriff staggered to his boots, lifted his fists, and Smoke decked him for the final count. Cart hit the dirt and didn't move.

Smoke washed his face and hands in a horse trough, picked up his hat, and settled it on his head. He looked up at Cart's deputies and pointed to the sheriff. "Get that trash off the streets and out of this town. And don't come back. You understand all that?"

"Yes, sir," they echoed.

Smoke jerked a thumb. "Move!"

The deputies grunted Cart across his saddle, tied him in place, and rode out.

"You do have a way of making friends, Smoke," Joe said, walking his horse over to the hitchrail and dismounting.

"Let's just say I leave lasting impressions," Smoke smiled the reply, shaking the rancher's hand.

"What a headline this will make!" Henry said. The editor of the *Barlow Bugle* grabbed up all his photographic equipment and hustled back to his office to develop the pictures and write the story.

"Stick around," Smoke told Joe. "We'll have some coffee in a minute." He looked at Sal. "When did Cart get here?"

"'Bout an hour ago. He was full of it, too. He had me and Jim plumb shakin' in our boots."

"I'm sure he did," Smoke said, noticing the wicked glint in the man's eyes. "I can tell that you haven't recovered yet."

"Right," Jim said, grinning along with Sal. "They're runnin' scared, Smoke. All of them up at Hell's Creek. Cart said that Big Max can't get a freight company to haul goods up to them. He's tryin' to get goods pulled in from that new settlement to the west of him . . . Kalispell; but the marshal over there told him to go take a dump in his hat. Or words similar to that."

Joe Walsh and his men laughed out loud, one of the hands saying, "Me and the rest of the boys talked it over, Smoke. When you need us, just give a holler. We'll ride with you and you call the shots."

"I appreciate it. Max won't stand still and get pushed around much longer. I expect some retaliation from Hell's Creek at any moment. Unfortunately, I don't have any idea in what form it might be." He told them all what he'd been doing that day, riding and warning those in the south end of the county . . . or as many as he could find.

"A man who would harm a kid is scum," Joe said. "I suggest we keep a rope handy."

A crowd had gathered around and they heatedly agreed.

Smoke let them talk it out until they fell silent. "You watch your children, people. Tell them not to leave the town limits. Not for any reason. Always bear in mind that we're dealing with scum. And these people have no morals, no values, no regard for human life. Adult or child. The farmers in this part of the county are breaking ground and planting. And they're doing it with guns strapped on. I don't want to see a man in this town walking around without a gunbelt on or a pistol stuck behind his belt. It's entirely conceivable that Max and Malone may even try to tree this town. If they do that, we want to be ready. Any woman here who doesn't know how to shoot, my wife will be conducting classes." He smiled. "She doesn't know that yet, but I'm sure she'll be more than willing to teach a class."

"You better watch out, Tom," a good-natured shout came out of the crowd. "Ella Mae learns to shoot, she's liable to fill your butt full of birdshot the next time you come home tipsy."

Tom Johnson grinned out of his suddenly red face. Tom liked his evening whiskey at the saloon.

"You're a fine one to talk, Matthew," the blacksmith yelled. "I 'member the time your woman tossed you out of the house with nothin' but your long-handles on."

The crowd burst out laughing and went their way. It was good laughter, the kind of laughter from men and women who had decided to make a stand of it. To not be pushed around and taken advantage of by thugs like Big Max Huggins.

"That laughter is good to hear," Joe said. "These folks have been down for a long time. I'm glad to see them back on their feet and standing tall." He paused to finish rolling his cigarette and light up. "And you're responsible for straightening their backbone, Smoke."

Smoke had been curious about something, and he figured now was the time to ask it. "Why didn't you do it, Joe?" he asked softly.

"Wondered when you'd get around to asking that. It's a

fair question. Me and the wife left right after roundup three years ago. Took us a trip to see San Francisco. Spent all summer in California. Up and down the coast. The kids is all growed up and in college back East. We left right around the first day of May and didn't come back until late September. Hell, Smoke, it was all over by then. Big Max had built Hell's Creek, him and Red Malone was in cahoots around here, and Big Max's outlaws had cut the heart right out of this town."

He dropped the cigarette butt into the street and toed it dead. "I spent the next year just protecting my herds and my land. Red tried his damndest to run me out. But I wouldn't go. I lost . . ." He looked at one of his hands. "How many men, Chuck?"

"Four, Boss. Skinny Jim, Davis, Don Morris, and John."

"Four men," Joe said quietly. "Good men who died for the brand. When Red finally got it through his head that I wasn't gonna be run out—and I can't prove it was Red doing it—he backed off and let me be."

"No way you can prove it was Red?"

"No. Not a chance. And I tried. That's on record at the territorial capitol. I raised some hell about it, and that, and with me and the boys fighting the night riders brought an end to it. They all wore hoods. Don't all cowards wear hoods or masks? I never was able to get a look at any of them." He smiled. "But I did recognize their horses. Unfortunately, that won't cut it in court." His eyes darted toward Sally as she stepped out of the hotel. "My wife is looking forward to you and your missus coming out. But I told her let's get this situation with Red and Max taken care of first, then we'll socialize."

"Yeah. My leaving town now, for any length of time, would not be wise. Hey! I got an idea. How about a community dance and box supper?"

Sally walked up. "You took those thoughts right out of my head, honey. Hi, Joe."

"Ma'am," the rancher touched the brim of his hat. "I think that's a good idea."

Smoke's grin turned into a frown.

"What's the matter with you?" Sally asked.

"It's not a good idea."

"Why not?" she asked.

"It would mean too many people would be leaving their homes unguarded. That might be all it would take for Max or Red to burn someone out."

"Oh, pooh!" Sally said, stamping her foot.

"Smoke's right. I didn't think about that. Must be getting old. Max and Red wouldn't pass up an opportunity like that. And we couldn't keep it quiet. It'd be sure to leak out."

Smoke began smiling again.

"Now what?" Sally asked.

"I know how to have the dance and avoid trouble—at least for the farmers and ranchers."

"How?" Joe asked. "What about Red and Max?"

"That's just it. We'll invite them."

Chapter 10

Joe Walsh rode back to the ranch, chuckling as he went. Smoke Jensen was not only the slickest gunhandler he'd ever seen, but the man was damn smart, too.

There was no way a western man was going to turn down an invitation for a box supper and a dance with some really nice ladies. And both Max and Red would know that if anyone's place was torched that night, the fires could be seen for miles and there was no way either of them would leave Barlow alive.

"Slick," the rancher said. "Just damn slick."

"I had my mind all made up to not like Smoke Jensen," one of his hands said. "But I sure changed my mind. He's a right nice fellow."

"Yes, he is, Curly. I had my mind all made up to dislike the man. I figured he'd be a cocky son. Shows how wrong a man can be."

"I can't wait for this shindig," another hand said. "Been a long time since we had a good box supper and dance."

"Be a damn good time to put lead in Max Huggins and Red Malone, too," Curly said. Curly and Skinny Jim had been close friends.

"Be none of that, Curly," Joe cautioned his hand. "Not unless they open the ball. Too much a chance that women and kids would get hit."

"I hate both them men," Curly replied. "With Jensen leadin' the pack, we could ride into Hell's Creek and wipe it out. I don't see why we don't do that."

"It might come to that, Curly," Joe said. "For sure, a lot of blood is going to be spilled before this is over."

"Just as long as the blood spilled comes out of Max Huggins and Red Malone and them that ride for them," Curly said. "I don't wanna die, but I'll go out happy if I know I got lead in Max or Malone."

Joe cut his eyes to the puncher. I'm going to have to watch him, the rancher thought. He's let his hate bubble very nearly out of control.

Sally and the ladies of Barlow met with the editor of the paper and designed and had printed dozens of invitations. Smoke made certain that Max Huggins and Red Malone received an invite.

Max stared at his invitation for a long time, being careful not to smudge the creamy bond paper. "What's Jensen doing this time?" he questioned the empty office. "He's got to have something up his sleeve." Then it came to him: If he attended this shindig and there was any trouble caused by his men, Max and Red would be gunned down on the spot; shot down like rabid skunks.

The big man was filled with grudging admiration for

Jensen. Slick. Very, very slick. If he and Red didn't attend, Jensen and the others would be put on alert that something was going to happen out in the county, and it would be open season for any Lightning rider or gunhand from Hell's Creek caught out after dark.

He sent one of his bodyguards to fetch Val Singer, Warner Frigo, Dave Poe, and Alex Bell to his office.

"Me and Red will be attending this shindig," he informed the outlaw leaders. "And there better not be any trouble out in the county. You hold the reins tight on your boys . . . and I mean tight."

"It might be a trap," Val pointed out.

Max shook his head. "No. I don't think so. The people of Barlow are going to let off a little steam, that's all." He waved the invite. "This is their way of insuring that they can do so without fear of any trouble." He eyeballed them all. "And, by God, there isn't going to be any trouble. Those are my orders. See that they are carried out."

Red Malone had recovered from his beating at the hands—or fists—of Smoke Jensen. He stared hard and long at the invitation. He laid it on his desk and stared at it some more.

Was it a trap? He didn't think so. But he had a week to nose around and find out for sure.

"We goin', ain't we, Daddy?" Tessie asked, looking and reading over his shoulder.

Red turned his head and stared at his daughter, all blond and pretty and pouty and as worthless as her brother, Melvin. He loved them both—as much as Red Malone could love anything—but realized he had sired a whore and a nut.

"I don't know," he told her. She pouted.

"Stop that, girl. You look like a fish suckin' in air."

Tessie plopped down in a chair and glared at him. "I got me a brand-new dress I got outta that catalog from New York, and I ain't had no chance to wear it. Now I got a chance to wear it and you tell me we might not go."

Red sighed. "Where's Melvin?"

"Same place he always is: shootin' at targets."

The boy was good with a gun, Red thought. Fast as a snake. But was he as fast as Jensen? Maybe. Just maybe the boy might do one thing in his life that was worthwhile: killing Smoke Jensen.

"Come on, Daddy!" Tessie said. "Let's go to the dance and have some fun."

Red stared at her, wondering whom she was bedding down with this time around.

The girl had more beaus than a dog had fleas.

"Pooh!" Tessie said. "I never get to do anything."

Except sneak out at night and behave like a trollop, Red thought. "I said I'd think about it," he told her. "Now go tell the cook to get dinner on the table. I'm hungry."

She sat in her chair and pouted.

"Move!" Red yelled.

She got up and left the room, shaking her butt like a hurdy-gurdy girl.

Red sighed and shook his big head. The only thing he regretted about his wife leaving him was that she didn't take those damn kids with her.

"Max has accepted," Sally told Smoke, holding out the note from Hell's Creek. "This came on the southbound stage a few minutes ago."

Smoke read the note and smiled. "One down and one to go. No word from Red yet?"

"No. Nothing."

"Smoke!" Jim's sharp call came from the outside. "Melvin Malone ridin' in. You watch yourself around this one. He's crazy as a skunk."

Smoke walked to the door and stepped out, after removing the hammer thongs from his .44's. He'd heard too much about Melvin to be careless around him. He watched the young man swing down from the saddle, being careful to keep the horse between himself and Smoke.

Smart, Smoke thought. He's no amateur.

Melvin stepped up on the boardwalk, studying Smoke as hard as Smoke was studying him. Melvin was about six feet tall and well built, heavily muscled. He was handsome in a cruel sort of way. He wore two guns, the holsters tied down. The spurs he wore were big roweled ones, the kind that would hurt a horse, and Melvin looked the type who would enjoy doing that.

"Jensen," the young man said, stopping a few feet away. "I'm Mel Malone."

"Nice to see you, Mel. What's on your mind?"

Killing you, was the thought in Mel's head. He kept it silent. Big bastard, Mel thought. Big as them books made him out to be. "My pa said to give you a message. We'll be coming to the dance and box supper."

"Well, I'm glad to hear that, Mel. Yes, sir. Sure am. You be sure and tell Red I'm looking forward to seeing him again. He is feeling all right, now, isn't he?"

The young man stared at Smoke for a moment. Was Jensen trying to be smart-mouthed? He couldn't tell. "Uh, yeah. He feels just fine."

"That's good. Your sister Tessie makes a pretty good box supper, does she?"

"My sister couldn't fry an egg if the hen told her how," Mel replied. "But the cook can fry chicken that'll make you wanna slap your granny." Why the hell was he standing here

talking about fried chicken with a man he was going to kill?
He stared hard at Smoke. Fella seemed sort of likable.

Smoke chuckled. "Well, some women just never get the
knack of cooking, Mel. Tell Red to take it easy now." Smoke
turned and walked across the street, leaving Melvin alone on
the boardwalk.

Feeling sort of stupid standing on the boardwalk all by
himself, the young man wandered over to the saloon for a
drink.

Sally watched it all from the window and she smiled.

"Smoke handled that just right," Jim said. "There wasn't
nothing else to be said, so he just walked off leavin' Melvin
standing there lookin' stupid. Which ain't hard to do, 'cause
he is."

"But good with a gun," Sally remarked, watching the
young man push open the batwings to the saloon. "I can tell
by the way he carries himself. He walks a lot like Smoke."

"He's almost as fast as Smoke, ma'am. But not quite as
good. But he's a dead shot, I'll give him that."

Sally felt just a twinge of worry that she quickly pushed
aside. She had known what Smoke was when she met and
later married him. She had long ago accepted that wherever
he went, there would be men who would call him out. The
West was slowly changing, but it would be years before
gunfighting was finally banned.

When Melvin left town, Smoke was leaning up against
an awning support watching him go. Smoke raised a hand in
farewell. Melvin looked at him, then cut his eyes away, re-
fusing to acknowledge the friendly gesture.

Smoke walked back to the office. Sally had just finished
cleaning and straightening it up. "What do you think of
Red's son, Smoke?"

Smoke poured a cup of coffee and sat down at his desk.

He sipped and said, "He's crazy and he's cruel. I'll have to kill him someday."

Little by little, in small groups, Red's hands began drifting back into town for a drink or a meal or to buy this or that. So far, Red had not tried to buy any supplies from Marbly. The rancher was going to be in for a rude shock when he did.

Red's hands caused no trouble when in town. They had all noticed that every man in town was packing iron: the bartender, the editor of the *Bugle,* the store clerks . . . everybody. And they promptly took that news back to Red.

Red digested that bit of information with a sigh. "Then that's it, John," he told his foreman. "We've got to make a move and do it quick, before the town really gets together and runs our butts out of the country. And they'll do it eventually. Believe me."

"Before the dance, Red?"

Red shook his head. "No. After it. Maybe a week after it. Max has got some long-distance shooters comin' in from Europe. They was invited to come in here for a hunt long before Smoke Jensen showed up. They should be here this week. Early next week at the latest. We'll get things firmed up with Max after the party."

"Take Jensen out first?"

"I don't know. I think it'd be better to start working on the townspeople. I just don't know. Whatever Max decides to do, we got to back him up. That's the deal we made and I always keep my word." He looked around him and sniffed, a look of distaste crossing his face. "What in the name of God is that horrible smell?"

"The cook is tryin' to teach Tessie how to cook. Tessie is fixin' supper, so I'm told."

"Oh, my Lord. I'll eat with you boys tonight. What the Sam Hill is she cookin', skunk?"

"Fried chicken."

"She must have left the feathers on."

Henri Dubois and Paul Mittermaier were blissfully unaware of what was taking place in Barlow and Hell's Creek. They had seen the sights of St. Louis and were now ready to board the train west.

What they did not know was that they were under surveillance by agents of the U.S. Federal Marshal's office. They knew of the situation building in Barlow and Hell's Creek, and they also knew that with just a little help, Smoke Jensen would handle it and they would not have to get directly involved. The marshals sent a wire to the nearest town to Barlow, and the message was forwarded to Smoke Jensen by stage.

Smoke opened the envelope and read: Mercenaries left St. Louis this a.m. No charges against Dubois or Mittermaier. They are unaware of what is taking place in your area. Watch your back and handle situation as you see fit.

It was unsigned, but Smoke had a pretty good idea what federal office had sent it.

He showed the message to Jim and Sal. Neither man could understand why Smoke was smiling. Jim asked him.

"They have to come right through here, boys." He walked to a wall map and put his finger on a town south of them. "This is rail's end. From here to Barlow is either by horseback or stage, and I'm betting they take the stage."

"And you got what in mind?" Sal asked.

"Any trouble that happens out in the county, you boys handle it. Starting day after tomorrow, I've got to meet the stage."

"I wonder what he's got in mind?" Jim asked Sal after Smoke left the office.

"Be fun to watch, whatever it is."

"You reckon the Frenchman and the German will see the humor in it?" Jim asked with a grin.

"Somehow I doubt it. I really do."

"The saloons are runnin' out of whiskey," Max was informed. "And the boys is gettin' right testy."

Max took a long pull on his stogie. "Yeah, and I had me five boxes of cigars on that shipment Jensen seized, too. So what else is new? *I* can't find any freight haulers to handle our orders. The only option we have is some outfit out of Canada, and by the time all the red tape is over with, it'll be six months before we get any supplies."

Alex Bell shifted in the chair. "Max, the boys ain't gonna stand still for this very much longer. They all got cash money to spend and nothin' to buy. The women is raisin' holy hell 'cause the boys is unhappy. Somethin' has got to pop, and damn soon."

Max Huggins's little empire was crumbling at the edges and he didn't know what to do about it. For the umpteenth time since Jensen entered the picture, the thought that he should pull out entered his brain. And for the same number of times, the thought galled him; but with each revival of the thought, the intensity of the sourness was somewhat lessened as common sense fought to prevail.

"I'll talk to the boys," he finally said to Alex. "Damnit!" he cursed, pounding a fist on the desk and scattering papers. "He's just one man. Just one man! He's not a god, not invincible. There has to be a way."

"There is," Alex said. "Me and Val and the others been talkin'."

Max waited, staring hard at the outlaw gang leader.

"Wipe the town out. Kill every man, woman, and child. It can be done, and you know it."

"Damnit, Alex," Max said, struggling to maintain his patience with the gang leader. "This is 1883, man. The country is connected by telegraph wires and railroads. Ten years ago, I would have said yes to your proposal. But not now. I think the press would pick it up, and the public would be up in arms and all over us. We'd have federal marshals and troops in here before you could blink."

"Fires happen all the time, Max," Alex pointed out. "We pick a night with a good strong wind and that town would go up like a tinderbox. You think about that."

"The people would still remain, Alex."

"Maybe not. Maybe not enough of them to do any good. Lots of folks die in town fires. And charred skin don't show no bullet holes. By the time the newspapers got 'hold of it, them folks would be rottin' in the ground and nobody could do nothin' about it."

Max jabbed out his cigar in an ashtray. With a slow expelling of breath, he said, "We may have to do that, Alex. It's a good plan, I'm thinking, but very risky." He stared hard at the outlaw. "Have you ever killed a child, Alex?"

"Yeah. I gut-shot a kid durin' a bank stickup; squealed like a hog at butcherin' time. I shot him in the head to shut him up. I shot half a dozen or more ridin' with Bloody Bill Anderson. All the boys has. It ain't no big deal."

Max nodded his head in agreement. He had killed several children—accidentally and deliberately—during his bloody life. And as Alex had stated: It was no big deal. He had no nightmares about it. They got in the way, they were disposed of. It was all a matter of one's personal survival.

The plan that Alex was proposing would have to be very carefully worked out. There could be no room for error or miscalculation. And the men involved would have to be chosen carefully, for if word ever leaked out, nationwide condemnation would be certain to follow—quickly. It was a good plan, but very chancy. Very chancy.

"What do you think, Max?"

"It would take a lot of planning, Alex. And the men would have to be chosen carefully. The ones who don't ride on the raid must never know what took place. Now, then, is that possible?"

The outlaw and murderer thought about that. Slowly, he shook his head affirmatively. "Yeah. Forty men could pull it off. Any more than that would be too many. Most of the men here would keep their mouths shut about it. Out of the whole bunch, maybe ten might blab later on."

"Dispose of them now, Alex," Max gave the killing orders. "Once that is done, we start planning on destroying the town."

Alex rose with a grin on his face. "My pleasure, Boss."

Chapter 11

Something nagged at Smoke as he walked through the town. He walked up and down the streets, on the board-walks wherever they were, on the dusty paths where they had not yet been built.

Something was wrong, and Smoke could not pull it out of his brain. Then it came to him. The town lacked adequate water barrels for bucket brigades in case of fire.

Swiftly, he walked back to his office and sent Jim out to round up Tom Johnson, Judge Garrison, and several others in the town.

"What's the drill in case of fire?" he asked bluntly, as was his way.

"Why . . ." Tom looked puzzled. "There isn't any."

"There will be by dark. Judge, alert the people. I want water barrels by every store and every house; buckets placed nearby. And I want those barrels to stay full at all times. We have an old pumper down at the livery stable. See that it's checked out and the hoses inspected for leaks. Benson," he looked at the blacksmith, "you're in charge of the fire brigade."

The blacksmith nodded his head. "You're thinkin' Max might try burning us out?"

"That's exactly what I'm thinking. I'll start rounding up volunteers to clear out the brush and other cover that surrounds the town. I'll ride out to Joe's place and see if he'll lend us some hands to help. Check out and destroy any place where sharpshooters could hide and pick us off. Get on it now, Sal."

The man quietly left the room.

"Max would do it, too," Judge Garrison said. "He told me when he first confronted me that if I didn't do exactly as he said, he'd pick out a child and kill her in front of me. I didn't like what I was doing, but I figured it was the only way to save some children's lives."

"I understand, Judge." Smoke leaned back in his chair. "If we can get most of this done by the dance night and keep a close eye on Max to check his reaction, we can know pretty well that he had burning us out in mind. Then he'll have to come up with another plan."

"He will," Judge Garrison said. "The man is totally and utterly ruthless."

"What are you gonna do with them mercenaries when they step off the stage, Smoke?" Jim asked.

"Oh, welcome them to town, Jim," Smoke said with a smile. "Roll out the red carpet."

That afternoon, Smoke met the southbound stage and was pleased to see it was full, with several men riding on top. The driver handed the mailbag to Marbly's wife—who was the town's postmistress—and seeing there were no passengers departing Barlow, he hollered his team forward.

Those men perched precariously on top gave Smoke

some extremely dirty looks as the stagecoach pulled out. Its next stop would be a way station some fifty miles south, where it would change teams, another stop near Salmon Lake for food and a fresh team, and then on into Missoula, some one hundred twenty-five miles from Barlow.

"Stage was full today," Mrs. Marbly noted, handing Smoke a letter posted from Kalispell, addressed to Sally Jensen, the Grand Hotel, Barlow, Montana Territory. "That means some are giving up on Hell's Creek."

"That it does, ma'am," Smoke said. "Those were all gamblers riding on top. The inside was filled with saloon girls. When the gamblers and the wilted roses start leaving a town, it's like they say about rats leaving a ship. It's about to sink."

"Good riddance to bad rubbish, I say," Mrs. Marbly said. "I'm not an evil-hearted person, Marshal Jensen. My motto is if you can't say something good about a person, don't say anything at all. But that motto has been sorely put to the test by those hooligans and trash up at Hell's Creek. If God were to strike them all dead, I would dance on their graves, Lord forgive me."

She walked back into the store. A good, decent woman who had been pushed just too far, one time too often. Smoke knew she carried a Smith & Wesson pocket .38 in her purse. And he had no doubts but that she would use it.

He took the letter back to the hotel, gave it to Sally, and waited until she had read it.

"You guessed, of course, that it was from Victoria?"

He nodded his head.

"This was posted yesterday in Kalispell—that's only thirty miles away from Hell's Creek—but it's still fast service. There have been a rash of killings in Hell's Creek. Outlaws killing outlaws. One of them managed to escape from the town and came to Robert for treatment. He told Robert that

Big Max had ordered the killings. He didn't know why, but that something big was up. Then the man died. Robert—he's no fool—took the body back into Hell's Creek and told Big Max he had found the body on the road and thought it should be reported to the authorities. Big Max thanked him for being such a civic-minded person and told Robert he'd take care of it. Max knows that Robert is scared to try to leave because of the threats made against Lisa. What does it mean, Smoke?"

"Probably that Val Singer and Warner Frigo and the other gang leaders are getting rid of those they feel might not be able to keep their mouths shut once this something big goes down. So much for honor among thieves."

"And this something big is . . . ?"

"Probably a raid against the town. A raid that includes killing everyone here. Sally, have the hotel pack me a bait of food. I'm going to take a little trip. I should be back by late tomorrow afternoon. I'll arrange for Jim and Sal to meet the stage in case Dubois and Mittermaier should arrive; but I think it's still a couple of days early for that."

"Where are you going, honey?"

"To get the one thing this town needs, Sally." He grinned. "A doctor."

Smoke had checked the land office and knew where the Turner spread was located. He spared his horse, resting often, and rode into Big Max Huggins's country well after dark. He avoided the town by several miles and pulled up at what he hoped was the Turner spread about ten o'clock.

He circled the house to see if they kept a dog and was relieved to find they did not. Smoke picketed Star and slipped up toward the house. He flattened himself against the woodshed when the front door opened and a man stepped out. The man closed the door behind him and stood in the front yard, breathing in the cool night air.

"Dr. Turner?" Smoke called softly.

The man spun around, startled.

"Take it easy, Doctor," Smoke said. "I'm friendly. I'm going to walk toward you, both my hands in plain sight. OK?"

"Who are you?" the doctor demanded.

"The name is Jensen. Smoke Jensen." Smoke walked closer.

"Hold it right there!" the doctor warned. "I have a gun."

"No, you don't," Smoke replied, stepping closer. "And even if you did, it's doubtful you'd know how to use it."

Smoke stopped a few feet from the man and stared at him. "If you're Smoke Jensen, tell me about yourself."

"My wife's name is Sally. We live in Colorado on a spread we named the Sugarloaf. My wife went to college back East with your wife, Victoria. Sally calls her Vicky. Vicky lost her parents while she was in school and had to work very hard to get through. You have one child that lived, Lisa. Your wife can't have any more children. Sally got a letter from Vicky today, telling us about the recent killings in Hell's Creek and the outlaw who staggered up to this ranch and told you about it. You got this ranch by befriending an old man who was visiting back East. You . . ."

"Enough." The doctor held up a hand, visible in the faint light of a quarter moon. He smiled and stuck out the hand for Smoke to shake it. "Welcome to our home, Mr. Jensen."

Smoke shook the hand. "We don't have much time, Doctor. Things are going to blow wide open around here very soon, and you and your family have got to get clear. Let's go in the house and talk."

Lisa was in bed, asleep. Vicky was introduced to Smoke. She stepped back and inspected him, good humor in her eyes. Smoke liked her immediately. He would reserve judgment on the doctor.

"Sally always could pick them," Vicky said. "You are one hell of a man, Smoke Jensen."

"Vicky," her husband said in a long-suffering tone.

Smoke laughed. "Relax, Robert. Sally can occasionally let the words fly herself. I can see why these two were friends at school."

"How about some coffee and something to eat, Smoke?" Vicky asked.

"That would be nice. While I'm eating, you two can pack." That stopped them both in their tracks. Robert asked, "Pack? Where are we going?"

"Getting out of here." Smoke found the cups and poured his own coffee. Very quickly, he explained what was going on. "As far as your ranch goes, if Max burns the buildings down, you've still got the land. You don't have any cattle or any hands. You can always rebuild. You can't do anything from the grave. So pack. We're pulling out."

Smoke drank his coffee and ate a sandwich. Then he went outside and hitched up the teams to a wagon and a buggy. He helped the doctor load his medical equipment onto the wagon, then their luggage and a few possessions from the house. Lisa was awake and wide-eyed as she solemnly stared at the most famous gunfighter in the West.

"I'm surprised Lisa doesn't have a dog," Smoke said.

"I did," the little girl said, sadness in her voice. "Patches was his name. A man killed it a few months ago."

"A rather unsavory character named Warner Frigo rode up into the yard and shot him," Robert said. "It was another one of Max Huggins's little not-too-subtle warnings."

Smoke knelt down and, with a gentleness in his voice that surprised Robert and Vicky, said to Lisa, "We'll get you another dog, Lisa. It won't take the place of Patches, I know that. You'll always remember him. But you can love your new puppy, too. How about it?"

"I'd like that, Mister Smoke. I really would."

Smoke picked her up with no more effort than picking up a feather pillow and smiled. "First thing after we get you all settled is a new puppy, Lisa."

"Frigo is a bad man," the girl said. "He's awful. Only cruel people kill dogs who aren't doing them any harm."

"That's right, Lisa. That's exactly right. Don't you worry about Frigo. I'll take care of him." He set her back down and said, "Let's go, people. We've got a long haul ahead of us."

Vicky walked through the house once more, and there was sadness in her eyes. "I've grown to love this old house, this land with the mountains and the eagles and all its vastness." She blew out a lamp, plunging the room into darkness. "I pray that Max and his hooligans will let the house stand." She sighed and squared her shoulders. "But if they don't . . . we'll rebuild."

"That's the spirit," Smoke told her. "But you might decide to relocate down in Barlow."

"Why would we do that?" Robert asked.

"Because I intend to destroy Hell's Creek, that's why."

Because with the wagons they would have to come within a half mile of Hell's Creek, Smoke wrapped the horses' hooves in sacking when they got close. Out of habit, he checked his guns, loading them up full. The action did not escape the eyes of the doctor and his wife. Lisa had fallen asleep in the back of the wagon, lying on a soft comforter and wrapped up in a blanket, for the night was cool.

"Rumor has it you've killed twenty-five men, Smoke," Robert said.

"Closer to two hundred, I reckon," Smoke corrected.

"Two hundred!" the doctor blurted out. "Two hundred men?"

"Killed twenty-five when I was about nineteen or twenty,

I think I was. They raped my wife and then killed her and our son. I tracked them down to a silver camp on the Uncompahgre and read to them from the Scriptures, so to speak."

"You were only nineteen?" Vicky breathed the question.

"Maybe twenty. I don't remember."

"So young," Robert muttered.

"Oh, I dropped my first man when I was about seventeen, I think I was. After Pa died, an old mountain man named Preacher took me in and raised me. It was a shooting just west of the Needle Mountains. They call the place Rico now. Two men braced me in the trading post. Pike and another man. Never did know his name. I killed them both."

Robert and Victoria listened in silence, their mouths open in shock and fascination, their expressions much like one would wear while gazing at a rattlesnake.

"Me and Preacher, we rode over to what's now called Pagosa Springs—that's Indian for healing water. Two men called me out over there. Man named Haywood and another fellow who was Pike's brother." Smoke tied another piece of sacking in place. "I dropped Haywood and let Pike's brother live. I only shot him twice, in the leg and the arm.

"Me and Preacher rode on over to La Plaza de los Leones; that's on the Cuchara River. It's now called Walsenburg. You see, I was looking for the men who killed my brother and my pa. Killed seven that day and hung one. Casey was his name.

"We drifted on over to Canon City, looking for a man named Ackerman. He found us, him and five of his gang. Killed five, left one alive."

"Lord Jesus," Robert said softly. "That's thirty-three men."

"Oh, I haven't even gotten started yet," Smoke said. "Me and Preacher, we spent the winter back at Brown's Hole, then come spring we drifted out again. That summer I met Nicole and we got married. Sort of. Within a year it all fell to pieces. Bounty hunters got lead in Preacher and I thought they'd killed him. They did kill Nicole and the baby. That's when I rode up to the silver camp with hate in my heart."

"And there have been many more dead men since then?" Robert asked.

"More than I can count, Robert. They just keep coming at me. It was early spring in . . . oh, '74 I think it was. I rode over into Idaho looking for the rest of the men who killed my pa and my brother. Town called Bury. I was going by the name of Buck West."

The horses' hooves muffled, the small party moved out.

"A man called Big Jack braced me at a trading post. His partner buried him out back. I rode on. I had ten thousand dollars on my head at that time, and a lot of bounty hunters were hard after me.

"It was in Challis that two gunhands called me out in the street. I think their names were Carson and Phillips. After I killed them, the marshal asked me to leave. I don't blame him, and I left.

"I rode into Bury with no one knowing who I really was. I was looking to kill the last of the three men who killed my pa and brother: Josh Richards, Wiley Potter, and Keith Stratton. Sally was teaching school there. I saw my sister Janey for the first time in ten years. She was Richards's mistress. She didn't recognize me right off.

"I was walking Sally back to her home when two gun-handlers braced me on the street. Dickerson and Russell. I dropped them both.

"Things turned both tragic and funny after that. Sally lost her job school-teaching and went to live in a whorehouse."

"A whorehouse!" Victoria almost shouted the word. "Sally in a whorehouse?"

Smoke chuckled. "Yep. Oh, she didn't work there. She just lived there."

"My heavens!" Robert muttered.

"Ol' boy on the SRP payroll braced me. I don't remember his name. I had to kill him. It was that day that Janey recognized me as her brother." Smoke cut his eyes and turned his head. He held up a hand for the wagons to stop.

"What's the matter?" Robert asked.

"Something out there," Smoke said.

"How do you know that?"

"Star's ears just came up. A horse is as good as a dog about warning you."

They all heard the clop of horses' hooves and watched as two men rode out of the darkness and up to their wagon.

Both of the men had guns in their hands, the hammers jacked back.

"Well, now," one said. "Ain't this a sight? The doctor and his pretty wife tryin' to slip out, and Smoke Jensen leadin' them. Look here, Jensen. Look down the barrel of the gun that's gonna kill you!"

Chapter 12

Ail Robert or Vicky would remember in the retelling of the event was a series of roaring gunshots. What they did not know was that at the sound of the horses' hooves, Smoke had wrapped the reins around the saddle horn and filled both his hands with .44's.

And neither Robert nor Vicky had seen the third man; but Smoke had.

It was all over in two heartbeats. Three men lay dead or dying on the ground. Robert started to climb down from the wagon.

"Sit down!" Smoke's words were sharp. "Pick up those reins and whap those horses on the butt. We've got to move and do it fast."

"But those men . . ." Robert protested.

Smoke knee-reined Star up to the wagon. When he spoke, his words were low and savage. "Mister, do you want to see your wife and little girl spread-eagled on the ground, being raped, over and over again, until dawn?"

"No. Of course not! But . . ."

"Then shut up and drive this wagon." Smoke slapped one horse on the butt and the team jumped forward, the doctor hanging onto the reins. "Go, Vicky!" Smoke shouted. "Stay on this road south. Don't get off of it. I'll catch up in about an hour. Move!"

Smoke jumped off Star and grabbed the outlaws' rifles from the saddle boots. He jerked off their gunbelts and swiftly loaded the two Winchesters and the Henry up full.

"You gotta help me!" one gut-shot outlaw moaned. "I'm hard-hit."

"That's your problem," Smoke told him. "You were going to kill me, remember?"

"You're a heartless bastard, ain't you, Jensen?"

"No," Smoke replied, levering a round in each chamber of the rifles. "Just a realist, that's all. Now either shut up or die; one or the other."

He left the man moaning in the road and, leading Star, got himself into position in the rocks above the road, in the center of the curve, several sticks of capped and fused dynamite beside him. He made him a little smoldering pocket of punk to light the fuses and waited. He could hear the pounding of hooves, the riders coming hard.

He lit a fuse and judged his toss, placing the charge about fifty feet in front of the laboring horses. The dynamite blew and the horses panicked, throwing riders in all directions. Most of them landed, rolled, and came up on their boots, running for cover. Several lay still, badly hurt and unconscious.

Smoke worked the lever on the Henry as fast as he could and knocked down half-a-dozen riders. He grinned when he saw where many of the gunhands had taken shelter. He poured dirt over the smoldering punk to kill it and left his position, working his way back and then up to about a hundred yards above the road.

He lit another stick of dynamite and tossed it in the middle of a rock pile above the men, then another stick. The explosions jarred the rocks loose and sent them bouncing and crashing onto the men below.

Smoke ran for Star, jumped into the saddle, and was gone into the night. It would take the outlaws anywhere from thirty minutes to two hours to round up their horses.

When he caught up with Robert and Vicky, he halted the parade.

"What did you do back there?" Robert asked, his eyes wide. "We heard explosions and shots."

"I showed them the error of their evil ways and put them on the path of righteousness."

Vicky laughed out loud.

"In other words, you killed them?"

"Lord knows, I sure tried. We'll go on for a few miles and then stop and make camp."

"But those men of Hell's Creek . . . they'll be after us, won't they?"

"Not that bunch," Smoke assured the doctor. "I took the guts right out of them back yonder."

Five miles farther, off the road and camped in a little draw, Smoke drank his coffee and ate a cold sandwich. Lisa had tried to stay awake but finally closed her eyes and was sound asleep.

"Tell us the rest of the story," Victoria urged.

"Where was I?" Smoke asked.

"Killing people," Robert muttered.

Smoke suppressed a chuckle. He had a hunch the doctor

was made of stronger stuff than he appeared. "Well, on the day in Bury that my real identity got known, I was trapped in the town. I'd just left the whorehouse talking with Sally and was coming up an alley when I was braced. That ol' boy let it be known that he was gonna collect that thirty thousand dollars that Potter and Richards and Stratton had put on my head. After I shot that fella, I told him to be sure and tell Saint Peter that none of this was my idea."

Robert was shaking his head but listening intently.

"Before I got out of that alley, another gunny braced me. I left him on the ground and got back to my horse. I put the reins in my teeth and charged the mob that was comin' up the street, led by a crooked sheriff name of Reese.

"Drifter—that was my horse—killed one with his hooves and I shot another gunhand name of Jerry. Me and Drifter scattered gunhands all over the main street of Bury, left that town, and linked up with Preacher and a bunch of old mountain men that was camped up in the mountains outside of town. Let me see . . . there was Preacher, Tennysee, Audie— he was a midget—Beartooth, Dupre, Greybull, Nighthawk— he was an Indian . . . a Crow—Phew, Dead-lead, Powder Pete, Matt—he was a Negro. Matt was the youngest of the bunch and he was about seventy.

"We blew the road bank in and trapped those in the town. Wasn't but two ways in or out, and we closed them both. We gave the citizens a chance to leave and a lot of them did. In the days that followed, before I met a bunch in a ghost town, we got Sally and the wilted flowers out and then I went headhunting."

"How many men did you kill during those days?" Victoria asked.

"Any who tried to kill me, Vicky. A half a dozen or so, I imagine. On that day we burned down Bury and I met

Richards and his bunch in that ghost town, the first man to brace me was a man called Davis. Then Williams and Cross. Then a hired gun name of Simpson faced me. Then there was Martin and a man I didn't know. Rogers and Sheriff Reese came after me. I plugged Rogers and Reese's horse crushed him. I shot Turkel off a rooftop and Britt shot off part of my ear." He lifted one hand. "This part. I dropped three more. Britt, Harris, and Smith. Then Williams got lead in me and I blew Rogers to hell with a shotgun. Brown come up and I dropped him.

"I used my knife to pick the lead out of my leg and wrapped a bandana around it. I believe there were three more left. I plugged two and used a rifle to blow a hired gun name of Fenerty out of it."

Smoke's voice softened as memories filled him, taking him back years. Robert and Victoria could practically feel the pain of those years as they strained to hear him.

"All right, you bastards!" Smoke yelled, tall and bloody in the smoky main street of the ghost town. "Richards, Potter, Stratton. Face me, if you've got the nerve."

The sharp odor of sweat mingled with blood and gunsmoke filled the still summer air as four men stepped out into the bloody, dusty street.

Richards, Potter, and Stratton stood at one end of the street. A tall bloody figure stood at the other. All their guns were in leather.

"You son of a bitch!" Stratton screamed, his voice as high-pitched as a woman's. "You ruined it all. Damn you!" He clawed for his pistol.

Smoke drew, cocked, and fired before Stratton could clear leather.

Potter grabbed for his gun. Smoke shot him dead, holstered his pistol, and waited for Richards to make his play.

Richards was sure he could beat Smoke. He had not moved. He stood with a faint smile on his lips, staring at Smoke.

"You ready to die?" Smoke asked the man.

"As ready as I'll ever be, I suppose." Richards's hands were steady. There was no fear in his voice. "Janey gone?"

"Yeah. She took your money and pulled out."

Richards smiled. "That's one tough babe, Jensen."

"Among other things."

"Been a long run, hasn't it, Jensen?"

"It's just about over."

"What happens to all my holdings?"

"I don't care what happens to the mines. The miners can have them. I'm giving all your stock and the lands they graze on to decent, honest punchers and homesteaders."

A puzzled look spread over Richards's face. He waved his hand at the carnage that lay all around them. "You did . . . all this for nothing?"

Someone moaned, the sound painfully inching up the dusty street.

"I did it for my pa, my brother, my wife, and our baby son."

"But killing me won't bring them back!"

"No. But it will insure that you never do anything like that again."

"I can truthfully say that I wish I had never heard the name Jensen."

"You'll never hear it again after this day, Richards."

"One way to find out, Jensen." He drew and fired. Richards was snake-quick but he hurried his shot, the lead digging up dirt at Smoke's boots.

Smoke's shot hit the man in the right shoulder, spinning him around. Richards grabbed for his left-hand gun and

Smoke fired again, the slug striking the man in the chest. He struggled to level his pistol. Smoke shot him again, the slug hitting Richards in the belly. Richards sat down hard in the street.

Smoke walked up the street to stand over the man. Richards reached out for the pistol that had fallen from his numb hand. Smoke kicked it away.

Blood filled the man's mouth. The light began to fade around him. Richards said, "You'll . . . meet . . ."

Smoke never found out whom he was supposed to meet. Richards toppled over on his face and died.

Robert and Vicky were silent for a few moments after Smoke had finished his story.

Vicky said, "And after that?"

"I got Sally and we took off, heading for Colorado. We've been there ever since." Smoke tossed the dregs of his coffee into the night. "We best get some sleep. We still got a pull ahead of us come morning."

Smoke led the wagon and buggy into Barlow. The group was met with cheers from the onlookers. Draper was there with his camera, taking pictures.

"I must admit," Robert said, "I rather like the welcoming committee."

Sally rushed out of the hotel and the two women hugged each other. With Lisa in tow, the ladies disappeared into the hotel. They had a lot of catching up to do.

"I'm teaching the women of the town who don't know much about guns to shoot," Sally told her friend. "Classes are this afternoon. Do you have any jeans?"

"Britches?" Vicky looked horrified.

"Sure. It's a changing world, Victoria. We'll get you some at Marbly's."

"Everything's been quiet, Smoke," Sal said, walking up. He shook hands with the doctor, his eyes sizing the man up. He took note that the doctor did not wear a gun.

"Do I pass inspection?" Robert asked with a smile.

"Won't know that until the shootin' starts."

"I've done more than my share of hunting, I assure you," Robert replied stiffly.

"Deer don't shoot back," Sal said, then walked off.

Robert looked around him. The people standing around them were all friendly-looking and he had shook a lot of hands. He also had noticed that every man was armed. Every man. Including the editor of the *Bugle*. No doubt about it, the doctor thought. This town is braced for trouble.

"Mrs. Jensen told us what you were doing yesterday, Smoke," Tom Johnson said. "We fixed up an office for Dr. Turner. It's right next to his house."

Smoke grasped the doctor by the shoulder. "You and Victoria get settled in, Robert. Big doings come Saturday night." He smiled. "The town is throwing a party."

Forty-eight hours before the dance and box supper, Smoke met the northbound stage and knew he'd hit pay dirt when two nattily-dressed men stepped off to stretch their legs. They were the only two passengers on the stage. Northbound business had dwindled since Smoke had arrived in Barlow and pinned on a badge. The two men were dressed like dandies but their eyes, cold and emotionless, gave them away.

Henri Dubois and Paul Mittermaier.

Smoke had talked with the driver several days before, setting things up, and the driver nodded his head at Smoke's glance. "It's gonna be about an hour 'fore we pull out, boys," he called. "I got to change this cracked brake lever and one of the pads. Yonder's the saloon. I'll give a hoot and a holler when I'm ready to go."

The team was led away, team and coach heading for the barn.

Henri and Paul headed for the saloon. One of the Circle W hands, Wesson, had agreed to his part in the action. He walked toward the men and slammed a shoulder into the big German.

"Watch where you're goin', stupid!" Wesson said.

"Get out of my way, you ignorant lout!" the German replied.

"What the hell did you call me?" the hand faced him.

"Back off, Paul," Henri said softly.

"What's the matter?" Wesson said with a sneer. "Your buddy have to do your fightin' for you?"

Paul drew back a fist and Wesson popped him on the nose. Henri gave Wesson a blow to the jaw just as the saloon cleared, all of Joe's hands pouring out. The Circle W crew then proceeded to kick the snot out of the pair of assassins, leaving them unconscious on the street.

"Clear out," Smoke told them. "I'll see you all come Saturday night. Thanks, boys."

"Our pleasure, Smoke," Curly grinned around the words. He looked down at the unconscious and badly battered men. "Them ol' boys won't be doin' much of anything for a week or two. Maybe longer."

The Circle W crew rode out of town. "Now what?" Jim asked.

Smoke grinned and reached into his coat pocket, pulling out a bottle of opium-based elixir. "I bought a full case of this from a drummer last week. By the time these two wake up, they're going to be on a train, heading back East. Come on, help me drag them off the street."

They dragged the unconscious men into an alley and stripped them of their duded-up clothes, dressing them in filthy, ragged shirts and jeans. Henri moaned and tried to sit up. Smoke popped him on the noggin with a cosh he'd taken to carrying and the Frenchman laid back down.

With the two men now dressed like bums, Smoke poured a half bottle of knock-out medicine down each of their throats and placed them in the back of a freight wagon.

"Keep them unconscious," Smoke told the grinning freighters who had been more than willing to participate in the game. Anything to get rid of Max Huggins and his gang of outlaws. "When you get down to Helena, pour a bottle of the elixer down them and toss them in an empty eastbound railcar. They'll be somewhere in Nebraska when they wake up."

"Will do, Smoke," the freighter told him. "Don't worry about a thing. Man, this is more fun than I thought it'd be. We was lookin' forward to seeing a shoot-out; but, hell, this is better." Laughing, the freighters pulled out, joining other empty freight wagons on the pull back south.

"Now what do you have in the back of that devious mind of yourn?" Sal asked, unable to wipe the grin off his face.

"Let's go inspect their luggage. I want to see these fancy guns that were going to be used to kill me."

Sal whistled when Smoke opened the gun cases. Both men had seen rifles of this type before, but neither had seen one so duded-up. They were Winchester high-wall, falling block rifles. Single shot.

Smoke hefted one. The rifle had been reworked and the balance was perfect. The telescope was about two feet long, and the shells looked like either the German or the Frenchman or both had carefully and painstakingly loaded their own.

"That bullet would travel about three miles before it knocked you down," Sal said, inspecting one cartridge.

"You know," Smoke said, "most guns are tools. A man uses one snake-killing, or varmint-killing, or to protect himself or his loved ones. I've driven tacks and nails in horseshoes with the butt of my pistols. But these rifles are meant for only one thing."

"Yeah," Sal agreed, closing the lid to the gun case. "Mankillin'."

Chapter 13

The people started coming into town for the dance and box supper during the middle of the day on a beautiful Saturday afternoon.

Most would spend the night camped under their wagons, or in the wagon bed under canvas if it was raining. A few took rooms at the Grand Hotel.

Just before dusk, Smoke had taken his bath and dressed in a black suit, white shirt with string tie, and slipped into his just-polished boots. He strapped on his guns and looked in on Sally. She had dressed in a simple gingham outfit; but with Sally, she could make a flour sack look good.

She gave her hair a final pat and turned to Smoke. "Are you expecting trouble tonight, honey?"

"Yes, I am. When Joe Walsh's crew meet up with Red Malone's Lightning crew, anything is apt to happen."

"All the crews coming in?"

"As far as I know. Joe really stripped his herds this

spring, keeping mostly young stuff. So night-herding is not that essential."

"Shooting trouble?"

"No. We've taken care of that. All guns will be checked upon entering the dance area. If any object to that, they can carry their butts back home. If any trouble starts, it will be fists."

"But you and Sal and Jim will be armed?"

Smoke smiled. "Oh, yes, honey."

"This promises to be quite an interesting night."

"That . . . is one way of putting it, yes."

They walked down the stairs and were a head-turning couple, Sally a beautiful woman and Smoke a strikingly handsome man in a rugged sort of way.

They joined Dr. and Mrs. Turner in the hotel dining room for coffee.

"I will say this, Smoke," Robert said. "I find the people of Barlow a refreshing change from the hoodlums and rowdies of Hell's Creek. We both like it here."

"I'm glad you do. And I hope you decide to stay. It's going to be a growing little town."

"But you and Sally will eventually move on?"

"Oh, yes. Back to the Sugarloaf. It's home. We'll get this situation straightened out here and be back home in early fall."

"Will there be trouble tonight?" Vicky asked.

"Probably," Smoke gave her an honest reply. "But it won't be gunplay."

"Anyone from Hell's Creek made an appearance yet?" Robert asked.

"Not to my knowledge. But they'll be along. They can't afford not to show up."

They looked up, and Tom Walsh and his Circle W crew rode in and dismounted. Tom drove the buggy, sitting beside his wife. Mrs. Walsh joined the ladies in the dining room, while Smoke and Dr. Turner stepped outside to join Joe and his crew.

"All right, boys," Smoke spoke to the Circle W hands. "This is the way it's going to be this night. When you enter the dance and box supper area, you check your guns with Mrs. Marbly. The only people who will be armed will be me and my deputies. And I've appointed several special deputies for this night. Anyone who doesn't think they can abide by that rule, haul your ashes out of town."

"Suits me," Curly was the first to speak. "But it's gonna be interestin' to see you take Melvin Malone's guns offen him."

"I'll take them," Smoke replied. "Or tomorrow his dad will be burying him."

Tom Johnson, one of the special deputies, rode in from the north, just as Benson, another of the special deputies, rode up from the south end of town. Johnson said, "Big Max and half a dozen of his gunslicks coming in."

"Red Malone and his crew are just outside of town," Benson added.

"Get your shotguns, boys," Smoke said. "Line up with me on the boardwalk."

Johnson, Marbly, Benson, and Toby got sawed-off shotguns and lined up in front of the hotel, two on each side of Smoke. Jim and Sal stood a dozen yards off, one on each side of the five. They too were armed with Greeners.

Smoke knew some of the men who rode in with Max: Alex Bell, Dave Poe, Val Singer. He did not know the others with them. But he knew the breed: hired guns.

"I don't like this," Val muttered, eyeballing the shotgun-armed men on the boardwalk.

"Relax," Max told him. "It's just a show of force."

"Hell of a welcoming committee, Boss," John Steele said.

"Don't nobody do nothin' stupid," Red Malone said to his men. "Them express guns would kill everybody in the whole damn street. Let's find out what's going on."

One of Red's hands was driving the buggy with the elegantly gowned Tessie. She took one look at Smoke and said, "Oohhh, I think I'm in love!"

In heat would be more like it, the hand thought. But he kept that to himself.

Tessie's exploits were known throughout the entire county and several adjacent counties.

The crews of Max and Red swung their horses and faced Smoke and his deputies.

"Good evening, gentlemen, Miss Tessie," Smoke said. "Welcome to Barlow."

"What's the idea of all this force?" Red demanded in a loud voice.

Smoke ignored him. "It's a beautiful night, people, so we decided to move everything outdoors. The dance area is roped off, as is the box supper area. We have plenty of chairs and benches for your comfort if you didn't bring blankets to sit on. That tent set up just before you enter the entertainment area is where you will check your guns."

Smoke had stepped off the boardwalk as he was speaking, moving close to Mel Malone.

"I'll be damned if I'll check my guns!" the young man said.

Smoke jerked him off his horse, slapped him twice, ripped the gunbelt from him, and tossed guns and belt into a horse trough. He did it so quickly no one had a chance to interfere.

Smoke faced the young man as he spoke to his deputies. "Anybody who makes a grab for a gun, start killing the whole bunch of them."

Hammers were eared back on the sawed-off shotguns and the muzzles leveled at the mounted men.

"Now, hold on!" Red bellowed. Sawed-off shotguns at this range would tear them all apart.

Smoke grabbed Melvin by his fancy shirt and jerked him close. "You say one more word to me about what you're not going to do, sonny-boy, and I'll break both your goddamn arms so you'll never be able to pick up a gun again. You understand me?"

For the first time in his life, Melvin Malone knew real fear. It clutched at him, souring his stomach. He looked into the eyes of Smoke Jensen and saw death staring back at him. Death rode a fiery horse and the grim reaper wore the face of Smoke Jensen.

"Yes, sir," he said quietly. "I understand." Then rage overrode fear and the young man made up his mind. He carried a hide-out gun behind his belt buckle.

Smoke released him. He was expecting a sneak-play from the young man and was ready for it.

Mel grabbed for his Remington over-and-under .41 derringer and Smoke hit him. Smoke's big fist smashed into the young man's face, flattening his nose and knocking him flat on his butt in the street. Before Mel could shake the birds and bells and buzzing bees out of his head, Smoke had rolled him over and clamped handcuffs tight around his wrists.

Smoke straightened up. "Take him to jail, Jim. The charge is disorderly conduct, disturbing the peace, and attempted murder of a peace officer. Bond, if any, will be set by Judge Garrison in the morning. That's it, people. Check your guns with Mrs. Marbly and have fun."

Smoke walked back onto the boardwalk, turned, and faced the mounted men.

Red cut his eyes to the south. A dozen men, all armed with rifles, stood in the street, blocking any escape. Max followed the glance, grunted, and then looked toward the north. Another dozen men, all heavily armed, blocked the north end of the street.

"I think," Alex Bell said with unusual restraint, "that we'uns better check our guns and get ready for the dance."

"We'll do that," Red said, swinging his gaze back to Smoke. "And there'll be no trouble in this town tonight. Not by any of my people. But you'll not try my boy on them charges, Jensen."

"He'll be tried, Red. And if convicted, he'd do his time in the territorial prison. Now hear me well, all of you. The days of lawlessness are over in this town. The days of any of you riding roughshod over decent, law-abiding people have ended. Pull in your horns and act right, or die. That's the only choice I'm going to give any of you. If any of you cause trouble at tonight's festivities, I'll kill you. I'll shoot you down like a rabid skunk and drag your carcass off and stick it in the first hole I come to. And if it's the lime pit of an old privy, that'll do just fine. Now stable your horses and check your guns."

Max was the first to move. He backed his horse and rode to the livery stable, Red and the others following. And it was a silent following. Not one of them doubted that Smoke Jensen meant every word they'd just heard him say.

In the stable, Val Singer said, "I'd hate to think I had to spend eternity in a shit-pit."

"And Jensen would do it, too," Alex Bell said.

"We got to do something about Jensen, Max," Dave Poe said. "And we got to do it damn quick."

"I know. Did you boys notice anything riding into town?"
No one had.

"Then open your damn eyes!" Max snapped at them.

"Look around you. You're supposed to be gunfighters, men who live by your wits. Hell, boys, there are water barrels everywhere. Full barrels. With buckets close by. This very stable is where the town used to keep their pumper. It's gone. That means that Jensen outguessed us . . . again. He guessed we might try to burn him out, and they're prepared for it.

"Did any of you see the clearing of brush that's been done around the town? And up on the ridges where a sharp-shooter might hide? There is no place. Not anymore. The town is ready for an attack."

"Where is them high-priced sharpshooters from Europe that was comin' in?" Val asked.

"I don't know," Max admitted. "They should have been here by now. Unless . . ." he mused aloud. Then he shook his head. "No. Jensen had no way of knowing they were coming in. And neither one of them carries a sidearm . . . where it can be seen. He'd have no reason to pull them off the stage. I can but assume they are on their way in."

One of the gunslingers unbuckled his gunbelt and draped it over his shoulder. "Well," he drawled. "Let's go be good little boys and check our guns and dance with some real ladies, and then we'll eat some home cookin' for a change."

Smoke stood on the edge of the lantern-lighted perimeter and let Curly from the Circle W and a redheaded hand from the Lightning brand slug it out. He had no idea what had started the fracas, but as long as no guns were involved, he had told his deputies to let the men fight, but to just keep it away from the ladies.

"Anybody that would work for Red Malone would eat road apples," Curly told the puncher.

The hand flattened him.

Curly jumped up, butted the puncher in the stomach with his head, and both of them went rolling across the dirt. Curly came up on top and proceeded to rearrange the redhead's face for him.

Smoke finally pulled the man off the Lightning puncher. "That's enough, Curly. He's out of it. Kill him and the matter becomes something other than a fistfight."

The blacksmith, Benson, grabbed Curly and led him off to a horse trough. Benson, strong as a grizzly bear, picked Curly up and dunked him headfirst into the trough several times.

"Now cool down, man," Benson told him. "Your sweetie's box is gonna be comin' up soon. You miss the bid on it and she'll never speak to you again." Benson was holding him by his boots, upside down.

"You do have a point," Curly sputtered. "Now turn me a-loose."

"You sure?" Benson asked.

"Damn right, I'm sure."

Benson turned him loose and Curly dropped headfirst into the horse trough.

Everybody gathered around, including Max and Red, had a good laugh at that.

Curly came up for air, sputtering and cussing.

Smoke walked to where Dr. Turner was kneeling down beside the moaning cowboy.

"He'll be all right," the doctor said. "His nose is broken and he's lost some teeth, but I can't find any broken ribs. He'll be sore for a few days. Barbaric method of settling arguments," he added.

"Beats the hell out of guns," Smoke told him.

"You have a point," the doctor conceded.

The rest of the evening went smoothly, with no more trouble. The bidding on the boxes was fast and sometimes heavy, depending on whether two young men were courting the same young lady. Smoke bid on Mrs. Walsh's box and Joe bid on Sally's, and everybody seemed to have a good time. Even Max got into the spirit of things and was laughing and telling jokes to the ladies . . . clean jokes.

After everyone had eaten and the dancing began, Max walked over to Smoke, standing in the shadows.

"You really think you've got the bull by the horns, now, don't you, Jensen?"

"Or riding a tiger."

Max chuckled. "Yes. The old East Indian proverb. I know it. And you surely must know, Smoke, that we of Hell's Creek are not simply going to give up and desert the town."

"You'd be smart if you did."

"No way, Jensen. You've backed us into a corner. We have to fight."

"If you say so."

"Innocent people will be hurt . . . killed."

"That's usually the way it goes." He turned slightly to face Max. "Take some advice, Max: Pull out. Break up your gangs and leave the country. If you stay, I'm going to have to kill you. You must know that."

"Or I'll kill you."

"A lot of men have tried that, Max. I've soaked up a lot of lead in my day. I'm still here."

"Oh, I think Melvin is as good as you are. And you'll never bring that boy to trial, Smoke."

"Maybe not. We'll have to see, won't we?"

"And maybe I have a couple of aces in the hole, Smoke."

"By the names of Henri Dubois and Paul Mittermaier?" Max's smile was not in the least pleasant to look at. The big man sighed in disgust. He had been counting on the back-shooting pair.

"I've got their fancy rifles locked up in my office. Those

two are halfway back to New York City by now. They're so doped up it'll be days before they even know who they are, much less where they are."

Max chuckled. Outlaw, killer, thief, he nevertheless had a sense of humor. And while he did not like being bested, he could still appreciate—however reluctantly—the method that was used in doing so.

"Slick, Jensen. I keep underestimating you. I've got to stop doing that. Jensen, what is the point of your interference? Is this what you're going to do for the rest of your life, stick your damn nose in other peoples' affairs?"

"I hope not, Max. To tell the truth, my wife and I came up here to visit friends. Nothing else."

"Dr. Turner and his wife," Max put it together. "I should have guessed. Sure. Who else in Hell's Creek would your wife want to associate with? So, now Barlow has a doctor and we don't. What's next, Jensen?"

"Your packing up and pulling out."

"That is something I will never do, Jensen."

Smoke shrugged his heavy shoulders. "You've noticed the cleanup around the town, the new water barrels." It was not put as a question. "You've seen where we've fixed up our pumper. And you've seen how the people are all armed and willing to stand shoulder to shoulder to fight you and Red Malone. Don't you feel it in your guts, Max? Can't you see you're not going to win this one?"

Max felt it, all right. He'd been sensing it for several days. Riding into Barlow had been depressing. The town was clean and neat, with swept boardwalks and washed windows and shrubs and flowers planted around the homes. Not like Hell's Creek, where litter was ankle-deep in some spots and the gunhands lived in shacks and tents and squalor. The stench of unwashed bodies was something one grew accustomed to in Hell's Creek. The people here took pride in their town. Here, in Barlow, there was a better class of people and good water.

Of course, that's all Hell needed.

Max's eyes flickered to the lush little body of Aggie, doing a reel with that pig-farmer's boy, Elias. His blood grew hot with perversion.

The quick glance did not escape the eyes of Smoke, who filed it away.

"I'll go down with my town," Max said, his voice husky with sudden desire. "If indeed we are to go down at all. And that certainly remains to be seen."

"Men like you never learn, Max. Civilization is fast spreading throughout the West. The people aren't going to tolerate men like us much longer."

"Us?" The statement confused Max. "Us!"

"Sure, Max. Us. I'm tolerated because I'm bringing a change to this town. When you and Red are either dead or run out of the territory, the people won't want me around. I'm a gunfighter, Max. The smell of gunsmoke lingers around me like some sort of invisible shroud. Just like the smell of perversion lingers around you."

Max's head jerked up. "What the hell do you mean by that, Jensen? Perversion?"

"You touch that Feckles girl and I'll kill you, Max. I'll ride right into Hell's Creek and shoot you. As God is my witness, I'll do it."

"She's a woman, Jensen. She might be a child in mind, but she's got the body of a woman." Max knew he ought to shut his big mouth, but arrogance worked his tongue.

"You're pure crud, Max. I know that you lusted after both Victoria and Lisa. Tell you what, Max. I'm going to start sending out wires to a lot of law enforcement offices; I'm going to blanket your back trail and see what I can come up with. And I'm going to start with telegrams concerning child molestation and rape over . . . say, the past ten years or so. How does that grab you, partner?"

Max was thinking hard. He'd left a trail behind him, for sure.

If Jensen started digging, he'd soon put two and two together and Max would be forced to run. No question about that.

Max forced a laugh. "You do that, Jensen. My back trail is clean."

"We'll soon know," Smoke spoke the words softly. "It'll take me about a week to find out."

Max could scarcely control his wildly raging temper. He stared at Smoke for a moment and then spun on his boot heels, hollering for his men to get their gear and mount up. They were leaving.

"What's with Big Max?" Joe Walsh asked, walking up.

"I touched a festering boil," Smoke told him. "And it's just about ready to explode."

Chapter 14

Over coffee the next morning in his office, Smoke told Jim and Sal and Judge Garrison what had brought on Max Huggins's sudden departure the night before.

"Let me start canvasing various law enforcement agencies, Smoke," Judge Garrison said. "I have many more contacts than you. I should have something within a week, probably in less time than that."

"Good, Judge. Get right on it, will you?"

"Immediately." The judge left the room and walked over to the telegraph office. He would be very busy for the next several days. Judge Garrison did not set a bond for Melvin Malone. He said the attempted murder charge meant he did not have to set a bond. Melvin would stay in jail.

"You're dead, Jensen," Melvin hollered from his cell. He rattled the barred door. "You're a dead man walking around and you're just too stupid to know that."

"Shut up, boy," Smoke called. "You're only making things more difficult for yourself."

"Son of a bitch!" Melvin yelled. "That's you, Jensen. Low-life, no-good . . ."

Smoke tuned him out.

"You know Red is gonna try to bust him out," Sal said.

"Sure. Once he hears no bond was set, he'll try force. Maybe as soon as tonight."

"You want us to set up cots and sleep here?" Jim asked.

"No." Smoke's reply was quick. "Red, so I'm told, likes to use dynamite. That's how he drove all those small farmers out that were settling around his holdings. He might decide to use explosives here. Too risky for us to sleep in."

"Hell, Smoke!" Sal said. "He uses dynamite, he might blow up Melvin tryin' to get him out."

Smoke shook his head. "We won't be that lucky, Sal." Smoke cut his eyes to the window in time to see John Steele riding up, the point man for several wagons, coming into town for supplies. They pulled up in front of Marbly's General Store.

"Oh, boy," Jim said. "Here it comes."

Smoke stood up and reached for his hat. "Yep," he said, heading for the door. "Storm clouds are gathering and it's about to rain trouble all over us. Let's go, boys. I wouldn't want to miss this."

The three men crossed the street just as John Steele was entering Marbly's store. They stepped up onto the boardwalk in time to hear John's shout of disbelief.

"What the hell do you mean, you little worm?" John roared. "My money is no good? My money is as good as anybody's, and by the Lord, you're going to sell me what I want."

"Get out of my store," Marbly stood his ground. "I don't

want you or any of your scummy crew in my place of business. Get out, I say!"

John reached across the counter and grabbed Marbly by the shirtfront. Mrs. Marbly jerked an axe handle out of a barrel and honked it across the top of John's Stetson-covered head. John's eyes rolled back in his head and he sank to the floor, out cold. One of the Lightning hands jerked out a gun and aimed it at the woman. Smoke dusted him through and through with a .44 slug. The force of the slug knocked the cowboy to one side and into a showcase. He died among women's underthings, his head on a corset.

The townspeople reacted immediately to the shooting. The street filled with armed men. The remaining Lightning crew held up their hands in a hurry, not wanting to get plugged from every angle.

Smoke holstered his .44 and pointed to John Steele. "Drag him to jail." He looked at Marbly. "You going to press charges?"

"Damn right!" the shopkeeper said, considerable heat in his voice.

"Charge him with assault and battery," Smoke said to Sal. "Jim, get the undertaker."

Smoke stepped outside and faced the Lightning crew. "This town is off-limits to you and to anyone who works for Red Malone—including Red. I am officially banning any and all of you from Barlow. Take the word back to Red."

"Big talk, Jensen," the hand sneered at him. "I'll see your hide nailed to the wall afore this is over."

Smoke reached up and took off his badge, handing it to Marbly. "You want to try it now, cowboy? Guns or fists, it makes no difference to me."

The cowboy, who was going by the name of Dan since he was wanted in several states for cattle rustling and armed robbery, among other things, hesitated.

Smoke smiled, knowing he was giving the man no way out. It was the way of the West that when challenged, you had but two options: fight or be branded a coward. Smoke did not like the code but, in this case, felt he was justified in invoking it.

Dan took off his gunbelt and handed it to a Lightning puncher. He flexed his arms and looked back at Smoke. "You mind if I warm up a little first?"

"I don't care if you do the Virginia reel," Smoke told him, and that got a laugh from the gathering crowd, both men and women. "You probably can't dance any better than you can fight."

The crowd roared with laughter and Dan flushed in anger.

"I think I'll just clean your clock," Dan said.

"Then come on, cowboy."

Dan tried a sucker punch that brought no response from Smoke. He hooked a left that Smoke blocked and tried to follow through with a right that Smoke flicked away.

Smoke jumped lightly off the boardwalk and waved Dan down to join him.

"Stand still and fight, damn you!" Dan yelled.

"Oh!" Smoke said. "I see. That's what you want. I thought you were still warming up."

The crowd loved it and roared their approval.

Dan didn't think it was a bit funny and stepped in close. Smoke rattled his teeth with a left and put a knot on his head with a right. Dan backed up, shaking his head and spitting out blood.

"I'm waiting to fight," Smoke taunted him.

Dan charged him with a shout of defiance, and Smoke stuck out a boot and tripped the man, sending him sprawling into the dirt of the street.

The Lightning cook sat his seat on the wagon and shook his head. Dan was gonna get the crap beat out of him for sure, and just as soon as that was over and done with and they got back to the ranch, Cookie was packin' up his kit and gettin' the hell gone from the Lightning brand. His oldest boy had been forever trying to get him over into Idaho to help on his horse ranch. This time, by God, he was going. Hadn't oughtta a stayed this long with this pack of screwballs.

That thought had just crossed his mind when Dan got up from the dirt and went charging and yelling toward Smoke Jensen. The cook grimaced as Smoke poleaxed the puncher with a solid right fist that turned Dan around and sent him stumbling out into the street.

As a matter of fact, the cook thought, there ain't no reason to go back to the ranch. I just got paid, I got my best clothes on, I'm wearin' my gun, and I ain't got nothin' back there no good for anything no how.

The dull smack of Smoke Jensen's fist again connecting with Dan's jaw prompted Cookie to climb down from the wagon seat and walk up toward the stage office. He had more than enough money in his pockets to get a room at the Grand and buy his ticket over to Idaho. Hell with Red Malone and his foolish boy and the whole damn crazy bunch out at Lightning.

Cookie turned in time to see Dan whip out a knife. "Stupid, Dan," he muttered. "Now Smoke's gonna kill you."

"I'll gut you, Jensen," Dan screamed his rage and frustration. He stepped closer.

Smoke reached behind his right hand .44 and pulled out a long-bladed Bowie knife. "You sure this is the way you want it?" Smoke asked him.

Dan moved closer, working the blade from side to side. He tried to fake Smoke but Jensen wasn't falling for it.

"Don't do this, Dan!" one of the Lightning crew yelled. "It ain't worth it."

Dan pressed on, curses rolling off his tongue. He swung the blade and Smoke parried it, the metal clanking as the razor-sharp knives met.

Smoke stepped in and cut Dan from earlobe to point of jaw. "Drop the knife," he warned the puncher. "Mountain men raised me. I've been knife-fighting since I was sixteen."

"Hell with you!" Dan said as the blood dripped from the cut on his face.

"I don't want to kill you, boy," Smoke told him. "Give this up."

Dan moved in and Smoke cut his knife arm, opening him up from elbow down to hand. Dan screamed as the knife dropped from his numbed and useless hand.

"Get Dr. Turner," Smoke said to the crowd. "See what he can do with this fool."

Smoke wiped the blood from his blade and sheathed it. Turning to the Lightning punchers, he said, "You have one minute to get clear of this town. And don't ever come back."

Cookie watched from the boardwalk as the bleeding Dan was led to the doctor's office. "Told you so, boy," he muttered. "I learned fifty years ago to give mountain men a wide berth."

Cookie turned and walked into the ticket office. Idaho sure looked good to him.

Red Malone received the news of being banned from Barlow stoically. He had been expecting something like this, so it didn't surprise him.

But he was shook down to his boots at the news of John Steele being jailed. "How is Dan?" he finally asked.

"He ain't never gonna use his right arm again. Tendons was cut."

Red grunted. "Cookie?"

"He quit."

"Get my horse. I'm riding to Barlow."

"You want me to get the boys together?"

"No. I'm riding alone. Do it, Jake. I don't want to hear any arguments."

Red rode to the town limits and sat his saddle in the middle of the road. Malone was many things, but a fool was not one of them. Someone would soon spot him and take the news to Jensen. Smoke would ride out to see what he wanted.

In a couple of minutes, Jensen rode up and faced him. "Something I can do for you, Red?"

"Has bond been set for John Steele?"

"Fifty dollars. He's out, saddling his horse. He'll be along shortly."

"He hurt?"

"He's got a knot on his noggin and his pride is bruised, that's all."

Red nodded his head. "You'd a done Dan a favor if you'd gone on and killed him. A one-armed puncher ain't good for much, Jensen."

"That's his problem, Red."

John Steele came riding out, wheeled his horse up beside Red, and faced Smoke. The man was killing mad and it showed on his face, which was chalk-white with anger. Smoke knew that was the sign of a very dangerous man. A red-faced man usually meant all bluff and bluster, but one whose face was chalk-white meant he was cold inside.

"I want to see my boy, Jensen. He ain't much, I'll give you that, but he's still mine. You can have my gun and search me. Have a deputy there with us. But I want to see him."

"All right, Red. I wouldn't have kicked up any fuss at that. A father has a right to see his own. John, you ride on to the spread. Don't come back to town. I mean it. Your high-handed, roughshod ways of dealing with the people of Barlow are over."

"You and me, Jensen," the foreman said tightly. "Someday, just you and me."

"Shut your mouth and clear out, John. Don't dig your own grave."

John wheeled his horse and rode away.

"Did this . . . incident with John go down the way my hand said it did?"

"What'd your hand say about it?" After listening to a brief rundown, Smoke nodded his head. "That's about it, Red."

It was obvious that Red had more on his mind than seeing his son. Smoke got the impression Malone didn't even like the boy. He might love him, but he sure didn't like him.

"Where am I supposed to buy supplies, Jensen?"

"I don't know, Red. But if Marbly doesn't want you in his store, that's his right."

"You've pushed me up against a wall just like you're pushin' Max. Don't you think we'll push back, Jensen?"

"We're ready anytime you boys want to start the tug-of-war, Red."

"Damnit, man!" Red stirred in the saddle. "My boys will have to drive teams way the hell south of here for supplies."

"There's a way you can prevent that, Red, and you know it."

"There's two ways, Jensen. And you know the other way I'm talkin' about."

"You want to try it now, Red?" Smoke calmly laid down the challenge.

Red grudgingly smiled at the man's calmness and courage. He took a deep breath and shook his head. "I reckon not, Jensen. But you can't stick around here forever. You got to leave sometime. I'll wait."

"I'm betting you won't, Red. Oh, you might; I'll give you that. But sooner or later, your daughter is going to want some pretties from the dress shop or the general store, and she'll agitate you or someone else until you drive her in. One of your hands is going to get drunk and come rip-snorting in here. You or some of your crew or your kid will get sick and have to see the doctor or the man at the apothecary shop. Any of those things could blow the lid off. And one of them more than likely will."

"You'd stop me from bringing my girl or one of my men in to see the doctor?"

"That's right, Red."

"You're a heartless bastard, Jensen!"

"Oh, I wouldn't prevent the doctor from going out to your spread. Or you could bring them to this town limit and he could treat them. But after today, unless it's for a court appearance, neither you nor any of your family or crew sets a foot in Barlow."

Red curtly nodded his head. "I got a packet in my saddlebags for Mel. It's some readin' material and money so's he can buy himself some food from the cafe. Is that all right?"

"Suits me, Red."

Red unbuckled the straps and handed Smoke a small packet.

"You know I'll have to inspect it?"

"I know. It's a Bible, Jensen. That's the only book I could find in the house. Maybe he'll read it, maybe he won't. I reckon I should have."

"You think it's too late for that, Red?"

The rancher thought about that for a moment. "Yeah, I

think it is, Jensen." He shook his head. "That don't make no never-mind. I'll deal with the devil when I meet him. Jensen, either I'm gonna kill you, John Steele is gonna kill you, Max Huggins is gonna kill you, or somebody is gonna kill you for that bounty on your head . . . and you know there is one."

"So I've heard."

"And there you sit, just as calm and unconcerned as a hog in slop."

"That's me, Red. I don't worry about things I have no control over. I don't fret about too little or too much rain. That's in God's hands. And I don't worry about what you or Max and your scummy crews are going to do. Oh, I could take control of that, Red, by blowing you out of the saddle right now. But even though I've killed lots of men, I'm not a murderer and I don't force gunplay on people who haven't pushed me. So I just wait."

"Lemme see if I can get through to you, Jensen. The people in this town are little people. You and me and Max, we're big people. Big people have always had little people under their thumb. That's what makes the world go round, Jensen. Do you understand that?"

"I hear your words, Red, and you're wrong. But you'll never see that, though. If you lived in a big city, you'd be running a sweatshop, forcing decent people to work long hours under miserable conditions for little pay. That's just the way you are, I reckon. Lots of folks are like you and Max, Red. You're born that way. I call it the bad seed theory."

"Goddamn you, Jensen," Red flared. "I came out here in late '65 when this country was wild, man, wild! I built my spread with sweat and blood, a lot of it my blood. I fought Injuns and homesteaders and hog-farmers and white trash. I scratched and clawed and chewed my way to what I got. And I'll not see it tore apart in front of my eyes. I demand respect."

"You left out a lot of things, Red. You left out that you probably came out here running from the law back East."

Smoke knew he'd hit pay dirt from the expression on Red's face. The man looked like he'd been hit with a club. He ground his teeth together so hard Smoke could hear the gnashing. Red's face turned white and he fought to maintain control.

"You always were a liar and a cheat and a thief and a womanizer. I'm told you beat your wife so often and so savagely she finally had enough and quit you. Now I add all that up, Red, and do you know what the total is?"

Red stared at Smoke. He was killing mad but smart enough to know if he dragged iron, Jensen would beat him. Red was good with a gun, but no match for Smoke Jensen.

"So add it up and tell me what you come up with, gunfighter," Red spat the words.

"Scum," Smoke said softly. "One hundred percent stinking scum."

"I'll spit on your grave, Jensen."

"I doubt it."

"Goddamn you, Jensen!" Red flared. "Who gives you the right to pass judgment on me? You're nothin' but a gunhandler. You made your money killin' people. What in the hell gives you the right to think you're better than me?"

"Oh, I don't think I'm better than you in the Biblical sense, Red. We're all going to have to stand before our Maker and be judged."

Red's face had regained much of its normal color. He wore a puzzled look as he spread his hands wide. "Then . . . ?"

"Red, I could stand here and try to explain the differences

between us until I fell off my horse from exhaustion. No matter what I said, I'd never get through to you. So I'll tell you this: If you're not going to change your murdering, thieving ways and try to live a decent life, if you're not going to fire the scum from your payroll and run them out of this country, I suggest you go make your peace with God. Go make out your will and leave your ill-gotten holdings to Tessie."

"Tessie! Hell's fire, man. She'd go through my money like a whirlwind. I'll leave my holdings to my son."

"He won't be around very much longer, Red."

"Huh?"

"If he beats the charges—and he probably will; Judge Garrison says the attempted murder charge is pretty flimsy— he'll come after me. And I'll kill him. Then you'll go on the prod, and I'll put you down. The way I see it, Red, any way it goes, you're looking at a grave." Smoke glanced at the packet in his left hand. "I thought you wanted to see your boy?"

"I changed my mind. I got some ruminatin' to do, Jensen. I got to think on what all you've said this day. I don't know whether you're the bravest man I ever met or just damn crazy. But if you wanted another enemy, Jensen, you just made one with me."

"See you around, Red."

"You set foot outside this town, Jensen, you better be wearin' a gun."

Smoke smiled. "I'm wearin' one now, Red."

Red shook his head and wheeled his horse, heading back to his ranch.

Smoke rode back to the jail and inspected the contents of the packet. Exactly what Red had said. He rifled through the pages of the Bible to check for a derringer or a knife, then tossed the money and Bible to Melvin.

"Your dad brought you some reading material, kid."

Melvin began tearing out the pages.

"What are you doing, boy?" Smoke asked. "That's the holy Bible."

"Damn heathen," Sal muttered.

Melvin grinned. "Tell my pa thanks, Jensen. I needed something to wipe my butt with."

Chapter 15

Melvin Malone was released from jail, the attempted murder charge dropped. Sal picked up the torn pages from the Bible and carefully disposed of them, muttering about heathens and those doomed to the pits of hell.

A week passed, with no retaliation from either Max Huggins or Red Malone. But the townspeople did not relax; they knew an attack was coming. They just didn't know when or how.

Smoke received an unsigned telegram telling about the further misadventures of Paul Mittermaier and Henri Dubois. It seems the pair had been arrested and jailed in Kansas City for strong-arm robbery. They told some wild tale about being beaten and drugged in a small town out west, and then waking up in an empty railroad car. They claimed they were really foreign tourists, over here to do some buffalo hunting.

The judge laughed at them and sent them off to prison for a couple of years.

Smoke sent the wire to Max Huggins.

On a warm and bright summer's day, Aggie Feckles walked into a field on the outskirts of town to pick flowers for the kitchen table.

Several hours later, Martha showed up at the marshal's office, nearly hysterical.

Smoke didn't need a crystal ball to know what had taken place. He sent a boy over to the hotel for Sally, so she could look after Martha, and began stuffing his saddlebags with items he might need when he declared war on Hell's Creek.

"We'll get a posse together," Judge Garrison said.

"No, we won't," Smoke nixed that idea. "That's what Max wants. They want a posse chasing after shadows and leaving the town undefended." He looked around him. Sally and Martha had gone over to Mrs. Marbly's. "If Aggie is still alive, I'll bring her back."

"If she's still alive?" the blacksmith, Benson, questioned.

"The lawyers have a phrase for it," Smoke replied. He glanced at Judge Garrison.

"Corpus delicti," the judge told the crowded room. "It means the facts to prove a crime. In a case this heinous—and we might as well say the word: rape—Max, if it is Max, would probably dispose of the body after the viciousness was done. He'd be a total fool to keep her alive. And Max is not a fool. Let's all hope and pray he's savoring the anticipation and has not completed the act."

Smoke walked out of the office and stepped into the saddle.

Judge Garrison followed him out. "Smoke, I've received some confirmation about Max Huggins's back trail. I was on my way over to tell you when I heard about Aggie. He's wanted back East. Mostly for rape of young girls. He then killed them. In several states."

"Do you have the warrants?"

"That'll take some time. Probably a month or better. It's a time-consuming process, Smoke."

Smoke shook his head and grimaced as he picked up the reins. "Aggie doesn't have a month, Judge. Looks like this is going to be western justice. See you."

He rode out of town, heading north.

Smoke stopped at the Brown farm and pulled the farmer off to one side, briefing him.

Brown's face tightened. "I'll try to keep this from Elias. The boy is sure sweet on that girl; no tellin' what he'd try to do. Damnit!" the man cursed. "What kind of filth would do something like this?"

Ellie brought them coffee and her husband told her what had happened.

"That poor child. How much hope do you hold out for her, Mr. Jensen?"

"Not much. Max will probably do the deed and then kill her. It's a pattern of his."

She frowned and said, "I'm a God-fearing woman, Mr. Jensen. But I have to ask this: Why doesn't society hang men like Max Huggins and others who do these terrible things? Why are they allowed to live?"

"I don't know, ma'am. It has something to do with a movement started back East. Something about the worth of a criminal's life or some such drivel as that. God help us all if it spreads out here."

They all turned at the sounds of a horse approaching. Pete Akins was coming up the road. He saw Smoke standing in the farmer's yard and turned in, closing the gate behind him. The gunfighter dismounted and walked over to the group.

"I'm out of it, Smoke," he said, taking off his hat in the presence of Mrs. Brown. "Bell and Frigo and some others grabbed the little Feckles girl and hauled her to Max Huggins. My gun may be for hire, but I'll be damned—'cuse the word, ma'am—if I'll have a part in abusin' a child or botherin' a good woman. If you want another deputy, you got one, Smoke."

"I had a hunch you'd come around, Pete. Where is Aggie being held?"

"She ain't bein' held nowhere, Smoke. She's dead. Max done his evil and give her to the men. Made me sick to my stomach. I'd ridden over to Kalispell for supplies; came back right in the middle of it. I just got out of Hell's Creek with my hide on."

"Are they planning on attacking the town, Pete?"

"If a big enough posse rides out, yeah. They got men on the ridges with signal mirrors to tell yea or nay. I figured I'd ride in and warn the townspeople."

Smoke scribbled a short note and handed it to Pete. "This will keep someone in the town from shooting you, Pete. I'm going to go show the citizens of Hell's Creek what hell is really like."

"You want some company?"

Smoke shook his head. "This is something I want to do myself. How many people pulled out with you?"

"No one, Smoke. There ain't nothin' but trash left up there. Men and women. There ain't no kids in the town. Not a one. Even that so-called minister up yonder took his turn with that poor child. When she went crazy-actin' after all the horribleness, Frigo shot her."

"You keep an eye on Elias, Brown. Hog-tie the boy if you have to."

Smoke stepped into the saddle and was gone.

* * *

The outlaw and gunslinger experienced the chill of a cold sweat as the muzzle of the .44 was pressed against his head. He'd just stepped out of the privy and was slipping into his galluses when the muzzle touched his head.

"If I think you're lying to me," Smoke's voice was as cold as the invisible grip of death that touched the hired gun, "I'll stake you out and skin you alive. Do you understand?"

"Yes, sir. Jensen?"

"That's right, punk. Did you take part in the rape of Aggie?"

"Yes, sir."

"How many more?"

"Jesus, Smoke . . . everbody in the whole damn town. Includin' some of the women. She screamed and hollered until she couldn't holler no more. Went on all day. Then she went nuts in the head and Frigo shot her."

Smoke cursed under his breath. "How did you feel raping that child, punk?"

"I . . . liked it, damn you!"

"Yeah, scum like you would. They waiting for me down in town?"

"Yeah. They damn sure are. So go on down and git killed, Jensen. You . . ."

He never got to finish it. Smoke buried the big blade of his Bowie into the man's back and twisted it upward with all his considerable strength. Smoke slammed the man's face first onto the ground to stifle the scream building in his throat. He wiped the blade clean on the man's shirttail and sheathed the weapon. Smoke checked his guns, loading them full, then took the dead gunny's two Remington Frontier .44's, looping gunbelt and all over one shoulder. He made his way back to his horse and circled the town, keeping to the timber until he found a good spot to picket the animal.

He changed into moccasins, slung his saddlebags over his other shoulder, picked up his rifle, and began working his way toward the town. He knew they were waiting for him because of the silence of the usually raucous place. Lights were burning, but there was no laughter coming from any of the saloons.

And Smoke was determined that before he left that night, there would be no cause for joy in the town for a long, long time. If he could, he was going to destroy as much of Hell's Creek as possible.

He paused for a moment, listening. The old mountain man, Preacher, his mentor, had taught him many things, including patience. Smoke heard the faint jingle of spurs coming up the weed-grown alleyway. He pressed against the building. When the man drew close, Smoke hit him in the face with the butt of the rifle. The man dropped like a stone, faint moonlight glistening off his bloody and broken face.

Smoke walked on to a corral. He didn't want to hurt any animal; they could not choose their owners. He silently slid open the bars. When the action started, the horses would find the opening and bolt. He did the same at two other corrals. He glanced at the huge livery stable and decided to leave it alone. Men were probably lying in wait for him in there.

He slipped around to the back of a saloon, dug in a pocket of his saddlebags, and came out with six sticks of dynamite, taped together, already capped with a long fuse.

He softly entered through the back door. Now he could hear voices and the tinkle of glasses and beer mugs. But the conversation was low and the drinking was probably light.

Smoke thumbnailed a match into flame and lit the long fuse, placing the charge against the storeroom wall. With a smile on his face, he slipped back into the night.

Smoke planted two more charges on that side of the street before he was spotted by a man who'd stepped out of a back door to relieve himself.

"Hey!" the man shouted, turning and still spewing water.

Smoke shot him about five inches below the belt buckle. The man fell to the earth, screaming in agony.

"You'll not rape another girl," Smoke muttered, then dashed across the street, at the far end of town.

The saloon charge blew. Smoke saw one man thrown from the building, crashing through glass. He hit the street and did not move. Another man fell through the floor and onto the dusty walkway in front as the rear part of the poorly constructed building collapsed under the heavy weight of the charge.

The second and third charges blew, and chaos reigned for a few minutes as men and women poured into the street.

Smoke emptied the Remingtons into a knot of men, knocking them sprawling. He lit another charge, tossed that through a side window of a building, and dashed away. He collided with a man, recovered first, and pointed a pistol at the man's head.

"The body of the girl Aggie, where is it?" He jacked back the hammer. "And I'm only going to ask it one time."

"Sid tossed it into a backwater just off the river yonder. I swear to you I ain't lyin'."

Smoke jerked him to his feet. "Show me, you weasel. And you'd better be right the first time."

Keeping low, as the flames began licking at the dry timber of the destroyed buildings, the man led Smoke to a dry wash and from there to the slough. The naked body of Aggie was clearly visible.

"Get her, you crud," Smoke ordered, the menace in his voice chilling the man.

The man waded into the dark waters and pulled the girl to the shore.

"Pick her up and walk toward the timber," he ordered.

"But she ain't got nothin' on! That ain't decent!"

One look from Smoke's cold eyes convinced the man that he'd better shut his mouth and do as ordered.

"Where is the bastard?" Smoke heard the voice of Max Huggins plain in the night. "Find him, you fools. Find him and kill him!"

At his horse, Smoke had the man wrap Aggie's body in a blanket.

"What are you gonna do with me?" the man asked.

"Did you take a part in raping this girl? And don't lie to me."

"Yeah, I did. Ever'body did."

Smoke hit him with one big gloved fist. The man dropped like a rock.

The flames in the town were slowly being contained by a bucket brigade and one small pumper.

Smoke knew there was no point in taking the man back to Barlow for trial. Once away from Smoke Jensen's gun, the man would lie, denying any part of the rape. If a deal could be worked out, everybody in Hell's Creek would alibi for the other and nothing would be accomplished there.

Smoke left the man on the ground and picked up the slender, blanket-covered body of Aggie Feckles. Star didn't like the idea of carrying the dead, but Smoke managed to get into the saddle. He headed back for Barlow, taking a route first west, then cutting south, to throw off any pursuers. He doubted there would be many; they were too busy fighting the fires.

At a farmer's house, he borrowed a horse and tied Aggie across the saddle. He rode into Barlow just as dawn was breaking fair in the eastern skies. People began lining the streets, silently watching as he rode in, leading the horse with the body of Aggie across the saddle.

Dr. Turner came out of the hotel, where he had just given Martha a sedative, and walked over to Smoke. Smoke stepped wearily out of the saddle and gave the reins to Jim. The deputy led the animal to the stable.

A crowd began to slowly gather around.

"After they abused her," Smoke said, his words soft, "Warner Frigo shot her in the head and dumped her body in a slough."

"Pete Akins told us the rest of it," Judge Garrison said. A little bit of soap was still on his face. He had been shaving when the news of Smoke riding in reached him. "This is absolutely the most dastardly act I have seen in all my years on the bench."

"How much damage did you do in Hell's Creek, Marshal?" a citizen asked.

"Burned down about a half-dozen buildings. Got lead in maybe a dozen people. I used some dynamite, and the explosions probably killed another six or seven and put that many out of commission for a time. How is Martha?"

"She's sleeping," Turner said. "Victoria and Sally are with her now. I just gave her a sedative about fifteen minutes ago. She'll be groggy when she wakes up."

"The girl was shot at close range," Smoke told him. "The slug took off about half her face. Have the undertaker do his work and then nail the coffin lid shut. Let's spare Martha that."

The doctor nodded his agreement.

"I've got to get some rest. I'll see you all this afternoon." Smoke wearily climbed the steps to their suite after asking Toby to have a boy get water for a bath.

He hung up his guns, pulled off his boots, waited in his long-handles until the tub was filled, and then took a bath. Sally came into the WC and scrubbed his back.

Smoke slipped under the cool, fresh sheets and closed his eyes. He slept deeply and soundly and dreamlessly. He awakened just after noon and was finishing shaving when the sounds of gunshots and women screaming sent him running down the hotel steps.

Chapter 16

Max had not waited long to retaliate. The gunhands on his payroll and those who lived in Hell's Creek had hit the town hard from the north and were now preparing to strike again, from the south end. Several had thrown torches and two buildings were on fire; but the bucket brigades were working and the fires were being snuffed out before much damage could be done.

"Get into position!" Smoke yelled. "Just like we practiced. Move!"

The men and women of the town responded, quickly getting into battle positions on the roofs and behind shelter. The outlaws saw what was taking place and broke off the second attack before it could get started. They galloped south.

Smoke didn't need a fortune-teller to know where they were heading: to Red Malone's spread.

"Do we follow them?" Toby asked, coming out of the hotel carrying a rifle.

"Not a whole bunch of us. That's what they want. They'd set up an ambush point and nail us. Jim," he called, "saddle me a horse. Not Star. He needs a rest."

Smoke looked around. "Judge, deputize Pete Akins. Pete and Jim will stay here. Sal, come on. Let's do some head-hunting."

Sally pressed a couple of biscuits and salt meat in his hand while the hotel cook made a poke of food for the men to take with them. Smoke gulped down a cup of coffee and then was in the saddle, riding a long-legged buckskin with a mean look in his eyes.

"I know that horse," Sal said. "That's the stableman's personal ride. He's a good one."

Smoke nodded and the men were off, leaving the road just outside of town and cutting across country. From their tracks, it was clear that the outlaws had arrogantly elected to stay with the road, daring Smoke and any others to chase them.

The shortcut that Smoke chose was one pointed out to him by Jim; and Sal knew it as well or better. It would cut off miles getting to the Lightning spread. It was rough country; high-up country.

The men rode the mountain trails and passes in silence. A great gray wolf watched them from a ridge. Smoke spoke to the wolf in Cheyenne, one of several Indian languages that Old Preacher had taught him. Preacher had taught him that for man to fear the wolf was downright ignorant. Preacher had said that he'd never known of a man being attacked by a wolf unless that man was threatening the wolf or got too close to a fresh kill. Either way, according to Preacher, it was the man's fault, not the wolf's.

"Magnificent animals," Sal said, looking at the timber wolf. "But they don't make good pets worth a damn."

"They're not meant to be pets," Smoke agreed. "God didn't put them here for that. Damn stupid hunters keep killing them, and the deer and elk population suffers because of it. They're part of the balance of nature. I wish the white man would understand that. Indians understood it."

The wolf stood on the ridge and watched the men pass. Then it turned and went back to its den, where it was watching over the cubs while its mate hunted for food, which is a lot more than can be said for a great many so-called superior humans.

"There they are," Sal pointed out.

Smoke looked to his right and slightly behind him. A group of riders, tiny from this distance, rode far below them. About twenty-five of them.

"We'll be a good fifteen minutes ahead of them after we cut off up yonder," Sal said. "I know a place that'll be dandy for an ambush."

"Take the lead, Sal. I'll follow you."

The men rode down from the high country, the temperature warming as they descended from the high-up into a valley. Wildflowers had burst forth, coloring the landscape with brilliant summer hues.

Smoke was going to add some more color to the scenery: blood-red.

The two men left their horses safe within boulders and timber and, with their rifles, got into place. They were about fifty yards above the road. This was not the stage road, but an offshoot that led to and stopped at Malone's ranch, some miles farther on. They were on Lightning range.

Sal pointed that out.

"Good," Smoke replied. "Maybe they'll hear the shots and come to lend their buddies a hand. We'll lessen the odds against the town if they do."

Sal took that time to point out that should that occur, the two of them would be outnumbered something like forty to one.

Smoke grinned and patted the bulging saddlebags he'd taken from behind his saddle. "Have faith, Sal. If worse comes to worse, we'll blast our way out."

"There ain't a nerve in your body, is there, Smoke?"

"Oh, I've known fear, Sal." Smoke thought for a moment, then smiled. "Back in '69, I think it was."

Both men laughed, then sobered as the outlaws came into view, riding around a curve in the road, still too far away for accurate shooting.

"Wish we had brung one of them fancy rifles you took from them foreigners," Sal said. "We'd a sure tried it out."

Smoke eared back the hammer on his Winchester. "They'll be in range in about a minute. I'll take the left side, you take the right."

"Good," Sal said flatly. "I can recognize Ernie's horse from here. Ain't neither one of them worth a damn for anything."

"Here we go, Sal."

The men lifted the rifles to their shoulders, sighted in, took up slack on the triggers, and emptied two saddles.

The outlaws appeared confused as their horses reared and bucked at the gunfire and the sudden smell of blood. Instead of turning left or right, or retreating, the outlaws put the spurs to the animals' flanks and came forward.

"Like shootin' clay pigeons standin' still," Sal muttered, and emptied another saddle.

Smoke grabbed several taped-together sticks of dynamite from the open saddlebag, lit the fuse, and tossed it down the hill. The charge landed just above the road and blew, sending small rocks hurling through the air like deadly missiles.

Through the cloud of dust raised by the dynamite, Smoke and Sal could see a half-dozen more riderless horses, the outlaws on the ground, some of them writhing in agony with hideous head wounds and broken limbs, the others lying very still, their skulls crushed by the flying rocks.

Smoke and Sal started tossing the lead around. The dozen or so outlaws left in the saddle decided it was way past time to clear out. They put the spurs to their horses and were gone, fogging it to Red's ranch.

Smoke and Sal mounted up and rode down into the carnage, to see if anything could be salvaged. Sal rounded up the outlaws' horses while Smoke stood among the dead and wounded, making certain no one summoned up the courage to try a shot at either one of them.

They had just finished tying the dead across their saddles and securing the wounded on their horses when Red Malone and his crew thundered up, raising an unnecessary cloud of dust.

"What the hell are you doin' on my range, Jensen?" the man yelled.

"I'm a deputy sheriff of this county, Red," Smoke calmly told him. "And I'm carrying out my duties as such. You interfere and I'll put your butt in jail."

Sal had worked around; he now faced Red, a rifle pointed at the rancher's chest. The action did not escape Red, and he knew if trouble started, he would be the first one dead.

But he wouldn't, couldn't, leave it alone. "You got a warrant for the arrest of these men, Jensen?"

"I saw them attack the town of Barlow, Red. Me and several hundred other people. Those alive are going back to stand trial. Now back off."

All looked up as the sound of hooves pounding against the earth reached them. Twenty men from the town reined up, heavily armed, among them Joe Walsh and a half dozen of his hands.

"The town's secure, Smoke," Benson said. "We thought we'd ride out and give you a hand."

"It's appreciated. You men start escorting these bums back to town." Smoke and Sal swung into the saddle. Smoke looked at Red. "Their trial will begin in a couple of days. You and your men are still banned from the town. Keep that in mind, Red."

"Someday, Jensen," Red warned, his voice thick with anger. "Someday."

"Anytime, Red. Just anytime at all." Smoke lifted the reins and rode away.

The funeral of Aggie Feckles was an emotional, gut-wrenching time for all. Midway through the ordeal, Martha collapsed and had to be carried back to the doctor's office. Young Elias Brown had a very difficult time fighting back his tears. Just as the earth was being shoveled into the hole, Smoke cut his eyes and looked toward the north. Plumes of smoke were billowing into the sky.

"Max is burning you men out!" he called to Brown and his friends. "Let's ride."

They were too late, of course. It was miles to the collection of farmhouses and barns and other outbuildings. Brown had been completely burned out. Gatewood lost his house, but the other buildings were intact. Cooter lost his barn and smoke-house. Bolen's house was gone, and Morrison and Carson lost barns and equipment. All the farmers' cows and hogs had been shot, the chickens scattered and trampled.

"Goddamn a man who would do this!" Brown said. He squared his shoulders and added, "That sorry son will not run me out. We'll rebuild."

"And we'll help you," Tom Johnson said.

"Your credit is good at my store," Marbly said. "For as long as it takes."

"I have money put back," Judge Garrison told the farmers. "I'm good for loans."

Sally and Victoria had ridden out in a buggy. Sally said, "Smoke, I'm going to wire our family's board of directors back East. I think it's time Barlow had a bank. I'll get the first steps in motion this afternoon."

Smoke turned and smiled at her. "Good, honey. That's a great idea."

"Your wife owns a bank?" Marbly asked.

"Her family is one of the richest families in the nation," Smoke told the startled crowd. "They own factories, banks, shipping lines, railroads . . . you name it. If Sally says put a bank in Barlow, a bank will be put in Barlow." He turned to Jim Dagonne. "Let's go pick up some tracks and see where they lead to. As if we didn't know."

But the direction tbe marauders took did not lead toward Hell's Creek. They went north for a couple of miles, then cut toward the northeast, toward the flathead range and the glacier country.

"What's up there, Jim?"

"Man, that is rugged country. I understand they's talk in Washington about making a big chunk of it a national park. It's about a million or so acres. And the weather is unpredictable as hell. Storms can blow in there—even in the summer, so I'm told—dropping temperatures fifty . . . sixty degrees. They's mountains in there over two miles high and impassable."

"You've been in there?"

"I've been on the edge of it several times. Continental Divide runs right through it."

"Anything between here and there?"

"Tradin' post of sorts up ahead on the Hungry Horse. Some pretty salty ol' boys hang around there."

Smoke nodded. "We'll follow these tracks as long as we

can. We'll supply at the post. The nick in that shoe is a dead giveaway. That'll hold up in court."

"You plan on bringing them back?"

"Not if I can help it."

The country was so rugged and unsettled that the men could not make the trading post that day. They camped along a creek and dined on fresh fish caught with their hands, Indian style.

"Where'd you learn how to do that?" Jim asked after watching Smoke catch their supper by hand.

"I was raised by mountain men, Jim. A very independent and self-sufficient bunch."

"I've met a couple of real old men who was mountain men. I saw something in their eyes that made me back off and talk right respectful to them."

"Wise thing to do. A mountain man isn't going to take much crap from anybody."

They ate until they could hold no more, then rolled up in their blankets, using saddles for pillows, and were up before dawn, making coffee and talking little until they'd shaken the kinks out and had a cup of coffee you could float nails in.

"Who runs this trading post?" Smoke finally asked.

"Don't know no more. Man by the name of Smith used to run it. He might still. Smith ain't his real name. He's a bad one. Have to be bad to run a place like that. Got him a grave-yard out back of hardcases who tried to steal from him or brace him over one thing or another."

"Fast gun?"

"Nope. Sawed-off shotgun. And he don't hesitate none in usin' it, neither. He's got the worst whiskey you ever tried to drink. I think he adds snake heads to it for flavor. And I ain't kiddin'."

"I think I'll stick with beer."

"That would be wise."

They rolled their blankets in their ground sheets and were in the saddle as the sun was struggling to push its rays over the mountains.

They followed the tracks, and they led straight to the trading post on the north fork of the Flathead River. Both men had taken off their badges, had dusty clothing from the trail, and had not shaved that morning. Both of them had heavy beards, so they were beginning to look a little rough around the edges.

"If Smith is still here, is he going to recognize you?" Smoke asked.

"Probably. But he ain't gonna say nothing except howdy, 'til he figures out what I might be up to. How are we going to play this?"

"You just follow my lead."

"I's afraid you was gonna say that."

The men put their horses in the big barn behind the long, low trading post and unsaddled them, carefully rubbing them down and giving them a good bait of corn. *25 ceents a skoop,* the sign said.

"Yep," Jim said. "Smith is still here. You ever seen such outrageous prices?"

"It's the only game in town, partner."

"You called that right."

Smoke lifted the right rear hoof of each animal until he found the one with the chipped shoe. He smiled up at Jim. "We found our man."

"Men," Jim corrected. "I count six of them."

Smoke straightened up and, with a grin on his face, said, "Hell, Jim, don't look so glum. We got them outnumbered."

"If that's the way you count," Jim said soberly, "I shore am glad you don't count out my payroll!"

Chapter 17

The men took the leather thongs off their guns and stepped up onto the rough porch. With Smoke in the lead, they entered the dimly lit old trading post. The smell of twist tobacco all mixed in with that of candy, whiskey, beer, and ancient sweat odors that clung to the walls and ceiling hit them. They walked past bolts of brightly colored cloth, stacks of men's britches and shirts, and a table piled high with boots of all sizes. They passed the notions counter, filled with elixirs and nostrums that were guaranteed to cure any and all illnesses. Most of them were based with alcohol or an opiate of some type, which killed the pain for a while.

Smoke and Jim stopped at the gun case to look at the new double-action revolvers.

"Pretty," Jim said.

"I don't like them," Smoke said. "The trigger pull is so hard it throws your aim off. And if you have to cock it, what's the point of having one of those things?"

"Good question," his deputy agreed. "They look awkward to me." Something on the nostrum table caught his eye and he picked up a bottle of Lydia E. Pinkham's Vegetable Compound. He read the label, blushed, and put the bottle down. "The things they put on labels. I declare."

"Sally swears by it. Says it works wonders."

"You ever tasted it?"

"Hell, no! I did taste some Kickapoo Indian Sagwa a couple of years ago, back East."

"Did it work?"

"It tasted so bad I forgot what I took it for."

Smiling, the men stepped into the bar part of the trading post and walked up to the counter, in this case, several rough-hewn boards atop empty beer barrels.

Smith flicked his eyes to Jim and they narrowed in recognition. But he said only, "Howdy, boys. What might your poison be on this day?"

"Beer," Smoke said. "For both of us."

Both Smoke and Jim had quickly inspected the heavily armed men sitting at two pulled-together tables near a dirty window at the front of the barroom.

"Hadn't been up here in a long time,"Jim said after taking a pull from his mug. "I'd forgot how purty this country is. And how chilly the nights get."

"It do get airish at times," Smith agreed. "I got fresh venison stew on the stove and my squaw just baked some bread."

"Sounds good," Smoke said. "Jim?"

"I could do with a taste. Them cold fish we had for breakfast didn't nearabouts fill me up."

Smoke and Jim took their beers to a table across the room from the arsonists and began whispering to each other, knowing that would arouse some suspicion from the men who had torched the farmhouses and barns.

It didn't take long.

"What are you two a-whisperin' about over there?" one burly man called across the room.

Smoke looked at him just as the stew and bread was being placed on the table. "None of your damn business."

The man flushed and started to get up. One of his buddies pulled him back into the chair. "Let it alone, Sonny. They ain't worth our time."

"I ain't so sure about that," Sonny said, giving Smoke a good once-over. "I seen that face afore."

"That's Murtaugh talkin'," Smith whispered. "Watch your step, Jim. They're all bad ones."

"Now the damn barkeep's whisperin'!" Sonny yelled.

Smith turned and faced him. "It's my goddamn store, lunkhead. I'll whisper anytime I take a notion to."

"Who you callin' a lunkhead, you old goat?" Sonny hollered.

"You, you big-mouth ninny!" Smith fired back, moving toward the bar. There, he reached behind him and came around with a sawed-off shotgun in his hands. He eared back both hammers and pointed it at Sonny. "Now, then, mule-mouth, you got anything else you'd like to say to me?"

Sonny's complexion, not too good to begin with, lightened appreciably as he looked at the twin barrels of the express gun, pointing straight at him. Those around him took on the expression of a very sad basset hound, knowing that if Smith pulled the triggers, someone would be picking them up with a shovel and a spoon.

"I reckon not," Sonny finally managed to say.

"Good." Smith eased down the hammers and laid the shotgun on the bar. "That's just dandy. Use your mouth to eat and drink, and stop flappin' that thing at me."

With a scowl on his ugly face, Sonny turned away, but not before giving Smoke another dirty look.

The stew smelled good and tasted even better. The bread was lavishly buttered, and Smoke and Jim fell to eating.

"Bring us some of that stew," Murtaugh called.

"Dollar a bowl," Smith told him.

"A dollar a bowl! Hell, man, that's plumb unreasonable."

"Then go hungry."

"I'll take another bowl," Jim said. "That's fine eatin'."

"You better see the color of his money afore you dish up any more grub to him," Murtaugh said. "He don't look like he's very flush to me."

"You worry about your own self," Jim verbally fired across the room. "I got money, and I earned it decent."

"What'd you mean by that?" the arsonist asked.

"Just what I said."

"You sayin' I ain't decent?"

"You said that, not me. Now hush up. I'm tryin'to eat, not jaw with you."

Murtaugh gave him a dirty look. "Maybe you think you're hoss enough to shut me up?"

"Just as soon as I finish eatin', mister."

"Anybody busts up furniture, they pay for it," Smith said.

"They started this war of words," Smoke pointed out. "All we did was come in for a drink and some food."

"That's right," Jim said, spooning stew into his mouth. "Sad state of affairs when a man can't even eat without havin' to listen to all sorts of jibber-jabber from lunkheads."

"Now, I ain't puttin' up with no saddle-bum callin' me a lunkhead!" Murtaugh stood up. He walked across the room. "I better hear some apologies comin' out of that mouth of yourn, cowboy," he said to Jim.

Jim grinned up at him. His right hand was holding a spoon, his left hand out of sight.

Jim belched loudly. "There's your apology, big-mouth. Catch it and carry it back acrost the room with you."

Murtaugh cursed and swung a big fist at Jim's head. But Jim anticipated the punch and ducked it, coming out of the chair and driving his fist into the bigger man's stomach. Murtaugh bent over, gagging. Jim grabbed the man by his hair and slammed his forehead onto the tabletop. Turning the stunned Murtaugh around, and grabbing him by the collar and the seat of his britches, Jim propelled him across the room, dumping him onto the table he had just exited.

"You boys best look after him," Jim told Murtaugh's buddies. "He can't seem to take care of hisself at all."

Sonny looked around him. Smith was holding the Greener, hammers back, pointed at him.

Jim walked back to his table and looked at the spilled stew. "Get the money for this from Murtaugh," he told Smith. "It was his head that spilt it."

"I'll be damned!" Murtaugh said, and charged across the room at Jim, both fists whipping the air.

Jim picked up a chair and hit the rampaging Murtaugh in the face with it. The firebug hit the floor, on his back, and did not move. His face was bloody and several teeth had departed his mouth to take up residence on the floor.

"That does it," Sonny said, rising from his chair. He looked at Smith. "You gonna take a side in this?"

Smoke stood up, brushing back his coat, exposing his .44's. "Stay out of it, Smith. We're deputy sheriffs from down Barlow way. These men are wanted for arson and destruction of livestock. Any damage to your place will be taken care of."

"That's fair. I know Jim and you look familiar to me. Who you be, mister?"

"Smoke Jensen."

Sonny suddenly looked sick. And so did the other four with him.

"Have mercy!" Smith said.

"We ain't done nothin' to nobody and we ain't destroyed no livestock," Sonny said.

Murtaugh groaned on the floor and sat up. He blinked a couple of times and wiped his bloody mouth with the back of his hand. "What the hell's goin' on?"

"You're under arrest," Jim told him.

"Your aunt's drawers, I am!" Murtaugh's hand dropped to the butt of his gun at just about the same time Jim kicked him in the face. Murtaugh hit the floor again and this time he was out for the count.

Sonny grabbed for his gun and Smoke shot him in the belly. The outlaw stumbled backward and sat down hard on the floor, both hands holding his .44-caliber-punctured belly. He started hollering.

One of his buddies jerked iron and Jim took him out of the game with a slug to the shoulder.

The trading post erupted in gunsmoke and lead. The booming of .44's and .45's rattled the windows and shook the glasses behind the bar. Things really got lively when Smith leveled his Greener and blew one outlaw clear out of the barroom, the charge of rusty nails, ball bearings, tacks, and whatever else Smith could find to load his shells nearly tearing the man in two, picking him off his boots, and tossing him out a window.

One outlaw, gut-shot and screaming in pain, dropped his pistols and went staggering out into the other room. He died underneath the table holding five-cent bottles of Dr. Farrigut's elixir for the remedying of paralysis, softening of the brain, and mental imbecility.

When the dust and bird-droppings from the ceiling and gunsmoke began to clear the room, three arsonists were dead, one was not long for this world, and Murtaugh was again trying to sit up, blood from his broken nose streaming down his chin. The punk Jim had shot through the shoulder was leaning up against a wall, moaning in pain.

"My, my," Smith said, picking out the empties from his Greener and loading up. "I ain't seen such a sight in two . . . three years. Things was gettin' plumb borin' around here. Them no-goods really burn some folks out?"

"Five families," Smoke told him, punching out his empty brass and reloading. "All good people. I suspect Big Max Huggins paid them to do it."

"I'll talk," the shoulder-shot outlaw hollered. "It was Big Max who paid us to do it. I'll testify in court. I'll tell . . ."

Murtaugh palmed a hide-out gun and shot the man between the eyes, closing his mouth forever.

Smoke slammed the barrel of his .44 against Murtaugh's head, and for the third time in about three minutes, the outlaw went to sleep on the floor.

"Gimme ten dollars for the winder and you give whatever else is in their pockets to them folks that was burnt out," Smith said. "That fair?"

"Plenty fair," Jim said. "The families will thank you."

Smoke tied Murtaugh's hands behind his back with rawhide and straightened up. "We'll help you bury this trash, Smith. Then I'll get a signed statement from you attesting to the fact that you heard that one"—he pointed to the man with a hole beween his eyes—"confessing as to who paid them. You won't have to appear in court."

"Good enough," Smith said. "Shovel's in the back. I'll get my old woman to sing a death chant for them. She's Flathead. Does a nice job of it, too. Right touchin', some folks say."

Smoke put all the guns in a sack and tied it to a saddle horn, while Jim readied the horses for travel back to Barlow.

The guns and horses and saddles they would give to the farmers who were burned out. The men had about five hundred dollars between them. That would go a long way toward rebuilding the homes and barns and smokehouses.

Morning Dove was still chanting her death song as they rode away.

Chapter 18

Judge Garrison read the signed statement from Smith.
"Will that hold up in a court of law, Judge?" Smoke asked.

"It will in my court," the judge said with a smile. "Besides, both you and Deputy Dagonne heard one man confess. Don't worry, Smoke. Just remember the name of the town the jury is going to be picked from."

Both men shared a laugh at that. Smoke said, "Any further word about Max Huggins's background?"

"Yes, but unfortunately, we can't use any of it. Some of the parties involved are still too frightened to testify. Others have moved away or died. While the authorities east of here know Max is guilty, they can't prove it."

Smoke thought about that for a moment. "But Max doesn't have to know that, Judge."

The judge looked puzzled for a moment, then smiled. "Of course, you're quite right."

"Let me think about how we can use that information, Judge. We've got Max bumping from side to side now, let's see if we can keep him that way."

"Good idea. I have trial scheduled to start Thursday for those who tried to shoot up the town. I want extra security, Smoke."

"You've got it, Judge. How about Melvin Malone's case?"

"His is the first one I try. This is . . . unusual for a judge, Smoke. But I want to ask your opinion. I can put him in jail. I can put him to doing community work . . . public service work it's now being called. But putting him to work cleaning the streets is only going to anger him further. Jail? Probably do the same thing. Or I can fine him. What do you think?"

Smoke rolled a cigarette and lit up. Finally, he shrugged his shoulders. "The boy wants to kill me so bad now it's like a fire inside him . . ."

"Is he that good?" the judge interrupted.

"I doubt it. He makes the mistake that so many would-be gunhandlers make: He hurried his first shot. I was born blessed with excellent eye and hand coordination, Judge. I was born ambidextrous." He smiled. "Sally taught me that word, by the way. The speed came with years of practice. I still practice. But I think the thing that keeps me alive—or has kept me alive all these years—is that I'm not afraid when the moment comes. I'm confident without being overly so. As to your original question fine him and let him walk for all I care."

The judge nodded. "It might buy us more time, if you know what I mean."

"I do. Kill Melvin now, and Red is very likely to blow wide open. The town is growing stronger every day. In another two weeks, it would take an army to overrun it."

"That's correct. And we owe it all to you."

Smoke waved that away. "I just propped you people up, that's all. Gave you all a little talking to and jerked you around and around. You all did the rest."

The judge grinned and rubbed the side of his face. "I never thought I'd see the day when I appreciated a slapping around, but I do, boy, I do."

"See you around, Judge."

Smoke stepped out of the judge's chambers and walked the streets of town. People waved and called his name as he passed. No doubt about it, Smoke thought. These folks are going to fight for their town. And they're probably going to have it to do . . . very soon.

He walked back to the jail and stepped inside. Murtaugh started cussing him as soon as he heard the jingle of Smoke's spurs. "You'll never hold me in this cracker box, Jensen. Soon as I can get my hands on a gun, you're dead, hotshot. You're dead, and that's a promise."

Smoke did not reply.

"I know a lot of things you don't, Jensen," Murtaugh kept flapping his mouth. "A whole lot of things."

Smoke waited.

Murtaugh laughed from his cell. "Have your trials, Jensen. Let that lard-butted judge bang his gavel and hand down his pronouncements. It ain't gonna make a bit of difference in the long run."

Murtaugh lay down on his bunk and shut his mouth.

Smoke got up and closed the door to the cell block.

"Have the others had anything to say?" he asked Sal.

"They've all been boastin' about us not keepin' them for very long. I been doin' some thinkin' about that. I think someone's gonna spring them after they've been sentenced."

"From the jail, you think?" Smoke asked.

Sal shook his head. "I don't know. I'd guess so. Max or Red ain't gonna take a chance of bustin' them away from the

prison wagon when they come to haul them off to the territorial prison. That'd bring too much heat on Max, and he
don't want that. So, yeah. I'd say they'll make their try just
after these hardcases are sentenced."

"We have until Thursday to make some plans. The judge
has requested extra security, so he thinks something is in the
works, too."

Pete Akins hitched at his gunbelt. "Max could have at
least seventy-five men ready to ride in ten minutes. He could
pull fifty more in here in two . . . three days. The folks in
this town are good people, and I mean that; I never did none
of them no harm and they know it. They've accepted me.
But they ain't gunhands, Smoke. If you know what I mean."

Smoke knew what he meant. Most of the men were good
shots with a rifle. But few of them had ever killed a man
close up. They had fought in the war; but that was, for the
most part, a very impersonal thing.

Smoke tossed the question out, "How many men does
Red Malone have on the payroll?"

"Thirty," Jim answered it. "He pays them all fightin'
wages. And there ain't no backup in none of them. They ride
for the brand and that's it."

"So we're conceivably looking at anywhere from a hundred to a hundred and fifty men."

"Or more," Pete added.

Smoke paced the office in silence, deep in thought. Finally, he stopped and faced his deputies. "He's got to try to
destroy the town. That's his only option. Killing me alone
won't stop the movement now. He can't let Sally's people
start up this proposed bank. That would bring the state and,
in some cases, the federal government into it . . . if anything
were to happen to it."

"Maybe there's another way to look at that, Smoke," Sal
pointed out. "Maybe Max wants the bank to start up. Rob

the bank, destroy the town, and haul his ashes out of the area and start up somewheres else. You can bet that he has someone in this town feedin' him information."

"Who?" Jim asked.

Sal shook his head. "That I don't know. It could be anybody. The swamper over at the saloon. The bartender, a store clerk . . . anybody who's hard up for money."

"Hell, that could be any one of a hundred people," Pete said. "Lemme tell you about Max. He's sneaky. He has one ear to the ground all the time. He hears about somebody seein' somebody else's wife, he holds that over their head. He finds out about somebody bein' wanted, say, back in Ohio, he uses that for leverage. Max can be smooth. He might have loaned someone in this town money when he first come here. Money's tight right now. Maybe they couldn't repay him like they said they would. Man, he could have half-a-dozen people in this town feedin' him information."

Smoke turned and looked out the window. It might be Jerry at the saddle shop. Lucy at the hotel. The boy down at the stable. One of the farmers scattered around this end of the county. One of Joe Walsh's hands. Then it came to Smoke; but he kept his suspicions to himself, hoping they would not prove true.

He left the office and walked over to the hotel. He sat with Sally for a long time in their suite, talking, exchanging ideas. At first she tought his suspicions to be perfectly horrible. Then, gradually, she began to agree. When Smoke left, both he and Sally wore long faces.

Smoke walked the streets, looking hard into the face of every man and woman he passed. Had to be, he thought. I didn't see it at first because I wasn't looking for it. But as he spoke and waved to another citizen, heading out of town, the family resemblance was just too strong to ignore.

There it was, staring him right in the face and saying good morning to him.

"You have to be joking!" Judge Garrison said, recoiling back in his chair.

"No. I'm ninety-nine percent certain. It has to be, Judge. Look at the person."

The judge drummed his fingertips on his desk. He shook his head and sighed. "Now that you mention it, I can see it. My God. I would have never put it together. It was all a sham on this person's part."

"It had to be, Judge. Looking back, it all went down too smoothly, with no arguments."

"And you propose to do what about it at this time?"

"I don't know. From all I've learned by association, this individual does not appear to be a bad person. Rather likable, actually. Let's just sit on this for the time being, Judge. See what develops."

"Just between us?"

"You, me, and Sally are the only three in town who know or who suspect."

"You think it's just this one person?"

Smoke sighed. "I hope so. But how can we be sure?"

"We can't."

Smoke stood up and put on his hat. He told the judge about Sal's suspicions as to when an attack to free the prisoners might take place.

The judge nodded his head in agreement. "I think he's right. They wouldn't want to attack the prisoner wagon from the territorial prison; that might bring the state militia down on their heads. They'll strike here, Smoke. Bet on it. We'll just have to be ready for it."

"We'll be ready," Smoke assured him. "I'm going to deputize all of Joe Walsh's hands and Brown and Gatewood and the other farmers in that area just in case Max tries a diversion to pull me out of town."

"That's a good idea. If trouble comes—and it would be a diversion—north of town, Brown and his friends could then legally handle it. Same with trouble south of town. I'll draw up papers making them full deputies. That will make it official and part of the record."

"The trial going to be in the new civic building?"

"Yes. I expect a large crowd to attend. Oh, by the way, the Marblys' dog had puppies about six weeks ago. Mrs. Marbly said to tell you to stop by and pick one out for Lisa Turner."

"I'll do that right now. See you, Judge."

Marbly grinned at Smoke. "I'm afraid they're mutts, Marshal. But they sure are cute. Come on, I'll show them to you."

"Mutts is right," Smoke said, squatting down by the squirming, yelping litter. "That one," he said, pointing. "The one with the patch around his eye."

"Her eye," Mrs. Marbly corrected.

"Whatever. I like that one."

"Lisa will love it. Tell Mrs. Turner she's paper-trained and completely weaned."

"Victoria will love that, I'm sure." Smoke picked up the puppy, who promptly peed all down his shirt from excitement and then licked his face to apologize, and carried the squirming mass of energy over to Dr. Turner's house.

Lisa was so happy she cried—she named the pup Patches—and ran out in the backyard to play.

Since it was not proper for a man to be alone in a house with a married woman, Vicky invited Smoke to take coffee with her on the front porch.

"I love everything about this town, Smoke," she said

after the coffee was poured. "The people are so friendly and they accepted us immediately."

"Yes. They're good people. Where is Robert?"

"On a call out in the country. He left early this morning and said he wouldn't be back until late. He wanted to check on the families who were burned out."

"Anything serious?"

Vicky laughed. "Not really. One of the kids came down with chicken pox and gave it to all the other kids who hadn't as yet had it. A lot of them are having an itching good time."

Smoke grimaced, remembering his own bout with chicken pox as a boy back in Missouri.

"Are you expecting trouble when the trial starts, Smoke?"

"I won't lie to you, yes, I am. Either during the trial or just after the sentencing. Security will be tight. Are you planning on attending?"

"I . . . don't know. I doubt it. I don't want Lisa to have to hear all that—there will probably be some pretty rough language at times—and if I went, I'd have to leave her alone, and I won't do that."

"I think that's wise. Sally isn't going to attend either. I'll ask her if she'll come over and stay with you. If there is trouble, Sally—as you've seen in the shooting classes—can handle a six-shooter with either hand. And won't hesitate to use one."

Victoria shook her head. "Sally certainly has changed since our days back at school."

"Out here, Vicky, one must change. Believe me when I say that the West will be wild for many years to come. People out here resist change; they fight it. It's the sheer vastness of the West that makes laws so difficult to enforce. Here it is 1883, and there are still many areas that remain largely unexplored. Millions of acres for outlaws to run into and hide. Oh, it's getting smaller with each year that passes.

Law enforcement people are being linked by telegraph and train, but the gun still remains the great settler of troubles."

"When will you hang your guns up, Smoke?"

"When a full year passes and no one comes after me looking for a reputation. When newspapers and magazines and books no longer carry my name."

Victoria smiled. "What you're saying is, you will never hang them up."

"I'm afraid that's true."

"Would you like to hang them up?"

"Very much so." He looked at her and smiled. "For one thing, they're heavy."

She laughed aloud at that, then sobered. "What value do you place on human life, Smoke?"

"The highest value I can accord it, Vicky . . . for those who respect the rights of others; for those who can follow even the simplest rules of society. I don't prejudge on the basis of what a person has contributed to our society, but whether a person has taken away from it. None of us are obligated to create fine art or music, or invent things that better mankind. We're not obligated to do anything to improve society. What we are obligated to do is not take away from it." He waved one big hand. "There is an entire subculture out there with only lawlessness on their minds. To hurt, to steal, to kill, to maim, to destroy. They don't give a damn for your rights, or my rights, or Lisa's rights to live life and enjoy it in relative safety and comfort. They want what they want and to hell with anything else. They spit in the face of law and order and decency. If those types of people get in my way, I'll kill them."

Although the day was not cool, Victoria shivered. It did not escape the attention of Smoke.

"You think I'm half savage, don't you, Vicky?" he asked.

"I don't know what my thoughts are about you," she

replied honestly. "You bring Lisa a little puppy and then talk about killing human beings. You are a philosopher and yet you've killed at least a hundred men. Probably twice that number. You respect law and order, and yet carry the name of gunfighter. I think you are a walking contradiction, Smoke Jensen."

He smiled. "I've been called that, too, Vicky."

"What are you, Smoke Jensen? The Robin Hood of the West?"

"I don't know whether I'm that or that fellow who went around sticking his lance into windmills."

"Don Quixote. No, I don't think you and Don Quixote have much in common. You get quite a lot accomplished . . . in your own rough way."

"It's a rough world, Vicky. There is a saying out here: A man saddles his own horse and kills his own snakes. Now, only a few species of snakes are harmful, and a rattlesnake will usually leave you alone if you don't mess with it. But these two-legged snakes we have surrounding us right now are the vicious kind. They are capable of thinking, know right from wrong, but still want to strike out and sink their fangs into anyone who gets in their way or tries to block their lawless behavior. They have had their chance to live decently. They looked at a decent way of life and chose to ignore it. And they've made that choice dozens of times. Nobody forced them into a life of crime. They chose it willingly. As far as I am concerned, that means they gave up any right to demand compassion when they're caught. If they face me, they are going to get a bullet."

"The West frightens me, Smoke. I like the people in this town. But even they carry guns."

"Then go back East, Vicky. Go back where you have a uniformed police officer on every street corner and it's getting to be when a criminal is caught, the punishment is light or nothing at all."

"But they're human beings, Smoke!"

"They're garbage, Vicky. Rabies-carrying rats whose diseased fleas are hopping onto everyone who gets close to them."

Smoke stopped talking as a tall stranger on a painted pony rode slowly into town. The stranger cut his eyes to Smoke, sitting on the porch, and smiled.

Smoke stood up. "Time to go to work, Vicky. Max is pulling in the heavyweights now."

"What do you mean?"

"That's Dek Phillips. A hired gun from down Texas way originally."

"Why is he here?"

Smoke stepped off the porch. "To kill me."

Chapter 19

Victoria gasped and put one hand to her mouth. "But . . . you're the marshal! A deputy sheriff!"

"That doesn't mean anything to men like Dek. When this is over, Vicky—the war, I mean—and Max Huggins and Red Malone are either dead or have pulled out, go on back to Vermont or wherever you came from. Maybe I'm judging you hastily. But I don't think you're cut out for the West. Excuse me now, Vicky. I got to go stomp on the head of a snake."

"You're going to arrest him?"

"I'm probably going to kill him."

"But he hasn't done anything!"

"That's right. So I'll just crowd a little bit and see what he's got on his mind. If he wants to ride on out, I'll let him. Thanks for the coffee. See you, Vicky."

Smoke walked over to his office. Sal, Jim, and Pete were

standing out in front. Dek's horse was tied to the hitchrail outside the saloon.

"We seen him ride in," Sal said. "You know him, Smoke?"

"I know him. From years back. He's a no-good."

"We agree on that," Pete said. "I'd hired on for fightin' wages down in Arizona some years back. I seen Dek shoot a nester woman in the back. I drew my wages and left. But give the devil his due, Smoke. He's good. He's damn good."

"I've seen him work. Yeah, he's good. But the problem is he knows it and it's swelled his head. He stopped working with his gun years ago, letting his reputation carry him."

"By the way," Jim said. "I been hearin' shootin' every mornin' for the past week or more. From outside of town. Real faint like. Sounds like someone practicin'. Reckon who that is?"

Smoke stepped off the boardwalk. "Me," he said. He walked across the dirt street to the saloon and pushed over the batwings, stepping into the dimness.

The bar had cleared of patrons when Dek walked in. His reputation was known throughout the West, and unlike Smoke, he liked all the hoopla. Smoke walked to the bar and faced Dek, leaning against the other end of the long counter.

"Jensen," Dek said. "I hear you been throwing a wide loop here of late."

"What of it?"

"Some folks don't like it. So they got ahold of me to cut you back to size some."

"And you figure you're the man for the job, huh?"

"I figure so."

"Anybody ever tell you that you were a damn fool, Dek?" The gunfighter flushed, then fought his sudden anger under control and smiled at Smoke. "That won't work, Jensen. So save your little mind games for the two-bit punks."

"That's you, Dek."

Dek carefully picked up his shot glass and took a small sip of whiskey, gently placing the drink back on the bar. "You've had all those books written about you. I even seen a play some actors put on about you once. Made me want to puke."

Smoke waited. He'd played this scene many times in his life. Dek was working up his courage.

The barkeep said, "Can I pull you a beer, Marshal?"

"Yes, that would be nice. Thanks, Ralph. A beer would taste good."

Dek tossed a coin on the bar. "On me, barkeep. It's gonna be his last one."

"It's on the house," Ralph said. "And I 'spect the marshal will be comin' in tomorrow for his afternoon taste."

Dek didn't like that. His eyes narrowed and his left hand clenched into a fist. Slowly, he relaxed and picked up his whiskey. Another tiny sip went down his throat.

Ralph slid the beer mug up the bar and Smoke stopped it with his hand. He took a healthy pull, holding the mug in his left hand. He wiped his mouth with the back of his hand and took several steps toward Dek.

Dek watched him, the light in his eyes much like that of a wild animal, filled with suspicion.

Smoke stopped and said, "Why, Dek?"

"Huh? Why? Why what, Jensen?"

"Why do you want to kill me?"

"That's a stupid question! 'Cause there's money on your head, that's why."

"What good is it going to do you dead?" Smoke took another few steps.

"Huh? Dead? You're the one gonna be dead, Jensen. Not me. Now you're crowdin' me, Jensen. You just stand still. Back up and drink your beer."

Smoke took another step. He was almost within swinging distance. "You got a mother somewhere, Dek?"

"Naw. She's been dead. Now, damnit, Jensen, you stand still, you hear me?"

"No wife for me to write to?"

"Naw. Why the hell would you want to write to my wife even if I had one?"

"To tell her about your death, that's why." Smoke took two more steps.

"Jensen, you're crazy! You know that? You're as nutty as a road lizard. You . . ."

Smoke hit him in the mouth with a right that smashed the man's lips and knocked him spinning. Smoke jerked the man's guns from leather and tossed them behind the bar. He stepped back, raising his fists.

"Now, Dek. Now we'll see how much courage you have. Come on, Dek. You think you're such a bad man. Fight me. Stand up, Dek. I don't think you know how. I don't think you have the guts to fight me."

Dek cussed him.

Smoke took the time to pull riding gloves from behind his gunbelt and slip them on. He laughed at Dek. "Oh, come on, Dek. What's the matter? You afraid I might kick your big tough butt all over this town in front of God and everybody? You afraid somebody might see and laugh at you?"

"That'll be the day," Dek snarled, raising his fists. "You ain't about man enough to put me down."

"We'll sure see, Dek. But there is one thing that puzzles me."

"What's that?"

"Are you trying to talk me to death?"

Cursing, Dek charged Smoke. Smoke ducked a wild swing and tripped him. Grabbing Dek by the collar and by the seat of his pants, Smoke propelled him through the batwings and out into the street, Dek hollering and cussing all the way. On the boardwalk, Smoke gave a mighty heave and tossed Dek into the dirt.

Dek landed on his face and came up spitting dirt and cussing and waving his arms.

Smoke stepped in and gave Dek a combination, left and right, both to the face, which staggered the gunfighter and backed him up, shaking his head and spitting blood.

A crowd began gathering, grinning and watching the fun. The women tried to frown and pretend they didn't like it, but from the gleam in their eyes, they were very much enjoying watching one of Max Huggins's men get the tar knocked out of him.

"Knock his teeth down his throat, Smoke!" Mrs. Marbly hollered.

"Yeah," the minister's wife shouted. "Smite him hip and thigh and bust his mouth, too, Marshal."

Dek looked wildly around him. He looked back at Smoke just in time to catch a big right fist smack on his nose. The nose crunched and Dek squalled as the blood flew. Dek backed up, trying to clear his vision.

Jensen didn't give him much chance to do that. Smoke waded in, both big fists working. He busted Dek in the belly and connected with a left to the man's ear that guaranteed him a cauliflower for a long time . . . not to mention impairing his hearing for the rest of his life.

Dek connected with a punch that bruised Smoke's cheek and seemed only to make him stronger.

Dek suddenly realized that Smoke was going to cripple him; was going to forever end his days as a gunfighter, and was going to do it with his fists, not his guns. He looked for a way out. But several hundred people had formed a wide circle around them. There was no way out. He was trapped.

"Gimme a break, Jensen," he panted the plea. "I ain't never done nothin' to you to deserve this."

Smoke almost laughed at him. The man had been hired to kill him and was now asking for a break. Dek Phillips had killed women and children and brought untold grief and suffering to many, many others. And he was asking for a break.

Smoke gave him a break. He stepped in close and with one powerful fist broke several of Dek's ribs.

Dek yelped in pain and involuntarily lowered his guard. Smoke knocked him down with a left to the jaw.

Smoke stood over him and said, "You know what I'm going to do, Dek. Are you going to lay there like a whipped coward while I kick you to death, or get up and fight?"

Dek slowly got to his boots. "You're a devil, Jensen," he panted, blood dripping from his face. "You got to come from hell." He flicked a fake at Smoke but Jensen wasn't buying it. Dek swung a looping right that Smoke ducked under and danced away.

"Stand still, damn you, Jensen!"

Smoke's reply was a right to the jaw. Even those in the rear of the crowd heard Dek's jaw break.

Smoke began to deliberately and methodically ruin the man. He gave him his overdue punishment for all the good lives he had taken over the years, and for all the misery and heartbreak he had caused.

The crowd no longer cheered. They stood in silence and watched with satisfaction in their eyes as Max Huggins's man was beaten half to death in front of their eyes. Vicky Turner stood in silence, shocked by the brutality taking place in front of her eyes. Sally Jensen stood beside her. The wife of Smoke Jensen knew fully well what her husband was doing, and she approved of it. Men like Dek Phillips could not understand compassion because they possessed none. They understood only one thing: brute force. That was the only thing they could relate to. And Smoke was giving Dek a lesson in it that he would never forget.

When Dek Phillips finally measured his length in the dirt and did not get up, Smoke walked to a horse trough and bathed his face and hands. He straightened up and said to Pete, "Tie him across his saddle and take him to the edge of Hell's Creek."

"The man is injured!" Robert Turner shouted. "He needs medical attention."

"Shut up, boy!" Joe Walsh spoke from the edge of the crowd. He had ridden up unnoticed and sat his saddle during the final minutes of the fight. "Dek Phillips just got all the attention his kind deserve." The crowd muttered their agreement with that.

Sal said, "This ain't back East, Doctor. The laws are still few out here. You're a nice fellow, I'll give you that, but you got some adjustin' to do if you're gonna make it out here. You might feel sorry for a rabid dog, but you don't try to comfort it. You just kill it. You best learn that."

His face stiff with anger, Dr. Robert Turner took Victoria's hand and left the street, walking back to his office.

Pete rode out, leading the horse with Dek Phillips tied across the saddle.

Joe Walsh told several of his hands to accompany Pete, to act as guards in case some of the scum at Hell's Creek tried to waylay him.

Smoke walked back to the hotel to bathe the sweat and grime from him and change into fresh clothing.

Henry Draper, editor of the *Barlow Bugle,* headed back to his office to write the story of how the mighty hired gunfighter Dek Phillips had fallen under the fists of Marshal Smoke Jensen. He knew he could sell the story to dozens of newspapers back East. The reading public loved it.

The crowds broke up into small groups, talking over and rehashing the fight. With each victory they were stronger as a town, becoming closer-knit. The advance party from back East was due in the next day, and soon they would have a bank. Max Huggins would continue trying to destroy them—they all knew that—but they all sensed he would fail. And they owed it all to one man: Smoke Jensen.

Max Huggins had just come from the bedside of Dek Phillips. The horse doctor who had attended the gunfighter had said the man would probably live, but he would be marked forever. His jaw was broken, his ribs were cracked, one arm was broken, a lot of his teeth had been knocked out. And worse, the horse doctor said, Dek Phillips's spirit appeared to be broken.

"The trial will probably last two . . . three days," Val Singer broke into Max's thoughts. "It'll take a good two weeks for the prison wagon to get around to pickin' up the boys. By that time, the bank will be operatin'. We hit the bank, loot the town, lift us some petticoats and have some fun with the women, and then strike out for greener pastures. What'd you think, Max?"

Max was thinking about Smoke Jensen. For three weeks, the big man had been exercising, running several miles a day and working out. He might not be able to beat Smoke Jensen with a gun—and that was up for grabs, for Max knew he was one of the best with a short gun—but there was no doubt in Max's mind that he was the better fighter of the two.

But how much time did he have? His informant in Barlow had sent him word that Judge Garrison and Smoke Jensen were gathering up old arrest warrants on him from his days back East. Two or three weeks might be cutting it very close.

And his informant had also told him that old warrants were being looked at against Red Malone. If the authorities back East came through, the rancher would have to run with Max. And Max knew the man would never agree to do that. The man would stand his ground and die with a six-shooter in his hand. He was too bullheaded to do anything else.

With a deep sigh, Big Max turned his attentions to the group of outlaws in his office. "Yes," he said slowly. "We're out of time here. Smoke Jensen has beaten us. Red may not see it that way, but I do. Smoke has used fists and guns to bring civilization to our doorstep."

Max eyeballed the group, one at a time. Val Singer, Warner Frigo, Dave Poe, Alex Bell, Sheriff Paul Cartwright. "We're all wanted men, maybe not under the names we're using now, but wanted nevertheless. Two or three weeks is going to be cutting it awfully close. But I understand that is the way it's going to have to be. Monies have to be in the bank before we hit the town. To hell with those in jail. If we can get them out during the raid, fine. If not, that's all right, too. Are we in agreement with that?"

They were in agreement.

"The next problem," Max said, "is where do we run to?"

Everyone had a different idea. Cartwright couldn't go back to California. He was wanted out there. Singer couldn't go east. He was wanted in six or seven states in that direction . . . And so it was with them all.

Max waved them silent. "All right, all right! Enough. It might be best if we split up after the raid anyway. We'll pick a place to meet and divvy up the loot, and then split up. And boys," he eyeballed each of them, "I shall be personally leading this raid."

The outlaws all exchanged glances. Max had master-minded a lot of raids, but none of them had ever known him to lead one. They were curious, and Val Singer put that curiosity into words.

"I have plans for a certain lady in that town," Max said with a smile. "I want her to know a real man just once in her life . . . just before I kill her."

"Well, if you gonna be draggin' some squallin' petticoat around with you," Warner Frigo said, "I think it's best we do split up. We're gonna have enough money to divvy up to buy the best women in any crib in the world."

"Yeah," Dave Poe said. "That don't make no sense, Max. It's too risky. Once we're out of this area, when words gets out about harmin' a woman, they'll be posses lookin' for you all over the place. And you do have a tendency to stand out in a crowd," he added dryly.

"It'll die down. It always has before. Hell, don't you boys get righteous on me. You've all raped before. Besides, you don't even know who I have in mind."

"Sure we do," Alex Bell said. "Has to be the doctor's wife, Victoria Turner."

Max smiled. "Nope. Her name is Sally. Sally Jensen."

Chapter 20

The trial of the outlaws and the arsonist went off without a hitch. Judge Garrison handed down the toughest sentences he could under the law and the territorial prison was notified. The returning wire said it would be two or three weeks before the wagon could come and pick them up.

Smoke noticed the now-familiar buggy rolling out of town, heading north. He walked to the livery, threw a saddle on Star, and headed out, staying to the high ground, which oftentimes ran parallel to the road but high-up.

He trailed the buggy to within a few miles of Hell's Creek and watched as Max Huggins rode out to meet it. Max and the driver of the buggy sat for a long time on a log, talking, Huggins with one big arm around the other person's shoulder.

That night he told Sally about it. She shook her head in disgust. "Things are just never what they seem to be, are they, honey?"

"This thing isn't, that's for sure. Problem is, I don't know what to do about it. No laws have been broken. The only thing broken will be the faith of the townspeople."

"And a broken heart when the other partner in the marriage learns of it," she added.

"Yeah. If they don't already know about it."

"I hadn't thought about that. Oh, Smoke, I just can't believe that. Just thinking about it makes me sick!"

"I'll have to face one or the other pretty soon, I reckon. And I'm not looking forward to that. Well, let's get off of it. How's the bank coming along?"

"I just got word this morning. It'll open for business next Monday morning. The money will be coming in day after tomorrow. And it will be heavily guarded."

She handed him a telegraph and let him read it. He whistled. "That's a lot of money."

"Yes. And that will be too good an opportunity for Max to pass up."

"I wish you and Victoria would get out of here, Sally. The two of you go on back to the Sugarloaf."

She shook her head. "No. I'm staying. We'll leave together, Smoke."

He had expected that answer so it came as no surprise to him. "I'd say I have two weeks before Max hits us. Maybe three. But no longer. I think those rumors the snitch carried to him about those old warrants back East has him spooked. And I'm told that Red Malone is getting jumpy, too."

She smiled at him. "The Sugarloaf will look good, won't it?"

"You bet." He got up and found his hat. "I'm going to prowl the town for a while."

"Anything wrong?"

"No. I just want to check around."

"I'm going to read. If you're late, I'll leave the lamp low."

Smoke walked down the stairs and through the lobby, speaking to the night clerk at the desk. The Grand Hotel was full, for with the coming of the paper, a doctor, two lawyers, and a half-dozen new businesses, the town was experiencing a growth unseen since its inception.

The saloon was doing a land-office business and had hired two nighttime waitresses and a piano player. The piano player was banging out a tune, the melody floating on the night air.

Pete walked up, spurs jingling softly. "Horse tied out of sight down by the creek," he told Smoke. "I never seen the brand before. Fancy riggin'. Rifle is gone from the boot. We might have us a back-shooter in town."

"You tell the others?"

"Goin' to now."

"OK. Watch yourself."

Pete gone, Smoke stepped back into the shadows created by the storefront and lifted his eyes, inspecting the rooftops of the buildings across the street. He squatted down and removed his spurs, laying them behind a bench on the boardwalk.

Standing up, he freed his .44's and slipped into an alleyway, walking around behind the buildings. He paused at the alley's end, staying close to the hotel's outside wall. He listened, all senses working overtime.

Smoke watched a man come out of a privy and walk into the hotel, through the back door. The lamplight inside flashed momentarily as the door opened. Smoke closed his eyes to retain his night vision. He opened his eyes and walked on, slipping around the buildings.

He angled around Martha's Dress Shoppe and came out behind the cafe. A slight movement ahead of him flattened Smoke against the back wall of the cafe, eyes searching the darkness. He caught a faint glint of moonlight off what appeared to be the barrel of a carbine—short-barreled for easier handling. Smoke waited, muscles tensed. He pulled his right-hand .44 from leather and, with his left hand over the hammer to reduce the noise, cocked it.

The man behind the gun stepped away from the building, and for an instant, Smoke could see his face. It was no one he had ever seen before. The man was clean-shaven, his clothing dark and looking neat. The man took a step, a silent one. He wore no spurs.

Slowly, Smoke knelt down, carefully stretching out on the cool ground to offer the man less of a target. "You looking for me, partner?" Smoke softly called.

The man turned and fired, the slug striking the wood of the building some four feet above Smoke's head. Smoke fired, the .44 slug hitting the rifle and tearing the weapon from the man's hands. The gunman ran back into the darkness.

"Yo, Smoke!" Sal called from the street.

"I'm all right. Stay under cover. I'm thinking this man is not alone." Smoke rolled to his left as some primal warning jumped through his brain.

Two fast shots, coming from different weapons, tore up the ground where he had been lying.

Smoke caught the muzzle flashes of one of the guns and snapped off a fast shot. The gunhand screamed as the slug ripped his belly and sent him tumbling off the roof of the saddle shop. He hit the ground and did not move.

An unknown gunhand stepped out of his hiding place behind Smoke and leveled his pistol. Jim and Sal fired as one from the main street, both slugs striking the man, knocking him off his boots.

Smoke rolled and came up on his feet, behind a tree. Both his hands were filled with .44's, hammers back. A slug ripped the night, burning through the bark of the tree, knocking chips flying. Smoke stepped to the other side of the tree and fired twice, left and right guns working. The man doubled over, both shots taking him in the stomach. Smoke ran to him and kicked the dropped guns out of his reach. He knelt down beside the hard-hit man just as his deputies came running up.

"You're not going to make it," Smoke told the bloodied man. "Who hired you?"

The man grinned through his pain. "Told the boys we was gonna be buckin' a stacked deck comin' after you." He groaned. "But the money was just too good to pass up."

"Whose money?" Smoke asked.

"You go to Hell!" the man said, then closed his eyes and died.

"This one's still alive!" Sal called, kneeling beside the man who had fallen off the roof. "But not for long. I think his neck's broke."

"Hell, that's Blanchard," Pete said, looking down at the man. "I thought he was in prison down in New Mexico." He knelt down. "Come on, Blanchard," he urged. "Go out clean for once in your life. This is your last chance, man. Who hired you?"

Two dozen people, men and women, in various dress, including nightshirts and long-handles, had gathered around.

"Huggins from over to . . . Hell's Creek," the dying man gasped. "Pulled us up from Utah. We rode the train. Me and Dixson. Dee was . . . he rode over from Idaho."

"Dee Mansfield?" Smoke questioned.

"Yeah."

"That his horse down by the crick?" Sal asked.

"Yeah. He . . . Gettin' cold and I can't . . . move my hands."

Dr. Turner pushed through the crowd and knelt down, looking at the man. It was a quick look. Blanchard had died.

The doctor stood up and faced Smoke. "When is this carnage going to end, Jensen?"

"Whenever Red Malone and Max Huggins call it off," Smoke told him. He spotted the undertaker. "Haul them off," he said. "OK, folks, show's over. Let's break it up."

"No, it isn't," Tom Johnson said, walking up. "Melvin Malone just rode into town. He's calling you out, Smoke."

"Damn!" The word exploded from Smoke's mouth. "I knew that kid would cut his wolf loose someday." He punched out his empties and loaded up full. "Sal, clear the streets."

"I demand an end to this barbaric practice of justice at the point of a gun!" Dr. Turner said. "Just arrest him, Marshal. You don't have to kill him. You have the manpower to overwhelm him."

Smoke looked at the man in the dim light. "You . . . demand, Robert? Who in the hell do you think you are, anyway? Demand? Overwhelm him? How? He's come to kill, Robert, not talk. He'll shoot anyone who tries to disarm him."

"You don't know that, Smoke. That's just conjecture on your part. Law and order must prevail out here. It's past time."

"Why don't you go disarm him, then, Doctor?" Sal suggested.

"I . . . uh . . . I'm not a lawman," the doctor said, his face coloring. "That's your job."

"Yeah, right," Sal's reply was dour. "I think that was the reason I hung up a badge the last time I wore one."

Smoke turned his back to the doctor and walked away, his deputies moving with him, the crowd following along.

"He's in the saloon," Tom called. "You goin' to kill the punk, Smoke?"

"I hope not," Smoke muttered.

"There might not be any other way, Smoke," Jim pointed out.

"I know. But I can always hope."

Smoke stepped up onto the boardwalk and pushed open the batwings. The piano player stopped his pounding of the ivories when he spotted Smoke. The waitresses moved as far away from the bar as they could get. The long bar was already void of customers. Only Melvin stood there, a whiskey bottle in front of him, his right hand close to the butt of his Colt.

"Come on in, Jensen," Melvin said. "I'll buy you a drink."

"You were banned from this town, Melvin. Leave now and I won't toss you in jail."

"You'll never toss me in jail again, Jensen. Me, or anyone else for that matter."

"Boy, don't be a fool!" Smoke snapped at him. He knew that his plan to move close enough to slug the young man was out the window. Kill was written on Melvin's face, and his eyes were unnaturally bright with the blood lust that reared up within him. "I've faced a hundred young hot-shots like you. They're all dead, boy. Dead, or crippled."

Smoke could tell that Melvin was not drunk. The young man had enough sense about him to lay off the bottle before a gunfight. Alcohol impaired the reflexes.

Melvin laughed at the warning.

Smoke was thinking fast. He had been warned that Melvin was very, very quick and very, very accurate, so any idea of just wounding the young man was out of the question. When Melvin dragged iron, Smoke was going to have to get off the first shot and make it a good one.

"Boy, think of your father," Smoke tried a different tact. "Your sister. Think what your dying is going to do to them."

"Me, dying?" The young man was clearly startled. "Me? Oh, you got it all wrong, Jensen. You're the one that's going to be pushin' up flowers, not me."

"Listen to me, boy," Smoke said, doing his best to talk some sense into Melvin. "You . . ."

"Shut up!" Melvin yelled, stepping away from the bar. "You're a coward, Jensen. You're afraid to draw on me."

A coldness touched Smoke. A coldness that was surrounded by a dark rage. It sometimes happened when he was looking at death. It was a feeling much like the ancient Viking berserkers must have experienced in battle.

"I tried, boy," Smoke's words were touched with sadness. "Nobody can say I didn't try."

"And that's all you're gonna do in this fight," Melvin sneered the words. "Try to beat me. You've had a long run, Jensen. Now it's over. Now my pa can stop worryin' about his back trail and we can get on with our lives."

"All but one of you," Smoke corrected the young man.

"Huh?"

"Your life is over."

With a curse on his lips, Melvin's hands flashed to his guns and he was rattlesnake quick. But Smoke's draw was as smooth as honey and lightning fast. Melvin got off a shot, the slug blowing a hole in the barroom floor. Smoke's first shot took the young gunslinger in the belly. Melvin's second shot grazed Smoke's shoulder, burning a hole in his shirt and searing his flesh. Smoke shot the young man again, the slug turning Melvin. Still he would not go down.

Melvin lifted his left-hand Colt and fired, the slug smashing the bar. Smoke shot him again and Melvin went down to his knees, still holding his Colts.

Smoke stepped through the swirl of gunsmoke and walked to the young man. He kicked the guns from his hands and stood over him.

"I beat Blackjack Simmons and Ted Novarro," Melvin moaned the words. "Holland didn't even clear leather against me."

"They were fast," Smoke spoke the words softly.

"But you . . ." Melvin gasped. "You . . ."

He toppled over on his face and began communicating with the afterlife.

Smoke punched out his empties and reloaded. "Jim, get word to Red that he can come in and take his boy home. Just Red. Anybody else of the Lightning brand tries to enter this town, I'll toss them in jail or leave them in the dust."

The young deputy left the barroom and walked to the stable, saddling his horse for the night ride.

"Knowing Red as I do," Sal pointed out, "he just might come bustin' up here with all his hands, figuring to burn down the town."

"If he does, it'll be the last thing he'll ever do," Smoke said. He looked around the barroom. "I want ten men on guard at all times tonight. Take some water and biscuits with you when you go to the rooftops. Go home and get your rifles." He looked at the barkeep. "Shut it down, Ralph."

"Will do, Marshal. I'll clean up and then get my rifle to stand a turn."

"Thanks, Ralph."

The body of Melvin Malone was carried to the undertaker and the lamps in the saloon were turned off. The men of the first watch were getting in place on the rooftops as Smoke, Sal, and Pete walked the boardwalks of the town, rattling doorknobs and looking into the darkness of alleys.

Smoke passed Robert Turner on the boardwalk as the man was going home. The doctor did not speak to the gunfighter.

"Yonder goes a scared man," Sal said. "Something about that fella just don't add up to me."

Pete said, "I been thinkin' the same thing. He looks familiar to me, but I swear I can't place him."

"Think of Max Huggins for a moment," Smoke told the men.

"What do you mean, Smoke?" Sal asked.

"Max Huggins is Dr. Robert Turner's brother."

Chapter 21

Smoke swore his deputies to silence about the true identity of Dr. Turner, then went to the hotel to catch a few hours' sleep. He was up long before dawn. Smoke dressed quietly, letting Sally sleep, then went down to the jail to bathe his face and hands and shave. He walked out onto the silent boardwalks and leaned against a support pole. Jim had arrived back in town after delivering the news. He said Red did not take the news well. Smoke sent the man off to bed and then rolled a cigarette, waiting for the arrival of Red Malone.

Just at dawn, the hooves of a slow walking horse drummed over the wooden bridge at the south end of town. It was Red Malone, and he had come alone.

Red reined up and stared at Smoke through the gray light of dawn. The man's face was hard and uncompromising. "I come to get my boy, Jensen."

Smoke jerked a thumb. "He's over at the undertaker's, Red."

"I'll get my boy buried proper, Jensen, and then you and me, we'll settle this."

"Why settle anything, Red? Your boy came to me, looking for trouble. Thirty . . . forty men heard me practically beg him not to draw. He was a grown man and he made his choice. He tossed the dice and threw craps. Bury your boy and put the hate out of your heart."

Red stared at him for a long moment. Then, without another word, he turned his horse's head and rode slowly up the street, toward the undertaker. A few minutes later, Melvin was tied across the saddle of his pony, the horse carrying its owner for the last time.

As he rode slowly past Smoke, Red turned his head and said, "I'll be back, Jensen."

"I'll be here, Red."

Smoke waited until the sounds of horses had faded to the south, then walked across the street to the hotel dining room for breakfast. Red was going to work himself up into a murderous rage, then gather all his hands and attack the town. He would get with Max Huggins and work it all out. Max and his men would attack from the north, Red and his bunch from the south. Smoke was sure of it.

After breakfast, Smoke walked up and down the town's streets, telling people what he felt was coming at them. They had all felt that sooner or later they would be attacked. They took the news stoically. Benson, the blacksmith, summed up the town's feelings. "We'll be ready, Marshal."

The town braced for trouble, and Smoke went to see Dr. Robert Turner.

The doctor met him at the door. "If you're hurt, I'll treat you, Smoke; I'd do that for any man. But other than that, you are not welcome in this house."

"I see," Smoke said, standing on the small porch. "Does that include my wife, too?"

Robert hesitated. Women were held in high esteem back East, but nothing compared to the way they were almost revered out here in the wild West. "Sally is welcome here anytime, of course."

"You just don't like my barbaric ways, is that it, Doc?"

"Something like that, yes. All this killing is quite unnecessary, you know."

"No, I didn't know that, Doc. What am I supposed to do when a man confronts me with a gun? Kiss him? Let me tell you something, Doc. This will probably change over the coming years, and in a way it'll be a sad thing when it does; but out here, a coward can't make it. Now, there is a reason for that. If a man is a coward, then there is a good chance that he's also a liar and a cheat. Not always, but often that's true. You see, Doc, out here, a man's word is his bond. If a man's word can't be trusted, what good is he? So no man wants the title of coward branded on him. Too much goes with it. Are you beginning to understand what I just said?"

"Of course, I understand it. It's still stupid, primitive, and barbaric."

"Victoria home?"

"No. She went shopping."

"That's good. 'Cause I just don't believe she knows the game you're playing."

Robert stared at him for a time. The doctor's eyes were unreadable. "I don't know what you're talking about, Jensen."

"You're a liar."

Robert didn't back up. "I'm no gunhand, Smoke. And I certainly can't whip you with my fists, so I'm not going to try. Does that make me a coward?"

Smoke chuckled. "No. But I didn't call you that to provoke a fight. That's a bully's way. And I'm not a bully. I called you that to get your attention. Have I got it?"

"Yes. I believe you could say that." Robert stepped out onto the porch and waved Smoke to a chair. "What's on your mind?"

"Your brother, Max Huggins."

Robert was so shaken he missed the seat of the chair and went tumbling to the porch floor. Smoke helped the man up and into the chair. Robert was ghost-white and his hands were trembling.

"You want me to get you a drink of water?" Smoke asked.

"That would be nice. Yes. Would you?"

"Sure." Smoke went into the kitchen, pumped a glass full of water, and took it to the man.

Robert drank the glass empty and sighed heavily, as if a load had been taken from him. "How did you find out about Max?"

"By looking at the two of you and guessing. I knew someone had been leaking information out of town, so I followed you one day. Now, then, what do you intend to do about it?"

The man shrugged. "Victoria doesn't know, Smoke."

"All right. Neither Sally nor I believed she was a part of it."

"How many people know?"

"Me and Sally. Judge Garrison. My deputies."

"When the townspeople find out, I guess I'm through in Barlow, right?"

"I imagine so. You and Victoria, you're not cut out for this kind of life, Robert. The West is not for people like you. It's still plenty raw out here. You and Victoria, you both want all the pretty things that are scarce out here. Women wear gingham out here, not lace. Coming up here from train's end, me and Sally took our baths in creeks. I can't work up a picture in my mind of you and Victoria doing that.

Killings are common out here, Robert. Not as common as they used to be, but people will still travel a hundred miles to see a good hanging."

The city doctor shook his head at that and grimaced in disgust.

"And then there is the little matter of your brother to take into consideration."

"Max is my brother. Can't you understand that?"

"He's also a thief, a rapist, a murderer, and God only knows what else. And accept this, Doc: I intend to kill him."

"Judge, jury, and executioner, right, Smoke?"

"Sometimes that's the way it has to be, Robert. And you're no better than Max, are you, Robert?"

"What do you mean by that?"

"There was no old rancher that you befriended back in the city, was there, Robert?"

The doctor's silence gave Smoke his reply.

"I suspected as much. Max killed that rancher and then had the letter forged. The letter you showed your wife."

"He never said, and I never asked."

"Didn't you even care?"

"Yes," the doctor's reply was spoken low. "Yes, I cared. I came out here in hopes of changing my brother, making him see that what he was doing was wrong. Evil. Our parents died two years ago, four months apart. They left quite a sizable estate; it all came to me. Of course, they had written Max out of the will years before. I even offered Max half of the estate."

"Sally thought you were a poor struggling doctor."

Robert laughed, a bitter bark that held no humor. "Hardly. I assure you I have plenty of money."

"And Max told you he would change his evil ways and become a fine upstanding citizen." It was not a question.

"Yes, he did, and I believed him."

"All that crap you told Victoria, that she wrote to Sally, about Lisa and Victoria being lusted after by Max. All that was a lie?"

"No. No, it wasn't. He told me he wanted my wife. And he told me he would use Lisa to have her."

"And you still defend the sorry no-good? Jesus Christ, Robert, what have you got between your ears? Mush?"

"I owe him my life, Smoke. Three times, I owe him. And I owe him my family fortune."

"You want to explain that?"

"A gang of thugs set on me when I was a boy. They had knives. Max whipped them. Every one of them. Later, when I got a—a woman in a family way, her father had me cornered, with a gun. Max killed him."

Smoke looked at the man, amazement in his eyes. "You're a real swell fellow, Robert. You know that?"

Robert could not miss the sarcasm in Smoke's tone. "She was just trash. So was her father."

"You did see the child through school, I hope?"

"Of course not. Don't be ridiculous. I told you, she was trash. Anyway, she moved away. I have no idea where she and the brat might be."

Smoke took off his hat and shook his head in disbelief. Robert was as bad, in his own way, as Max. He wondered if Victoria knew about any of it. He didn't think so. At least, he hoped not, for Sally's sake. "Go on, Robert." Smoke put his hat on and leaned back in the chair, rolling a cigarette. "It's such a heartrending tale."

"Yes. It really is, isn't it?"

Smoke looked at him to see if the man was serious. He was. Smoke sighed and waited.

"The third time Max saved my life I was in college. He

was on the run from the law—had been for years—but he was back East at the time. I had a rather unpleasant experience with a brother. . . ."

"You have another brother?"

"Oh, no. This was a fraternity brother at school."

"What the hell is that? Never mind. I don't want to know."

"I beat the young man quite severely about the head with a brick. It was over a woman, of course. Max finished him off for me."

Smoke was jarred right down to his boots. The good doctor, Robert Turner, was crazy. Insane. Smoke had read of people who had, or professed to have, two or three or more personalities. This was, he believed, the first time he'd ever met one of those people. He sincerely hoped he would never meet another.

"Finished him off? What do you mean, Robert?" Smoke knew exactly what he meant, but he wanted to hear the words out of Robert's mouth.

"Killed him, of course. Oh, the young man was dying anyway. Max just took the brick and beat his head in with it. I was appalled, of course. I abhor violence of any kind."

"Yeah. I can sure see that."

"It was in the dead of winter. And my heavens, but it was cold. Max took the body and threw it into the river, after tying several heavy objects to it. We're brothers, you know. Brothers help each other."

"Yeah. Right."

"It was just after that when my father got into his . . . ah . . . predicament. Max took care of that, too. Then he headed west. He always kept in touch with me, though. We're brothers, you know."

"How did he take care of your father's . . . ah . . . troubles?"

"Killed my father's mistress. She was attempting to blackmail Father. That would have done poor Mum in had she ever found out about it."

"I'm sure it would have, Robert." It's just about doing me in listening to it, he thought.

Robert sat up straight in his chair and clasped both hands to his knees. "Well, my good fellow. I certainly am glad we had this little chat. I feel so much better now that I realize what an understanding man you are." He stood up, a broad smile on his face. "I must go see my patients now. They need me, you know? It's such a nice feeling to be wanted."

Robert walked back into the house, took his doctor's bag, and got into his buggy, clucking the horse forward. Smoke sat on the porch and watched the doctor drive out of town.

"The man is nuts," Smoke said. "Crazy and dangerous. Very dangerous."

He was sitting on the porch when Vicky strolled up, her arms filled with packages. She did not seem surprised to see Smoke sitting there. He helped her with her packages, then waited on the porch for her to come out of the house.

"Are you waiting for Robert?" she asked.

"No. I had a long chat with Robert. He just left. I was sitting here . . . ah . . . sort of catching my breath after our conversation."

"Whatever in the world do you mean, Smoke?"

Smoke did not know how to handle this. He was not the type of man who relied on finesse. His way was straight ahead and get the job done.

He shook his head and stood up. "Nothing, Vicky. It was just that our conversation got a little deep for me. Medical stuff."

"Oh! Are you ill? Is Sally all right?"

"Both of us are fine. Where is Lisa?"

"Playing with a friend." She smiled. "Don't worry. The kids are well guarded."

Smoke nodded. "Vicky, could I ask you some questions without your getting angry?"

"Why . . . of course." She studied his face. "It's Robert, isn't it?"

"Ah, yeah. It is." Smoke really didn't know how to get into this.

"He's a good man, I believe. But a very strange man at times. It's . . . and please don't think I'm criticizing him or talking behind his back; I've tried to discuss this with him. . . ." She paused. "It's almost as though he is several different people in one body. Do you know what I mean?"

"Yes, Vicky, I do."

"I've been worried about him ever since we came out here. My goodness, I haven't even told this to Sally. You're easy to talk to, Smoke."

"Has his . . . ah . . . behavior been sort of odd, Vicky?"

"Why . . . yes. That's it. You've noticed it, too?"

"Oh, yeah. I sure have. He sort of . . . ah . . . rambled, I guess you'd call it, while talking with me."

She stared at him for a moment, then rose from the chair and walked to the edge of the porch. She stood for a moment, looking at the mountains in the distance. Smoke could hear her sigh. "I don't know what to do, Smoke," she said. "I don't have a penny of my own money. I am totally dependent upon Robert. He has violent mood changes. I'm frightened of him, and so is Lisa." She turned to face Smoke.

"I know he used to meet Max Huggins in town. I thought that very odd. And I have no idea what they discussed. Except . . ." she flushed deeply, ". . . me."

"And Lisa," Smoke said, taking a chance.

"Yes. Max came to the ranch lots of times. Robert would laugh and joke with him. Usually outside, away from me. But sometimes in the living room. I never could understand the . . . well, call it a bond between them."

"They're brothers, Victoria."

She fainted, falling off the porch.

Chapter 22

S moke yelled at a passing boy to run to the hotel and fetch Sally, then go to his office and tell his deputies to get over here.

The boy took off like he had rockets on his feet.

Smoke picked Vicky up and placed her on the couch in the living room. He was dampening a cloth at the kitchen pump when Sally ran in.

"What happened?"

"She fainted after I told her that Max Huggins and Robert were brothers."

"I'm surprised she didn't have a heart attack. Give me that cloth and go outside."

Smoke went outside and sat on the porch. Sal, Jim, and Pete had just arrived, out of breath from unaccustomed running in high-heeled boots. They were typical cowboys; anything that could not be done from the hurricane deck of a horse they usually tried to avoid.

"What's up, Smoke?" Pete asked.

He brought his men up to date. Judge Garrison rolled up in his buggy and joined the men in the front yard.

"That poor woman," the judge said. "She certainly has a heavy cross to bear."

"Judge," Smoke said, "can you get Robert declared insane?"

"All I have to do is sign my name to a piece of paper. He'll be taken to the state hospital for the insane."

One of Joe Walsh's hands rode up and dismounted. "Say, Smoke, I just seen Dr. Turner headin' north toward Hell's Creek. He was putting the whip to that horse of his. He was shoutin' and cussin' as he drove. Damn near ran me down. I hollered and asked him what was the matter. He said he had to get to his brother. What brother's he talkin' about? I didn't know he had any kin out here."

"We just found out that he and Max Huggins are brothers," Smoke told him.

The cowboy's eyes bugged out and his mouth dropped open. "Holy crap!"

Smoke turned to the judge. "Get all the legal action going that needs to be done, Judge. Committing Robert, and seeing to it that his estate is in Victoria's hands."

"Easily done, Smoke. I'll have the paperwork done in an hour and wire his banks back East. You get into his strongbox or files and find out where and how much. Have the papers sent to me."

Smoke walked back into the house.

Sally had opened Victoria's bodice and placed a cool cloth on the woman's head. Her eyes were open and she seemed alert. Smoke pulled a chair up close to the couch.

"I'm sorry, Vicky," he said. "But I just didn't know how else to tell you."

"It's all right, Smoke. I'm glad you did. It answers a lot of questions I had in my mind. Now I can see the family resemblance."

Smoke told her what the cowboy had seen. "Judge Garrison is going to have him committed, and we're going to get Robert's estate in your hands. I need to know where he keeps his documents, bank books, and so forth."

"I'll show you." She fastened a few buttons on her bodice and sat up on the couch.

"You best lay back down," Smoke told her.

"No." She smiled and stood up. She was steady on her feet. "If I'm to be a western woman, I've got to learn to be strong."

Smoke returned the smile. "I thought you were leaving, heading back East?"

"I'm staying," Vicky said. "I want my daughter to be raised out here. The town needs another schoolteacher, and that is what I was trained to be."

Sal had entered the room. He took one look at Vicky's open bodice and blushed. Turning his back to the woman, he said, "I sent Pete over to fetch your girl, ma'am. They'll be along directly."

"Thank you, Mr. . . ."

"Just Sal, ma'am."

Vicky buttoned up her bodice. "You may turn around now, Sal."

"Thank you. I feel sorta stupid standin' here talkin' to a wall."

"That was kind of you thinking of Lisa."

Sal blushed. "Wasn't nothin', ma'am."

"It is to me, I assure you. Well!" She patted her hair and got herself together. "I have to assume that Robert is not coming back. So I think what I'll do is this: If you all will leave me alone for a time—Sally, will you look after Lisa for a few minutes? Good, thank you—I'll have myself a good cry and then start putting my life back in order."

Sal was the first one out the door. Women made him nervous, unpredictable creatures that they were.

"Man ought to be horsewhipped leavin' a good woman like that one back yonder," Sal said to Smoke as they all walked back to the office.

Sally looked at Smoke and winked at him. "Sal, what are your plans when we leave here?"

"Why . . . I don't rightly know, ma'am. Why do you ask?"

"The county is going to need a sheriff," Smoke picked up on what his wife was leading up to. "And you've been a fine deputy. How's about I recommend you to Judge Garrison."

"You mean that?"

"Are you interested?"

"Sure. But how 'bout these boys?" He jerked his thumb at Pete and Jim.

"Well," Smoke said with a smile, "I think Pete is going to try his hand at ranchin', seeing as how he's been tippy-toeing around the Widow Feckles, the both of them making goo-goo eyes at each other."

Pete's face suddenly turned beet-red. "I just remembered something. I got to go see about my horse," he said, and walked across the street.

"How about you?" Sal asked Jim.

"I like this deputy sheriffin'. Sure beats thirty a month and found sleepin' in drafty bunkhouses. It's fine with me, Sal."

"Good. It's settled then. Judge Garrison has papers declaring the election of Cartwright to have been illegal, and the man has no more authority. He's going to post election notices starting tomorrow. And you're going to be the only candidate."

"What are you gonna do?" Sal asked, clearly startled at the rapid turn of events.

"Retire from law enforcement and hang around to see the fun. A badge is too restrictive for me, Sal. I like room to roam."

"In other words, you're gonna take the fight to them."

"Why, Sal," Smoke said with a serious look on his face, "you know I wouldn't do anything like that."

"He occasionally tells tall tales, too, Sal," Sally told him.

"Judge Garrison did what?" Max jumped to his feet.

"Declared my election as sheriff illegal and they had an election down to Barlow yesterday," Cartwright said. "Sal is the new sheriff."

"He can't do that. We weren't advised of any election."

"Yes, we were." Cartwright held out a piece of paper. "One of the boys found this tacked to a tree just outside of town."

Max snatched the paper from him and squinted. "Hell, you can't read it without a magnifying glass!"

"That's sure enough the truth and that's what I done, too. It's a legal paper, telling the citizens of Hell's Creek about the election."

Max sat down and cussed. Loud and long. He wadded up the notice and hurled it across the room. He had never before been stymied at every turn, and it was an unpleasant sensation that he did not like.

"Well, you can still be town marshal of Hell's Creek."

"Big deal," Cartwright said sarcastically. "We got no protection now, Max. We don't know what's goin' on in Barlow now that your brother moved in with you. And the boys is gettin' right edgy."

"About what, Paul?"

"They're wantin' to hit the town now and get out. The bank's in place, ain't it?"

"Not yet. Monday morning is still the target date. We'll double our money if we wait until everybody there has dug up the money they've buried or pulled it out of mattress ticks. Tell the boys to calm down."

Cartwright left and Max turned in his chair, looking out his office window. His main concern right now was what he was going to do with Robert. His younger brother was getting unpredictable. He was like a goose, waking up in a new world every morning. Most of the time he was lucid, but other times he was crazy as a loon. Of course, he had always known his brother was nuts, walking a very fine line between genius—which he was—and insanity—which he certainly was.

But he was family, and family looked out for each other. As best they could, that is.

"You just sign right here, Victoria," Judge Garrison said, "and Robert's estate will be under your control."

Victoria signed and she became executor over Robert Turner's estate, thus insuring that she and Lisa would not be thrust penniless into the world.

Sal was now the officially elected and legal sheriff of the county, and Smoke had turned in his badge.

While Smoke respected the law, he was also well aware that there were hard limits placed upon it when dealing with the lawless. As a private citizen, he had shed himself of those limits. Now he could meet Max Huggins and Red Malone on an equal footing.

Smoke bought supplies at Marbly's General Store—including a sack of dynamite—and made ready to hit the trail. In addition to his .44 Winchester, he carried a Sharps .56 in

another saddle boot. Two days after the election, Smoke
kissed Sally good-bye and swung into the saddle. Star was
ready to go; the big black was bred for the trails and was
growing impatient with all this inactivity.

"I won't ask how long you'll be gone," Sally said.

"Two or three days this time around. I'll be back in time
to see the bank open."

He headed north, toward Hell's Creek, to see what mischief he could get into. He had heard rumors that Big Max
Huggins thought himself to be unbeatable as a bare-knuckle
fighter. Smoke knew that the man could be formidable; just
his size would make him dangerous. But Smoke also knew
that many big men rarely knew much about the finesse of
fighting, depending mostly on their strength and bulk to
overwhelm their opponents.

The trick would be to catch Big Max by himself. Smoke
didn't trust anyone left in Hell's Creek not to shoot him after
he whipped Max—and he knew he could whip him. He'd
take some cuts and bruises doing so, for Max was a huge
and powerful man. But Smoke had whipped men just as big
and just as tough; men who knew something about boxing.

Smoke stayed off the road, keeping to the mountain trails,
enjoying the aloneness of it all. He rested and ate an early
lunch above a peaceful valley, exploding with summer colors. Deer fed below him, and once he spotted a grizzly am-
bling along, eating berries and overturning logs, looking for
grubs. Squirrels chattered and birds sang their joyful songs
all around him.

Then suddenly it all stopped and the timber fell as silent
as a tomb. The deer below him raced away and the grizzly
reared up on his hind legs, testing the air. The bear dropped
down to all fours and skedaddled back into the timber.

Smoke had picked a very secure position to noon, with

Star well hidden. He did not move; movement would attract attention faster than noise.

Soon the horsemen came into view, about a dozen of them, riding through the valley. Smoke moved then, getting his field glasses out of the saddlebags and focusing in on the men, being careful not to let the sun glint off the lenses.

He knew some of them—or had seen them before. They were hired guns—hired by Max Huggins. The men were riding heavily armed, carrying their rifles across the saddle horns. Smoke could see where many of them had shoved extra six-shooters behind their belts.

The route they were taking would lead them straight to the farm complex of Brown and Gatewood and the others. Those families had taken enough grief from Huggins and Red Malone and their ilk, Smoke thought, returning to Star and stowing the binoculars.

He decided he'd trail along behind the hired guns and add a little spice to their lives as soon as he was sure what they were up to.

Smoke decided not to wait when he saw the men reach into their back pockets and pull out hoods. They reined up and slipped the hoods over their faces.

They were about three miles from the farm complex. No man elects to wear a hood over his face unless he's up to no good; but still Smoke held his fire. He was looking down at a pack of trash, that he knew. But so far they had done nothing wrong.

He left them, riding higher into the timber and getting ahead of the gunslingers. On a ridge overlooking the valley where Brown and the others were rebuilding, Smoke swung down from the saddle and shucked the Sharps .56 from its boot. He got into position and waited.

He didn't have long to wait. The raiders came at a gallop,

riding hard and heading straight for Brown's farm, guns at hand.

Smoke leveled the Sharps and blew one outlaw from the saddle, the big slug taking the man in the chest and flinging him off his horse, dead as he hit the ground.

Brown, his wife, and their two sons had been working with guns close by. The four of them, upon hearing the booming of the .56, dropped their hammers and shovels and grabbed their rifles, getting behind cover. They emptied four saddles during the first charge, and that broke the attack off before it could get started. The outlaws turned around and headed back north. They had lost five out of twelve, and that had not been in their plans.

They were about to lose more.

They headed straight for Smoke's position, at a hard gallop. Smoke leveled the Sharps, sighted in, and squeezed the trigger. Another hooded man screamed and fell from the saddle, one arm hanging useless by his side, shattered by the heavy .56 caliber slug. He stood up and Smoke finished him.

The hooded raiders were riding in a panic now, not knowing how many riflemen were hidden along the ridges. Smoke lifted the Sharps and sighted in another, firing and missing. He sighted in another man and this time he did not miss. The raider pitched forward, both hands flung into the air, and toppled from the saddle.

Smoke walked back to his horse, booted the rifle, and mounted up, riding down to see if any of the outlaws on the ground were still alive. Two of them were, and one of them was not going to make it. The second man had only a flesh wound.

Smoke jerked the hoods from them and glared down at the men. "You'll live," he told the man with the flesh wound. He cut his eyes to the other man. "You won't. You got anything you'd like to say before you die?"

Brown and his family had gathered around. The sound of the galloping horses of the farmer's neighbors coming to their aid grew loud. Soon the men of the entire complex had gathered around the fallen raiders.

"How'd you know?" the dying man gasped out the question, his eyes bright with pain, his hands holding his .56-caliber-punctured belly.

"I didn't," Smoke told him. "I was having lunch on the ridges when you crud came riding along."

"What'd you gonna do with me?" the other outlaw whined.

"Shut up," Smoke said. "You get on my nerves and I might just decide to hang you."

"That ain't legal!" the man hollered. "I got a right to a fair trial."

Cooter snorted. "Ain't that something now? They come up here attackin' us, and damned if he ain't hollerin' about his right to a fair trial. I swear I don't know where our system of justice is takin' us."

"Wait a few years," Smoke told him. "I guarantee you it'll get worse."

"I need a doctor!" the gut-shot outlaw hollered.

"Not in ten minutes you won't," Gatewood told him.

"What'd you mean, you hog-slop?" The outlaw groaned the words.

"'Cause in ten minutes, you gonna be dead."

He was right.

Chapter 23

Smoke helped gather up the weapons from the dead raiders. Brown and the others in the farming complex now had enough weapons and ammo to stand off any type of attack, major or minor.

"They got their nerve comin' back here," Cooter said as they dug shallow graves for the outlaws.

"And we'll keep comin' back," the outlaw trussed up on the ground said. "Until all you hog-farmers are dead." He had regained his courage, certain he was facing death and determined to face it tough.

"You're wrong," Smoke told him, stepping out of the hole and letting one of Cooter's boys finish the digging. "Take a look at these men around you, hombre. Even without my guns, they'd have stopped the attack. I don't know whose idea this was, but I doubt if it was Max's."

The young man on the ground glared at him but kept his mouth closed.

Smoke had an idea. "Can you read and write, punk?"

"Huh?"

"You heard me. Can you read and write?"

"Naw. I never learned how. What business is that of yours?"

Smoke walked to his horse, dug in the saddlebags, and found a scrap of paper and the stub of a pencil. He wrote a short note and returned to the outlaw. Folding the paper, he tucked it into the raider's shirt pocket and buttoned it tight.

"That's a note for Big Max. You give it to him, and to him alone. I'll know if you've showed it to anyone else." That was a lie, but Smoke figured the outlaw wouldn't. "You understand?"

"You turnin' me loose?"

"Yeah. With a piece of advice. And here it is: Get gone from this country. Give the note to Max and then saddle you a fresh horse, get your kit together, and haul your ashes out of Hell's Creek. We know Max and Red are going to attack the town. That is, if the old arrest warrants on his head don't catch up with him first. And they might." Another lie. "The town is ready for the attack, hombre. Ready and waiting twenty-four hours a day. We know the bank is tempting. But don't try it; don't ride in there with them. The townspeople will shoot you into bloody rags. There's nigh on to six hundred people in and around Barlow now. Six hundred." That was also a slight exaggeration. "And there are guards standing watch around the clock, ready to give the call. It's a death trap waiting for you."

"You say!" the outlaw sneered, but there was genuine fear in his voice that all around him could detect.

Smoke jerked the man to his feet, untied his hands, and shoved him toward his horse, who had wandered back toward its master after running for a time. Pistols and rifle and all his ammo had been taken from the raider.

"Ride," Smoke told him. "And give that note to Max."

The man climbed into the saddle and looked down at Smoke. "I might take your advice. I just might. I got to think on it some."

"You'd be wise to take it. I'm giving you a break by letting you go."

"And I appreciate it." He tapped the pocket where Smoke had put the message. "All right, Smoke. I'll give this to Big Max, and I'm gone. You'll not see me again unless you come around a ranch. That's where you'll find me . . . punchin' cows."

"Are there any kids in Hell's Creek? Any decent women?"

The man shook his head. "None at all. There ain't nothin' there 'ceptin' the bottom of the barrel—if you know what I mean."

"Good luck to you."

"Thanks." The man rode north, toward Hell's Creek.

Smoke swung into the saddle. "Before you boys bury that crud, go through their pockets and take whatever money you find. You earned it."

"Don't seem right, takin' money from the dead," Bolen said.

"They won't need it," Smoke assured the man. "Near as I can figure out from reading the Bible, there aren't any honky-tonks in Hell."

Big Max Huggins opened the folded piece of paper and read. He read it again and began cussing. He ripped the small note into shreds and did some more fancy cussing. All of the cussing leveled at and centered around Smoke Jensen.

The note read: MAX, YOU STUPID, HORSE-FACED PIECE OF HOG CRAP. MEET ME TOMORROW AT THE WEST SIDE OF THE SWAN RANGE BY THE CREEK.

NO GUNS. I'M GOING TO STOMP YOUR FACE IN WITH FISTS AND BOOTS. COME ALONE IF YOU HAVE THE GUTS WHICH YOU PROBABLY DO NOT HAVE, BEING THE COWARD THAT YOU ARE.

Max let his temper rage for a few moments, then began to calm himself. He sat back down behind his desk and smiled. Max had killed men with his fists and felt very confident that he would do the same with Smoke Jensen.

This is what you've been training for, isn't it? he thought. Yes, of course it is. How to play it? The fight will be rough and tumble, kick and gouge. That isn't what you meant and you know it! he mentally berated himself.

Jensen had slighted his courage, for a fact.

Max folded his hamlike hands behind his head and leaned back in his chair. How to play it? Well, there was only one way: He would play it straight. He would go alone.

Jensen had tossed down the challenge; Jensen had implied that he did not have the courage to meet him alone. Well, he'd show that damn two-bit gunfighter a thing or two about courage.

Jensen had chosen well, Max thought. He knew exactly where Smoke would be: on the flats just above the creek. Good level place for a fight.

Max would go in alone, but he would be armed; to do otherwise would be foolish. Once there, both men would shuck their guns together, each in plain sight of the other. Then, Max smiled, I will beat Smoke Jensen to death with my fists.

Smoke camped on the flats. On the afternoon before the fight—if Max showed up, and Smoke felt confident he would—Smoke prowled the area, picking up and throwing away every stick and rock he could find. He walked the area a dozen times, looking for holes in the ground that might trip a man. He memorized the natural arena. Then, sure he had done everything humanly possible, he cooked his supper and made his coffee. He rolled into his blankets just after dark and went to sleep with a smile on his lips.

What he was doing he knew was foolish. It was male pride at its worst. But when two bulls are grazing in the same pasture, one is going to be dominant over the other; that was nature's way. And Smoke had been raised too close to the earth to attempt to alter nature's way.

The fight would really accomplish nothing of substance. Smoke knew it, and Max probably knew it, too. If he didn't, then the man was a fool.

Smoke knew that what he ought to do was to kill Max Huggins just as soon as the man stepped down from the saddle. But that wasn't his way, and Max probably realized it. If Max came, and came alone, then he was going to follow the same rules.

It promised to be a very interesting fight.

Smoke was up at dawn, boiling his coffee and frying his bacon. He ate lightly, for he knew the fight might take several hours until the end, and he did not want to fight on a full stomach.

At full light he looked out over the flats, and far in the distance he saw a lone rider approaching. From the size of the man, he knew it had to be Max Huggins. He lifted his field glasses and scanned the area all around Max, to the rear and both sides. He could pick up no sign of outriders. Big Max was coming in alone.

Max rode up to the flats and dismounted. He was wearing two guns, tied down. Smoke stood up from his squat and hooked his thumbs behind the buckle of his gunbelt.

"How do we play this, Max?"

"It's your show. You call it."

"First we untie, then we unbuckle and put them over here, next to my bedroll."

"That sounds good to me."

The men untied, unbuckled, and laid their guns on the ground, next to Smoke's bedroll.

Smoke pointed to the battered coffeepot and two tin cups. "Help yourself. It's fresh made."

"Thanks. That'll taste good." Max squatted down and poured two cups. With a smile, he handed one cup to Smoke and said, "If it's poisoned or drugged, then we'll go out together."

"It's neither," Smoke said, and took a sip of coffee. "It's just hot."

The men sipped and stared at each other in silence. Max broke the silence. "How'd you put it together about Robert?"

"Family resemblance is strong. Then I followed Robert one day and saw you together."

"He's quite insane, you know." It was not a question.

"Yes, I know. What are you going to do with him?"

"I honestly don't know, Smoke."

"Judge Garrison has legal papers ordering him committed to the asylum."

Max's face hardened. "Robert will never be confined in one of those places. They're treated worse than animals in there."

"You better think of something to do with him after you're gone."

"Oh? Am I going somewhere?"

"Yes. You're either going to leave this area voluntarily, go to prison, or I'm going to kill you."

Max chuckled, then laughed out loud. "Damn, but you are a gutsy man, Smoke Jensen. If the circumstances were different, I could really like you."

"There is nothing about you that I like, Max."

Max chuckled again, and it was not in the least forced. "That's a shame. I'm going to both enjoy and regret beating you to death."

"Don't flatter yourself. I've whipped bigger and better men than you in my time."

Max cut his eyes, looking at Smoke. The man was all muscle and bone. Max upgraded his original estimate of Smoke's weight. His arms and shoulders and chest and hands were enormous. Max probably had a good sixty pounds on the man, but he guessed accurately that Smoke would be quicker and able to dance around with more grace than he.

"I'm not surprised that you came alone," Smoke said.

"I do have some honor about me," Max replied stiffly.

"Honorable men do not make war against women and children. Neither do they rape young girls."

"Aggie was a mistake," Max admitted. "But both Robert and I—we get it from our father—have hot blood when it comes to girls. It's a failing, I will admit."

Smoke wondered how many young girls had suffered and died at the hands of the man he faced. And once again the thought came to him: I ought to just shoot him.

Smoke sipped his coffee, holding the cup in a gloved hand, and stared at Max Huggins from the other side of the fire.

"I guess it's about that time," Smoke said.

Both rose as one and tossed the dregs of their coffee to the ground. They tossed the cups to the ground and walked away from the campsite. Max flexed his arms and wiggled his hands and did a little boxing shuffle with his feet.

"That's cute," Smoke told him. "Where'd you learn that? From a hurdy-gurdy girl?"

"You're going to be easy, Jensen. That's one of Jem Mace's moves."

"Somehow I think he did it better. You looked kind of stupid."

Max stepped in quickly and tried a right at Smoke's head. Smoke sidestepped, but not to the side that Max anticipated, and the left that followed the right almost jerked him off his boots when it exploded against thin air.

"Damn, you're clumsy," Smoke told him.

Max charged in and Smoke was forced to back up. Smoke knew that if Max connected solidly with that big right, it would hurt. Max drew first blood with a sneaky left that bloodied Smoke's mouth; but Smoke moved away too quickly for the right he threw to connect. Smoke's left did connect against Max's belly and it was like hitting a tree.

He danced back and let Max follow him. Neither man had as yet worked up a sweat or was even breathing hard. Both of them knew that this fight could last a long time.

Max snaked a right that almost connected. Smoke smashed a left uppercut that jerked Max's head back and stopped him for a couple of seconds. Before he could fully recover, Smoke danced away.

Blood was leaking out of one side of Max's mouth as he followed Smoke around the flats. Smoke suspected the big man had bitten his tongue due to that uppercut.

Suddenly Max dropped his fists and charged, trying to catch Smoke in a bear hug. What Max got was a combination left and right to his face, followed by a boot to his knee that staggered him. Before he could catch his balance, Smoke had hit him twice more, both times on the face. Max felt blood running down from his nose and the sensation infuriated him. He stepped in and busted Smoke on the jaw with a hard right, and then a left to the belly that hurt the smaller man.

Smoke backed up, shaking his head, for Max had a punch like the kick of a mule.

Max sensed victory too soon, but with good reason. Never had he had to hit a man Smoke's size more than twice to put him down. He stepped closer to put the finishing touches to one Smoke Jensen, and Smoke knocked the crap out of Max Huggins.

The hard right fist connected flush on the side of Max's jaw and put the big man down on the grass. He was astonished! He wasn't hurt, just simply astounded that Jensen had actually knocked him down.

Max was further astonished when Smoke backed up, allowing the man to get to his feet. Smoke was fighting ring rules.

"Just as long as you do, Max," Smoke said after correctly reading the man's expression.

Max nodded and stepped in, raising his fists. So it was boxing that Jensen wanted, hey! Well, he would sure oblige the man.

Both men were wary now, each of them knowing the other could do plenty of damage. They circled each other, Max with his fists held high, Smoke with his left fist held wide from his body and his right fist just in front of and to one side of his head.

He's no boxer! Max thought gleefully. Not with a stupid stance like that. Now I have him. Now I have him.

What Max got was a left fake that he brushed aside and a powerful right that barreled through and busted him flush on the mouth. He felt his lips split and the blood gush. The left that he had brushed away caught him a smashing blow on the side that hurt the big man, backing him up.

Smoke pressed in, hitting the man with a flurry of blows to the arms and shoulders as Max could do nothing but cover up until he caught his wind. And the blows were bruising. Smoke pounded the man's arms, hurting and bruising them, taking some of the power from them. Max finally had to lower his guard and shove Smoke from him. The move got Smoke off him for a moment, but it also earned Max a smashing blow to the head.

Max saw an opening and took it, handing Smoke a one-two combination to the head. The blows popped Smoke's head back and bloodied his mouth. The left had caught him above the eye and opened a cut.

Smoke backed up, shook his head, and then plowed right back in, pressing the attack. He drove a right fist in that caught Max on the nose, and the big man felt the already injured nose break. The blood poured. Smoke didn't let up. He smashed a left and right to Max's head that rocked the big man back on his heels. Max got in a hard right that shook Smoke down to his boots, staggering him.

Max jumped at Smoke, intending to boot the man to the ground. One boot did catch Smoke on the leg, bruising the flesh but not putting him down. Smoke countered with a kick of his own that caught Max on the shin and brought a yelp of pain from the man. Smoke jumped in and blasted another left and right. The left took Max on the side of the jaw and the right hit him flush in the mouth.

Max grimly spat out part of a broken tooth and came on, both fists held high.

Smoke hit the man in the belly and took a left hook to his head for that move. Max followed the hook with a heel-drop that sent Smoke to the ground. Max tried to kick him. Smoke rolled away and came up on his boots, a hard light in his eyes.

Max had expanded the fight, moving away from ring

rules with that attempted kick. If that were the way the man wanted it, so be it.

Max swung a looping right. Smoke caught the forearm and wrist and threw the man to the ground, then stepped in and gave Max a vicious kick to the kidney that brought a howl of pain from him. Smoke brought his balled fist down hard on Max's neck just as the man was trying to get up. The blow knocked him flat on the ground. Smoke went to work with his boots, stomping and kicking. One boot caught Max flush in the mouth, and the force of the kick shattered the big man's front teeth, top and bottom.

With a scream of rage and pain, Max flung out his hand and caught Smoke's jeans leg, tumbling the smaller man to the ground. Smoke rolled and came up on his boots before Max could get to his feet and apply the boots to him.

For a full minute the men stood toe to toe and slugged it out, with each of them giving and receiving about the same amount of damage. But Smoke could tell the bigger man was losing some of his power. Max was fighting with his mouth open now, sucking in air in great gasping gulps. Smoke had known nothing but hard work all his life. Max had spent the last fifteen years either sitting behind a desk, planning his evil, or sitting at a poker table, cheating those who played the game of chance with him.

Smoke sent a crashing right fist through Max's guard, a punch that knocked the big man to the ground. Smoke stepped in and kicked the man in the butt just as he was trying to get to his feet. The butt-kick knocked Max sprawling, sliding facedown in the dirt and the grass.

"You know what I'm going to do, don't you, Max?" Smoke asked, standing over the man. Max tried to get to his feet and Smoke kicked him in the butt again, knocking the big man down to the ground.

"I'm going to rearrange your face, Max." Smoke walked around to the front of the struggling giant of a man. "When I get tired of hitting you, I'm going to kick your face in." Max knew he was whipped, knew Smoke was going to stomp him into the ground. "I've had enough," the big man said, blood dripping from his mouth.

"I imagine Aggie said something along those lines, didn't she, Max?"

"She was trash! Nester trash."

Smoke kicked him in the belly with all the power he could get behind the boot. Max's body arched upward off the ground and he screamed in pain.

Smoke backed away and let the man struggle to his feet. Big Max stood before him, swaying slightly. "Fight, you sorry bastard," Smoke told him.

Max lumbered forward and walked into a straight right that he felt all the way down to his toenails. Smoke followed that with a left that turned Max's head and loosened teeth. Smoke didn't let up. He began to work on Max's belly, driving hammer blows to the man's guts. Max backed up, unable to throw a punch that would stop Smoke Jensen. He landed several punches, but they had no power behind them. Smoke shifted his area of punishment. He began working on Max's face. The face of Big Max now began to resemble a raw side of beef that someone had worked over with a sledgehammer. His nose was flattened, one ear was swollen and pulpy, his mouth was a ruined mess, and both eyes were closing. Still Smoke Jensen continued to punish the man.

Max searched frantically around him for a weapon—a club, a rock, anything! He found nothing. Smoke had carefully cleared the area. He tried to run and Smoke pursued him, leaping onto his back and riding the man around the area like some sort of beast of burden. It was the most humiliating thing that Big Max Huggins had ever been forced to endure.

Max finally collapsed onto the ground, his strength gone. Smoke stood over him. The smaller man had taken his licks. One eye was almost closed, and blood was leaking from his nose and mouth. But he was on his boots and ready to fight.

Max heard the words: "You got a choice, Big Man," Smoke told him. "You either get up and fight, or as God is my witness, I'll kick you to death."

Max struggled up. He turned and faced Jensen, lifting his fists. Max charged in a last-ditch effort to grab the smaller man and break his back.

Smoke stepped to one side and buried his fist into Max's belly, doubling the man over and bringing a painful retching sound from his mouth. Smoke's fist struck the man on his ear and Max experienced a roaring in his head. Another fist came up, seemingly from the ground, and slammed into his battered face. That was followed by a right fist that crashed into his nose. Smoke's fist hammered his lower back and smashed into his rib cage, sending waves of pain through the man as his kidneys took the brunt of the blows.

Max was beyond mere pain. This was an agony new to him. He had been moved into a sea of solid hurt. It was nothing like he had ever experienced before. His shirt had been torn from him sometime during the fight, and his upper torso was bruised and bloody.

Still Smoke Jensen would not back off. Big Max Huggins stood like a giant oak that was being battered by the elements, his huge arms hanging by his sides. He could not find the strength to lift them.

Smoke knocked him down and Max painfully climbed to his boots to face his tormentor. He turned in time to catch another huge right fist to his already ruined and swollen mouth.

Through eyes that were now nothing more than swollen slits, Max could see Jensen smiling at him. He had never seen a smile that savage on Smoke's face. Jensen's eyes were cold, killing cold. Max watched as Jensen measured him. He knew with a soaring feeling of relief the fight was soon to be over.

Smoke started his punch somewhere down around his ankles, and when the gloved fist exploded against his head, Max's world turned black.

The big man lay stretched out on the ground. Unconscious.

Chapter 24

Smoke muscled Big Max across his saddle and tied him there. He looped Max's gunbelt on the saddle horn and slapped the horse on the rump, sending it on its way back to Hell's Creek.

Smoke packed up and headed for the high country, making camp not five miles from Hell's Creek. He had plans for that town. Smoke ached all over and his hands were swollen. He looked for and found the plants he sought, carefully picking them and boiling them in water, then soaking his hands. He stayed snug in the camp for two days, resting and eating and treating his hands until the swelling had gone down and he was ready to go.

Smoke had spent the time in the hidden camp not only resting and treating his hands and the cuts on his face, but also capping and fusing the dynamite, tying them into three—stick bombs. Star was rested and restless and eager to hit the trail.

At dawn of the third day after the fight on the flats, Smoke swung into the saddle and pointed Star's head toward Hell's Creek. He had it in his mind to destroy that town and as many people in it as possible.

The startled gun hands who watched as Big Max's horse walked slowly up the muddy and rutted main street of Hell's Creek could not believe their eyes. They were further astonished—and some a little frightened—when they untied Max and lowered him to the ground.

To a man, none of them had ever seen a person beaten so badly as was Max.

Robert Turner snapped out of his befuddlement of the moment and slipped back into his role as doctor. He ordered Max carried to bed and ran for his bag. Robert had taken one look at his brother's battered body and knew the big man was hurt—how seriously he would know only after a thorough examination.

"Not seriously," he finally said with a sigh, leaning back in the chair by his brother's bed. "No ribs are broken that I can detect, but his face will never be as it was. Smoke Jensen did this deliberately. This is the most callous act I have ever witnessed. Jensen deliberately set out to destroy my brother's handsome looks."

Robert looked around at the outlaws. "Well, my mind is made up. I have never believed in violence, but this"—he looked down at the sleeping Max, the sleep brought on by massive doses of laudanum—"has to be avenged."

Val Singer seized the moment, guessing what this crazy galoot had in mind. "What do you plan to do about it, Robert?" he asked.

"Why . . . I plan to step into my brother's boots and lead

the raid against Barlow, that's what. What do you think about that, Mr. Singer?"

The outlaw leaders had to fight to hide their smiles. Of course, they'd let sonny-boy here lead the raid. Of course, they'd go along with it. For with Max out of the picture, they could ravage the town, rob the bank, and would not have to share a damn thing with Big Max Huggins. And before they left the country, they would kill Robert Turner.

So much for honor among thieves.

"That's a damn good idea, Robert," Dave Poe said. "I like it. I really do. When do you think we ought to hit the town?"

"Tomorrow morning, just as the bank opens."

"I like it," Alex Bell said.

Smoke had left his horse in timber on the edge of town, and he worked his way up a dry creek bed, coming out behind a privy. He ducked back down as two men walked to the outhouse, chatting as they walked.

"This time tomorrow, Larry," one of them said, "Barlow ain't gonna be nothing but a memory, and we'll have had our fill of women and be a damn sight richer."

"Yeah, and we won't have to share none of it with Big Max. That's what makes it so rich to me."

Smoke listened, wondering what was going on. Tomorrow! They were going to hit the town tomorrow?

"Goofy Robert said he'd give Max enough laudanum to keep him out for a day and a half. He'd give it to him just before we pull out."

"Who's gonna kill that nut?"

"Hell, who cares? Sometime during the shootin' one of us will plug him. I've got me an itch for some of them women in that town."

"Me, too."

The men stepped into the two-holer and closed the door.

Smoke made his way back up the wash, swung into the saddle, and headed for Barlow.

He stopped at Brown's house to rest his horse and to tell the farmer to warn the others about the raid the next day.

"You want us in town, Smoke?" Brown asked.

"No. I want you men to load up full and be prepared to defend yourselves in case they decide to attack you first, although I don't think they will."

"We'll be ready." He smiled, his eyes on Smoke's bruised face. "Who won the fight?"

"Big Max is still unconscious," Smoke told him with a grin.

"Glad to hear it."

Smoke mounted up and headed for Barlow. He hit the town at a gallop and yelled for people to gather around him. "It's tomorrow morning, people," he shouted, so all could hear. "The men of Hell's Creek are going to hit the town at nine o'clock, to coincide with the bank opening. Start gathering up guns and ammo, and make certain the pumper is checked out and the fire barrels are full."

He swung down from the saddle and handed the reins to the boy that helped out at the livery. "Rub him down good and give him all the corn he wants, boy." Smoke handed the boy a coin and Star was led off for a well-deserved rest.

Smoke stepped up on the boardwalk in front of the sheriffs office, while others gathered up the rest of the townspeople. Smoke stayed in hurried whispered conference with Sal, Judge Garrison, and Tom Johnson for a few minutes, until the whole town was assembled in the street.

Judge Garrison, Sal, and the mayor agreed with his suggestions, and Smoke turned, facing the crowd. "All right, folks," he said, raising his voice so all could hear. "Here it is. There is a good chance that a rider was sent out to Red Malone's spread before I slipped into Hell's Creek and overheard the outlaws' plans. Red will probably attack us from the south at the same time the raiders hit us from the north. We've got to be ready to hit them twice as hard as they hit us. Jim has already left to warn Joe Walsh and his people. I told Jim to tell Joe to stay put and guard his ranch. Red hates him as much as he hates us. So it's going to be up to us to defend this town and everything you people have worked for. That's all I have to say, except start getting ready for a war."

The crowds broke up into small groups, each group leader, already appointed, waiting to see where they were supposed to be when the attack came.

"Tom," Smoke said, "you and your group take the inside of the bank. Take lots of ammo and water."

"Will do, Smoke," the mayor said, and moved out to get ready.

"One group inside Marbly's store. Toby, you and your people will defend the hotel. Benson's group will take the livery. Ralph, you and your bunch will fight from the saloon. The rest of them know where to be and what to do. Let's start getting ready."

Sal looked at Smoke's battered face and commented, "Need I have to ask who won the fight?"

"Big Max didn't," Smoke said, then walked toward the hotel for a hot bath, a change into fresh clothes, and to rest beside Sally.

"I'd give a pretty penny to have seen that scrap," Sal said.

"Yeah," Pete Akins agreed. "He must have hurt him bad for Max not to be leadin' the raid come the morning."

"How many men are we facing tomorrow?" the owner of the cafe asked.

"Nearabouts a hundred from Hell's Creek," Pete told him. "Maybe more than that. And all of Red Malone's bunch. We'll have them outnumbered, but bear this in mind: Them we'll be facin' is killers. Ninety-nine percent of the townspeople ain't." He looked hard at the cafe owner and at the other group leaders. "You pass the word, boys: Don't give no mercy, 'cause you shore as hell ain't gonna be gettin' none from them that attack us."

Smoke took a long hot soak in their private bath in the suite, then napped for an hour. He dressed and began cleaning his guns, loading rifle, shotgun, and pistols up full. He took his spare pistols out of wraps and cleaned and oiled them, loading them up. They were old Remington Frontier .44's, and Smoke had had them for a long time. He liked the feel of them, and was comfortable and confident with them in his hands.

"Early in the morning," Smoke told his wife, "you go get Victoria and Martha and the kids. Bring them back up to this suite. We'll be up long before then—the cafe and hotel dining room is going to open about four o'clock to feed those that don't eat at home—and we'll rearrange the furniture in this suite to stop any bullet. I'll have a boy start bringing up water to fight any fires that might start. Their plan is to destroy the town, so they'll be throwing torches."

Sally sat at the table with her husband, oiling and cleaning her own guns. "Vicky doesn't know anything about pistols," she said. "But Martha does. We'll have rifles and shotguns ready. How about Robert, Smoke?"

He shook his head. "I don't want to kill him, honey. I can't justify killing a crazy person unless there is just no other way out."

"I've been reading that there is some new treatment for the mad. But insane asylums are just awful."

"I know. I mean, I've heard they are. Chain them down like wild animals until they die." He rose from the table and buckled his gunbelt around his lean waist, tying it down. "I'm going to roam the town."

Everybody was pitching in to secure the town. The new bankers just arrived from the East were nervous about the upcoming fight but doing their share in carrying water, moving barricades in place, and anything else they were asked to do. And Smoke could also read excitement in their faces.

Sal caught up with him. "Where are you going to be come the mornin', Smoke?"

"I'll be lone-wolfing it, Sal. Moving around. Did you see to it that everybody had a red bandana?"

"Everybody that will be behind a friendly gun will have one tied around their right arm. They was a darn good idea of yours. That's gonna help keep us from shootin' our own people."

"The dust and smoke are going to be bad when it starts. So I would suggest we water down the main street just before the bank opens. What do you think?"

"Another good idea. I'm gonna miss you and Sally when y'all pull out."

"You'll handle it, Sal. And, Sal? . . ."

The sheriff turned to face him.

"Martha and Vicky and the kids will be with Sally in our suite come the morning. So you won't have to worry about Victoria."

Sal blushed and headed across the street. Smoke smiled and continued his walking tour.

The saloon had been turned into a fort, as had the livery stable and barn. Marbly's store was barricaded, and anything that might be broken had been taken from the shelves and stored in wooden boxes. Smoke nodded his approval and walked back to the hotel. The waiting was going to be hard.

"Way I see it," John Steele said to Red Malone, "we just ain't got much of a choice."

"We have no choice," the rancher said. "We both have

warrants on us in other states. The town has to be destroyed, and everybody in it dead and buried in deep graves. We'll toss the bodies into the fires and burn them before we bury them. The authorities, if any show up, won't be able to prove a damn thing."

"Some of our men rode out today, right after the rider from Hell's Creek left. Said they wasn't havin' no part of killin' women and kids."

Red snorted his disgust. "We don't need them. We're better off without them."

What neither of them knew was that the hands who had left in disgust over making war against women and kids were riding toward Barlow, to join the defenders of the little town.

"After Barlow is burned out," Red said, "the outlaws will scatter to the wind. We'll ride and burn down Hell's Creek. We'll blame everything on Max's bunch. Hell, we can even say that we sided with the townspeople in trying to fight them outlaws off. We'll take some of our own men dead, for sure. We can point their graves out to the investigators as proof."

"That still leaves Joe Walsh and his crew," the foreman pointed out.

"We'll deal with them. We've got them outnumbered three to one. Soon as Barlow is done and over, we'll ride for the Circle W and clean out Walsh and his crew."

John smiled a death's-head grin. "Then we can wipe out all them damn hog-farmers and other nesters, and the valley will once again be ourn."

"Yeah." Red rubbed the stubble of beard on his jowls. "And some of them nester girls ain't that bad looking. We can have some fun with them." He laughed. "Be just like old times. . . . Hey, John, remember them days?"

John Steele joined in the laughter. The men were in high spirits as they walked out of the house to sit on the porch.

"Just let me get Jensen in gunsights," Red said. "All I need is one shot. Front or back, it don't make no difference to me."

The town of Barlow rolled up the boardwalks early that evening. Far earlier than usual. Everyone wanted to get a good night's sleep before the storm struck the next morning.

Red's Lightning hands who had rebelled against fighting women and kids had ridden in, holding up a white handkerchief—well, it was almost white—and Smoke, along with Judge Garrison and Mayor Johnson, met them in the street.

"We done quit Red," the spokesman for the group said. "We ain't havin' no part in killin' women and little kids. If you want our help, we're here."

"How do we know you weren't sent in here by Red to start shooting us in the backs come the attack in the morning?" Tom asked.

"That's a good question," the hired gun said. "And I don't know how to answer it."

"I do," Sal said, stepping off the boardwalk and into the street. "Howdy, Cobb."

"Howdy, Sal. We all right proud of you, you bein' elected sheriff and all. Me and Benny and Hale and Stacy here, we got to talkin' about that this mornin'. After that no-good from Hell's Crick come talkin' to Red this mornin' about killin' the women and kids and burnin' this town down. We couldn't do that, Sal. You've ridden some trails with us; you know we're not that kind of men. Oh, we've hired our guns out—just like you've done, for fightin' wages. But there ain't none of us ever made war agin' nobody 'ceptin' grown-up men. And we ain't about to start now. Smoke, I guess that's the only answer we can give you."

Smoke smiled and nodded his head. "It sounds good to me, boys."

"Me, too," Judge Garrison said. He wore two guns belted around his expansive waist. Two old Remington .44's—the Army model. Both guns looked to Smoke as if they'd seen some action. "There'll be stars in your crown for this, boys."

Stacy shifted in his saddle. "I don't know about that, Judge. I just don't want no more black marks agin' me in the Judgment Book. The Good Lord knows I got aplenty of them already."

"You boys stable your horses and meet me in the hotel dinin' room," Sal said. "Glad to have you with us."

"Right will prevail, Smoke," Judge Garrison proclaimed. "Sometimes it just takes an outsider to prod those oppressed into action."

Smoke looked at the .44's belted around the judge's waist. "When is the last time you fired those, Judge?"

The judge smiled. "I came out of the War Between the States a colonel, Smoke. Of cavalry. I had my law degree when I enlisted. I fought through nearly every major campaign." He smiled. "With Lee. I graduated VMI, sir."

"Then I won't worry about you, sir."

"Coming from you, that is high praise. Tell me, since I haven't had a chance to ask, how did you leave Max Huggins?"

"Unconscious and tied across his saddle."

The judge walked away, shaking with laughter. His booming laughter could be heard up and down the main street of Barlow.

Chapter 25

Smoke was up and dressed for war long before dawn. He wore his customary two pistols in leather, his two spares were tucked behind his gunbelt, and he carried an American Arms 12 gauge sawed-off shotgun, a bandoleer of shells slung across his chest, bandit-style.

He and Sally had breakfast before the sun was up, and then he walked Lisa and Victoria back to the hotel, Lisa carrying her puppy, Patches, in her arms. Pete escorted Martha Feckles and the boy to the suite, and the women made ready for war.

The men tied red bandanas around the upper part of their right arms. Since there were no females among the raiders who were riding to attack them, the women dressed in their customary attire. More than a few of them, including Mrs. Marbly, Victoria, Sally, and Martha, wore men's britches.

Sal's eyes bugged out when he saw Victoria. "Lord have mercy!" he said. "What's next?"

"The vote," Smoke told him.

"You have to be kidding! Votin' is men's business. Women don't know nothin' about pickin' politicians."

"You'd be surprised," Smoke said.

Smoke walked the town, inspecting each water barrel—and there were many. He checked to see if the buckets were ready in case of fire. They were. He checked each store that was to house fighters. They were ready and willing, even if many of them were scared. Mrs. Marbly, a very formidable-sized lady, had found herself a pair of men's overalls, and when she bent over, she looked like the rear end of a stage-coach. But she handled the double-barreled shotgun like she knew what she was doing. Smoke concluded that he wouldn't want to mess with her.

Pete was still in shock after seeing Mrs. Marbly in men's overalls, bent over.

"Close your mouth, Pete," Smoke told him. "Before you suck in a fly."

Jim was stationed two miles out of town, on a ridge, a fast horse tied nearby. As soon as he spotted the dust of the raiders, he was to come hightailing it back into town and give the warning.

Smoke walked to the north end of the town and leaned up against a hitchrail. He rolled him a cigarette and lit up, waiting for the action to start.

He looked back up the wide street. It was void of any kind of life. The horses were stabled safely and the children's pets were in the house, out of harm's way.

Smoke watched as a water wagon rolled down the street, then back up, watering the wide street to keep down the dust. He clicked open his watch: eight thirty. He walked on down the street, coming to a nearly collapsed old building; a relic of a business of some sort that had failed. This was the last building on either side of the street. Smoke stepped up on the porch and pushed open the door. Rusty hinges howled in protest. He stepped inside and looked in both rooms of the structure. He tried the back door, working it several times to make certain he could exit that way. There was not a window-pane intact in any frame, so he did not have to worry about being cut by flying glass. He sat down on the dusty floor and waited.

At eight forty-five, Jim came fogging into town from his post. Smoke heard him yell, "Here they come, folks. And there's plenty to go around." He rode into the livery stable and disappeared.

Smoke eared back the hammers on the sawed-off and knelt by the window. Moments later, he could feel the vibra-tion through the floor, the faint thunder of hundreds of hooves striking the ground.

As the pack of outlaws drew closer, Smoke stared in amazement. Robert was leading the bunch. He wore a pith helmet, the leather strap tied under his chin, and was waving a sword. God knows where he had found either article in Hell's Creek.

The raiders, more than a hundred strong, thundered into town. Smoke let Robert and a few behind him gallop past, then he gave both barrels of the sawed-off to the outlaws.

The hand-loaded charge of nails and buckshot cleared a bloody path in the middle of the outlaw horde. Smoke dropped the shotgun and jerked out his Colts, cocking and firing as fast as he could; deadly rolling thunder erupted from the small collapsing building on the edge of town. Horses began milling around, confused and frightened and riderless. Bodies lay in the street.

A wounded outlaw, his hands filled with guns, staggered up on the porch. He spotted Smoke and leveled his guns. Smoke gave him two .44 slugs in the chest and the man's days of lawlessness were over.

Smoke quickly reloaded his Colts, shoved fresh shells

into the express gun, and ran out the back door, turning to his right.

"Red and his bunch are attacking from the south!" he heard the faint shout over the roar of battle.

Smoke ducked into the space between a home and a business and ran to the street. A hatless and bearded man stepped off the path and turned to face Smoke. Smoke pulled the trigger of the sawed-off, and the force of the charge lifted the outlaw off his boots and knocked him out into the street. Smoke ran to the edge of the street and gave the other barrel to a cursing raider. Blood smeared his saddle and the man hit the street, dead.

Smoke filled both hands with Colts and began emptying saddles. From the sounds of shotgun fire coming from the bank building, and the number of bodies littering the street in front of the bank, the Easterners were having a duck shoot and doing a damn fine job of holding their own.

Smoke stepped back and reloaded the pistols and the shotgun.

"Forward, men!" he heard Robert shout, the cry coming from behind him. "Slay the Philistines."

Smoke turned around. Robert was charging him on horseback, waving his sword. Smoke ducked the slashing sword that could have taken his head off and swung up behind Robert as the frightened horse reared up, dumping both men on the ground. Robert lost his sword and Smoke gave him a one-two combination that dropped the man to the ground, out cold. Smoke tore the pith helmet off and used the leather chin strap to bind Robert's hands behind his back. He used the man's belt to securely bind his ankles, then rolled the doctor under a building. Smoke picked up his shotgun and stepped back into the fray.

Two raiders, apparently having lost their appetite for any further battle, came racing up the street, heading north.

Smoke stepped out and gave them both barrels of the sawed-off. Two more saddles cleared.

Smoke stepped up on the boardwalk and ran toward the center of town, reloading the shotgun as he went. He turned down an alleyway and entered the hotel through the back door, muttering curses because the rear of the building was not guarded.

Just above him, on the second floor, Warner Frigo had kicked open the door to the presidential suite and was looking down at Lisa, huddled on the floor, holding her puppy close.

"Well, now," the outlaw said with a sneer. "Won't you just be a juicy little thing to have."

He holstered his guns and reached down for her, lust in his eyes.

"You'll hurt no more children and kill not another child's pet," Warner heard the woman say.

He looked up. Sally stood in the foyer, holding a sawed-off in her hands, both hammers eared back.

Warner's lips peeled back in an ugly smile. "I'll have you after I taste little-bit here."

"I doubt it," Sally said, then pulled both triggers. The force of the blast knocked Warner off both boots and sent him flying into the hall. He hit the hall wall and slid down to the carpeted floor. The wall behind him was a gory mess.

Smoke looked up as the shotgun went off. If anyone had tried to mess with Sally, they picked the wrong woman. He went up the stairs to check it out.

He saw Warner's body and stuck his head into the foyer. "Everybody all right in there?" he called.

"Just dandy," Sally said. "Would you please remove that garbage from the hall, darling?"

"Sure." Smoke dragged Warner's body down the hall and threw him out the second-story window. The downward hurtling body hit Sid Yorke and knocked him out of the saddle. The outlaw stared in horror at what was left of Warner Frigo.

He looked up at Smoke, standing behind the shattered window, grinning down at him. Sid lifted his pistol, and Judge Garrison, standing in his office, fired both Remington .44's, the slugs knocking the man to his knees. The outlaw died in that position, his hands by his side. His hat fell from his head. The wind picked it up and sailed it down the street.

Sal stepped out from his position just as John Steele was rounding a corner.

"Hey, John!" Sal called.

The foreman of the Lightning whirled in a crouch, both hands by his holstered guns.

"You always bragged how good you was," the newly elected sheriff said, his voice carrying over the din of battle and the whinnying of frightened horses. "You wanna find out now?"

John dragged iron. He was far too slow. Sal put two slugs in his belly before Steele could clear leather.

"I guess now you know," Sal told him.

"You sorry . . ." John gasped the words. He never got to finish it. The foreman fell off the boardwalk and landed in a horse trough.

"Have to remember to clean that out," Sal muttered.

Judge Garrison went out the back door of his office and came face to face with Paul Cartwright. The judge smiled at the man. "You used to love to lord it over me, Paul. You have guns in your hands. Use them!"

The deposed sheriff's guns came up. Judge Garrison lifted his Remington Army Model .44's, and the muzzles blossomed in fire and smoke. Paul Cartwright fell backward, dead.

The judge reloaded and walked up the back of the buildings, conviction and courage in his eyes.

"Gimme all your goddamn money, you heifer!" Frank Norton yelled at Mrs. Marbly.

Mrs. Marbly lifted her shotgun and blew the outlaw out the back door.

"Nice going, mother," her husband said.

Larry Gayle knew it was a losing cause. He had been thrown from his rearing, bucking horse and was now cautiously making his way out of town . . . on foot. He'd find a horse. To hell with Barlow, Max Huggins, and the whole mess. There had to be easier pickings somewheres else was his philosophy.

"Going somewhere, Larry?" The voice spun him around.

Pete Akins stood facing him.

Larry lifted his Smith & Wesson Schofield .45 and got off the first shot. It grazed Pete's shoulder. Pete was much more careful with his shooting. He shot Larry between the eyes. He walked to the prostrate and very dead outlaw and looked down at him. He shook his head.

"Whoo, boy. You was ugly alive. Dead, you'll probably come back to haunt graveyards."

Ted Mercer stood facing Smoke Jensen. The outlaw felt a coldness take hold of him. His Colt was in his hand, but he was holding it by his side. Could Jensen beat him? He didn't know. He really didn't want to find out.

"You can drop that iron and walk," Smoke told him. "Change your life. It's up to you."

"You're only sayin' that 'cause you know you can't beat this."

"You're wrong. Ted."

"Your guns are in leather!"

"Drop it and walk, man. Don't be a fool."

"I think I'll just kill you, Jensen." Ted's hand jerked up.

He felt a dull shock hit him in the belly, another hammerlike blow beat at his chest. Impossible! he thought. No man is that fast. No man is . . .

Smoke walked up and looked down at the dead outlaw. "I gave you a chance," he said.

Fires had been started by the raiders, but they had been quickly put out by the ladies of the bucket brigades. The plans of the outlaws were put out as quickly as the flames. Lew Brooks jumped his horse over the body of a friend and went charging between buildings. Judge Garrison stepped out and gave the outlaw a good dose of frontier justice, not from a law book but from a .44. Lew hit the ground, rolled over, and came up with a .45 in his hand. Judge Garrison imposed the death sentence on the man, then calmly reloaded and walked up the alleyway.

Jake Stringer knew that John Steele was down and dead, along with several other Lightning men. He didn't know where Red Malone was. He tried to calm a badly spooked horse and climb into the saddle. But the horse was having none of that. The animal jumped away and left Jake on foot.

"Damn that hammerhead!" Jake swore. "I ought to shoot it."

"Why not try me?" Jim Dagonne said.

Jake turned. Jim's guns were in leather, as were his own. A smile creased his lips. "I enjoyed whuppin' you with my fists, Jim. Now I'm gonna enjoy killin' you."

Jim was no fast gunhand, but he was a dead shot. Jake cleared leather first and his shot went into the dirt at Jim's boots. Jim plugged the man just above the belt buckle. Jake sat down on the ground and started hollering.

Jim walked to him. He could see where the slug had exited out the man's back, right through the kidney. "You ain't gonna make it, Jake. You got anyone you want me to write?"

"I didn't even know you could write," Jake said, then fell over on his face and closed his eyes.

Ella Mae, Tom Johnson's wife, was struggling with a man who had less than honorable intentions on his mind. He ripped her bodice open and stared hungrily at her flesh. Momentarily free, Ella Mae ran to the kitchen, jerked up the coffeepot from the stove, and threw the boiling contents into the man's face.

The outlaw screamed and went lurching and staggering through the living room, finding his way out the front door, his face seared from the boiling coffee. He stumbled out into the street and was run down by another wounded outlaw, trying to get out of the death trap named Barlow. The burned outlaw fell under the hooves and lay still.

Clark Hall made the bank and hurled himself through the door. He came up on his boots just in time to face several men with shotguns. He had time to say one word: "No!"

Three sawed-off shotguns roared, and Clark Hall was literally torn out of his boots and thrown out into the street. The shooting stopped. An eerie silence fell over the town. Smoke stepped out into the street, the Remington Frontier .44's in his hands. The moaning of the wounded drifted to him.

Judge Garrison took charge. "Gather up the wounded, and we'll patch them up as best we can and then try them. We were forced to use frontier justice to stop this, but there'll be no unauthorized hangings. From now on we go by the book."

Ralph from the saloon was dead. Shot through the head. Toby at the hotel had taken a slug through his shoulder. Several other citizens were wounded, but Ralph was the only fatality. The streets and alleys of the town were littered with dead and wounded. Guns lay everywhere one looked and riderless horses milled around, not knowing what to do or where to go.

Henry Draper came out of his office at the newspaper, wearing two huge Dragoons belted around his waist. That would account for some of the booming sounds Smoke had heard and also some of the hideous wounds he'd seen. Draper set up his camera and began preparing for shots of the carnage. This was great stuff. The newspapers back East would eat it up.

Tom Johnson had wandered the main street, counting the dead and wounded. "Red Malone's not here," he said, walking up to Smoke and a group of others.

"How about his men?" Sal asked.

"Most of them are dead. I saw two of them riding out north early on. Looked like they were clearing the country."

"You have enough to do here for three men, Sal," Smoke said. "Besides, this is personal between me and Red. I'll get him. And I'll bring him in alive if I can."

"You better find him before Joe Walsh does," Jim said. "Joe told him years ago that if he ever caught him without his private army with him, he'd kill him."

"There is that much bad blood between them?" Smoke asked. "I knew they didn't like each other."

"Man, yeah!" Jim said. "He helped found this town—Joe, I mean. Him and Red don't like each other at all."

"Well, I'll be!" came the shout. "Here's that so-called preacher from up at Hell's Creek. He had him a torch and was right in the middle of it all."

"Dead?" Pete called.

"I'll say. Plugged through and through."

Smoke walked the littered street, looking at the dead and wounded. But Alex Bell, Ben Webster, Nelson Barrett, Al Martin, Dave Poe, and Val Singer were not among them.

That left a lot of very bad men still on the loose, but Smoke doubted that they would ever return to Barlow.

He walked to the hotel, kissed Sally and petted Lisa's puppy Patches, then told his wife, "I'll be back. I'm going after Red Malone."

"I'll go down and help with the wounded."

"See you when I return."

As Smoke was riding out, Jim said to Pete, "I wonder if he'll bring Red in alive."

Pete spat on the ground. "Not if Red tries to draw on him."

Chapter 26

Smoke rode easy, knowing there was no hurry. Red Malone was not about to run. But he wondered about Max. What would the big man do—that is, if he were still alive? Or had his renegades returned to Hell's Creek after their failure in Barlow and killed him? And that was highly likely.

Smoke rode on, keeping Star in an easy canter, sometimes walking him. But the big horse loved to run and they ate up the distance. He was soon on Lightning range and, within minutes, facing three Lightning cowboys. One of them was wearing a bloody shirt, due to a bullet graze on his arm.

"The people of Barlow are signing warrants right now, boys. Best thing you can do is just ride and keep on riding. If you think Sal and his deputies won't come out here to get you, you're flat wrong."

The cowboys looked at each other, then back at Smoke. One said, "You'll let us ride?"

Smoke jerked a thumb. "Ride on."

"I'll tell you this much," another said. "Red is alone. Except for that no-account daughter of his. But you won't take him alive."

"Thanks. But I'd hate to kill a man in front of his daughter."

One of the cowboys laughed. "Smoke, that girl is as low and mean-spirited as her pa. She don't give a popcorn poot for him. All she wants is the ranch. I believe she'd kill him herself if she got the chance."

"Thanks. I hope I don't see you boys again."

They grinned. "You won't!"

They rode out, taking trails that would skirt the town of Barlow.

When Smoke rode into the yard, Tessie was sitting on the porch. A shotgun lay on the porch floor. At the sight of him, she started bawling and squalling. As he drew closer, he could see that her dress was torn. She stopped crying long enough to expose more skin. Then she resumed her blubbering.

Smoke sat his saddle for a moment, staring at the young woman. "Where's your father?" he asked when there was a break in the hollering.

"He's dead!" she squalled. "In the house. He tried to attack me. He went crazy. I had to defend my honor!" She began a new round of wailing.

Smoke swung down from the saddle and walked up onto the porch. He really didn't know what to expect; maybe a trap. He just didn't know.

He opened the screen door and the smell of blood hit him hard. He walked through the house until he found Red, dead, sprawled in front of a safe in his study. The door was open, and greenbacks and small sacks of gold lay on the floor and in the safe.

Smoke grunted. Red Malone had been shot in the back at close range.

"Ohhh!" Tessie hollered from the front porch. "I'm shamed forever. My own father tried to as-sault me. Oh, the dishonor and disgrace of it all." She started blubbering.

Smoke looked down at Red. "I hate to say it, Red, but even you probably deserved better kids than you had."

He walked outside. Tessie honked her nose into a bandana and said, "What am I gonna do with this big ol' ranch? Why, I'm just a woman; I can't handle men's work."

"I certainly don't envy you, ma'am. Don't you have anybody else left on the ranch?"

"Just the cook. She's gone visitin' friends for the day. I suppose I could get her to help me bury Pa. You think he'll keep 'til late this afternoon?"

"I expect so, ma'am." Smoke stepped into the saddle.

"Are you just gonna leave me here all alone with my poor dead father? I could sure use some comforting." She batted her eyes at him. It was the most grotesque thing Smoke had ever seen—and he had seen some sights in his time.

"I'll explain to the sheriff what happened," Smoke said as he backed Star up. Damned if he was going to turn his back to this woman. "I'll sure do that."

When he had backed Star to the point where he was reasonably sure she could not hit him with the sawed-off, Smoke gave the big black his head. Star took off like the wind. The horse wasn't real thrilled with Tessie, either.

When Smoke arrived back in town, he told Judge Garrison and Sal what he'd seen out at the Lightning spread. Neither man seemed very surprised.

"She'll take every dollar from the safe, sell off the herds, and be gone in a month," the judge prophesied. "And good riddance to bad baggage."

Smoke looked around. Most of the bodies had been tossed in wagons and were being hauled off to be buried in a mass grave. Half the men in town were working with shovels at the gravesite.

"Wagons coming," Jim announced, pointing to the north.

As the wagons neared, Judge Garrison said, "Saloon girls, gamblers, and assorted riffraff from Hell's Creek. Rats leaving a sinking ship."

"No," Smoke said. "A burning one. Because that's what we're going to do in the morning."

"Suits me," Tom said. "I'll ride with you."

"Keep moving," Sal told the lead wagon. "And don't stop until you're in the next county. And he won't want you, either, 'cause I'm fixin' to wire the sheriff and tell him about you scum."

One of the ladies of the evening, sitting in the back of the wagon, gave him a very obscene gesture with a finger.

"I'll jerk you out of that wagon and hand you over to the good ladies of this town," Sal warned her. "And they'll shave your head and tar and feather you."

The shady lady tucked her finger away and stared straight ahead.

The wagons rumbled out of sight.

"Why wait until the morning?" Pete asked. "Hell, Smoke. Let's ride up there and put that town out of its misery right now."

Smoke was curious to see what had happened to Big Max. "All right. Let's ride."

* * *

The band of men had stopped at Brown's farmhouse and asked if the farmers wanted any of the lumber in the town before they put the torch to it.

To a man, they shook their heads. "Thanks kindly, but no thanks," Gatewood said. "We just want shut of that den of thieves and whores and hoodlums."

The men rode on, Smoke, Pete, Tom Johnson, Judge Garrison, and half a dozen more of the town. They were heavily armed, for no one among them knew what awaited them in Hell's Creek.

Desolation.

As they topped the ridge overlooking the town, they could all sense the place was empty, completely void of life.

"Let's check it out," Smoke said.

The men inspected every building. The town was deserted. There was no sign of Big Max Huggins. Smoke looked at the safe in Max's quarters. The door was open and there was no sign of forced entry. So Max had found the strength to open it and ride.

Smoke found a coal-oil lantern, lit it, and tossed it into the squalor that someone had once lived in . . . and from all indications, it had housed several women. The building was quickly ablaze. The other men were doing the same with coal-oil-soaked rags. Soon, the fierceness of the heat drove them back.

In half an hour, the town of Hell's Creek, Montana, was no more than an unpleasant memory.

The men headed back toward Barlow, for a hot bath, a good meal, and some well-deserved rest. The day's events would alter their lives forever. For the good.

All that was left for Sally and Smoke were the good-byes to the people of Barlow and the ranchers and farmers out in the county. In the short time they'd been there, a lot had happened and they had discovered some friendships that would last forever.

Robert had been transferred to the territorial mental asylum and the doctors there had given him very little hope of ever recovering.

Through Sally's help, the new bank had agreed to loan Martha and Pete the money for a down payment on the Lightning spread. The two were married the day before Smoke and Sally were due to pull out.

Tessie Malone left the country the very day she sold Lightning to Pete and Martha.

Much to Sal's embarrassment, Victoria announced that the newly elected sheriff had proposed marriage to her and that she had accepted. Victoria had also accepted a position of teaching at the new school.

The other new schoolteacher in town, a cute little redhead, was making goo-goo eyes at Jim Dagonne. Bets were that he'd be roped and hog-tied before summer's end.

Smoke and Sally had said their good-byes to Joe Walsh and his wife.

The town of Barlow had been quiet for a week. Not one shot had been fired, not one fist had been swung in anger. Sal commented that it was just too good to last.

That proved true when one of Joe Walsh's hands came fogging into town, pale as a ghost and so excited he could hardly talk. He'd found Smoke Jensen's body on the trail. Sally Jensen was missing.

Chapter 27

Smoke was not dead, but had the bullet that grazed his skull been one millimeter more to the right, the slug would have blown out his brains.

He was back on his feet the next day, over the protestations of the new doctor in Barlow, and strapping on his guns.

Every able-bodied man in Barlow had been on the search for Sally and her kidnapper or kidnappers. They had ridden back into town at dawn, weary. They had lost the trail.

All Smoke could remember was that he and Sally and the packhorse had ridden down the edge of Swan Lake, intending to pick up the Swan River and follow it south to the railroad. They had stopped to water and rest their horses when Smoke's head seemed to explode.

That's all he could remember.

He swung into the saddle and pointed Star's head south, intending to backtrack. He had a headache, but other than that, he felt fine.

"You're sure you don't want some help?" Sal asked.

"No. A big posse is too easy to spot. Besides, Sally will leave messages along the way; messages and markers that would make sense only to me. It's Big Max, I'd bet on that. I was instrumental in bringing down his little empire, so now he intends to destroy as much of what I hold dear as possible. See you, Sal."

Smoke rode easy, down to the south end of the lake. There he dismounted and began searching the area, using tactics taught him by the old mountain man, Preacher. He worked in ever-widening circles, on moccasin-clad feet. By mid-afternoon he had picked up the trail—the true one, not the one that had been deliberately left for the posse.

The trail headed north by northeast. The lead horse was carrying a heavy load. That would be Max Huggins. Smoke recognized the hoofprints of Sally's mare. If they stayed on this trail, Smoke surmised, they were heading for glacier country.

Smoke doggedly stayed with the trail, taking his time, being careful not to miss a thing. He found where they'd camped at the base of and on the east side of Mt. Evans. Sally had left three stones in the form of an arrowhead, pointing toward the Flathead River.

Smoke followed, his head no longer aching and his strength having returned. He kept his fury under control—barely. He met a lone hunter, and the man took one look into Smoke's eyes and felt the chill of death touch him. The hunter backed off the trail and let Smoke pass with just a nod of his head.

The man would tell his grandkids that he had once seen Smoke Jensen on the prod, and that it was not a sight he ever wanted to see again.

On the east side of the South Fork Flathead, Max had met up with the tracks of a dozen riders. Probably the remnants of Max's gang, Smoke thought. Several miles farther, one rider had left the bunch. Smoke left the trail and circled. He picketed Star and worked his way back a bit on foot. He smiled when he saw who had stayed behind to waylay him.

It was the young man who had taken to calling himself Kid Brewer; the young man with a few pimples on his face who had made the obscene gesture at Smoke after the window-washing incident.

"Waiting for me, Kid?" Smoke called from behind the young man.

Kid Brewer whirled, his hands frozen over the butts of his tied-down guns. Smoke Jensen stood facing him, a Winchester pointed at his belly.

"You really shouldn't have taken a part in the taking of my wife, punk," Smoke told him. "Coming at me is one thing; taking my wife is something entirely different."

"Yeah," the young gunhand sneered at him. "So what do you think you're going to do about it?"

Smoke shot him. The .44 slug from the rifle struck the young man in the right elbow, knocking him down and forever crippling his gun hand. He lay on the cool ground, moaning and calling for his mother.

Smoke walked down to him and placed the muzzle of the rifle on the gunhand's left elbow. "If you think I won't leave you permanently crippled in both arms, you're crazy. Talk to me, punk."

Brewer looked up into the coldest eyes he had ever seen in all his young life. They so chilled him he momentarily forgot the pain in his shattered right arm. He began talking so fast Smoke had to slow him down.

When he had finished, Smoke smashed Brewer's guns, threw him on his saddle, and when the young man had stopped screaming after the jolting pain in his arm from the toss had lessened, Smoke gave him some advice. "If I ever see you again and you're wearing a gun, I'll kill you." He slapped the horse on the rump and the pony took off at a fast canter. Brewer was still screaming when Smoke mounted up.

Smoke backtracked and once more picked up the trail. He found where they had nooned and discovered Sally had taken stones and spelled out: O K. With a smile that would have backed up the devil, Smoke swung into the saddle and rode on.

He left the obvious trail and rode up into the high lonesome, into the east slopes of the Rockies. He dismounted and took his binoculars, carefully scanning the area below him. He scanned it once, then twice, and then a third time. He picked up the thin tentacle of smoke on the third try. He studied the area below him until he felt he had found a way in. He mounted up and headed down into the valley.

Nelson Barrett was enjoying a cup of hot coffee. His pleasure abruptly lessened when he felt the cold steel of a big Bowie knife against his throat. What made it even worse was the dark stain that suddenly appeared in the crotch of his dirty jeans.

"Talk to me, pee-pants," Smoke whispered. "And I'd better like what you have to say. 'Cause if I don't, I'll stake you out and skin you alive."

"Your woman's awright!" Nelson blurted. "There ain't nobody touched her. I swear it, man!"

"You were left here to do what?"

"Kill you!"

"Well, now. Is that a fact? What do you think I ought to do with you?"

"You let me ride, you'll never see me again, Smoke. As God is my witness, I promise you that."

Smoke took the knife from the man's throat and Nelson made a grab for his gun. Smoke jammed the big blade into the man's back and ripped upward with it. Nelson Barrett fell face-first into the small fire.

Smoke wiped the blade clean on Nelson's shirttail and poured himself a cup of coffee. He drank it slowly, then carefully put out the fire. He left Nelson where he lay and mounted up.

He crossed the Middle Fork of the Flathead River and rode into the area that would someday become the Glacier National Park. Smoke slipped into a jacket, for it had turned cold.

He plunged into a wild, beautiful wilderness. His thoughts turned to Preacher and how much the old man would have enjoyed the beauty of this rugged, lonesome country.

Then his thoughts lost all trace of beauty and turned savage and ugly as he followed the trail of Max Huggins and his dwindling gang of thugs and punks and human crap. He thought he heard a voice from out of the dark tangle of vegetation and pulled up, dismounting. He picketed Star and moved forward, both guns in his hands.

Al Martin, Dave Poe, and Ben Webster squatted around a campfire, boiling coffee and frying bacon.

"I cain't understand why Big Max don't go ahead and take the woman," Al said. "I would have."

"'Cause he'd have to knock her out cold to do it," Ben replied. "And that ain't no fun."

"He ought to just go 'head and shoot her," Dave opined. "She ain't never gonna be what Max wants her to be."

"I say we go on and kill Jensen, if that is him behind us, then kill Max, take his money, and have our pleasures with the woman," Al said. "There ain't nobody ever gonna find her body in this place."

Smoke stepped out and ruined the men's appetites. Both .44's belched flame and death, destroying the tranquility of the lovely forest in the high-up country.

Smoke dragged their bodies away from the fire and dumped them down a ravine. He pulled the picket pins of their horses and set them free. Smoke got Star and unsaddled him, rubbing the animal down and allowing him to graze for a time.

By that time, the bacon was done and the coffee was ready. Smoke drank and ate, sopping out the grease in the frying pan with a hunk of stale bread.

Smoke rolled him a cigarette and leaned back, enjoying the warmth of the fire. He poured another cup of coffee. If his calculations were correct, all that remained were Max, Val Singer, and Alex Bell. He moved away from the fire, laid his head on his saddle, and went to sleep.

He slept for a couple of hours, then rose and began circling the camp. He found another stick message from Sally. Three sticks laid out side by side, with four sticks next to them, in the shape of a crude D. Triple Divide Peak. Had to be.

Ol' Preacher had told him about this country, as had other old mountain men, and like most outdoorsmen, Smoke retained that knowledge in his head, a mental map.

He saddled up and took a chance, cutting straight east for a time, then turning north just west of what he felt was the Continental Divide. If he was right, and Max and what was left of his gang were not too far ahead of him—and he didn't think they were—he would make Triple Divide Peak ahead of Max.

Smoke pushed Star that day, but it was nothing the big horse couldn't take and still have more to give. Man and horse traveled through country that seemed as unchanged now as it was when God created the earth.

And Smoke could not understand why Max, with his love of cities and towns, hurdy-gurdy girls and parties, had chosen to come here, into this cold and vast wilderness.

He concluded that Max, like his brother Robert, had a streak of insanity running through him.

Smoke made camp that evening between Mt. Thompson and Triple Divide Peak. He loved this country, this high lonesome, where bighorn sheep played their perilous games on the face of seemingly untraversable mountains. Where cedars grew so tall they seemed to touch the sky. Where far below where he camped, heating his coffee over a hat-sized fire, he could see herds of buffalo roaming.

It all seemed just too peaceful a place for what Smoke had in mind.

But peaceful or not, he had come to find Sally, and get Sally he would. He rolled up in his blankets and went to sleep. Tomorrow was going to be a very busy day.

Smoke was up before dawn. He did not build a fire. He watered Star and left the big horse to graze. Below him, by one of the many small lakes that were scattered like jewels in this wilderness, he had spotted a campfire. Leaving his boots and spurs behind, Smoke slipped into his moccasins and picked up his rifle. He had it in his mind that he and Sally would be riding toward the Sugarloaf come noon.

Smoke moved through the thick underbrush and damp grass like a wraith. His clothing was of earth tones, blending in with his surroundings. From his high-up vantage point, Smoke had seen the second fire. That would be where Max and Sally were camped. Max had chosen to make his stand—if that's what he had in mind—on the flat of a sheer drop-off, maybe a thousand feet above where his two remaining gunmen were camped, waiting for Smoke Jensen.

"Let us not disappoint you, gentlemen," Smoke muttered. "I do hate to keep people waiting."

"No word from any of them we left behind," Val Singer said to Alex Bell. "That means that Jensen got them."

Bell said nothing for a moment. He sipped his coffee,

warming his hands on the tin cup. He was cold, he was uncomfortable, and he was scared. All along the way up into
this godforsaken country, they had left good men behind
them; men left there to take care of Smoke Jensen. But
Jensen had taken care of them, it seemed. The man was a
devil. Straight out of hell. Had to be.

"Let's get out of here, Val," he finally spoke. "To hell
with Max and the woman. Let's just ride."

"It's too late," Val said, the words soft.

"What the hell do you mean?"

"Jensen's here."

Alex looked wildly around him. He could see nothing,
only the seemingly impenetrable tangle of brush that was all
around them. "I don't see nothin'. I don't hear nothin'."

"No," the gunfighter said, standing up and working his
guns in and out of leather. "You wouldn't with Jensen. But
he's here."

Alex stood up, loosening his guns. "You're beginning to
spook me, Val."

"We shoulda left when Jensen showed up. We shoulda-
just pulled out and got gone. Now it's too late."

"That's right, Val," the voice came from the underbrush.
"Now it's too late."

Alex Bell jerked iron and emptied one gun into the thick
brush.

Laughter was his reply.

"Come out here and fight, damn you!" Alex screamed.

A .44 slug from a Winchester doubled him over, the slug
taking him just above the belt buckle. The second slug
turned him around and dropped him to the cold ground. His
gun fell from numbed fingers.

Val Singer had not moved. He stood tall, his right hand
close to the butt of his Colt. He waited.

Alex Bell moaned on the ground. Val ignored him.

Smoke stepped out of the brush. He carried the rifle in his left hand, his right hand by his side.

Val said, "I guess we do it now, don't we, Smoke?"

"I reckon."

"No point in my sayin' I'd just ride on out and leave you be?"

"Nope."

"You're a hard man, Smoke."

"Yep."

Val cussed him.

Smoke waited, tall and tough and cold-eyed.

Val jerked iron and Smoke shot him twice in the belly, once with his Colt and once with the .44 rifle. Smoke walked to the fire and poured a cup of coffee. He made a sandwich out of the nearly burned bacon and some bread wrapped in a cloth. He cut his eyes to Val Singer.

"We all make mistakes," the gun-for-hire said, his eyes pain-filled as he lay on the ground, both hands holding his punctured belly.

"Indeed you did."

"Gimme some coffee, Smoke."

"You're gut-shot. Worse thing in the world for you is liquid."

Val laughed bitterly. "I'm a good two hundred miles from a doctor. You think I don't know I've had it?"

Smoke poured Val a cup of the strong brew and handed it to him.

"Thanks," Val said. He took a sip of the brew and then screamed as the pain rose in waves.

To the west and above them, Sally had been working for several hours, rubbing the rawhide that bound her wrists against a rock. She felt the rawhide part and then, keeping her hands behind her, began to work circulation back into her hands.

Max turned to look at her. His face was a ruin. Smoke had destroyed the man's handsome looks with his fists. Madness shone in his eyes; madness combined with a burning hatred for Smoke Jensen.

"You heard the shots?"

"Yes."

"I'm next."

"I'm sure."

Max tried to smile. The broken bones in his face twisted his smile into a grimace. "I've got about an hour before Jensen can work his way up here. So I'll have you and then throw you off this cliff."

"I'm cold," Sally said. "May *I* scoot closer to the fire?"

"May I?" Max said mockingly. "My, how proper. Yes, Sally, you may."

Sally scooted to the fire's edge. Max turned his back to her, looking down into the valley below. Sally reached around and quickly untied the rawhide that bound her ankles, but left the rawhide looped around her boots.

Alex Bell sighed once and then died.

"Well, that's the end of it," Val managed to say, his voice thick with pain. "That's the last one of us 'ceptin' Max. And I 'spect you'll nail him, too. You gonna bury us, Smoke?"

"Nope." Smoke ate his sandwich and sipped his coffee.

"You just gonna leave us for the buzzards and the bears and the wolves?" The outlaw could not believe that Smoke really meant that.

"Yep."

"That ain't decent!"

"You're not a decent person, Singer. There is nothing decent about you."

"I was drove to a life of crime!"

Smoke laughed at him. "That's all horse-crap and you know it, Val. You chose your lifestyle willingly. So don't go out with a lie on your lips."

"I guess," the outlaw said, his voice weak. He looked around him and laughed bitterly. "All them books them folks back East write about the glamorous life on the hoot-owl trail. They don't know nothin'. All the outlaws I ever seen, me included, were dirty and hungry and cold and miserable ninety-nine days out of a hundred. But there ain't no point in wishin' I could change it, is there?"

"No, there isn't."

"Smoke?"

Smoke looked at him.

"You're a good man, Jensen. You got a good woman. I wish you both the best."

"Thanks, Val. You want to be buried with your boots on?"

"No. Gonna be hot enough where I'm goin'." He laid his head on the ground and closed his eyes.

Smoke waited for death to take the man.

"Max?" Sally whispered. She had taken a good-sized chunk of burning wood from the fire and stepped up behind the man. One end of the fire-brand was blazing hot.

Max turned and Sally hit him in the face with the burning end, then jammed the blazing wood into his open mouth. Max dropped his rifle and screamed, backing up. His boot hit a rock and sent him tumbling over the edge of the cliff. He screamed for a thousand feet.

Silence fell over the wilderness.

Sally rubbed her aching ankles and wrists, then set about making fresh coffee and slicing bacon. Her man would be along in about an hour.

*   *   *

Smoke rode into the flats and dismounted. He held his woman in his arms for a long time. She pushed him away and expelled breath. "What took you so long?"

"I buried Val Singer. Are you all right?"

"I am now. Come on, eat. I made fresh coffee."

The sun burst out of the clouds and mist of mid-afternoon. Sally looked across the fire at Smoke Jensen. "No point in starting out now. We can wait until morning."

"Oh? You have something in mind?"

She came to him and whispered in his ear.

Smoke took her in his arms. "Now that's the best suggestion I've heard in a long time."